In the Palace of the Khans

Peter Dickinson

IN THE PALACE OF THE KHANS

ISBN 978-0-9557805-8-5

First published 2012 by Peter Dickinson Books
This edition published 2013

cover image: Oleg Seleznev/iStockphoto

A CIP catalogue record for this book is available from the British Library

Peter Dickinson Books
Box 424
80 High Street
Winchester
Hampshire SO23 9AR
UK

www.peterdickinson.com

CHAPTER 1

Day 1. (28/7/2007, if you want to be exact, but Day 1's easier.)

Hi there. This is from Dara Dahn, capital of Dirzhan. That's way out east. Next but one and you're in China.

DD is a twin city, like Budapest (been there) and that place in the US (haven't). Looking out of my window, this side of the river's Dahn and the other side's Dara. That thing bang in the middle, right on the river (see photo), is the Palace of the Khans. Now, that is one cool building. That's where the President lives…

"But the man's a monster!" said Nigel's mother, not looking up from her book.

"What kind of a monster?" said Nigel.

"You don't want to know," said his father.

"How do you know what I want to know?" said Nigel. "We're all supposed to be keeping a blog for Mr. Udall. He doesn't want to plough through a lot of stuff about the height of mountains and the length of rivers. 'The President of the People's Thingummy of Dirzhan is a monster' would be a cool start."

"People's Khanate," said his father. "Hum. I shall have to think about that."

"If you don't tell me I'll put it in anyway and post a copy to the *Daily Mirror*," said Nigel. "'Ambassador's Son Calls

President Monster.'"

"And if I do you won't?"

"I'll show you before I post it so there's time to change anything you don't want me to say."

"You should be negotiating over this dam, not the crew we've got. All right. The deal includes not talking to anyone about what I tell you outside this room. We detected three listening devices inside the embassy when we first moved in, quite sophisticated ones."

"Wow!" said Nigel. "They wanted to know stuff about the dam, I suppose."

The dam was been a big deal for Nigel's father. He'd been Trade Secretary in Santiago until a year ago, and it didn't look as in he was ever going to get a move up. Dirzhan hadn't had an embassy at all then, only an office where the ambassador to Kyrgyzstan next door showed up once a month or so. Then the project for a British consortium to build an immense new dam in the Vamar Gorge had come up, and the British had decided that they'd better have a real ambassador on the spot. Nigel's father had dealt with one of the companies in the consortium before, so he got the job.

Dirzhan was in the back of beyond of Central Asia, but there was one big plus side. The President of Dirzhan had been so keen on having a real British ambassador in his crazy little country that he'd simply turfed out the owners of an old family hotel, large enough to hold an apartment for the ambassador as well as the actual embassy, and as a result here Nigel was having breakfast in a gorgeous room looking out over the roofs of Dara Dahn.

"You still haven't said what kind of a monster," he said.

"A monster of efficiency, I suppose. Sometimes he appears to have no decent human feelings at all. Apart, perhaps, from his affection for his daughter. If someone threatens his prestige or stands in his way he has them removed, which may well mean that they end up dead. Usually it's done by members of his bodyguard, but if he wants to make a special point of it he does it himself.

"In the early days of the dam project—before my time here—there was a disagreement in his cabinet about who should be the main contractors. Two of the ministers had taken bribes from an Italian bunch. They misjudged the situation and argued their case a bit too forcefully. The President gave them plenty of rope, until without warning he took a gun from a drawer and shot them both dead."

Nigel felt the blood drain from his face. There was something about people getting violently killed. It was the stuff of the old nightmares he still sometimes had. He'd never seen it happen in real life, of course, and in video games and films he'd learnt how to armour himself against the shock. But here, safe, relaxed, having a luxurious breakfast alone with his parents, his mother reading while she ate, his father holding forth about something while he spread his butter in an exactly even layer…

Neither of them seemed to have noticed. He pulled himself together.

"He's a Varak, from the north," his father was saying. "They're the smallest group, but they tend to hold positions of power because neither the East nor the West Dirzh, in the south, trust each other an inch. If they were to co-operate they'd run the country, but they can't, so they let the Varaki do it."

"Do *they* think he's a monster?"

"Hard to say. He's got complete control of the media, and ordinary people wouldn't tell an outsider what they think. My guess is that if there were ever such a thing as a free and fair election in Dirzhan he'd get about eighty per cent of the vote, simply because he makes the country function.

"He was a lecturer at Moscow University when the USSR fell apart twenty years ago, and his half-brother, who was the local chief of police in Dirzhan, seized power in the chaos and declared independence. He brought our chap back from Moscow and made him President to give a respectable façade to his regime. He then set about milking the economy for all it was worth.

"Our chap, the President, was not so happy. He was just as much of a thug as his brother, only a lot more intelligent. He wanted power, and he saw that he'd have much more power as the head of a prosperous, functioning state than a ramshackle, broke, falling apart one. He wasn't interested in stashing millions of dollars away in Switzerland.

"There was only one way the disagreement could end, and he got his blow in first. It is widely believed that he arranged to have his brother strangled and watched it happen on CCTV. He then rushed in and shot the men he'd hired to do it and announced that he, personally, had foiled a coup attempt against the regime but had arrived too late to save his brother.

"The media trumpeted the story to the world, but I doubt if many Dirzhaki believed it. It's a weird little country—one foot in the age of the internet and the other one still in the middle ages."

"Can I put that in my blog?"

"Um. I suppose so, provided you don't say I told you. Anyway, the Dirzhaki had been here before. Khan after khan in the old days had most of the men in his family killed off as soon as they moved into the palace."

Nigel was ready for it this time.

"But the Varaki didn't like it," he said in a no-big-deal kind of way.

"Oh, they'd have taken it in their stride—like I said, it was what they were used to. At least the men he'd shot had only been Dirzh."

"I suppose that's pretty monstrous, but…"

"He's a monster all the same. Tell him about the snow ibex," said Nigel's mother, still not looking up from her book. It didn't mean she hadn't been listening. She read like breathing. She could do other things at the same time.

"I was coming to that. At first glance it seems to be true crazy-monster behaviour, but in fact it fits into the same pattern. I sent you a postcard of a snow ibex, didn't I, Niggles? It's a species of goat found in these northern mountains, nothing to do with the true ibex though it's a very handsome creature. In the old days it was a royal beast. Only the Khans were allowed to hunt it. The villagers were well rewarded after a successful hunt, but if no animals were found the head man of the village was staked out to die, on the grounds that he'd been allowing poachers to operate. The communists put a stop to that, and the ibexes were hunted almost to extinction for the sake of the rams' horns, which are highly prized in Chinese medicine. When the President staged his coup the numbers were down to down to the last eighty-odd animals. It's still an endangered species, but the numbers are now up in the hundreds, thanks entirely to him."

"What's so monstrous about that? It sounds like good-guy stuff."

"He does quite a bit of good-guy stuff if it suits him. He doesn't waste billions buying high-tech fighters and tanks. He's much more likely to spend it on schools and hospitals. He has total control over what gets taught in the schools, mind you. If a teacher steps out of line he doesn't just get fired. He disappears. Same with journalists, even more so.

"The business about the snow ibexes came up when he declared that Dirzhan would henceforth be known as the People's Khanate. As President he obviously had inherited the rights and privileges of the khans, and henceforth only he would hunt the snow ibex.

"Those last animals were confined to one remote valley, where the villagers were not in the habit of paying much attention to edicts from Dara Dahn. So the hunting continued, though by that time it might take a skilled hunter two or three weeks to track and kill a ram. They were utterly unprepared when the President showed up and told them that he had come to hunt the snow ibex. Unsurprisingly, with only eighty animals left, none was found for him to hunt. The headman of the local village was staked out and died in the night—Dirzhan winters are harsh as they come. The village was searched, all the hunting rifles were burned, any householder with an ibex skull was hanged in his own doorway."

Again Nigel was ready.

"Wow! That's monster stuff all right. This was up in the mountains, so they were Varaks too?"

"Varaki. My guess is that he wanted to show the Dirzh that nobody gets any favours unless it suits him."

"What happened next year? Did he shoot one?"

"I must go now. I'll get Roger to show you the CD. And think about this business with his daughter, Niggles. I can get you out of it if you don't feel like it. No problem."

It wasn't true and they both knew it. He needed to keep the monster sweet.

"Oh, I'll go all right…"

"Nigel!" said his mother. "At least wait till…"

"No, Mum. I don't expect there are a lot of kids for me to hang out with here. It'll be interesting, even if it's only just once. Provided I hit it off with her, of course. I wonder if she plays chess. Do I get to meet the monster?"

"He will certainly want to cast an eye over you," said Nigel's father, checking his tie in the mirror by the door and rearranging a wisp of pale hair. "You'll be chaperoned all the time you're with her, by the way. I believe he used to play chess in Moscow, I don't know how well, though I doubt is there's anyone in Dirzhan with the nerve to beat him. Shall I tell Roger to lay it on?"

Nigel's mother sighed, slid a marker into her book and put it on the pile.

"I suppose so," she said to his departing back. "I'm sorry, darling. The diplomatic community here is tiny, and it's hard to make friends outside it. There just isn't anyone your age who'd do."

"Except the President's daughter, with luck. Has she got any brothers and sisters? Is there a Mrs President?"

"Yes and no. They're semi-separated. They married when he was in Moscow, and their sons were born there. She's Russian, of course, and she doesn't like it here. She can't speak the language, no ballet, no opera, so she lives in Moscow with the boys. One's at university and the other must be just about finishing at high school. They can speak Dirzhani—the President's insisted on that—but all their friends are in Moscow, and so on, so they come back as little as they can get away with.

"Is she pretty, this daughter?"

"I think so, in a Dirzhani kind of way. They're different anyway, Dirzhani girls. A lot of them get married off soon as they're fifteen. They don't get much say in who to...

"Goodness, is that the time? I thought you'd be sleeping much later, but if you can keep yourself occupied till eleven, I'll take you to the market, which is the real thing, not at all Hollywood. Dara Dahn will be an oven after lunch, but it'll be a bit more bearable up in the hills. I've found a falconer who'll show you his birds and if you're interested he'll give you some lessons."

"Oh, cool!"

"We'll have to take a bodyguard, I'm afraid. You get used to it. The thing you've got to remember about them is that they're only pretending they can't speak English. So be careful what you say in front of them. After that..."

"It's all right Mum! You don't have to look after me every hour of every day. Anyway, I've got my blog to get started on. Stop fussing. What sort of thing do you do at the weekends? Can we get up into the mountains and bird-watch and stuff?"

"Of course. There's a super little hotel at Forghal, with good fishing for Nick and ponies we can hire and scramble around on them with our binoculars..."

"That means two bodyguards, one for us and one for Dad."

"Nick will slip ours a fifty and tell him to hire his own bloody pony if he wants to come along. He won't. I've got to go now too, darling. See you at eleven."

In the holidays Nigel liked to have breakfast in his dressing-gown. It gave him a sense of freedom from the endless pressure of time during school term. He'd set his alarm, and the hell with jet-lag, so that he could have breakfast with his parents. It was almost three months since he'd last seen them. Always before they'd been in big cities—Madrid, Athens, Santiago—where they'd lived in ordinary houses with Spaniards or Greeks or Chileans for neighbours and his father had gone to work in the British embassy, like going to the office.

This time his father's appointment had come out of the blue, and the Foreign Office had had to scramble Nigel into an English boarding school. He'd been to a Spanish school in Santiago and spoke English the way his parents did, so he'd felt a bit of an outsider, coming in late, with his silly posh voice and his stupid name and hopelessly uncool slang. He'd gone to his aunt Helen or his sister Libby for most weekends and then, at the end of term, had flown out to join his parents in Dirzhan.

Despite the jet-lag Nigel had enjoyed having his breakfast at a beautifully polished table in his cosy old dressing-gown, being waited on by a maid in a spotless white apron; and now, clean and dressed, he was standing at the living-room window gazing out over Dara Dahn. It was built either side of a river that flowed into a large lake he'd seen from the aeroplane flying in last night. This side of the river was Dahn and the far side Dara. The embassy was air-conditioned, but the roofs of Dahn, tumbling down to the river below him, already glared with heat in the morning sun. In the clean upland air he could see for vast distances beyond Dara on the opposite slope, first a range of lion-coloured hills, and much farther away real mountains, with a faint glimmer against the pale blue sky that might be snow-peaks.

He couldn't see much of Dahn itself except its roofs, mostly wavy yellowish tiles, with zigzag patterns of purple ones worked into them. Minarets rose here and there. ("The Dirzhaki are nominally Muslim," Google had told him, "but few other Muslim communities accept them as such.") But Dara was displayed before him. It looked a bit like Istanbul in some ways—they'd been there once on a long weekend from Athens—but somehow wilder, stranger, with even more secrets. There were some interesting old buildings and some hideous new ones. The best and the worst of these were a glorious, ornate, gold-coloured building with five blue domes, spreading along the waterfront; and, further up the hill, a huge pale grey vertical slab like a giant's tombstone.

A tap at the open door behind him. He turned.

"Do I intrude on your meditation?" said Roger.

He was the Third Secretary. There wasn't a First or Second Secretary—the Embassy wasn't important enough. Tim O'Hara, the Commercial Secretary, looked after the Vamar Dam stuff and Roger did everything else. Youngish, round without being obviously plump, smiley, soft spoken. The big thing about him was that he had a passion for languages and he'd learnt Dirzhani for the job.

"What's that horrible thing there?" said Nigel.

Roger put a CD and a blue folder on the table, and answered without coming to look.

"The People's Palace, I expect. Typical bit of Stalinist architecture."

"It looks like a tombstone."

"Spot on. Monument to the sterility of the communist ideal. They turned the old Palace of the Khans—that one with the blue domes—into a museum, but President Dharviu moved back in there as soon as he took over."

"What's it like inside?"

"That's one of the things I came to see you about. Do you know what your plans are for tomorrow? Your mother seems to have disappeared."

"She said tomorrow was blank."

"Then you may be seeing for yourself. The President's daughter will be prepared to receive you at ten o'clock."

"You'll have to clear it with Mum. She wasn't keen, really, but she said OK in the end. What's the problem? They can't do anything to me, can they? Hold me as a hostage to get what they want on the dam deal, or whatever?"

"He's not that kind of a fool. It'd be something much subtler than that. The CD will give you a bit of an idea, perhaps. I won't spoil it for you. We'd better deal with this other stuff first if you'll come over here."

He opened a folder and began to sort out papers and envelopes onto the table.

"This is an official document in both Dirzhani and English, signed by your father and stating that you are a British subject and have diplomatic immunity. This is five hundred-dollar bills and ten thousand-dzhin notes. This is some local money in smaller denominations. This is a list of telephone numbers. Remember if there's trouble that someone's quite likely to be listening. This is a mobile that works here some of the time, though the signal's extremely patchy. Landlines are purely local. There are masts in Dara Dahn and some of the larger towns, but…"

"I've got my own."

"Won't work here. The sticker on the back's a special license to use an internet connection. That's so they can monitor what you're saying and come after you if you get out of line…"

"How'm I going to post my blog?"

"You can do that from the office here. Don't worry. One gets used to it. Finally, for real emergencies this is a number we want you to memorise. It isn't difficult."

Nigel frowned at the pencilled number. 1491 8191 6601. Not difficult…?

"Try backwards," said Roger.

Ah, of course. William the Conqueror, end of World War One… um…

"Dunkirk?" he guessed.

"And Battle of Britain. All that. Now, that's a secure line, routed via satellite to London and back directly to us here in the embassy, so that the signal then sounds to anyone listening in as if it's coming from there. We've just had the system put in for when the dam project is in full swing. It takes a bit of a while to get through. If there's anything wrong you'll hear a bit of canned piano music, and you ring off at once. Otherwise your father will answer, or Tim or me if he's out. Keep it short. There'll be longish pauses while the signal goes to and fro."

"This is all for real?"

"'Fraid so. Dirzhan is that sort of country, but with luck you'll never need it. What else? Oh yes. Tell me if you want to go out and I'll find you a bodyguard. And wear a hat of some sort. A baseball cap will do, with the peak down over the back of your neck. The sun's hotter than you think, and anyway it's the custom."

They chatted for a bit about Nigel's flight, and he left. Nigel put the notes in his new money belt and the rest of the stuff back in the folder and with very mixed feelings settled down to watch the CD. He wanted to know what happened. Also to see what the monster looked like. He wasn't so keen to watch a rare and beautiful animal getting shot. That must be how it had ended—the monster would never have let a video of an unsuccessful ibex hunt get out. On the other hand Nigel's father must have known how he'd feel about it… And then Roger's last remark… Reluctantly he pressed the "Play" button.

It wasn't the amateur, hand-held job he'd expected, more like a TV travel ad. There were titles in Dirzhani with translations below—English, Russian and Chinese. Background music, hunting horns—Nigel had heard it before—Haydn? Mozart? One of that lot. Anyway, it didn't sound at all Dirzhani—not that he'd any idea what Dirzhani music did sound like. Then he was looking at a steep rocky snow-strewn hillside, sunlit and dotted with patches of scrub. Snow-covered mountains above. A line of men and women, tiny with distance, working their way down towards the camera, pausing wherever the line reached a scrub-patch and thwacking it with the staffs they carried while the rest of the line moved on into an arc, ready to drive whatever emerged from the scrub on down the hill.

The camera swung to the hunting party, four men screened from further up the slope by a bank of brushwood. One was a cameraman. Another carried two guns. The other two were watching the beaters over the top of the hide. One of them lowered his binoculars and turned towards the camera. The focus closed in on him, a stocky, muscular figure. Bare-headed, with dark close-cropped hair. His smooth skin was a pale, yellowish brown, and he was wearing a brown winter coat with a lot of pockets. Below that, breeches and stockings.

Without obviously posing he stood as if he was confident that people would want to look at him. Of course they would. He was President of Dirzhan, wasn't he?

The other watcher raised an arm and pointed up the hill. The President turned to look. The bearer handed each of them a gun and the camera swung back to the hillside. Five white animals were racing down it in great flowing bounds, utterly sure-footed over the rocky surface. The line of beaters broke into a run but were soon outdistanced

The view cut to another camera, and Nigel was looking over the President's shoulder along the line of the hide. The camera swung to show the ibexes leaping towards a gap about thirty yards further on. They were quite obviously goats, the largest he'd seen, a ram, two nannies and two kids, almost as white as the snow. The ram had a thick black mane like a pony, and all of them had black muzzles and black tails. The ram was leading the group. It was half again as big as the nannies, with magnificent coiled horns. The camera switched to slow motion as it leaped through the gap. It was in mid-air when the President's gun twitched slightly with the recoil of the soundless shot.

The ibex had heard it, of course. In the dance-like, slowed-down movement Nigel saw it already trying to turn aside. It landed, swerved and bounded away.

Missed! Both of them! The other hunter had been out of sight, but he must have been there as a back-up to make it look like a successful hunt even if the President shot wide. But surely in that case he'd have been a crack shot... Nigel couldn't see what they were up to because the view had cut back to the other camera, not in slow motion, following the ibexes across the slope.

Without warning, between bound and bound, the ram seemed to miss its footing, stagger, reel aside, collapse, try to rise, collapse again and lie still. The nannies and kids raced past.

The camera closed in on an inert white mound, half hidden by a boulder, then cut to the foremost beaters rushing towards it. They lined themselves up a respectful few paces away, and stood waving their fists in the air like goal-scoring footballers, as if they themselves had heroically slain the creature. The President came into view, strode round the fallen ibex and turned to face the camera. This time he was posing, the great hunter, the Khan of Dirzhan, exercising his ancient privilege and so setting the seal upon his khanship.

Nigel stared at him. Why didn't he feel absolutely sick? It should have been obscene, disgusting, but, but... Those subtitles. The President was planning to show the world what he'd done. There'd have been an international outcry, the last thing he wanted before the major fuss there was bound to be about the dam. And he wasn't stupid, Roger said. "*The video will give you a bit of an idea, perhaps. I won't spoil it for you.*" He waited, frowning.

At last the President looked down at his victim, knelt beside it on one knee and gently eased something out from under the coarse mane. He rose and held it up. The camera closed right in. It was some kind of small dart.

(Oh, of course! Nigel kicked himself now for not having got it.)

Cut to a night scene. The same wintry hillside, but with a dozen good fires blazing. Villagers feasting around them. The President and four other men eating more formally, with chairs and a folding table. In the foreground, the drugged ibex. As the camera watched it raised its head, stared, started awkwardly to its feet and staggered away into the dark.

The villagers were all on their feet too, shouting and cheering. One of the men at the table clapped his hands for silence. An older man, clearly one of the villagers, made a short speech and raised his goblet to the President. With silent shouts of applause the feasters drank to their Khan, who answered with a rather longer speech, waited for the applause and held up his hand.

Solemnly he picked up a small object from the table, presented it to the man who had just spoken and kissed him on both cheeks. They were standing there face to face, with the firelight dancing across them, when the video ended.

Nigel returned to the start and watched it again, looking for clues. The gun had a sort of bulge at the end of its barrel, presumably for the dart. It couldn't be very accurate. Lucky shot to hit the ibex in the neck, so that it didn't show as it bounded on. No, of course not. It had really been shot by somebody hidden much nearer on the far side, and the fake dart planted after the ibex had fallen. He started again at the beginning. Yes, the shadows were wrong—too long. That scene must have been shot at least an hour later than the one showing the hunt. He was watching the closing moments again when his mother came back.

"I suppose that's the village headman," he said. "Do you know what he's giving him?"

"Actually he's a professional actor. But the headman really did get a purse of gold, worth as much as a pair of ram's horns, Nick says."

CHAPTER 2

Day 2.

Hi there. Well, I've now been in an ordinary Dirzhani house—not that ordinary, actually, really posh, right on the river, belongs to this guy—I'll call him Mr G—who's something big in Dara Dahn. He got together with my dad at some sort of a meeting and when Dad said I was coming on a visit he asked if I could hang out with his daughter a bit, help polish up her English. I'll call her Luana...

Nigel's father and the two Secretaries were British. Otherwise all the tiny embassy staff were "local". Tim's and Roger's wives were really British too but counted as local; they were embassy secretary on alternate days while the other one had their kids. Nigel's mother's secretary, Ivahni, was a Dirzhak who spoke good English. Most of the guards and servants spoke a bit of English. And then there was Rick, who really was local, and really was British.

He was the embassy driver. Before that he'd been general odd-job man at the FO's Kyrgyzstan outpost in Dara Dahn. His parents had come to England from Antigua, and he'd been born in Leeds. He'd gone into the army when he'd left school, but had got sick of the racial harassment and dropped out. Then he'd met and married a Dirzhani girl who was working as a cleaner at the hospital. He'd come back to Dirzhan with her as soon as it split off from the USSR and got himself made driver and odd-job man and pretty well everything else in the new FO outpost in Dara Dahn. He'd lived there for fifteen years now, and had two daughters. He wore a smart navy blue uniform and cap and held himself like a soldier. He liked to talk, and still did it in what Nigel guessed was a Leeds accent.

Now he spoke in Dirzhani to the bodyguard, who opened the rear door of the plush old embassy Rover and climbed in.

"You come up in front with me, sir," said Rick, holding the passenger door for Nigel. "Khan dun't like to be kept waiting, but we've a bit of time over so I'll take you down through the old town, and tell you what's what."

"You can call me Nigel if you like," said Nigel as Rick settled into the driver's seat. The car wasn't air-conditioned, so they kept the windows open.

"Suits me," said Rick. "Not in front of your dad, mind. Dun't give a flip for himself, but in Dirzhan he's H.E. the British Ambassador, and we got to keep standards up, even when there's nobody looking."

"You must like living here."

"Not half. I'm quids in here. I mean that, literal. Pound here will buy you two, three times what it would in England, less you've a taste for fancy foreign shoes and such. They cost all right. Besides, I'm somebody here. I get a bit of respect. Nothing like that for me back home."

He broke off to shout a greeting to a man leading a donkey-cart loaded with sawn timber up the steep, crowded, cobbled street. Most of the older men had thick, bushy beards and were wearing a kind of floppy turban, a long loose jacket and baggy trousers. All the women had shawls over their head or some kind of veil or even one of those long all-over cloaks that that covered them from head to toe except for the bit around their eyes.

"Those are burkas or something, aren't they?" said Nigel.

"Dahli, we call 'em," said Rick. "Dahl's a bit different anyway, seein' we're Dirzhaki. We're like that."

There were teenagers of both sexes in T-shirts and jeans, but all the girls, even kids not much older than toddlers, had shawls over their heads and the boys wore caps. And they kept apart, boys together, girls together.

"What would happen if I said hello to a girl I didn't know?" he asked. "Would they lynch me?"

"Know her or not, no difference," said Rick. "Don't try it, 'less you want your face spat in."

There didn't seem to be any shops, but every open space, however small, seemed to have a sort of mini-market in it, with a few stalls. And there weren't any advertisements, apart from enormous posters of the President on every blank wall. The man with the donkey-cart shouted cheerfully back as the two ancient vehicles edged past with millimetres to spare.

"Third cousin of Janey's—that's the wife," explained Rick. "'Nother thing about being here—you get real families. Like it was back in Antigua, 'cording to my mum. England, you get folks dun't know how many kids their brothers an' sisters got, pretty well."

"What do they think about the President? Do they all call him the Khan, like you did?"

Rick took his right hand off the steering-wheel, lowered it as if he was fiddling with his seat belt, and pointed urgently with his thumb towards the back seat. Nigel had forgotten about the bodyguard.

"Yeah, he's the Khan all right," said Rick. "Never had a President did 'em any good. Doubt the old khans were much better, but they've forgot about that. They respect this one. He's done all right by them, anyone can see. Hospitals, schools, steady jobs, food in the markets. Step out of line, mind you, deal drugs, anything like that, and you'll get it in the neck.

"Getting there soon, lad. That's it across the river—fancy bit of building, dun't you think?"

Without warning they had emerged into openness. It was as if the narrow, twisting street down which they had been driving, with its higgledy-piggledy houses, had been chopped short to create a modern tree-lined boulevard running beside the river. The trees were saplings, and the glass-walled offices and government buildings looked only a few years old.

The water-front opposite was utterly different. The river was about the size of the Thames in London, and along its further shore the buildings were any old age and crowded right to the water: wharves with derricks; the backsides of a couple of mosques, built as if they hadn't expected to be looked at from this direction; warehouses; one or two cafes actually fronting the water; a few ordinary little houses like those in the old city; and in the middle of it all, looking across at this handsome new boulevard, the Palace of the Khans.

Nigel thought it was the most beautiful building he'd ever seen, more beautiful the Empire State in New York or the Parthenon in Athens or Hagia Sophia in Istanbul. It was three tall storeys high, built mainly of a pale, fawn-coloured stone, exactly right to support the astonishing blue of the domes—lapis something, he vaguely remembered—a big one at the centre and two smaller ones either side. They were bordered with gold round their lower rims, ribbed with gold and topped with little golden spires. The entrance doors were set back under an archway reaching almost to the rim of the central dome and supported by two pairs of blue lapis-something pillars. Four narrower arches ran up the façade on either side, filled in with a delicate carved-stone lattice, a pattern like frozen flames.

"Wow!" said Nigel. "What's it like inside?"

"Never been, meself," said Rick. "You're one of the lucky ones. S'posing you come out again, o' course."

It was a joke. Didn't mean anything.

Two turbaned sentries stood at the top of the steps, with their guns slung behind their backs and purple sashes running slantwise from shoulder to hip over their khaki uniforms.

"You wait there, lad," said Rick. "We're on parade again."

He got out, walked round in front of the Rover, climbed the three steps and spoke to one of the sentries, then came back, opened the passenger door, saluted as Nigel got out and handed him his shoulder-bag.

"Thank you, Rick."

"Very good, sir."

Self-consciously Nigel climbed the five steps alone. Both sentries saluted as he reached the top. He knew the form from having seen his father go through this sort of thing, so he raised his hand in acknowledgment and was about to show them his pass when a man in a dark suit and purple tie came out of the doorway and walked up with his hand outstretched. Nigel tried to put his pass in it but the man took it with his other hand and then shook Nigel's.

"The President is expecting you, Mr. Rizhouell," he said in a high, anxious voice. "Avron Dikhtar. I am under-secretary to the President-Khan. I hope you have recovered from your journey."

He was a small man, pale faced, dark haired, already going a bit bald, though he can't have been that old. Apart from the actual name his English was pretty good. He'd probably been practicing. So had Nigel.

"I am honoured to be invited," he said. "The flight was fine, thank you."

"Will you please to come this way."

There was no lobby. The doors led directly into an enormous hall, just as stunning as the outside. There the day had been bright and clear, but this was a different sort of brightness, a rich dazzle and glitter sparkling from ten thousand polished surfaces, softened here and there by huge, deep-coloured hangings, all lit by hidden lights. The middle section rose to the full height of the central dome, with lower sections on either side. The only daylight came from a row of windows ringing the base of the dome.

Nigel would have liked to stop and look but Mr. Dikhtar led him briskly across the hall, up a few steps to a broad, stage-like dais and on up a magnificent staircase to a pillared gallery running round three sides of the central section of the hall. They turned left at the top and followed the gallery round to a door guarded by another two sentries.

"I regret the necessity, Mr. Rizhouell," said Mr. Dikhtar, "but it is a routine for all visitors to the private apartments. Please give me your bag and raise your arms above your head."

Nigel did as he was told, and the sentry leaned his gun against the doorpost and systematically ran his hands all over Nigel's body. When he got to his belt he grunted and spoke.

"You are wearing a money belt, Mr. Rizhouell?" said Mr. Dikhtar.

"Er…my proper one's bust," said Nigel.

It was half true. The buckle had started to come unstitched, but it didn't show. He'd bought the money belt in the airport because he thought it was a cool gadget, like his Swiss Army knife and his compass and his monocular for bird-watching and his travelling chess set. He was a sucker for that sort of thing.

Mr. Dikhtar spoke to the guard, who grunted again and went on with the search, finishing by checking the soles of Nigel's sneakers. He straightened, grinning, and rumpled Nigel's hair in a fatherly fashion. Nigel's face must have shown what he thought about it, because Mr Dikhtar spoke sharply to the guard before he handed him the bag.

"Er…I'm afraid that's got my Swiss Army knife in it," said Nigel.

Mr Dikhtar just nodded and waited. The guard checked the license on the back of the mobile and put it back. When he found the knife and the monocular and showed them to him he took the knife and put it in his pocket.

"I will return it to you when you leave, Mr. Rizhouell," he said.

"You may keep the eye-glass."

The guard handed Nigel's bag back and picked up his gun. The other guard opened the door.

The hallway beyond it felt and smelt and looked like the lobby of the suite in the expensive modern hotel in Santiago where Nigel had once waited for his father to come out of a meeting. Even the wild-life pictures on the walls and the faint reek of cigar-smoke were spot on. Still, this was different. He was about to meet the monster. His heart started to hammer.

Mr. Dikhtar tapped on one of the half-dozen doors.

"A pleasure to have met you, Mr. Rizhouell," he said, handing Nigel his pass. "I will see you later and give you back your knife"

"Thank you," said Nigel, and turned to the opening door.

Just inside the room, waiting to close it behind him, smelling of some kind of strong, musky scent, stood…

What?

Man or woman? The bald, mottled head emerged from a loose long-sleeved ivory surcoat. The skin of the face was almost the same colour, creased with tiny wrinkles and shrunken to the shape of the bone beneath. Out of that deadness one living eye gazed at Nigel. The other was filmed with grey goo.

With a shaking hand Nigel held out his pass. The right sleeve rose like the wavering fin of a tropical fish, thin fingers reached out from its folds, took the pass and held it up for the eye to peer at and gave it back, then beckoned Nigel to follow him across the room to where a man and a girl were sitting on a sofa. He was reading some documents and she was watching *The Simpsons.*

The man pressed the mute button but the girl snatched the remote from him and pressed it again. He slapped her hand and took it back, turned the volume way down and handed it back to her, then rose. He was the President.

He was wearing a black open-necked shirt, slacks and sandals. He was shorter than he'd seemed on the video. He looked at Nigel, unsmiling. Nigel met his gaze for a moment, and looked down.

Apart from the force of that gaze there didn't seem to be anything special about him. Pass him in the street, and you mightn't have noticed him. But standing there facing him for only a couple of seconds Nigel became strongly aware of something else. Nothing tangible, but there all the same. Like the hum of a PC on stand-by, so faint that you notice it only if the room is utterly silent. The purr of the monster in its lair.

The monster held out his hand to be shaken.

"G-good morning, sir," said Nigel as he took it and let go. "Er…It's good of you to ask me to meet your daughter."

"You know who I am?"

"Yes, sir. You're the President-Khan of Dirzhan."

Now the man smiled.

"Merely the President, internationally," he said. "The Khan is for local consumption."

"It sounds good, sir."

"Ah, a diplomat's son, evidently. So you are Nigel Ridgwell—a tongue-twister for us Dirzhaki."

He was obviously proud of his English, and had made a much better shot at the name than Mr. Dikhtar, but he still spoke with a definite accent.

"I bet there's a lot of Dirzhaki names I'd make a mess of, sir."

"Dirzhani names. Dirzhak is the noun, Dirzhaki its plural. Yes, of course. But you have been here only one day. How did you spend it?"

"I watched the video of your ibex hunt in the morning, sir. That was a cool trick you played."

"It was more than a trick, Nigel. It was a necessity."

(Nigel knew that already. His father had spent most of supper last night filling him in on stuff he might need to know when he met the President. Like the Greens making a lot of fuss about the dam internationally because there was some kind of fish-owl that lived in the gorge and the new dam would drown out its habitat. The President had made the video to help get them on his side.)

"'Cool'? That is still current?"

"Yes, sir. People say 'wicked' too."

"Do you?"

"Sometimes, sir."

"Not to my daughter, please. And then, after the video?"

He couldn't possibly want to know—just wants to get me talking, Nigel thought. Some kind of test, heaven knows what.

"My mother took me to the East market," he said. "Then in the afternoon we went and visited a falconer who's said he'll give me lessons…"

"I have eagles in my falconry, Nigel."

"Wow! That's because you're the Khan? Like the snow ibex?"

The President didn't reply at once, then nodded. It wasn't an answer to what Nigel had said. It meant that he had passed the test, whatever it was.

"You know the actress Helena Bonham Carter?" said the President.

"I've seen something she was in, sir. I can't remember what."

"I have a CD of *The Wings of a Dove*, but it is unsuitable. Do you remember the manner in which she speaks?"

"Very upper-class, lady-of-the-manor, isn't it?"

"That is how I wish my daughter to speak English. I learnt the language in too much of a hurry. I did not have the patience to acquire a good accent. I do not wish to have my daughter's English corrupted by this sort of thing."

He flicked a hand towards *The Simpsons* chattering away on the vast TV.

"I get teased at school for having a nobby accent, sir."

"Excellent. That is exactly how I wish my daughter to speak. With a nobby accent. This idiot programme is almost finished, and then I will introduce you. Forgive me. I have work to do."

He returned to the sofa, picked up his file of papers and started to read.

Nigel gazed round the room while he waited. He had a bit

more control of himself now. He thought he'd coped OK with the monster. The weird old man—it must be a man, he'd decided—who'd met him at the door had returned to his post beside it and was sitting motionless on a sort of high stool with his one good eye gazing directly at Nigel. It made him feel uncomfortable, so he looked elsewhere.

It was a strange room, a kind of mix between the amazing entrance hall below and the boring lobby just outside. Two large windows in the far wall looked out through the stone lattice towards the river and the embankment beyond. The other three walls were covered with pale green and gold carved panelling, obviously old. Each of them was framed by a painted climbing creeper, twisting around itself, with small bright birds here and there among the leaves. The vaulted ceiling was pale blue, ribbed with gold. But the furniture was almost all modern, comfortable but dull. One exception was an ornate chess table, with the pieces arranged on it ready to be played. Nigel went over and looked at it. The squares were black marble and mother-of-pearl. The pawns were fierce-looking warriors, the rooks were elephants with men in little turrets on their backs, the knights were horsemen, and so on.

The President looked up.

"You like it?" he said.

"Oh, it's awesome, sir! But it would be difficult to play with. You have to be able to recognise..."

"Of course, for serious chess. You play?"

"Yes, sir. I'm in the school team."

"Excellent. I like to relax during my luncheon. We will play then."

"I think my mother's expecting me back for lunch, sir."

"Not 'luncheon'?"

"Only if you're very old-fashioned, sir."

"I am. My secretary will call your mother. You may speak to her yourself, if you wish."

"I'm sure it will be all right, sir."

("The President of Dirzhan is a monster. I played chess with him." Wow! Except that Dad wouldn't let it through.)

"My secretary will let you know. Ah. Now, Taeela, pull yourself together and behave as your mother would wish. You have a guest to welcome. Nigel, this is my daughter Taeela. And this, my dear, is Nigel Ridgwell."

The girl had uncurled from the sofa, deliberately unwilling, like a cat disturbed from its slumbers. She pouted and snarled at her father in Dirzhani.

"Say it in English, please, my dear," said the President, unperturbed. "You must not cut our guest out of the conversation."

"I tell him he choose you for your name because it is difficult to say," she said, still pouting theatrically.

"I hate my name, if you want to know," Nigel said, speaking a little slower than usual. "I look like a Nigel, I sound like a Nigel, I am a Nigel. And Ridgwell only makes it worse. I wish I'd been called Terry or Wayne or Darren or something. I'm Nick at school, but I can't be at home because that's what everyone calls my dad. Actually he's even more of a Nigel than I am."

She'd stopped pouting, and was just looking at him now, almost in the same way her father had done, but without the purr of power. She had a green headscarf framing a face that wasn't exactly pretty, but interesting, slightly pudgy and browner than her father's, with heavy jet-black eyebrows and long eyelashes. Her eyes were dark and lively. She was wearing a loose, patterned green dress with a skirt that reached to her ankles.

"Terry is nice name," she said thoughtfully.

"OK. Terry it is. Terry and Taeela. We sound like a circus act. It's all right, sir. I shan't ask her to wear spangled tights."

The President actually chuckled.

"The eunuch would certainly disapprove," he said.

There seemed to be a sort of relief in his tone, as if he'd been waiting to see what his daughter would make of this new toy he'd given her. It took Nigel a moment to realize what he'd actually said.

"Eunuch, sir? I thought..."

"There are still a few eunuchs in isolated parts of the Middle East and Islamic Africa. Here the last khan was not deposed by the Russians until nineteen thirty-seven. Fohdrahko was born in nineteen twenty-six, he believes. He will be with you all the time you are with my daughter. Do not pity or patronize him, Nigel. It is the custom. It gives him purpose. He is also, by the way, highly intelligent. Now I must go. Someone will come to fetch you to my office at twelve fifteen."

He turned and left.

Nigel half expected Taeela instantly to turn the TV back on. He must have glanced towards it, because she shook her head and pointed up over his right shoulder. He turned and saw a closed circuit camera mounted up in a shadowy corner of the ceiling.

"My father see me all the time," she said with an exaggerated sigh. "You make him laugh. What do you say to him? A circus, yes? I know circus. Elephants and tigers, yes?"

"And acrobats and clowns and trapeze artists."

"Trapeze? I do not know this."

"Um. Trapezes. They are just bars of wood, swinging from ropes, high up in the air. Taeela holds onto one..."

He raised his arms and gripped an imaginary bar, then mimed the actions with his hands, as if he'd been wearing glove-puppets

"...and Terry holds on to the other with his knees, so he's upside down. They're wearing glittery tights, close to their bodies. They get the swings going. Together, apart. Together, apart...

"Now Taeela lets go of her swing and flies through the air. Terry catches her. And now they are both swinging from Terry's trapeze. I told your father I wouldn't make you wear glittery tights. He said—I don't know his name—Foh-something..." he nodded towards the eunuch sitting on his stool by the door, "...Your father said he would not approve of tights."

"Fofo!" she said, laughing delightedly. "No, he does not approve!"

She called to the eunuch and he rose from his stool and came over.

"This is my friend Fofo," she said. "He lives in the palace very long time. He knows many, many secrets."

Nigel held out his hand and the old man took it, but instead of shaking it he raised it to his lips and kissed it gently. It was a very expressive gesture, formal but at the same time warmly welcoming. The old eunuch was Taeela's guardian. For him she must have been the last of a long line of women and girls he had watched and protected, and so, perhaps, the most precious. The kiss told Nigel that he had passed another test, been judged, and accepted.

Taeela laughed again and flung her arms round the eunuch and hugged him. He stood for a little while nodding his head slowly and smiling at Nigel, then gently released himself and went back to his stool.

Taeela bundled herself up like a puppy into the corner of the sofa and patted the cushion beside her.

"Not close," she said. "Fofo..."

She laughed and shrugged and rolled her eyes.

Nigel was happy to settle onto the other end of the sofa. He'd never been comfortable with girls and their private language of gestures and glances.

"How do you want to do this?" he said. "I suppose we just talk about stuff and see how we get on. Do you want me to tell you when you get a word wrong? It'll slow things down no end."

"No, no! This is not lesson. I do so many lessons. No! We... just talk about stuff and see how we get on."

She got it dead right. He could even hear a whisper of his own voice saying the words.

"Tell me where you are born," she said.

"In London, but I don't remember anything about it because we moved to Madrid before I was one. I was a mistake, if you want to know. My sisters are much older than me—Libby's grown up and married now, and Cath's at university—and my parents didn't mean to have another one.

"I don't remember much about Madrid either, just one particular smell. There's a sort of magnolia. Most of the year it's big boring bush—almost a tree—but then suddenly in summer it produces these amazing huge white flowers—this big—and absolutely reeking of some kind of lemon syrup. One whiff of the right thing and I'm back in this stifling hot little courtyard full of dusty sunlight and this smell. And that's Madrid."

"I know this tree, Terry. No, is stupid, this. I call you Nidzhell. You teach me how I say it..."

The morning slid by. At one point a small, dumpy woman brought in a tray with a jug of ice-cold fizzy fruit drink and some crisp little almond biscuits. At another, when he was talking about his time in Santiago, she said "This is good...great! I get...I'm getting two lessons in one time. English, Geography. I tell...I'll tell my father."

He noticed the self-corrections with satisfaction, and even more so how, by the time she was talking about her own earlier life, she was saying things like "I'm" and "Don't" as smoothly as if she'd done so always. She went to a little school in the palace, with ten other kids, roughly her age. Both girls and boys, which apparently wasn't the custom in Dirzhan. Only the President could have got away with it, Nigel guessed. She loved riding, and had her own ponies both in Dara Dahn and at a hunting lodge in the hills. Nigel was taken by surprise when the eunuch answered a tap on the door and Mr. Dikhtar was standing just outside with a phone handset in one hand and the other beckoning him over.

"The President-Khan is ready to receive you, Mr. Rizhouell," he said. "I have spoken to your mother. She would like you to call her."

He dialled a number and handed the telephone over.

"Nigel?"

"Hi, Mum. I'm having a great time. I'm just going off to play chess with the President. Is that scary or is it scary? I like Taeela a lot. I have to say that because she's listening."

Taeela looked up and came scampering across holding out her hand for the mobile, the picture of affront.

"Hang on, mum. She wants to talk to you. You mustn't believe a word she says."

Taeela snatched the handset.

"Mrs. Rizhouell? No. It is Nigel you must not believe. I tell the truth, always. When he come home he'll say terrible things about me. They are not true. Can he come again tomorrow, please, so I tell him how bad he is?"

He heard his mother laugh as she answered, and took the phone back.

"That sounds all right," she said. "Enjoy your chess, darling. I'll see you later. They're driving you home, apparently."

The President's office was right round the gallery on the other side of the Great Hall. Once again Nigel had to have a body-search before he was let through. Inside, the layout was the same as that in the private apartments, with an almost identical inner lobby. The cigar smell was stronger, and the walls were hung with photographs of the President doing things like watching a parade or coming down the steps from a neat little jet with a group of bigwigs waiting to greet him.

Another door, and beyond it an office like any old office apart from the panelled walls and the vaulted ceiling. Desks, filing cabinets, a man and a woman using desk-top PCs, another man talking on the telephone. They glanced up from their work as Nigel was led through. One of the men raised his thumb and grinned at him. Another door…

Nigel halted, startled by the shock of change. It wasn't the office itself. That was much as he'd expected, with the President sitting at a big desk under the window, and behind him, seen through another of the stone lattices, the vista of the river with the steep-piled houses of Dahn. What stopped him was the wall of cigar-smoke that billowed through the doorway.

The President noticed. He shrugged and stubbed out the thin black cigar he'd been smoking.

"I will spare you," he said. "I cannot work without it, but we will eat and play in my study with the windows open. You said you play for your school, Nigel. Are the others in your team about your age?"

"No, sir. They're all older than me."

"So you play bottom board?"

"No, sir. Second."

"An experienced player, then. You do not think I need to give you a piece by way of a handicap?"

"Uh…Let's see how it goes, sir."

The study was a fair-sized room, also looking out over the river. There were bookshelves, easy chairs, a music centre and TV. At the back of the room was a table set out with plates, cutlery, glasses, a jug of juice and a beer-bottle, and several little dishes of food.

"Help yourself," said the President. "The food is all local. These are little fish from our lake, pickled in sweet vinegar, and those are the eggs of our mountain quail…"

Nigel did as he was told, taking a little of anything the President recommended. He was too nervous to feel hungry. The air in here was mercifully fresher, though the President himself still reeked. The chess table was set up under the window, with low tables beside each chair for the trays. The President took his over and sat, then waited for Nigel to do the same. He picked up a couple of pawns, juggled them between his hands and held out his closed fists. Nigel chose the left. Black.

"I can spare forty minutes," said the President said, putting a stopwatch down beside the board. "We will play two minutes a move, maximum, but faster if possible."

He advanced his queen's knight's pawn one square and clicked the watch. Nigel pushed a centre pawn two squares and did the same. The President shifted his bishop onto the empty pawn square to threaten it. Nigel was surprised. It was a flashy sort of opening, Mr Harries had told him, but schoolboys are always trying that sort of thing, so he'd met it before. He merely supported the pawn, then continued to occupy the centre, developing his pieces and at the same time blocking the President's attack down the diagonal. They castled on opposite sides and exchanged a couple of pawns.

The centre of the board was already becoming congested when for the first time Nigel took his two minutes. He wasn't thinking about how to win the game, but whether to. He hadn't worked it out exactly, but he thought he could do it in about eight moves, most of which would seem merely to be countering the President's coming attack. What had his father said? "*I believe he plays, I don't know how well, though I doubt is there's anyone in the country with the nerve to beat him.*"

Scary? Not necessarily. The President can't have seen the threat, so he'd never know if Nigel simply played on without putting it into action.

He couldn't bring himself to do it. He bit his lip and made a couple of what looked like nothing-much moves. Now, he thought, and swallowed convulsively. His heart started to pound.

The President launched his attack as if nothing had changed. When the massacre was over he was a knight for a pawn up but Nigel had his rooks doubled on a half-open file. Confidently the President shifted his remaining bishop to threaten Nigel's queen. Instead of retreating Nigel advanced her along the diagonal and took the bishop. As the President's hand was hovering to retake with a protecting pawn he saw what would happen. Move the pawn and the file would be fully open. Another move and Nigel would have his front rook on the back rank. Check. The knight could retake, but Nigel's second rook would take it in turn and the President's king would be trapped in its own fortress. Checkmate.

A really good player would have resigned two moves ago, but then a really good player wouldn't have got into that mess.

Abruptly the President stood, turned to the window, snatched a handkerchief out of his pocket and sneezed violently into it, a real trumpet-call of a sneeze. He turned, shaking his head and wiping his eyes with the handkerchief, and then folded it fussily and put it back into his pocket. As he was about to sit down there was a tap at the door.

He looked towards it, frowning, and called out. A man came in with a phone in his hand. The President took it and asked an irritable-sounding question. A pause, and then he sighed, shrugged and turned to Nigel.

"My apologies, but I must break off," he said brusquely. "Something urgent has come up. We will play again some time."

He spoke to the man, who answered briefly and left. The President had started to put the pieces away and Nigel was about to do the same but as soon at the door closed the President stopped.

Nigel looked up. The President didn't do or say anything, but stood there motionless, looking down at him.

Now he was really scared.

"You were about to checkmate me," said the President.

"Yer…yes, sir."

"You realise what this means to me, to be beaten, by a child, my guest, in my own palace?"

"Yer…yes, sir. I…almost…"

"Decided not to make the queen move? To let me overwhelm you a few moves later? And yet you did it. Why? Pride? Vanity?

To have beaten the President of Dirzhan? Something to boast about to your friends?"

"Oh, no, sir! That queen sacrifice—I hadn't even been thinking about it. It was just there, all set up, ready, and I sort of noticed it. I've never done one before. I could see it was going to work. Then…I knew what it meant—I could have just retreated the queen and fought you off—it'd have been a close thing—but I couldn't do it. It would have been a kind of…cheating, I suppose. I felt if I did it I'd never be given a present like that again."

"Cheating whom?"

"I…I don't know…The game…You too, sir, I suppose. You've done me proud, having me here, letting me visit your daughter—it's a terrific honour. I'd have been doing something sneaky, behind your back…"

He ran out of words and waited. His right hand was trembling. He couldn't stop it.

"My daughter appears to like you," said the President. "She has asked you to return tomorrow?"

(How…? Oh yes, of course. Mr. Dikhtar must have told him.)

"…er…Yes, sir…If that's all right."

"I asked you to play chess with me to see if you knew enough about the game to teach her. She is anxious to learn and I do not have the time."

"I'll try if you like, sir."

"And what do you propose to tell your parents about our game?"

"I'll say…I'll say we were still slogging it out when something came up and you had to go."

The President nodded and turned to the door, but paused with his hand on the doorknob.

"We will play again soon," he said. "And you will play your best. No 'cheating'. And I will beat you."

Nigel sighed, shuddered, and finished putting the pieces back in the box. Jet-lag swept over him with a rush, but by the time

Mr. Dikhtar came to take him down to the car his hands had almost stopped trembling.

He got his favourite meal for supper, grilled lamb chops, with chips and French beans and mushrooms. His mother had cooked it herself, to make sure the embassy's Dirzhani chef didn't mess it up with spices and sauces, but it all seemed to be subtly different from what it would have been in England. Surely a French bean is a French bean wherever you eat it, but these seemed to be French with a Dirzhani accent. His father was working late downstairs and didn't come in to supper till Nigel was well into his second helping.

"At last!" said his mother. "I've been bursting to know how Nigel got on at the palace, but it didn't seem fair to ask him to tell us twice."

"Suits me," said his father. "Reheats are seldom as good as the original dish. Well, Niggles, what did you make of the girl?"

"No, start at the beginning," said his mother. "Rick dropped you at the door and saw you taken inside, he says. Then what?"

Nigel took them through it in detail. His mother interrupted with questions and comments, about the eagles, for instance: "That's an outrage! Those magnificent birds, shut up in a mews!"

"It's probably the most effective way of protecting them," said his father. "Shepherds are going to think twice about putting out poison bait for the Khan's birds. Go on, Niggles. No, wait. I take it that apart from that interesting comment about the video you didn't discuss much by way of matters of state."

"He isn't there as a British spy, Nick! Absolutely not! I'd never have agreed…"

"As you say, absolutely not. But neither is he there as a channel through which the President can pass on information, or more likely misinformation, to me. If anything of that kind were to come up, I don't want to know about it. I think in fact the President will co-operate.

"And since we're on the subject, about your blog—odious word—Niggles, I think you'd better not say anything about your visit to the palace."

"Oh, but…."

"It isn't just that there's a lot of people back home who wouldn't be happy about the idea of the British ambassador cosying up with a ruthless dictator…"

"That's how I feel," said Nigel's mother.

"…I've a fine line to tread right here. Because of the dam project it is important that I should be on reasonable terms with him, but it is equally important that I shouldn't give the Russians the slightest excuse for claiming that I'm in any way close to him. Since the war in Georgia they've become increasingly hostile to anything that might be construed as Western interference in any of the states on their border that used to be part of the old Soviet empire. Only a few years back they persuaded Kazakhstan to turf the Americans out of an important airbase there. No doubt they've been putting similar pressure the President to let them take the dam project over. They'll find him a tough nut to crack—he won't stand for interference from anyone—but if he has a weak spot it is his daughter. Your visits to her may seem trivial in the light of world affairs, but in the hands of a skilled propagandist they could cause considerable embarrassment."

"I wasn't going to say he was the President, Dad. Just a rich guy with a swank house on the river."

"Ah…In that case…You'll show me when you've finished?"

"All right. Shall I go on?"

Was almost beating the President at chess a matter of state? The President seemed to think so. Nigel was pretty sure that that monstrous sneeze had been a sort of get-me-out-of-this signal. The interruption had been just too neat to be for real. Anyway, he'd already worked out what he was going to tell his parents, and it didn't make any difference what his father had just said.

"I took him a bit by surprise, I think. He only wanted to play me to see if I was good enough to teach Taeela, so maybe he was a bit careless. Out of practice too. We were about level when something came up and he had to go.

"And really that was it. Oh, yes, one thing, Mum. Any chance there's a video here Taeela might want to watch with people talking posh in it? Like Helena Bonham-Carter, he said."

"I'll look."

CHAPTER 3

Day 3.

Back to Mr G.'s in the morning...

This time one of the palace cars came to fetch Nigel. The driver didn't speak English, or pretended not to, and drove him along a boring modern ring-road, over a different bridge and round to the back of the palace, then through an archway guarded by sentries into a huge central courtyard, with a pillared arcade running all the way round it.

He parked in the far corner, got out, opened the door for Nigel, muttered what must have been the Dirzhani for "This way," and led him to a side door. A bored guard checked Nigel's pass, rootled a bit in his bag, frowned at the video of *The Railway Children*, shrugged and handed the bag back. The security seemed to be much slacker down here than it was at the main entrance. He did a perfunctory body-search and let Nigel in to a small modern hallway whose only feature was the door of a lift-shaft, with a key-pad on the wall beside it. Not bothering to hide what he was doing the guard pressed in a stupidly simple code, 9876. The door sighed open and he gestured to Nigel to enter, then leaned in, pressed the "2" button and withdrew as the door closed. Somewhere up at the top of the shaft a buzzer sounded.

The lift started upward.

When the door opened again Nigel stepped out into far end of the lobby in the Khan's private apartments. The door of the living-room was already ajar. Taeela came running to it and flung it wide, but stopped there and did her pout.

"You…you're late!" she said.

He looked at his watch.

"I'm three minutes early."

"Three minutes early is late!"

"OK."

Her new toy, he thought, as he followed her into the room. The eunuch, on his stool just inside the door, greeted him with a smile and a slow, deferential nod. He smiled back and raised a hand in greeting. Boys, he wondered. Apart from school, does she get to meet boys at all? If so, how do they cope with it, the precious daughter of the Khan, the eunuch listening to every syllable, watching every gesture with his sleepless single eye? They'd be out of there as soon as they got the chance, wouldn't they? Not much fun for her.

"Can I call him Fofo?" he muttered as he sat down

She glanced towards the door, frowned and shook her head.

"Then you must teach me to say his name."

"Fohdrahko."

The aitches were tricky. She kept him at it until she was satisfied, then called the eunuch over.

"Say it to him," she said.

Nigel rose. He didn't want to have his hand kissed again, so he put his palms together in front of his face as he'd seen Indians do, bowed his head slightly and said "Greetings, Fohdrahko."

The eunuch copied the gesture one-handed.

"Khanazhan Nigel," he said carefully.

Taeela clapped her hands.

"I teach…taught him how he…how to say your name. Khanazhan means little khan. Now you can call him Fofo."

She spoke in Dirzhani to the eunuch, who gave a silent laugh, bowed his head again to Nigel and returned to his stool.

"What would you like to do?" said Nigel. "My mother's found a film you might like to watch. If we get bored I could start teaching you chess."

"Cool," she said experimentally.

As soon as the film started Fohdrahko brought his stool over and settled behind the sofa. Watching it was a slow process because Taeela kept pausing it to ask Nigel questions about stuff she hadn't understood, or simply to explain what people were saying to Fohdrahko. She was starting to sound like Jenny Agutter when the servant came in with the drinks and biscuits. They were still only half way through, but she switched the TV off.

"Enough," she said. "Now you teach me chess."

Mr. Harries used the school team to help teach beginners, so Nigel knew the drill. First he showed her the moves, and how to take pieces and what check and checkmate meant and so on. Then he set the board up, giving her the black pieces, and advanced his king's pawn.

"Your turn," he said.

"What I…do I do?"

"Anything you like, so long as it's legal. I won't be trying to beat you, I'll be trying to keep the game going. It's just so you can get a feel of how it works."

The first game took about five minutes. In the second he started saying things like "I can take that knight with my bishop unless you protect it with that pawn." By the third she'd stopped moving almost at random and was beginning to play more intently, starting to make a move, taking it back (Mr. Harries let beginners do that), defending her pieces with other pieces and so on.

As they set up the pieces for the next game Nigel said "We'd better make this the last one. I'll have to go soon."

"I will play ve-ry slow-ly. This time I am black."

In fact she played only a little slower, and that because she was thinking more. When there were only a few minutes left he said "Are you sure you want to do that?"

She stared at the piece she'd just moved, and shrugged.

"Why not?"

He advanced a pawn to fork her knight and rook.

"You've got to lose one of them," he said.

She glared at him and shifted the knight.

"I like my little horses," she said.

"You mustn't think like that," he said. "That rook was much better placed, and it'll be stronger once the board's a bit clearer. You've got to get used to the idea of giving pieces up, any piece, if it's worth while. There's nothing more exciting than a good queen sacrifice."

"Show me."

"Next time. I'll have to think it out."

"No, show me now. This game is stupid."

Impatiently she picked her queen up and handed it to him.

"Oh, all right. But if the driver..."

"I tell him to wait."

"Oh, all right."

Because it was fresh in his memory and he could do it without thinking he quickly set up the position at the end of yesterday's game.

"Now look," he said. "I've got a strong attack on your king here. It's your move. The first thing you're going to do is..."

There was a tap at the door and the rustle of its movement across the carpet. It wasn't the under-secretary coming to tell Nigel the car was ready. It was the President.

Nigel rose. Taeela rushed across the room, grabbed his hand and started to pull him towards the board.

"Come! See!" she said. "Nigel is showing to me how I sacrifice my queen!"

He came and stood, gazing down at the board. Nigel's throat was taut, his mouth dry. He had to stop his tongue from continually licking his lips.

"You gave her the black pieces?"

"Yes, sir. Uh, she had them already. Uh, I'd forked her knight and rook…"

He stumbled through to the end of his explanation.

"Why this position?"

"It was a game I'd, uh, studied not long ago so I didn't have to think it out."

Another tap on the door and swish of its opening.

"Tell the driver to wait," said the President without looking round. "Very good, Nigel. Continue the demonstration."

Nigel managed to take a grip of himself. It was going to be all right. This time, anyway. He turned to the board.

"Now," he said. "It's my move. I attack your queen with my bishop. Either you'll have to move her away or use her to take my bishop, but if you do that I'll take her back with this pawn. What do you do?"

"I move her…but you say no?"

"Look what happens if you move her. Something like this…"

Rapidly he shifted the pieces through several moves.

"Now you see, you've still got your queen but you've lost more pieces than I have and I'm pretty sure to beat you soon. But…"

He put the pieces back.

"So I take the bishop, like this, with my queen?"

"And I take her with the pawn. You've lost her. But look at your rooks."

It took her a few seconds to see the point. She picked the front rook up and banged it down in his back rank.

"Check!" she shouted, and a moment later "Checkmate!"

"A queen sacrifice," said the President quietly. "Extremely satisfying. Except when it happens to you."

"You tell me I am your queen," said Taeela pertly. "Often you say this. So you sacrifice me, because it is satisfying? You tell me, marry the son of the British Ambassador because it will be good for your stupid dam."

"You should not tease your guest like this. It is not manners. Besides, Nigel may have views on the matter."

He turned to Nigel and raised his eyebrows.

"Er…well…of course you wouldn't sacrifice her for anything or anyone," he said. "Chess is only a game—all you've got to do is win. And anyway Fohdrahko wouldn't approve."

"Three excellent answers for the price of one," said the President. "All you have to do is win, so you will sacrifice your best pieces to achieve that. As your father my aim is to secure your happiness and well-being. As President my aim is to secure the happiness and well-being of Dirzhan. These two purposes are not part of the same game. May I never need to choose between them."

All the lightness of his tone was gone. For the first time Nigel felt that he had a glimpse of the man behind the mask of power—the man behind the monster behind the mask, if you wanted to look at it that way. Taeela reached up and stroked the back of his hand with her fingertips. He took her hand into his own, squeezed it gently, and let go.

"You do not choose," she said. "You ask me, 'Who do I wish I…wish to marry?' Then I choose. Am I right?"

She had dropped her habitual pertness and spoke as if she meant what she said almost as earnestly as her father had. His face went blanker than ever.

"Well, we must not keep our guest waiting to be taken home," he said.

Taeela refused to have the subject changed.

"First, tell me I am right, Dudda."

He said nothing for a while, then sighed.

"Yes, you are right. I do not sacrifice my queen, though I lose the game."

"Word of the Khan, Dudda?" she said, dead serious now, and offered him her hand, palm up. He hesitated briefly and took it between his.

"Word of the Khan, Taeela," he said.

"It is spoken, Khan," she answered, still utterly solemn, then swung round laughing, triumphant, and it was a game again.

"Nigel, you are witness. You will come again tomorrow?"

"If you like. But I'm afraid I can't do Saturday or Sunday. We're going up to the mountains for the weekend."

"Pooh! Nothing is to do in the mountains?"

"There is for us. My father is nuts about fishing, and my mother and I will go bird-watching. She says they've found a really nice old hotel at—I've forgotten the name— it begins with an F. For- something."

"Forghal," said the President. "I must take you there one day, my dear. The hotel is a true relic of the Czarist days…I am afraid there may be problems about that, Nigel. I will call for the latest reports and telephone your father. Meanwhile I think the driver is waiting for you in the lobby. We will see you tomorrow."

Nigel told his mother what the President had said as soon as he got back to the embassy.

"Oh, I hope not," she said, "but it's the sort of thing that happens here. Somebody gets drunk in a bar and says something stupid about the President and they close the whole area off and do a house-to-house search and so on."

"Are there actually any terrorists? Bombings and stuff?"

"Not like that, not so far. I suppose these days there are fanatics about wanting to turn Dirzhan into a proper Islamic state, though everyone else thinks the Dirzhaki are hopeless heretics and don't even count. You'll have to ask your father—he'll be up for lunch in a few minutes, though I doubt if he's heard anything about Forghal yet. It can't be that urgent."

She was wrong on both counts. He was half an hour late and

came in with an odd expression on his face. He didn't say anything until he'd sat down.

"The good news or the bad news?"

"The President told Nigel there might be a problem about Forghal," said Nigel's mother, "so I suppose the bad news is that we're not going there because the area's closed off."

"Right, but I doubt if that's true. Roger called the hotel this morning to check our bookings were OK, and they didn't say anything."

"Then why on earth…? Unless he doesn't want us to go to Forghal for some reason, I can't imagine what."

"Because he wants us to go somewhere else?" said Nigel. "And that's the good news?"

"You're spoiling my fun," said his father. "Care to guess what?"

"I don't know. We were chatting away about going to Forghal, and he started telling Taeela what a nice old hotel it was, and then, all of a sudden he pretty well closed right down and sent me packing."

"So the good news is…"

"That we're still going somewhere we can fish and bird-watch…He's taking us out to the thingummy gorge to look at the fish-owls so he can show the British Ambassador how much he cares about them?"

"I worry about you, Niggles. You really are too bright to live long. Yes, he's invited us to his hunting lodge for the weekend. That's something in itself. It's the old hunting lodge of the khans, not that far from the Vamar gorge, so we'll be flying up in a couple of helicopters on Saturday morning, then driving over to the gorge that evening to have a look at the fish-owls."

"In the dark?" said Nigel's mother.

"He's already got a project set up to study the birds with a view to providing them with a fresh habitat further down the gorge. There'll be night vision binoculars and so on. The project director—

I've met him—he's a very live-wire little German—looks like a cross between an Old Testament prophet and a garden gnome—he'll be on hand to tell us what's what."

"You've already accepted?"

"Difficult not to. It would be a considerable snub. Mostly he uses the lodge as a private retreat. I believe he took the President of Kyrgyzstan out there when he came on a state visit a few years back, but that was very much the exception."

Nigel could hear the purr in his voice. The visit would be a real plus for him at the Foreign Office.

"Is Taeela coming?" said Nigel.

"Indeed she is. He specifically asked me to remind you, Lou, that she mustn't be left alone with Nigel, or indeed with any member of the male sex over the age of four, including himself, but it's all right if you're there too."

"What a crazy mind-set. Helicopters and sophisticated economics and CCTV and this! Poor girl. Am I going to have to dress for dinner, Nick?"

"Not if we're going owl-watching, I imagine. But we'd better take something presentable, just in case. There's limited baggage-space in the helicopters, so a car will come for our stuff on Friday morning and take it up by road. Oh, one other thing. Don't tell anybody where we're going. Anybody at all. Even here in the Embassy."

"I bet you I hear about it at the next wives' lunch," said Nigel's mother. "These things always come out. They'll be green with envy."

"This is serious, Lou. I've promised the President that none of us will breathe a word about our visit until we're safely back in Dara. By the best intelligence we've got there've been two foiled assassination attempts in the last eighteen months."

"Wow!" said Nigel. "Who by?"

"Could be any of a number of people. The odds are it's something to do with the dam. According to rumours it was the Moscow mafia, hoping to muscle in on the project if the President isn't in the way. But it's just as likely to be home-grown Dirzhaki, some of them pretty high up in the administration, who've got the same idea. And then there'll be some of the military who'd like to be able to order absurd numbers of tanks and aircraft in the arms market because of the kick-backs that go with them. And there's even an old clan feud still active. You know what the great Dirzhani epic is called, Niggles? *The Vengeance of the Khan.* They still think like that."

"Have you got it?"

"There's an English translation in the library. I found it pretty unreadable. I hope you're both happy about this."

"Anything to get out of Dara for a couple of days," said Nigel's mother. "I was in the market before ten, and it was stifling already. Rick says according to the local radio it's going to get worse."

"That's all right, then. Now I've got to gobble and go. Tell me what you're up to this afternoon."

"I thought we'd go and look at the caves. At least it will be cooler in there."

CHAPTER 4

Day 4 was yesterday

Mr G's again in the morning, but then I got a crummy great headache and Mum made me go to bed. Sorry about that…

(He didn't like lying, but it was the best he could do.)

It seemed even hotter next morning by the time the driver dropped Nigel off at the back entrance to the Palace. The same guard was there, half-lounging in the strip of shade below the wall while he chatted to a young woman, presumably one of the palace servants. He had a piggy, pleased-with-himself face. When Nigel offered him his pass he just glanced sidelong at him and waved it aside and opened the door, making no attempt to search him, and gestured to him to go on in. He grunted something that probably meant "Wait" and returned to the girl.

Nigel went in and waited. He'd forgotten to have a pee before he left the embassy and was beginning to notice the fact. Several minutes passed. He was already late. The need to pee was becoming urgent. The hell with it, he thought, and keyed in the code. The lift doors opened, and closed behind him as soon as he pressed the 2 button.

The lift went down, not up, and stopped with a jolt. The lights went out. Close by outside an alarm bell clanged alive. His heart hammered. It's all right, he himself kept telling himself. Just a lift malfunction. They'll come and get me out.

After a while he settled down into a corner, stuffed his thumbs against he his ears to damp down the headachy clamour of the bell and played through his game against the President in his head to fight the urge to pee.

The bell stopped as suddenly as it had begun. He took his thumbs out of his ears and rose. He could hear a man's voice, close outside, giving orders by the sound of it. The doors sighed open and he was bathed in glaring light.

He staggered back, blinded. Rough hands grabbed him, hustled him out and flung him on the floor. A man shouted an order, urgent.

"I'm English!" he croaked, just managing not to wet himself. "I can't speak Dirzhani. No Dirzhani."

Silence. Hesitation. The glare vanished, replaced by ordinary electric light. Blinking, he made out soldiers standing above him, staring down. Two guns were pointing at him. He began to reach for the pass in his pocket, but was instantly grabbed again, and hoicked to his feet. One of the men felt in the pocket, found the pass, looked at it and handed it to the man who seemed to be in command.

He too looked at it, unclipped a handset from his belt and tapped in a number. When it was answered he spoke for a while, answered a question, waited, spoke again, and passed the handset to Nigel.

"Mr. Rizhouell?"

"Mr. Dikhtar? Yes, me. I'm terribly sorry. I didn't realise…"

"Please tell me what happened. Your driver reports that he left you at the door and passed you over to the guard on duty there."

"That's right…"

Nigel started to explain in detail.

"You knew the code for the lift door."

"The guard let me see him tapping it in yesterday. 9876. It was so simple I couldn't help noticing."

"Understood. Please pass me back to the guard sergeant."

The guard sergeant listened to the handset briefly, switched it off and clipped it back on his belt. He gestured to Nigel to go into the lift, then started giving orders to the other men.

Nigel waited shuddering with released tension and desperate by now for a pee. His headache got worse. To distract himself he tried to work out what must have happened. The simple security code was a trap. There must have been something the guard did yesterday after the door had closed. Yes, that buzzer, signalling that everything was in order. Without that the lift would have gone down, like today, trapping whoever was inside it safely in the basement.

So it looked as if the guard was going to be in serious trouble, and the poor servant-girl too, probably. It really didn't seem fair, especially on her. But if there'd been two assassination attempts in the last eighteen months…

At last the guard sergeant came in, closed the door, took the lift up a floor, opened the door, pressed the 2 button, and nipped out before the door closed. The buzzer sounded overhead and the lift rose, stopping at the second floor. Mr. Dikhtar was waiting in the lobby, not looking at all smiley. The air-conditioning was on, but his upper lip was shiny with sweat.

"You have behaved somewhat unwisely, Mr. Rizhouell."

"I didn't know what to do. Taeela doesn't like to be kept waiting."

"The guard denies that he kept you waiting more than a few seconds, while he finished some official business with the young woman."

"That's nonsense! It was more than five minutes. I looked at my watch. And they were chatting and laughing."

"One moment," said Mr. Dikhtar, reaching for a wall telephone.

"I've got to go to the bathroom," said Nigel. "It's really urgent."

Mr. Dikhtar pointed at a door as he picked up the handset, and

Nigel darted off. By the time he came back Mr. Dikhtar was trying to be smiley again, but not convincingly.

"Fortunately we have corroboration for your account," he said. "The car was logged in at the entrance eight minutes before the alarm sounded. That being the case I have to apologise on behalf of the President for the insolence of the guard's behaviour. But at the same time I must ask you not to speak to anyone about what has happened. If the precautions we take to protect the President became known, they would cease to be effective. I am afraid this applies even to your father. It is not that the President does not trust him personally, but…"

"It's all right, Mr. Dikhtar. I'm just here to help Taeela with her English. My father doesn't want me to get involved in anything else. If I happen to pick up interesting stuff here, he doesn't want to know."

Mr Dikhtar stared at him unbelievingly and shrugged.

"That is a wise arrangement," he said. "I will tell the President."

"What about Taeela? She must have heard the alarm. I've got to tell her something."

"She is aware of the precautions that involve her safety and will have taken the appropriate action."

He moved along the corridor, hesitated, and tapped on the door.

"I will see you later, Mr. Rizhouell," he muttered, and stood aside as it opened.

Inside the room almost nothing had changed, but the atmosphere was completely different. The television was on, *Charmed* this time; Fohdrahko was closing the door, Taeela sitting on the sofa. But he wasn't smiling and she was hunched and scared and the room prickled with tension.

"What happens? What happens?" she whispered, rising to her feet.

He forced himself into movement, crossed the room and settled onto the arm of the sofa, trying to look a bit more relaxed than he felt.

"It was mainly my fault, I suppose," he said, "but I didn't want to keep you waiting and I was desperate for a pee…"

"What is pee?"

"Go to the loo…er, toilet, bathroom, whatever you call it."

Her eyes widened.

"You talk about this? To me? A woman?"

"Er, yes. I suppose so. Shouldn't I have?"

She laughed suddenly, and the tension eased.

"I am learning so much from you," she said. "Go on."

It was a relief to tell someone who he felt was on his side. He went through the story in detail, only toning down his rough handling a bit, but making no bones about how scared he had been. It took a while as she stopped him every couple of sentences so that she could translate to Fohdrahko. Nigel had been ready for her to find it comic, which it had been in a way, the whole elaborate machinery of the palace gathering itself to suppress a harmless kid.

But Taeela didn't see it that way at all. She said something to Fohdrahko, and took Nigel's hand in between hers.

"But this is horrible for you, Nigel," she said earnestly. "Did they hurt you?"

"I'll get over it. But it was pretty scary while it was happening… Look, Taeela, there's one thing you could do. I don't feel too bad about the guard. He wasn't doing his job properly, and then he tried to make it look as if it was all my fault. But the woman he was talking to—could you try and see that they aren't too tough with her?"

"Was she pretty?"

"I didn't notice."

She shook her head pityingly and rose from the sofa.

"Nigel, you are too much…much too…nice," she said. "OK. I telephone Avron Dikhtar."

While she was talking to Mr Dikhtar Nigel looked round the room, puzzled. She would have taken the appropriate action, Mr Dikhtar had said. What? There was only the one door, nowhere obvious to hide, and the windows were barred by the stone lattice close outside. All he could think of was that there might be some kind of James-Bondish device which would shoot out of the floor at the touch of a button and bar the door with inch-thick bullet-proof steel, but he couldn't see any sign of it.

Taeela put the phone down and laughed.

"Poor Avron," she said. "He is so afraid of my Father, what he will say. I tell him...told him I will make it OK. Do I say 'OK' to my father, Nigel?"

He blinked at the change of subject.

"Er...I think he'd prefer 'All right,'" he said. "What about the woman?"

"She will be only warned," she said. "And she will be told that it is at your asking that she isn't more punished."

"Great. So what would you like to do now? I've brought a tape of another film my mother thought we might enjoy..."

Unsurprisingly the rest of the morning was rather flat. Nigel's headache came and went. His mother would have something for it. What was he going to tell her? Blame it on jet-lag? They watched *The Four Feathers* for a while, played three games of chess, chatted. He told her about school and the other kids, and his teachers and the gossipy rumours about them. It was an effort to keep it going. As he'd guessed, she didn't have any real friends her own age, but she talked about her visits to Moscow, and her mother and her brothers.

"Don't you miss them?" he asked.

She shook her head.

"They do not belong here. They are Russians. My brothers like the hunting lodge, but when they come they are visitors. Tourists. When I go to Moscow, it is the same. In Moscow I am the tourist. My mother didn't want another child. Always she is kind to me, but she cannot love me."

"I've been lucky. I was a mistake too, but my parents seem to love me OK."

"Oh, I am not a mistake. My father looked at my brothers. He saw that they were Russians. He said to my mother, give me another child, a Dirzhak, and then you can go to Moscow. I am the price of her freedom. She told me this herself."

He stared at her, appalled but fascinated. She had been speaking apparently lightly, but she wasn't joking, as if the fact that her mother couldn't love her wasn't any more than that, a simple fact, like the direction in which a river runs or the height of a mountain.

"You don't mind?"

She shrugged.

"My father loves me, and that is enough. He is Dirzhak, and I am Dirzhak. When I am older, we will choose a man for me to marry, but when my father dies I will be Khan."

"Is that possible?"

"We will make it possible. There were two Princess Khans in old times. My father has promised me."

She waited for a response, but he couldn't think of anything to say. Taeela frowned at him, puzzled, concerned.

"Are you well, Nigel?"

"Sorry. It's just a bit of a headache."

"Those stupid guards!"

"They were just doing their job."

"Here, you must lie down, and Fofo will make you his medicine. Then I send for the car to take you home."

The medicine was bright yellow and pungent as garlic. It got up Nigel's nose and made him sneeze till his head rang, but it must have had something effective in it, because he was almost asleep by the time he staggered up the embassy steps. His mother wasn't happy about it but decided not to risk giving him paracetamol on top of it, so let him go straight to bed, where he slept through a series of vividly crazy dreams and woke, clear-headed and hungry, just in time for supper.

Day 5,

Two visits this time, one to Mr. G's and one to Rick's. He works at the embassy. Couldn't have been differenter…

There was a new guard on the courtyard entrance next morning, who went punctiliously through the security drill, never looking Nigel directly in the eye. After what had happened yesterday, Nigel felt very on edge until the lift stopped at the second floor, and there was Fohdrahko waiting for him, smiling as he murmured his formal greeting, making the whole extraordinary world of the palace seem safe and ordinary for him, as it was for Taeela.

It stayed that way all morning, comfortable without being boring. They talked, then watched part of a Harry Potter movie. Taeela was very disappointed to learn that even without the magic Hogwarts wouldn't have been anything like the school Nigel went to.

"Maybe when my granddad was a kid," he told her.

It was slow going again, because she kept stopping the film to ask questions and explain stuff to Fohdrahko. She was fascinated by Hermione.

"Do you think she is pretty, Nigel?"

"I suppose so. She's an actress. It's her job to look hot."

"You suppose so! Oh, Nigel! You…you…Do you suppose I am pretty? Hot?"

"It isn't the most important thing, that's all. I like you. That's what matters. I wouldn't mind if you were plain as a boot, which you aren't. As a matter of fact I'm meeting a couple of girls this afternoon. I'll make a special effort to notice if they're pretty."

"Two girls? English girls? What they do…are they doing in Dirzhan?"

"They were born here. Their mum's Dirzhani, their dad's English, except he's taken Dirzhani citizenship. He loves it here. He's the driver at the Embassy. He brought me down here first day I came, and he told me about his daughters."

He'd been leading her on, enjoying her pretence of outraged jealousy as much as she was, but now she didn't take it like that. Instead she stared at him with genuine amazement.

"You...you are the son of the Ambassador of the Queen of England and you have tea with one of your servants!"

"Rick's a good guy. He's knows stuff about Dirzhan which I bet my dad doesn't know. And I do want to meet ordinary Dirzhaki. I love coming here, and I think you're terrific, and I really hope we can stay friends somehow. But you're the daughter of the President Khan. There's no way you can be ordinary. No way this can be an ordinary home."

Taeela pouted dramatically.

"They will be plain as...two boots," she said, closing the subject. "Now we will play chess."

They did that for a bit, Nigel giving himself five seconds a move and Taeela taking as long as she liked. He was teaching her the Queen's Indian opening—because she liked the name of course—when the President came in, followed by the drinks and nibbles. But he didn't stay long or say very much, and when he left they put the chess set away and watched Harry Potter until it was time for Nigel to go home.

"Tomorrow we go to the hunting lodge," said Taeela.

"We're thrilled. Mum and Dad too. We're really looking forward to seeing it."

"Fofo says there will be thunderstorms. He is never wrong."

Later that afternoon they dropped Nigel's mother off at some kind of diplomatic charity do on the embankment and drove on through the stifling heat, past the palace on the far bank, then up into the old town opposite a ridiculous fairy bridge with little knobbly spires down either side, like the ones you see on the roof of a cathedral. As soon as they were round the corner Rick stopped the car, took a banknote out of his wallet, turned to the bodyguard, spoke a few words in Dirzhani and gave him the note.

The guard grunted and got out of the car.

"Don't want him waiting out in the road for us," Rick explained. "Makes the neighbours jumpy."

He drove on up a typical twisting street, crowded with people and stalls, and filled with the reek of spices and herbs and the rich sweet smoke of barbecues, and halted beneath an imposing poster of the President triumphing over his snow ibex.

"That's where I live," he said, gesturing at the street opposite. "Got to take you round the back, though. No room to leave the car in front."

A little further on he turned left into a side street and then nosed the Rover into an impossibly narrow slot that opened into a courtyard with a strange old tree in the middle, its twisting branches utterly bare until they reached a bunch of dark spiky leaves at their tips. Rick parked underneath it, left the car without bothering to lock it and led the way under a narrow arch into smaller courtyard, lined with pots of herbs and trailing flowers, filling the oven-like heat of the enclosed space with their scent.

"Ain't all mine," said Rick. "That's us, at the back there. That side's a little orphanage run by a couple of Greek nuns. Lord knows how they come here. Guy other side runs half the fishing fleet. Took me out in one of his boats once. They do it at night, with lamps. Good night, right time of year, fish pretty well leap into the boat. It's amazing."

By now they'd reached the far side of the courtyard. He opened a door into a high, dim corridor. Cool air streamed out into the open.

"'Nother good thing about this Khan," he said. "No power cuts. Old days, before he took over, barely worth having air-conditioning. Lucky to get six hours electrics in twenty-four, and then you didn't never know when it was going to come on. Hi, guys! We're home! Come and say hello to young Nigel.

"Speak English good as I do," he added. "Only they're not

used to boys. Janey rattles along her own way. She's got a lot of the words, but she's not got much use for the grammar."

They'd reached a point where the corridor opened into a wider hallway, with what was obviously the front door at the further end. Two girls came out of a door on the left, lined themselves up side by side and curtseyed to Nigel. They were wearing the same sort of clothes as Taeela, with shawls over their heads framing their very un-Dirzhani faces, both light brown, the older one a bit darker than her sister. He made a careful note of their looks, for Taeela. One was a year or so older than Nigel, and wore a bit of eye-shadow and pink lipstick. Her sister was about two years younger, with a more serious face, and no make-up.

He'd had twenty minutes coaching from Roger before he left the embassy, so he knew what was expected of him. He clasped his crossed hands in front of his chin and spoke his only words of Dirzhani.

"My blessings upon this house."

"I'm sorry about the accent," he added in English.

The girls stared at him, dumbly. The older one gave a get-me-out-of-this glance at someone just beyond the door at her side.

"OK, let's do it my way," he said. "I'm your Dad's friend, Nigel. Good to meet you."

No good. He was praying Rick didn't start apologizing for their shyness, when the person the other side of the door came into the hall, a small, pudgy, anxiously smiling woman.

"This is Janey," said Rick. "Dzhanayah ,if you're talking local. And since the girls won't, I'll tell you that's Lizhala there on the left and Nahdalin on the right. Lisa and Natalie to you."

"Happy with meeting you," said Janey. "Come in along."

The room was obviously only used for this sort of thing, musty and shadowy, lit by one small window and three heavily shaded lamps. The central table was covered with dishes of elaborate little cakes and pastries and crystallized fruit.

Nigel sat where Rick told him to and put his shoulder-bag on the floor beside him. Rick sat opposite. The girls hovered while Janey took a pair of silver tongs, picked up a tartlet from one of the dishes and put it on Nigel's plate. She handed the tongs to Lisa who did the same and passed the tongs to Natalie, who changed her mind several times before giving him what looked like a crystallized gooseberry.

Roger had briefed Nigel about all this. "They're called guest gifts," he'd said. "Once you've eaten under their roof their men-folk are obligated to protect you."

"All right, you can sit down now," said Rick. "And for Allah's sake loosen up a bit, will you? He ain't going to eat you."

Cursing him under his breath Nigel opened his bag and took out the return gifts Roger had given him. They all came in neat little gold boxes with the British royal arms on the lid. There was a framed photograph of the Queen for Janey and two silver clips of the royal lion and unicorn for the girls, which they all seemed pleased with, but not enough to break the ice.

Nigel did his best, but it was hard work. Janey was obviously jumpy. Rick kept making clumsy attempts to jolly the girls along. Nigel told them the sort of stuff he'd been telling Taeela about his own life, and what things had been like in Santiago, and his school, and so on, but they just stared at him, and gave brief, unwilling, whispered answers to his questions about their own lives and doings. They spoke good English, with Rick's accent.

He was getting desperate when he asked them about their school. No, there weren't any boys there. Yes, the teachers were women too. Except the Imam. He taught them about Islam and the Koran. What did he think about Lisa's make-up?

Suddenly an expression, a slight pursing of the lips, suppressing a smile, and the ghost of a giggle.

"He don't know," said Lisa. "We got to wear our dahli for him."

"Have you got them here? Can I see you wearing them?"

He'd said it on the spur of the moment, just to give all three a bit of relief from the desert of time still to be got through before he could decently leave. They jumped up and scuttled out as if that was all they wanted, but they weren't long gone. There was a sound of laughter and scuffling at the door as each tried to push the other one in first. Then they composed themselves and walked demurely in, lined themselves up and curtseyed again to Nigel, just as they had done in the hall.

But this time the movement was easy, almost graceful, and though when they rose all he could see of their faces was the two-inch slot around their eyes, there was something different about the eyes themselves. There was a new light in them, a quickness of glance, an impression that life was fun. Boosted by Lisa's eye-shadow the change was dramatic, but it was also obvious in Natalie. Without the veils she was clearly the plainer sister. Now you couldn't tell.

"How on earth do you eat?" said Nigel.

Another giggle, and they came almost eagerly back to their chairs, and each took something off one of the dishes and slipped it neatly into their mouths through an opening in the side of their veils.

"Must be tricky with soup," he said.

Another explosion of giggles, Lisa half-choking on her mouthful, while Natalie unhooked a corner of her veil and, still holding it to cover her face, with her other hand mimed sliding a spoonful of soup behind it.

"Must take a bit of practice," said Nigel.

"All right, that's enough, girls," said Rick. "You can take 'em off now."

"Can I try one?" said Nigel.

Lisa helped him into hers, wrapping it round him like a dressing-gown and fastening it with a couple of hooks at the shoulder. Fussily she adjusted the veil. He found he could see perfectly well, but that there was an interesting feeling of peeping out from a hiding-place.

"Now you can forget about me being a boy," he said. "I'm Nigella. Hi, Lisa. Hi, Natalie."

More laughter, almost hysterical now. Obsessed with the break-through he hadn't noticed what was happening the other side of the table. There'd been an edginess in Rick's voice when he'd told the girls to take the veils off, and now Janey had half risen from her chair, glowering, clearly about to explode, while Rick was making desperate calming gestures. Not bothering to fiddle with the hooks Nigel pulled the dahl off over his head and gave it back to Lisa.

"I'm terribly sorry" he said. "I..."

"Janey takes that side o' things dead serious," said Rick. "You'd been a grown man, she'd've been wearing one herself. You couldn't've known."

"Is serious," said Janey. "Please, not again."

"I'll remember," said Nigel.

Mercifully the ice stayed broken. Janey and the girls cleared tea away and Rick got out a box of small coloured hexagonal tiles with different symbols on them, spread them out on the table and explained the rules of the game to Nigel. It looked fairly simple, but it wasn't. Natalie was a demon at it, and was clearly going to win when the time came for him and Rick to go and collect Nigel's mother and take her back to the embassy.

As they crossed the inner courtyard, stifling after the air-conditioning, Nigel said, "I'm sorry about putting my foot in it with Janey over the dahli."

"Forget it," said Rick. "We'd had a bit of a set to 'bout it, matter o' fact. She wanted girls to wear 'em for your visit, but I put my foot down. Wasn't that way when we married, Nigel. OK, I converted to Islam 'cause it made things easier with her family, but neither of us took it that serious back then and I still don't, but she's got a lot stricter recent. There's a bit of that going around.

"Never used to see the full veil in the old days, but there's all sorts wearing them now, despite the Khan's dead set against it."

At the bottom of the hill and Nigel got out and waited while Rick fetched the guard out of a bar. It was early evening and they were right down by the river but he was streaming with sweat in the thick and breathless heat.

Fohdrahko had been right. He could smell the thunder in the air.

CHAPTER 5

Hi there. Sorry about the gap. Mr G invited us up to his hunting lodge in the mountains for a couple of days and there aren't any internet connections there, We'd flown up in his helicopter and landed in a storm and damaged to chopper so we had to stay on a bit. I could still write the blog but I couldn't post it till we got back to Dara Dahn.

So this is Day 6.

It thundered amazingly all night…

The embassy seemed to shudder to the non-stop bellowing explosions. Rain torrented down. It was impossible to sleep, but after a while the rain let up and Nigel got out of bed and watched the storm. He'd never seen anything like it before. Even in the heaviest thunderstorms there'd always been intervals of utter dark before the next dazzling shaft, but here the fierce light flickered and pulsed continuously across the roofs of Dahn and the massed buildings of Dara and the hills beyond, all beneath a layer of bulging cloud so dense that not even the glare that fell from it could lighten its blackness. A house had caught fire down by the river in Dahn, a blob of smoky orange on the bleach-white scene. Then the rain sluiced down again, sifting out shape and distance and leaving only the glitter of refracted dazzle.

They woke to a still, brilliant morning and breakfasted with the windows open so that they could relish the freshness of the rain-rinsed air. The telephone rang while they were eating. Nigel's father answered it, listened for a while and said "I think that should be possible. Hold on a moment."

He cupped his hand over the mouthpiece and said "It's the President's secretary. Apparently this is only a break in the storm but there would be time for us to fly up to the hunting-lodge now and then stay an extra night so that you can see the fish-owls tomorrow. Back by mid-day Monday. OK with you two? Great… . Hello. Sorry to keep you. Yes we can certainly do that. It's very generous of the President to suggest it… Right, we'll be ready. Good bye… Well, we're going to have to get a wiggle on. There isn't much of a window. A car will be coming to fetch us in three quarters of an hour."

Three helicopters were waiting side by side in the rain-washed courtyard of the palace. The two smaller ones were painted purple, green and gold, the colours of the Dirzhani flag. In the glittering sunlight they looked like expensive toys compared to the big drab military chopper beyond them. The President, with Taeela at his side, was waiting in front of them. Two lines of uniformed soldiers were drawn up to one side. Some of them were women.

"All very formal, by the looks of it," muttered Nigel's father as the car slowed. "I'll go first and hand you out, Lou, and introduce you to the President. You just tag along, Niggles."

It all went smoothly. Taeela curtseyed neatly but shyly to Nigel's mother when they were introduced. Then they separated into the helicopters strictly by gender, Nigel's mother and Taeela and three woman soldiers in one of the smaller ones, Nigel with his father and the President and three of the men in the other, and the rest of the guards in the big chopper.

Nigel had been in helicopters before, but never as luxurious as this. There was a big comfortable seat either side of the aisle in the front two rows of the cabin and more normal seats for the three soldiers behind. The President and Nigel's father took the first two and Nigel settled into the one behind his father and put on his padded headphones. The engine woke with a roar, the rotor doubled the clatter and the palace floated away beneath them. He found a station playing an odd sort of ethno-rap and cocooned himself in solitariness. Soon he could see on his right the last of last night's storm as a dramatic layer of darkness, edged with brilliant silver, blotting out the northern mountains. On the other side the next instalment was already massing on the horizon.

For a while he watched the landscape sliding away beneath them. They were following the line of the river valley, almost due west to judge by the position of the sun. A guard came round with drinks and Dirzhani-style nibbles. He was hesitating over the drinks when the President twisted in his chair and pointed at a flask. The yellow-green fluid was cold, oily, and sweetish, with a dry aftertaste that made you want to sip again. Good choice, he thought. Typical. He doesn't miss anything.

Dazed with the luxurious comfort and the steady drub of the rotor and the remains of jet-lag he wasn't aware of falling asleep, but then woke with a start to find that the sun had moved dramatically and was now almost directly behind them, which meant the river must have swung north-west. This looked as if it was just as well. At this new angle he could see that if they had continued along the previous line it wouldn't have been long before they'd run into the advancing storm. Even as it was, it seemed to be coming surprisingly fast.

It was difficult to look away. In the seat across the aisle from the President he could see his father watching it too. The music in the headphones was replaced by the President's voice asking a question, and one of the pilots answering. The President gave orders and switched to English.

"There has been a forecasting error. The storm system appears to have changed course. It is now too late to turn back. Our best course is to descend into the comparative shelter of the gorge a little way ahead, where we could travel faster, but at the risk of encountering unpredictable gusts. If we continue as we are we will not reach the landing pad before the full force of the storm is on us. Going by the gorge we have a better chance, and if we fail to make it we should at least be over the lake, where we can ditch in…"

The rest of the sentence was lost as the helicopter gave a violent lurch and the roar of the rotor rose to a bellow, almost deafening despite the ear-muffs. As it died away he continued.

"We must prepare for a forced landing. Ambassador, please signal to me whether you both know the emergency posture… Good. Your life jacket is inside your left armrest. There is a small-size one for Nigel. Put them on but do not inflate them. A guard will come round with a waterproof bag for each of you. Put in it anything that might spoil in water, and give it back to the guard with anything that might impede your exit. Keep your seat fully erect and your seatbelt close fastened.

"Please do not worry about Mrs Ridgwell. She and my daughter are in no greater danger than we are. My guards are an elite squad, the women especially. I will keep you informed of any further developments."

By now seriously scared, Nigel found his life-jacket, put it on and laced it firm, then sorted out stuff to give to the guard and tucked it into his back-pack. The helicopter lurched again and put its nose down. Nigel readied himself for the safety drill, but it levelled and fought its way on, though now barely above the tops of the dense-packed trees on either side of the river. A shaft of lightning glared close by, forcing his eyes shut, and all other noises were drowned by the bellow of its thunder. By the time he could see again they were well below the tree-tops.

He was moving into a crouch, ready for a landing in the river when he realised that it wasn't that they were still descending but that the trees were now growing from fissured yellow-grey cliffs that rose sheer from the water. The helicopter was bouncing like a 4 x 4 riding rough ground. With his heart pounding and his palms slippery he watched the cliffs stagger past, with the tumbling water spuming along below.

Leaning forward he could see his father gnawing his knuckles as he stared out at the cliff. That makes two of us, he thought. Then something seemed to seize hold of the helicopter, tilt it to the left and at the same time fling it towards the right hand cliff. He huddled into the emergency posture. The racket of the rotor arms rose to a battering roar. Instinct closed his eyes against the flying splinters of impact.

It didn't happen. He forced them open and watched the cliff recede as the tilt of the machine clawed it clear. Lightning blinked and blinked again. He sat back up shuddering with relief. Never in his life had he been this scared. Across the aisle his father leaned out round the back of his chair with a stiff grin on his face and raised a thumb. Nigel signalled back no more convincingly. Time passed, unbelievably slowly, until the President's voice, as calm as ever, came through the headphones again.

"I have been in touch with the other two machines. They have had to drop back clear of our turbulence, but are making good progress. In about ten minutes we will be over the lake."

The helicopter bounced on. Any moment he'd be needing a sick-bag. Just in time, the ride eased. The cliffs either side receded and they were over open water. Out of the right-hand windows, across the aisle, he could see the shoreline, a narrow band of tumbled boulders and above that a forested slope rising to a craggy ridge, and way beyond that mountains, with the massed clouds of the earlier storm piling against their peaks, and the sluicing rain below.

He turned the other way and saw that the gusts that had been buffeting them to and fro were only the outriders of the next instalment of the storm. That had almost reached the shoreline, a heavy cloud-mass riddled with lightning blinks and bearing below it an impenetrable curtain of rain. In the brief lull before its onset the helicopters were racing for the landing place.

The President was talking to the pilots again. He switched to English. "We are unlikely to arrive at the pad before the rain reaches us, and in any case a dry-ground landing in this wind would be extremely dangerous in fully laden machines. There is a sheltered wharf a few hundred metres below the pad. You can both swim… ? We will jump from the helicopter as near to the wharf as we can safely hover. Two soldiers will go first to help us ashore, then you, Nigel, you, ambassador, and myself. The remaining soldier will follow. The pilots will endeavour to land the helicopter at the pad, and if they judge it too dangerous will return and ditch and then swim ashore. Take nothing with you that will impede your exit. If the machine is forced to ditch we will salvage it later. Do not inflate your lifebelt until you are standing at the door and ready to jump."

They flew joltingly on over the churning water until the rain hit them. It was as if the helicopter had flown into something solid. A clattering crash, a violent sideways slam, a stammer in the steady rotor-racket, a roar from the engines, a sense of falling…

Nigel crouched into emergency again and waited for the impact of splashdown, but the helicopter staggered on, its nose tilted downward. It couldn't last. He remembered how frail it had looked compared to the hulking Sikorsky. Surely no machine ever built could take such a battering for long…

The movement changed, with the fuselage roughly level, but swaying erratically left and right. A soldier clawed his way past him. Then another. Me next, he thought. He straightened, felt for the belt-buckle and waited for the signal. The first soldier fiddled with a panel in the door and passed it to the second one, who slotted it into the seat across the aisle from Nigel. Inside the compartment it had covered was a large black rubbery package. The first soldier unfastened straps and heaved it clear for the other one to open the door. Rain sluiced in and a spume-laden gust buffeted round the cabin. The soldiers dragged the package to the doorway and tugged at a couple of toggles either side of it. It was already inflating as they shoved it through the opening.

The first soldier stepped into the doorway, paused for a moment judging the drop, and stepped out. The second one followed. Nigel unbuckled his seatbelt and rose as the remaining soldier brushed past him. The man reached the doorway, glanced out and down, and beckoned him forward. His father gave him a thumbs-up as he passed, and rose to follow. The nose of the helicopter bucked like a leaping salmon, flinging him backwards. A hand grabbed his elbow and stopped him falling.

"Thanks," he gasped idiotically as the President hauled him up, not letting go till the soldier by the door had got hold of his other elbow and dragged him to the doorway. He copied what the first two men had done, gripping the doorposts either side and poising himself in the entrance with the rain swirling over him in the downdraught from the rotor.

Now that it was all happening the brainless terror seemed to leave him. He leaned out into the deluge. The inflated life-raft was a dark patch in the foaming turmoil below, with the soldiers either side of it holding it clear of the area where he'd fall. He drew a deep breath, checked the position of the toggle on the life-jacket and stepped firmly out, grabbing the toggle as he fell and yanking on it as he went under.

He rose gasping and shaking his head, trying to clear the water out of his eyes. He was already swimming when one of the soldiers reached him.

"I'm OK," he shouted, before the man could start life-saving him. He struck out for the life-raft and grabbed one of the hand-holds around its side. When he looked up the President was already falling. The last soldier paused in the doorway holding a big pistol-shaped object which he raised above his head and fired. He tucked it in under his jacket and stepped out. The helicopter lifted away and the flare the soldier had fired glowed above them in the downpour just as Nigel's father reached the life-raft.

"Well done, Niggles," he gasped. "All right?"

"So far."

The President joined them and waited to get his breath back, then spoke, not shouting but loud enough to be heard above the clamour of wind and water.

"Will you now swim for the shore. The wharf is a few tens of metres away downwind. One of the men will lead the way, another will stay with you in case you need help. A large inflatable is on its way out to pick up Mrs Ridgwell and my daughter. I will stay here with the remaining man and wait for them."

Led by the soldier they started to swim. It was hard work, and impossible to tell whether they were making any progress at all. From time to time he lost sight of the others but then the wave swept past and they were there again. Something loomed through the murk, a dark shape on the water. The soldier ahead stopped swimming to wave his arms, yelling at the top of his voice. The shape veered aside and bucketed past, a fair-sized inflatable with a crew of four.

They swam on. Another dark thing loomed, too large for any kind of boat, and steady in the storm. A few more strokes and Nigel could see the waves foaming along the foot of a stone wall. No possible landing on that, though there were figures on top of it, pointing and shouting as they saw the swimmers. The soldier led the way to the right, round the end of the pier and into calmer water. Several men were lined up against the stone-work on the timber steps that ran up the side of the wall, the lowest waist deep in the water. The soldier moved aside, and waved Nigel on.

The man in the water reached out as he came, took him by the arm and helped him stagger up to the next man, and so on up the steps. Even the ones standing clear of the water were drenched with rain and spray, but they grinned cheerfully at him as they handed him on. His leg muscles were like jelly. Someone at the top tried to help him towards a big Humvee but he shook him off and turned and watched his father climb the steps, looking tired and shaky, and as glad as Nigel had been of the helping hand on his arm.

"Well done, Niggles. All right? Not Lucy's idea of a good time."

"How long till she gets here?"

"Not too long. The inflatable will be quicker than we were."

"Sirs wait in auto?" said one of the men. "Hotting is on."

"Good idea," said Nigel's father. "Come on, Niggles. We'll perish in this wind."

Nigel realised that he was shuddering with cold as he stumbled along the wharf. The Humvee's windows were one-way glass, reflecting the light. The man waiting beside it, as drenched as all the others, helped them out of their life-jackets and saluted smartly as he held the door for them.

"Thanks," Nigel mumbled, and scrambled into the lovely fug. His father squelched down beside him on the expensive leather, rubbed his sleeve up and down the fogged window and peered out.

"They'll be all right, Niggles," he muttered. "These people know what they're doing. There goes their chopper. Those pilots are brave men. Maybe it'll be a bit easier with the rest of us out of the machines.

"Wait… there's Lucy…"

All of a sudden Nigel was weeping. Furious, he dragged his sopping sleeve across his face.

"And the President…" said his father. "Where's the girl?…Oh, he's got her. Looking like she did this sort of thing every day of the week… Two, three more women in life-jackets. That'll be the guards. How many were there in the chopper?"

"Three, I think."

"That's it, then. God, that's a relief!"

From the break in his voice Nigel realised that he was weeping too.

CHAPTER 6

The bath was ready and waiting when Nigel had stumbled into his suite. An anxious old man called Drogo had shown him to the bathroom and told him by signs and a smattering of English to leave his clothes by the door, then nipped in and removed them as soon as Nigel's body was decently submerged.

He lay in the lovely warmth, listening to the come-and-go battering of rain against the window and the drum-rolls of thunder, and letting the life tingle back into his dead-meat muscles and the shock and panic drift away into the sweet-scented steam, until he heard a knock on the bathroom door.

"Your case is in your room, sir," said a man's voice. "The President will be ready to receive you in twenty minutes. I shall come and fetch you." The man's English was pretty good but with a strong accent.

"Fine," called Nigel. "I'll be ready."

His bedroom was twice the size of his parents' room at the embassy, with gleaming panelled walls, paintings of lakes and mountains, a log fire blazing in the grate and a faint odour of scented smoke. He dressed luxuriously in front of it, then watched the storm until he heard a knock on the door.

He had barely looked at the hunting lodge when they'd

staggered in from the lake. He'd had an impression of a long, low wooden building, big as several barns, vaguely seen through the downpour, and then a lot of shiny wood inside.

His parents' room was next to his on a landing at the top of a gleaming stairway. The man who had knocked—dark, stocky, black suit, purple tie, white shirt, white gloves—watched impassively as Nigel ran and hugged his mother, both of them laughing with the final release of tension. He gave them about twenty seconds, then coughed and waited for them to let go of each other.

"The President sends his regrets," he said. "He has been called away. The Khanazhana will receive you in the luncheon room. Please to follow me."

Taeela was standing at the window looking out at the swirling veils of rain and the storm-tossed trees. She turned as they entered and curtseyed, much more confidently this time, to Nigel's mother.

"My father is called out," she said. "The Sikorski is found at where the lake empties down the gorge. Our men radioed how they see it across the water on some rocks."

"Good lord!" said Nigel's mother. "Do they know about the men who were in it?"

"They make signals, but it is hard to see in the rain. My father has gone to see what is to be done. He is sorry to leave you. These are his people. He must look after them. Now we will eat. I hope you are hungry."

"Famished," said Nigel's mother.

It was a pleasant, medium-sized, wood-panelled room with two large windows looking out over the invisible lake. They sat at a table laid for five at one end of the room, leaving an empty chair at the head of the table. Two serving maids wearing dazzling white aprons over high-collared purple tunics with silver buttons brought them a series of dishes with half a dozen different sauces to try. Taeela didn't know the English words for most of the food, and her stiffness broke up into laughter as they tried to work out between them what everything was. At the same time her rather anxious English relaxed and she started talking much more as she used to when Nigel came to the palace. They were getting along fine when the President came in.

"Sit, sit," he said, as he strode to his place and settled into his chair. "I must apologise for having deserted you."

"Of course you had to," said Nigel's mother. "Taeela has looked after us beautifully. I hope your men are all right."

"It is hard to tell. The Sikorski came down in the water close to the entrance to the gorge and was blown onto the rocks on the far side. The men are all out and ashore. Their radio was damaged in the landing, but from their hand signals we understand that some of them are sufficiently injured to need medical attention. They have first aid supplies and my doctor was aboard, so he will be able to do what he can for them, unless he himself is injured. We will send down one of our inflatables as soon as the storm eases. The forecast is that it should do so briefly later in the day."

The maids had been offering him food while he talked, and he'd helped himself without apparent thought and started to eat, talking between mouthfuls.

"Forgive me," he said. "There are urgent arrangements to be made. It was as well we left the helicopters when we did. Both of them suffered damage on landing. With our extra weight it could have been much worse. One can perhaps be repaired, the other will need specialist equipment. Furthermore a section of the roadway has been washed into the lake. The place is passable on foot, but not by motor vehicles, so we shall have to wait until the storm system has blown past. If the forecasts are right this should be in two days' time, so it should be possible to watch the fish-owls on Monday, along with your visit to the dam site, if you can stay the extra day, and then return to Dara Dahn by road. I must in any case be back in time for the ceremony on the Thursday, which I trust you will also be able to attend.

"The alternative would be to skip the fish-owls and arrange for cars to meet us the other side of the landslip. That would gain us an extra day, or perhaps two, but in storm-weather the journey would be considerably more than the standard eight hours. The choice is yours. Mrs Ridgwell?"

"Oh, it won't be any hardship to stay, Mr President. I'd give anything to see the fish-owls, and if it means Nick gets a bit more fishing..."

"If I may just call the embassy, if that's all right, sir," said Nigel's father. "I doubt my mobile will work in the mountains."

"There is a secure telephone line. The major domo, Mizhael, will show you. But I must ask you, Ambassador, to say nothing that gives any indication of my movements, nor that our security guard is currently depleted and the helicopters out of action."

"No problem, sir. We arrived safely, and because of the weather are staying on an extra day. Of course I shall have to make a report of our visit to the dam site, but there's no reason I should say anything about the journey, except perhaps to mention the skill of the pilots in difficult conditions."

Ambassador-talk, thought Nigel. He's really laying it on.

He caught Taeela's eye and winked. She pursed her mouth, suppressing a smile, and glanced at her father. He must have noticed the exchange, for he paused with a forkful of fish half way to his mouth and looked at her severely.

"A lesson in diplomacy, my dear," he said. "You are going to have to play hostess this afternoon and see that our guests are amused. Mizhael will make any arrangements. Now, if you will forgive me..."

He rose, so they did too. One of the maids came across with a tray, picked up the remains of his meal and followed him out.

"So, what will we all do?" said Taeela brightly, already playing the hostess for all she was worth. "When the rain stops, His Excellency will catch fish for our supper, yes?"

"I don't guarantee to catch any," said Nigel's father, joining in her game.

"You will catch three fine fish for my supper, your Excellency. I wish this. Mizhael will tell the cook that you bring… are bringing them."

"Your wish is my command."

"Good. And Mrs Ridgwell and Nigel will look for birds. I will come too. We will ride my horses. What birds do you wish to see, Mrs Ridgwell?"

"Oh, anything. It doesn't matter."

"Come on, Mum" said Nigel. "You're talking to the Khanazhana. If she says you would like to see a great pink hoopoe, someone will make sure it happens."

"I don't think they get hoopoes up here, darling."

"Come on, Mum!"

"Oh, well. A black-throated kingfisher, I suppose. They're very local, but there might be some here."

"You shall see a black-throated kingfisher. I will speak to Mizhael," said Taeela, laughing. "Now I'll stop being the Khanazhana. I'm Taeela. I'm Nigel's friend."

"Well, in that case I'm Lucy and this is Nick. That's what Nigel's other friends call us. What about when your father is here?"

"Ah…Perhaps you ask him, uh, Lucy."

"As soon as I get the chance."

They'd lunched very late, and the rain and wind had begun to ease by the time they'd finished. A guard and driver were waiting for Nigel's father with a Jeep, and he was off before the last drops fell. When the sky cleared Taeela, in full riding kit and looking like an advertisement in a glossy country magazine, met Nigel and his mother in the front hall, and they were driven the few hundred yards to the stables, where three absurdly handsome ponies were waiting for them, along with a couple of bodyguards, a woman and a man, with two more ordinary-looking horses.

Nigel had ridden a bit in Chile, and his mother had apparently been horse-mad when she was a kid, but then got interested in too much other stuff to keep it up. Taeela, of course, rode like a princess, because that was what her father expected of her.

They followed a trail up through the trees, and out onto the open mountainside like the one on the video of the snow ibex, a vast slope twinkling with little rivulets after the rain and strewn with boulders, tussocks of scrawny grass clinging to whatever soil had lodged there, and scattered clumps of stunted bushes. Their emergence surprised a large bird that must just have caught some small mammal and started to tear it apart. It looked round with shreds of meat hanging from its beak, then lumbered into the air and soared away with the limp carcass dangling from its talons. A steppe eagle, Nigel's mother decided.

The track turned and led them slantwise across the slope. The air up here seemed magically clean. They could see for uncountable miles in every direction except to the south-west, across the lake, where about ten miles away the next instalment of the storm was working its way towards them.

There were plenty of birds to see, active after the rain. Taeela must have longed to put her beautiful horses through their paces and show her guests what they could do, but she kept to a sedate walk beside Nigel's mother, halting when she wanted to use her binoculars, borrowing them so that she could look too, and asking questions about the birds. Nigel, still stiff from his swim, was happy not to have to do anything more demanding. They'd already ridden as far as he felt like when he noticed the body-guards muttering to each other, and looking to his left he saw why. The thunder was already faintly audible

"Hey, isn't it time we turned back?" he said. "We don't want to get soaked."

Taeela stared contemptuously at the coming cloud-mass.

"No problem, mister," she said in her Bart Simpson voice, wheeled her pony round and set it to a rapid canter. Nigel's mother and the female guard kept up but Nigel followed more cautiously, and the male guard stayed with him. He'd expected Taeela to go careering down through the wood, but she reined in and waited for them to catch up then rode down at a sensible pace. The first rain-veil swept up from the lake as they reached the stables.

Nigel dismounted, groaning.

"Me too," said his mother. "I shall have to have another bath or I'll be stiff as a bench."

"And sore," said Nigel. "I didn't notice a lot of kingfishers, Taeela."

"All down by the lake. They take a lesson from your father, how to fish. I'll send my father's... what is the word? She rubs you, makes you better."

"Masseuse?"

"Good, I'll send her to you, uh, Lucy. After that she can punch Nigel."

"Isn't she amazingly sane?" Nigel's mother whispered as they went upstairs. "Considering the crazy life she leads."

He came down in an almost trance-like state of relaxation after his massage. The masseuse had turned out to be one of the maids who'd waited on them at lunch. Her name was Marizhka. She'd been bossy and unsmiling, and spoke no English, but whatever she'd done had really worked. His aches were almost gone, and he was hungry all over again after his ride.

He found Taeela and his mother sitting down to a full English afternoon tea laid out at one end of the sitting-room. A log fire crackled in the hearth, thunder rumbled overhead, lightning blinked and blinked again, the tree-tops thrashed to and fro, rain-laden gusts slammed like gravel against the windows.

Nigel watched the storm in dreamy contentment while the other two hunted for the birds they had seen in two of the local bird-guides his mother had found waiting for her in her room, one in English and one Russian. This worked perfectly, his mother consulting her notes and finding a candidate in the English guide, and Taeela looking it up under its Latin name in the Russian one and translating the entry. They were both obviously having a wonderful time.

Taeela specially. She can't have had anything like this before. How could she have any real friends, friends who could talk to her as if she wasn't the daughter of the President Khan? Let alone any grown-up? She and his mother had known each other… how long? About nine hours. And yet they were already acting like friends. For Taeela it must have been totally amazing.

Perhaps that was why he got on with her so well. He too didn't have any real friends. Most of the kids at school were friendly enough, but there was no one he regularly hung out with. Of course he'd only been at that school a few months, but even in Santiago, where they'd lived almost four years, there hadn't been anyone he really missed when they'd left. He wondered if he simply didn't do that kind of friendship.

Except for Taeela now. Really he hadn't known her that much longer than his mother had, but he was certainly going to miss her when he flew home in a few weeks, and next time he came out to Dirzhan he was going to look forward to seeing her almost as much as he did his parents.

How come she could do that to him? Because she was a girl? To be honest he was thankful for the strict Dirzhani rules against his getting too near her. It made being friends a lot simpler. Suppose she'd been a boy…

He day-dreamed contentedly until they put the bird-books away. Then they taught Taeela to play various card-games until Nigel's father returned from the lake with three fine trout which he insisted on presenting to Taeela with full ambassadorial pomp. It ought to have been embarrassing, but she obviously enjoyed it. They were all four playing *Oh Hell!* when the President returned.

"Please sit down," he said, and came across to see what they were doing. He too had that wild-weather look, and was walking with a slight limp.

"You've hurt your leg!" said Taeela.

"I twisted my ankle helping the men to drag a tree-trunk aside so that we could haul the inflatable down to the shore. Marizhka has done what she can with it. What game is this?"

"It's called… er… *Oh Bother!*" said Nigel.

"It is very good, very right," said Taeela quickly. "You must not capture the queen."

"Clearly you will have to teach me."

Taeela stared at him as if this was something that had never happened before. He ignored her.

"What news of the other helicopter, sir?" said Nigel's father.

"Mixed, but it might have been much worse. At least there is nobody dead. We took the inflatable up as far as the landslip on one of the trucks and dragged it down through the wood before the weather cleared. That left just time for two trips to pick up the men from the mouth of the gorge. As I say, nobody is dead, but there are two stretcher cases; one, most unfortunately, my doctor, with a broken leg, and one of the pilots with internal injuries which may be more serious. Two others have broken bones, but can walk, and two of the women and three more men will not be fit for duty for some days. Otherwise nothing much more than cuts and contusions. I have sent for a surgical team to come up by road and see to the pilot. By the time they arrive workmen from the estate will have built a usable pathway across the landslip.

"You have had a satisfactory afternoon, Ambassador?"

"Excellent all round," said Nigel's father. "Taeela will tell you."

"No doubt," said the President. "But first you must teach me this game. What is its real name?"

"It varies from country to country," said Nigel's father. "In England it is *Oh, Hell!* In Chile we called it *Diablo.* I now learn that in Dirzhan it is *Oh, Bother!* In fact it's only a variant of whist."

"I have played bridge. Show me."

He picked the game up at once and played seriously, thinking about it, trying to win. Till now Taeela had been playing almost at random, relying on her luck, but she too began to take it seriously—not, Nigel guessed, simply to win but because her father did, and she wanted to beat him. If she'd never played cards with him before this might have been her first chance, ever. Luck repaid her at last when she was able to discard the queen of spades on a trick he was forced to take, causing him to lose ten points.

"Now!" she cried. "See, I sacrifice my queen! I win!"

"Very good," he said. "But you must not tell anyone, my dear. It is a state secret."

She laughed, but he nodded, straight-faced.

Later they went up and got into their best clothes for dinner and met again in the living-room. This time Nigel was playing a rather sleepy game of chess with Taeela when the President joined them. He chatted to Nigel's parents for a while and then came over and glanced at the board.

"Do you want to play, sir?" said Nigel. "Later, I mean?"

"You will be too tired. It is likely to rain for much of tomorrow, so you will have plenty of time to rest."

"I'll do my best, sir. I want to win too."

"Excellent."

And this is Day 7. Not a lot to report. When they do storms in Dirzhan, they really do storms…

The forecast was spot on. All Sunday it rained as if it was never going to stop. At first the President was doing president-stuff in his office, so Nigel's father worked on a report, his mother wrote her Sunday letter to Granddad and Taeela did the same to her mother in Moscow. Nigel settled down with his laptop and tried to write yesterday's blog, but then spent most of his time just staring at the screen. There was so much he couldn't write about without letting on they'd been staying with the President in his hunting lodge. OK, the imaginary Mr G might have had a private helicopter and a lodge of his own… They could crash-land in the storm…

It was difficult to make it all seem real…

The four of them were playing Newmarket when the President came in for coffee, smelling of cigar-smoke, and told them that the surgical team had arrived and the pilot was seriously hurt but stable. He chatted to Nigel's mother about Tolstoy and Solzhenitsyn and guys like that, and then he took Nigel's father off for more than an hour to talk about world affairs or whatever, so Nigel got Taeela to tell him all sorts of ultra-cool stuff about weird old customs that still went on in Dirzhan to fill in the gaps in his blog.

"Now I'm afraid I must work again," said the President after lunch. "My falconer will come in half an hour to take you to look at the birds. We not only keep hawks and a pair of eagles. There is also a rescue aviary, so you may be able to see some of our local birds at close hand. You will go with them my dear, to translate? And later Nigel and I will play chess."

They settled down to the game immediately after tea. Nigel was nervous again, but not scared this time. The President was probably going to beat him, and that was OK. But he was afraid of not playing well enough. Taeela and his father came to watch.

His nerves left him as soon as they started to play. He had the white pieces. The game was all there was. The President played that way too. Dirzhan, the dam, the injured pilot, the constant danger to himself and his daughter—all that was somewhere else, unreal. Reality was concentrated into the thirty-two pieces on the board. The sense of unpredictable power that came from him was as strong as ever, but now it was focussed onto this single centre. If thought had been sunlight the board would have burst into flame.

After the first few moves of one of the standard openings, which they didn't need to think about, the game slowed. The position became complicated, with too many possibilities to work out. If you have white you have the advantage and you've got to attack or you'll lose it, Mr Harries said. To clear the way Nigel exchanged a knight for a bishop and sacrificed a pawn. Four moves later he'd lost the advantage and was still a pawn down.

That was OK by him. He was always happier defending, reacting to the other player's moves, waiting for him to make a mistake. Not much chance of that this time, he thought. But a few moves later, astonishingly, it happened. He stared at the board, thinking it must be a trap, but he couldn't see how. He was too tired to think clearly. Even in important school matches he'd never played at this intensity before. Might as well get it over, he decided, so he forced the rook exchange and took the extra pawn back.

The President played on as if that's what he'd been expecting to happen, but after another few moves he looked at his watch and then at Nigel, which he hadn't done since the game began.

"I think I ought still to win," he said, "but there is not enough time."

"I'll resign if you like, sir," said Nigel, relieved not to have made a fool of himself, and by the thought they could now stop playing.

"No. The position is not sufficiently clear. We will play again some time. I ought not to have lost that pawn."

"It was only a silly pawn," said Taeela.

"If I still had it I could have made it into a queen," said the President. "That should mean something to you, my dear."

The rest of the evening passed in a mild daze. They talked about the birds in the aviary and taught the President to play *Newmarket*. Then there was another terrific meal, which Nigel was too tired to pay attention to, though he was awake enough to notice how much his mother was enjoying talking to the President and how he was taking the trouble to see she did. He didn't remember going upstairs to bed, but when his mother came in to say goodnight he woke up enough to whisper "Do you still think he's a monster?"

"A very civilised monster," she said.

"Perhaps he's only a full-moon monster. Like were-wolves."

"He'd still be a monster, I'm afraid."

CHAPTER 7

Day 8

Fish-owl day, but not till the evening. Before that we mucked around in a speedboat, Luana and me, and did some target practice, popping balloons with a real pistol…

Again the forecast was spot on. Nigel was woken by a tactful cough from Drogo as he came in to open the shutters. Sunlight blazed in and unfamiliar birds whooped and whistled in the trees, against a faint background tinkling of the rivulets from two days' downpour scurrying down to the lake.

After breakfast the President worked, Nigel's father fished, and he and his mother and Taeela rode out to watch the falconers fly their birds. They all met up for lunch, happy and relaxed, as if they'd known each other a long time. But the President was the President, there, inescapable. If you'd closed your eyes you'd still have known he was in the room, by the way people spoke, by the feel of the silences.

In the afternoon he took Nigel's father off to visit the site of the new dam and Taeela and Nigel went out on the lake in the presidential speedboat. One of the female guards came along.

The speedboat was ultra-cool, like a vintage Rolls Royce, with a shiny varnished deck and brass fittings and padded leather bench seats and a searchlight on the bows. No vulgar outboard motors. Two vast aero engines under the after-decking purred into life as they nosed away from the quay. The purr became a bellowing boom, far too loud for speech. The bows rose, the stern dug itself down into the surface of the lake, and the shape of the hull flung it out in two wide-arching silvery wings of spray that spread themselves either side of the foaming wake as they roared out over the silky calm.

Nigel sat in front with the boatman, of course. He heard Taeela crowing with excitement behind him. He turned to grin at her, and saw her gripping the hand-rail on the back of his seat and bouncing up and down like a small child on a fairground ride. Beside her sat the guard, blank-faced, her gun held ready across her lap as she scanned the nearer shore, where clouds of startled birds rose from the reed-beds and the forest beyond, and further back the wave of their wake foamed into the shallows. When Taeela had had enough she tapped the boatman on the shoulder and gestured to him to slow down.

The spray wings vanished, the hull levelled and the speedboat drifted into stillness at the centre of the lake, part of its peaceful beauty. But not for long. The guard put her gun down, opened a locker and took out a packet of party balloons and a pump. Solemnly she started to inflate a red balloon. Beside her Taeela drew a pistol from an inside pocket, looked at Nigel and grinned.

"Wow!" he said. "Is it real?"

"Sure. It can kill a man. My father give… gave it to me. He says I must know to use it. It isn't a toy. So now I practise."

The guard knotted the neck of the balloon, leaned across Taeela and dropped it over the side of the boat. Taeela watched the plain red sphere drift away under the light breeze. When it was about ten yards off she raised the pistol two-handed, aimed carefully and fired. The two explosions were lost in each other, but the sphere had vanished and there was only a crumpled red something on the surface of the lake, still drifting away among the spreading ripples.

"You want to try, Nigel?"

"Sure."

"You know how to do this?"

"Never touched a real gun in my life."

"I show you. Hold it how I did."

She passed the pistol to him, holding it with the barrel pointing downwards and the butt towards him, and didn't let go till he'd got a comfortable grip. It wasn't a fancy weapon, plain black, solid-feeling, workmanlike, but precisely made. His sort of gadget. Only for killing people.

"Good," she said. "That is the safety. Raise the gun. No. Point it that way, good. Now you push the safety up with your thumb…"

Nigel could almost hear her father's ghostly voice behind hers, giving her the same instructions. The guard tied the balloon-neck and glanced at him enquiringly. He nodded. The balloon touched the water and drifted away.

He raised the gun, and did as Taeela had told him. It was harder than it looked. His aim kept straying as he swung too fast or too slow. There! Now or never. He moved his finger round the trigger, opened the safety and squeezed firmly. The shot slapped into the water beyond the balloon.

"Too high," said Taeela. "Again. Don't jerk."

The balloon was a smaller target now as it drifted further away, but at the same time the sideways movement was less. He managed to keep it steady in his sights long enough to fire more coolly, but missed again. Only just, though. The balloon bobbled perceptibly in the ripples of the splash.

"Enough," said Taeela. "It is too far away for my little gun."

"I bet you hit first time you tried," he said.

"No, I missed twice. I was ten only when my father gave me the gun. Nilzha will shoot your balloon. Then we will try some more. Cover your ears."

In a brief, brutal clamour Nilzha's AK obliterated the escaping balloon. Nigel gave Taeela her pistol and she popped a couple more balloons and gave it back to him. He took it reluctantly, certain that he'd miss again, and he did. But this time he'd been ready for it, so adjusted his aim and fired almost at once. The balloon vanished. With a sigh of relief he gave the pistol to Taeela.

"No thanks," he said next time she offered it to him. "You're the one supposed to be practising. Hope you don't ever need it for real."

It was meant as a half-joke, but she nodded seriously and settled to work, letting the balloons drift further away each time before she fired her first shot. She missed only three first time and got two of them with her second shot, but the last one drifted out of range. Nilzha abolished it with her AK, then rested the gun against the seat while she put the remaining balloons and the pump away.

Nigel craned to look at it. He hadn't seen an AK close to, but they'd done a module on them in Geog with Mr Udall last term. There were millions of the things in all the trouble-spots of the world, openly sold in market places, cheap as mobiles, being loosed off in celebration at weddings, protecting drug traffickers, terrorising villagers, status symbols in street gangs, ambushing food convoys, kidnapping tourists, and here, now, popping red balloons from a luxury speedboat in the middle of a peaceful lake.

Nilzha must have noticed his interest, because to his surprise she picked the gun up and offered it to him. He took it and weighed it in his hands. It was a workman's tool, no kind of a gadget. But also for killing people.

He lifted it to his shoulder and looked along its sights, aiming at a pine tree on the edge of the water. The stock was a bit long for him but otherwise it would have been comfortable to use, and held like that seemed lighter than it did in the hand. When he turned to give it back to Nilzha he saw that she had got the pump back out of the locker and was starting to inflate another balloon.

"It's all right," he said hastily. "I don't want to fire it. I just wanted to see what it felt like. Thanks."

She looked up, shook her head, said something in Dirzhani and went on pumping.

"She tells you that a boy is not a man until he has shot with a gun. You must do it, Nigel. It is an honour she gives you her gun."

(Oh, come on, Nigel. Don't be wimp. There were kids at school who'd give their iPods away to be able to say they'd fired an AK.)

"Oh well, fine," he said. "Tell her the right things for me, will you?"

Nilzha showed him the controls. Taeela translated.

"That is the safety. That is for quick shots and one shot only. She puts it to one shot only. She says the gun jumps when you fire it, and you're not big enough to hold it doing quick shots."

"One's fine," said Nigel.

He took the gun back, checked the safety and watched the balloon drifting away. When it was a decent distance from the boat he raised the AK to his shoulder, opened the safety, aimed carefully—much easier than with the pistol—and fired. All, till that instant, ordinary, or at least no stranger than a lot of what had happened to him since he came to Dirzhan. The gun was an inert metal object, he himself was interested but relaxed. But as his finger tightened on the trigger the gun leapt into life like a hound startled out of sleep. It was only a moment, and then it was inert metal again. And the balloon was gone. It could have been a life. He felt no elation as he handed the AK back to Nilzha.

After an early tea they left for the Vamar Gorge. It was an almost two-hour drive in one of the Humvees. One of the guards had a black eye and a plaster on her temple. The other one was Nilzha. The one-way glass in the windows gave the sunlit world a brownish tint. For some while they followed a bumpy dirt track beside the lake, then climbed steeply up a series of hairpins with waterfalls splurging down the crags on either side and eagles soaring in the gulfs of air below. Then down, past two shabby mountain villages where people came out of their houses to stare distrustfully at the Humvee. They joined a good new road and followed it for about twenty miles, then turned off, climbed, levelled over a pass, and there below them, under a sky already starting to glow pink and gold with sunset, lay Lake Vamar.

It was hardly a lake at all. From the top of the pass it looked more like a fair-sized river running along the bottom of a wider valley. To north and south the hills plunged down, but far enough apart to leave room at the bottom for two broad, gently sloping strips of farmland. Good land too, by the look of it, with a few fields still green. Even at this distance the villages looked far better built and kept than the ones they'd seen earlier. Three of them had their own little mosques. When the dam was finished they would all be far below the surface, and the people who had lived in those houses and worked those fields for generations would have been moved somewhere else. Roger had dug some reports and newspaper cuttings about the dam out of the embassy files for Nigel to look at. Seeing it now for real, it struck him as odd that there seemed to be rather more fuss about the fish-owls than there was about the people.

The road branched, ending at a large, almost empty parking lot just above the lake with a few temporary-looking buildings along one side. They found the President and Nigel's father in a well-equipped office, talking to a short, pudgy, bald man with a bushy beard called Herr Fettler, who was in charge of the fish-owl project.

They stayed there only long enough to shake hands with him,

and set off in both Humvees on a dirt track above the shore-line, with the lake a few fields away on their right. Where the valley narrowed and the farmland ended they got out and walked on along a twisting footpath with Nilzha leading the way and the other guard coming behind. Nilzha would trot ahead for a bit, then wait, gun at the ready, scanning the hillside, till the main party caught up. Then she trotted on again. Looking to his right where the path twisted back on itself to round an inlet he saw the rearguard doing the same, timing each run so that one of them was always on the watch while the other was on the move.

The bare hillside changed to woodland. The slopes on either shore became steeper and steeper, until they were cliffs. On this side of the lake there was a wooden walkway clinging to the rock-face, which ran sheer down to the water, but on the far side a jumble of fallen boulders ran along the base of the cliff. Both cliffs curved inwards until they were barely fifty metres apart. Beyond that gap the Vamar Gorge stretched away.

The walkway ended at a roofed hide, built like a log cabin against the cliff, open at either end and with a waist-high parapet on the side looking across the lake. Two more guards, men, were already there, waiting for them.

"Look at that view!" said Nigel's mother, getting her camera out.

He turned to see what she was talking about and found himself staring down the whole length of the lake, with mountains and sunset reflected in its stillness. Herr Fettler coughed a pay-attention bark.

"I bring you here," he said in a thick, difficult accent, "so you best see how the lake is made, and how high the new water is to be, and what is the problem with the birds. The dam is twenty kilometres further in the gorge, but the fish-owls they are here. To this lake they are unique. Here alone they can live.

"You look this way, please. You see the cliff across the lake? It is new rock, four hundred thousand years, nothing. So they are soft. But this cliff…"

He strutted to the back of the platform and slapped his hand dramatically against the rock-face.

"… it is one point six million years, very old, very hard."

Dutifully Nigel got his pad out of his pack and made notes for his blog about how hundreds of thousands of years ago the whole valley had been full of water, and crayfish had burrowed holes in the softer rock on the far side, until the water had broken through at the weak point where the two rock surfaces met, forming the gorge and lowering the lake surface, which allowed the owls to take the holes over.

Herr Fettler had a lot to say about the owls, fetching binoculars out of one of a line of locked chests and handing them round while he talked. The owls were unique to this place. They didn't pair for life. When winter came and the lake froze they spread out down into the valleys and lived by themselves, eating fish if they could get it but anything else, birds, mice, beetles and so on, if they couldn't. A lot of young birds didn't make it through the winter but those that did came back in the spring, when the lake unfroze. The males came first and held hooting competitions for the biggest holes in the cliff—Herr Fettler played a tape; it was the most amazing racket, like a traffic jam of police cars and ambulances all in a hurry—and then the females showed up and they got down to chick-production. Most owls lay only two or three eggs because that's all the young they can easily hunt for, but the fish-owls wanted as many chicks as there was room for in the nest-hole so that there was more chance of at least two of them getting through the winter. That was why the biggest holes were the best and why the lake was so vital because it swarmed with fish and the owls were going to have all these hungry beaks to feed.

Sometimes the parents hatched more chicks than there was room for in the hole, in which case the bigger ones pushed the smaller ones out. They drowned if they fell in the water and a predator usually got them if they fell on the rocks, but Herr Fettler's team checked each morning and if any were still alive they reared them by hand, ringed them and released them as soon as they were old enough to fish for themselves. Most winters a few came through.

It all made a mad sort of sense, Nigel thought, in the way even the craziest bits of natural history turn out to do. Mr Udall would like it anyway.

It was darker now. The sun was down behind the mountains, the whole eastern sky fiery with its going. Taeela was getting restless—perhaps she found Herr Fettler's accent hard to follow. She'd stopped listening to him and was studying the cliff face with her binoculars. She gave an excited squeak.

"I see an owl! Oh, it's gone!"

"Please now to be quiet," said Herr Fettler. "These owls are very shy from people. Now I give you night vision glasses. You need them soon."

He fetched the glasses from the chest, focussed them and handed them round. They were a bit different from binoculars, two tubes about the size of toilet-roll tubes laid side by side, with eye-pieces.

"Oh, everything's green," said Nigel's mother. "Does that mean we won't see… Oh, there's one! Isn't it beautiful! Oh, there's another! Goodness, it's caught a fish already."

The owls were streaming from the cliff now, spreading out, barely flapping their wings, floating in dreamy silence a couple of metres above the water. The whole surface of the lake was hazy with flies. As the fish rose to take them the owls would half fold their wings and drop like stones, their long finger-like talons stretching down to snatch the fish out of the water with barely a splash just as the spread wings neatly braked the fall and took the bird swinging away towards its nest-hole.

The effect was dance-like, beautiful, with the owls—there were three hundred and twelve of them this year, Herr Fettler had said—neatly spaced apart, all at the same level, as if there was a separate surface up there and they were floating on it until the moment came to perform their elegant aerobatic turn.

It was now late dusk, but the night vision glasses made everything as clear as if he'd been looking at it in extremely bright moonlight, except that it was all green. The cliffs were dark green, the sky pale green, the water silky green the owls themselves mid-green with paler undersides. A green world.

Fascinated, wondering how much detail he'd be able to make out at a greater distance than the owls, Nigel trained the glasses on the jumble of rocks on the opposite shore. They too were astonishingly clear, clear enough for him to notice when a rock next to the one he was looking at changed its shape.

He turned his glasses on it, and saw the notch between the two rocks fill in for a moment and reappear. Something was moving among the rocks.

"Oh, they're all going home!" said Nigel's mother.

"Something disturbs the owls," said Herr Fettler.

"I saw something moving over there," said Nigel. "I thought it might be a fox."

"Foxes the owls do not fear," said Herr Fettler. "It is perhaps a poacher."

"Everybody get down behind the parapet," said the President calmly. "Nigel, show me where."

He added a few words in Dirzhani, moved at a crouch to behind Nigel's shoulder and peered along the line of his night-glasses. Nigel swung them slowly to the left, searching, and saw a flicker of movement as a crouching figure scuttled across a sloping slab, unmistakably human.

One of the guards spoke, low-voiced, urgent—she must have seen it too. Then another, and the hide was filled with a clamour of gunfire.

"Stop!" screamed Nigel's mother. "You don't know! They might…"

A moment of silence, and then she was answered by the sharp crack of something whanging against the cliff face behind them, a brief whine and a cry from one of the guards. Nigel flung himself face down beside the parapet and lay there, terrified, while the clamour broke out again.

A command from the President and the guards stopped firing. He spoke in Dirzhani, a question. A woman's voice answered, gasping.

"Mrs Ridgwell, Taeela," he said as calmly as ever. "Lie against the parapet. Stay where you are, Nigel. Ambassador, Herr Fettler, please drag the chests to protect them and yourselves from ricochets. Keep your heads well down"

"Somebody was hurt," said Nigel's mother. "One of the guards."

"A deep graze from a ricochet," said the President. "Painful, she says, but not serious."

"I've done a lot of first aid," said Nigel's mother.

"Later," said the President. "We are in no immediate danger, but cannot retaliate, as our attacker or attackers are beyond the effective range of our…"

He broke off as something slammed into the timber of the parapet close above Nigel's head. He gulped and tried to shrink even further into the floor, unable to stop himself thinking that the shot had been deliberately aimed at him. Stupid. But if it had hit a join between the rounded timbers…

"… but not of theirs, evidently," the President went on, as if he hadn't been interrupted. "The question is, is there more than one man?"

In the silence that followed Nigel could hear his father and Herr Fettler grunting with effort as they heaved the chests across the rough timbers. The President spoke to the guards and was answered.

"Just the one, we think, with a hunting rifle and a night vision sight."

Nigel's father heaved a chest into place alongside Nigel's body.

"Not a specialist sniper's weapon, sir?" he said, trying to sound as calm as the President and not succeeding.

"A hunting rifle is much more likely," said the President. "There will be several in each of the villages. You spoke of poachers, Herr Fettler. I thought we had put a stop to the taking of owls."

"Yes that is stopped, Herr President. And a rifle he would not need. Ach, I see your thought. You are not bringing soldiers enough for to make safe the area. A hunter is over there, setting perhaps traps for squirrels. He recognises your Excellency from across the water. He does not want the dam building. There is much feeling in the villages. This man is a hunter. Not only traps he sets. He brings his hunting rifle. Yes, it is possible."

"It must be looked into," said the President. "For the moment we will assume it is the case. What time is moon-rise, do you know?"

"Twenty-two forty-eight local time, Herr President."

"Then we have time to wait for full darkness before we leave. If you are prepared to look at the guard, Mrs Ridgwell…"

"Coming."

"Please wait. I will tell you when we are ready. You have a hand-torch, Herr Fettler? And First Aid kit?"

"I fetch them, your Excellency."

Scrabbling sounds from the other end of the hide. An urgent whisper from Nigel's mother.

"Nick! Turn round so you can hear me."

Grunts and scrabbles. Nigel wriggled himself beside his mother's legs so that he could hear too. Anything to distract him from the pit of terror.

"…thinks it's one of the villagers…"

"Which it very likely is."

"Yes, but he's going to take it out on all of them, like he did on that village where they couldn't find an ibex for him to hunt. You've got to stop him. Before he gets to a telephone. You've…"

"We are ready for you now, Mrs Ridgwell. Keep yourself well down."

"Coming."

She rose and moved away, visible in a faint glow from the further end of the hide. Twisting his head Nigel could see the President and Herr Fettler kneeling there, spreading some kind of tarpaulin into a tent-like structure over the source of the light. The light itself and the wounded guard were hidden by the line of chests. She reached them and crawled beneath the tarpaulin. They lowered it over her and the light vanished

Behind him Nigel's father sighed.

"She's right, isn't she, Dad?"

"I'm afraid so. The trouble is, he's got to do something. If there were a possibility of finding the right man… I may be able to persuade him it will dish the dam project if he over-reacts. There's no way it won't come out, there's too much interest…"

"Wait, Dad. There's a bullet. It hit the parapet just where I was lying. On CSI they're always looking at bullets and saying which gun they came from. And thingummys—you know, the bit the bullet fits into…"

"Casings. Ah… Thanks."

It was pitch dark in the hide now. Time went by. Terror flooded back. Any worse, and he'd be on his feet and rushing yammering out onto the walkway. He twisted himself over and tried to count the stars sliding westward along the narrow slot of sky that was all he could see from this angle, but his mind kept slipping free to gaze into the pit and he kept dragging it back. At last his mother spoke briefly with the President and returned. He shifted to make room for her legs, then reached up, feeling around for her hand, ashamed to speak aloud of his need. She understood and grasped his and held it.

"How is she?" said his father.

"It's in her thigh. Fairly nasty. She was losing a lot of blood. I've managed to stop it, mostly. She's going to need to be carried back to the cars."

"Well done. What's he up to now?"

"Just waiting, I think. He says we can move in twenty minutes. What are you going to do, Nick?"

"Talk to him if I can," said Nigel's father. Then, raising his voice above a mutter, "May I have a word with you, Mr. President?"

"Certainly, Ambassador."

His footsteps receded. A brief question from the President, answered by Nigel's father. Nigel could hear the tone and shape of the sentences, calm, reasoning, official—ambassador-stuff—but not the words. A can't-be-done sort of objection from the President. Nigel's father dealing with it. That pattern repeated. And again.

Fighting the fear-demon, he strained to hear, catching just the odd word now and again, and then with a lurch he'd be back in the nightmare, out on the walkway, an open target, with a skilled marksman peering at him through the night-vision sight of a powerful rifle.

His father's voice fell silent. Taeela's voice now, saying two or three words in Dirzhani, the last one "Dudda." His abrupt, brushing-off answer. Her reply, not at all official, urgent, passionate, her whole soul poured into it, refusing to be silenced till she ended, gasping for breath.

Silence again. A guard slapped at an insect. Now the President, speaking English, even-voiced as before, but a slight difference in tone at first, as if he'd just made one of his odd, unsmiling jokes. (Now, of all times?) Then back to normal, doing more of the talking than before, making a series of proposals. Occasional comments from Nigel's father. Finish. Almost time to go. Nigel's heart was already thudding when his father came back.

"You did it?" whispered his mother.

"Best we could get. Thanks to the girl, really. She's watched CSI too, apparently. Gave him a chance to save face, not simply giving in to me. Of course it's in his own best interest if he wants the dam built. He's going to close the area off and do a house-to-house search for rifles. But he's agreed to let me send Tim up as an observer. And I'm going to have to move heaven and earth to get a forensics boffin and equipment in from home to check the rifles and bullets—they don't have the facilities here… sounds like we're moving—tell you later."

The President's voice again, an order in Dirzhani. A guard moved away along the hide.

And again, in English.

"We will now prepare to leave. I and my guards are wearing body armour, so we will walk in pairs, with the unprotected person on the right. Ambassador, if you would be good enough to help me carry the casualty…"

"Er…Of course, sir. Now?"

"When I have finished. The attacker may already have left, but we must assume he is still there. When we are ready the three guards will line up at the entrance to the hide. Mrs Ridgwell will position herself on the right of the first one, Nigel behind her, then Taeela. Nigel, your guard will not be in place yet as he is helping us to lift the casualty. Take hold of your guard's uniform so that you will remain in cover as they vary their pace. The Ambassador and I and the casualty will come behind you. Herr Fettler has agreed to stay until we are among the trees, when one of the guards will be free to return for him.

"Herr Fettler has a flare pistol for night photography purposes. When we are ready to leave I will tell you to close your eyes. He will then fire a flare on a low trajectory over the water, to destroy our attacker's night vision while we are actually leaving the hide. We will leave at brief intervals as soon as the flare reaches the water and is extinguished.

"Will you now take up your positions."

With a lurch of the heart Nigel let go of his mother's hand started to twist himself over, tangling with her legs as she did the same.

"Ouch!" she whispered as he fought himself loose. The strap of his shoulder-bag snagged on something and he wrenched it free. He scrambled over the chest and scuttled towards the paler rectangle of the doorway, now partly blocked by the dark shape of the leading guard. His mother limped past and positioned herself beside him.

Nigel stopped, still crouching down a little way back from her, next to the second guard, but was immediately shoved forward with an impatient mutter, leaving him with no one to protect him on his left, once he was out on the walkway. Nightmare. The marksman across the water...

Despairingly he looked over his shoulder for help and saw the pale oval of Taeela's face floating beside the dim shape of the guard.

Just in time sanity returned. The mutter had been that of a woman's voice. The President had actually told him that his guard wouldn't be in place when he reached the door as he would be helping lift the wounded woman. He could hear her gasping groan as she was settled into place on the linked hands of her bearers. By the time his guard arrived he'd got himself together enough to feel around on the man's uniform for a bit of web strapping to hold on to.

The President's voice again.

"Keeping hold of the guard beside you, will you now turn your faces to the wall. Close your eyes and cover them with your free hand."

Nigel obeyed. Determined not to be separated from his human shield he was already clinging so fiercely to the strap that the webbing bit into his palm. He felt the man move round as the President repeated the order in Dirzhani.

"We are ready, Herr Fettler."

There was an explosive whoosh from the back of the hide, then silence, then a sharper explosion from out over the water. The sudden glare reflected from the rock-face penetrated hand and eyelids. Darkness again.

"Go now!" said the President. "Drah!"

Nigel's mother and her guard were out onto the walkway before he had turned his head. Instinctively he tried to lurch into a run, but his guard grabbed his shoulder, held him, waited two endless seconds, muttered "Drah," and broke into a rapid trot, short steps that Nigel could easily keep pace with. The starlight glimmered off the long reaches of the lake, framed by the dark mass of the mountains among which it lay. But all Nigel was aware of was the imprisoning cliff on his right, and the walkway ahead, blocked by the dim shapes of his mother and her guard, getting quickly closer. They seemed to be moving at barely more than a stroll.

Now they broke into a run, but strangely slow and awkward. His mother could run better that that, for God's sake. Sometimes in Santiago he'd gone out with her on his bike and admired her handsome, easy lope. Not now. So the obvious thing was to catch up, yell at them to get out of the way and race on to the sheltering woods. Come on, come on, come on…

Instead his guard muttered something and stopped dead. Before Nigel could protest he muttered again and marched on, slowed after a few paces, speeded up, slowed, stopped, broke into a run, with a grunt of warning at each change and keeping a hold of Nigel's shoulder all the time, forcing him to do the same. It was clear from the firmness of the grip and the tone of the grunts that the man knew Nigel was on the verge of bolting and despised him for it. Shame and fury—fury with the man, fury with himself—joined terror in the churn of his emotions. He stumbled on, only aware of rounding the bend in the cliffs and seeing the woods coming nearer and nearer, until they stepped onto the packed earth of the path and into the greater darkness under the trees. The guard let go with a final grunt and started back along the walkway.

Nigel stood, gasping, gasps that were almost sobs, with a taste of vomit in his mouth. Looking back he could see Taeela and her guard silhouetted against the starlit water, just reaching the end of the walkway. She was trotting along, head high, one hand holding onto the guard beside her, the other lifting her long skirt clear of the timber so that she could run more easily. Her guard wasn't keeping hold of her. No need.

Unable to face her Nigel turned away and saw that the darkness wasn't as absolute as before. Further into the wood his mother was sitting by the path with her skirt pulled up above her knees. She had got her little torch out, screened by her body, and was feeling around on her calf with her other hand. Her guard watched her from the dimness beyond.

Nigel staggered towards them. His mother looked up.

"Oh, darling, thank goodness!" she said. "Wasn't that awful! Are you all right?"

"Don't know. I'm going to be sick," he said, and was, leaning against a tree so that the mess fell further down the slope. He turned, shuddering and chilly, and sat down beside her. The terror seemed to have gone with the vomit, but the anger and the shame were still there, churning. She put her arm round him and drew him close.

"That was awful," she said again.

Mercifully Taeela hadn't seen any of this, as she had stopped as soon as she was in among the trees to wait for her father. They sat in silence, waiting for the others. Now it dawned on him what his mother had been doing.

"You've hurt your leg!"

"Caught it on the corner of one of those chests while we were getting out from behind them. We got in a bit of a tangle, remember?"

He did now. He remembered how he'd fought clear of her, how she'd muttered with pain, limped to her place at the door of the hide, run so awkwardly along the walkway… He'd felt and heard and seen these things, but not once thought about them, or what had caused them, or anything except his own terror-driven urge to run…

"Ah, here they are at last."

He scrambled to his feet and, rather than face Taeela, watched her guard help the two men lower the wounded woman to the ground. She seemed to have fainted.

The President rose and turned.

"Mrs Ridgwell, we must…You are hurt?"

"Nothing serious, just a nasty cut," she said, rising and limping over. "I just need a plaster bigger than what I've got in my bag. It can wait. How is she?"

"Still losing blood, I fear."

"I'll look, shall I? But I don't think there's much I can do here. It'd be much easier back at the offices, with proper lights and water and everything. What we really need is a stretcher. With her wound where it is it isn't doing her any good, carrying her like that."

"We will construct one," he said after a pause, and started giving orders to the guards. One of the women took a hand torch out of a bulging pocket and ran off up the path, the other handed her torch to the President and returned to the start of the walkway, where she waited under the trees, gun held ready, silhouetted against the star-glimmer.

"If you and Nigel would help us look for suitable branches, Ambassador," said the President.

"Of course. Come on, Niggles. You can drag them back down."

Nigel jumped at the chance, not just to do something—anything—except drown in shame and terror, but also to get away from Taeela. He fetched out his own torch, and started to follow the three men up through the trees. To his dismay Taeela came scrambling up beside him.

"Oh, Nigel!" she gasped. "I was so scared!"

He halted, turned, and stared at her. Her eyes seemed huge as an owl's in the dim light. Her chest was heaving with the effort of the climb.

"Me too," he muttered.

"But…But…Oh, Nigel!"

Then, astonishingly, she started to laugh, took a pace towards him, caught her foot on something and lurched forward so that he had to grab her to stop her falling. She flung her arms round him and hugged him, her laughter now on a rising note, almost out of control.

He was fighting the urge to join her in her hysteria when he heard the crackle and squeal of wrenched timber from further up the slope. That steadied him enough to be able to push her away and grab her wrist.

"Come on. We're supposed to be helping. We'll talk later," he said, and started to drag her up the slope. The effort of the climb loosed the laughter-demon's hold, and by the time they reached the others she was merely panting.

There were two branches ready for them to take, which was easy enough with the slope in their favour. On the way down they met Herr Fettler and Nigel's guard climbing up to help, and at the bottom they found that the guard who had run off towards the Humvees had just returned with one of the drivers, bringing a first-aid kit, plus some tools and cord and stuff.

"I'm sure they've got plenty of people up there now," said Nigel's mother. "Why don't you stay and help me, Taeela? I could do with someone to hold the torch."

So Nigel, still bewildered by Taeela's reaction, climbed the slope with the guard and driver and then held a torch for one of the men while he hacked and trimmed. It didn't take long with several workers and the right tools, nor did the job of assembling what they'd collected into a usable stretcher back down by the path.

"What happens now, sir?" said Nigel's father as they watched the process.

"We return to the offices," said the President. "I must make some immediate telephone calls and Mrs Ridgwell will do what she can for the casualty. The rest of you will eat while you are waiting. Do you have any calls to make, Ambassador? Your mobile won't work from here but I have satellite communication with the palace. If you will give me Mr O'Hara's number I can instruct someone to warn him he may have to accompany the security squadron to Vamar tomorrow. Then you can brief him more fully from the lodge. Is there anyone else?"

"Not immediately, sir. It can wait till we're back at the lodge."

"Very well. I must apologise to you for our expedition having been so unfortunately interrupted."

"At least we did see the owls," said Nigel's mother. "That was wonderful!"

CHAPTER 8

They climbed out of their Humvee in front of the Owl Project office, and watched the guard unload the stretcher from the other one. Nigel's mother and Taeela headed off for the toilet.

"Me too," said Nigel's father. "Come on, Niggles."

"I'm all right."

"Might as well while you can. Come along."

There was something urgent in his voice. Anxiously Nigel tagged along. The toilets were separate from the other buildings, on the far side of the parking lot. His father slowed to let him catch up.

"Keep your eyes open, Niggles," he muttered. "We're not out of this yet."

"Uh?"

"The President's got a problem. He knows there's no way I can't put in a report on what's happened, however much I tone it down."

Nigel halted in his stride, his mouth opening and closing.

"But...but it was only one guy taking a pot shot at him because he didn't want the dam built, Dad. It wasn't a big deal. I mean...I mean it was an effing big deal for us, worst thing that's ever happened to me, but...but it wasn't like the guy was trying to overthrow the government."

"As far as we know, Niggles. Even that is bad enough from his point of view. Green issues were big back home at the last election, and the Greens don't want the dam built. They'll make a lot of this—evidence of how strongly the locals think about it, and so on and so forth.

"But there's another possibility. Doesn't it strike you as a bit too opportune that a man should be out there with a rifle and night sights good as that on an evening when, for the first time ever, the President arrived without enough guards to secure the area? What serious hunter tries to shoot game at that sort of range in the dark? What's more, sights that good really cost. And you don't find them in every corner gun-shop. You'd need a couple of days at least to lay it on."

He sounded much less jumpy now, talking about the danger they'd been in calmly, reasonably, as if it were something in a film they'd seen. It was his way of dealing with it, but it wasn't much help to Nigel.

"B...but that would mean..."

"Exactly. Somebody would have had to have passed the word on almost the moment the accident had happened—effectively as soon as the President had called the palace to tell them. I doubt if they could have done it even then, from scratch."

"You mean..."

"Either a big criminal organisation, or the military, most likely...Wait. They're coming out. I haven't said anything to Lucy about this yet. Don't want to worry her."

Nigel waited in the dark, shaking his head. It couldn't be true. It mustn't be true. Somebody in the palace...He barely noticed his mother and Taeela heading back across the parking lot.

His father didn't say anything more about it until they'd started to follow them. Then he broke into a rapid mutter.

"Look, there isn't time to tell you the whole thing. The point is, all this is going to be pretty obvious to anyone back home, no matter how much I tone my report down. If he's going to do anything to stop me it's got to be before I call home. The obvious thing would be for all three of us to have an accident on the way back to the lodge. I don't think it's at all likely—he'd be crazy to try it, but maybe he is a bit crazy deep down inside. Tyrants get like that, in the end."

"No, Dad! He isn't like that!"

"He is, Niggles. I've read the reports. I've only told you a bit of them."

"But Taeela would be devastated! She really hit it off with Mum."

"There's no reason she should know it wasn't an accident if she travels in a different car. I'd say he'd do it if he thought he could get away with it. I really don't think it's at all likely, but to be on the safe side, do your best to travel in the same car as Taeela if you get the chance. OK?"

"I suppose."

The guards had fetched cool-bags and a hamper from the Humvees and were spreading food and cutlery out on a folding table, and Herr Fettler was fussing around finding stuff for them. The President had disappeared to make his telephone calls. The wounded guard was lying on a mattress on the floor with Nigel's mother kneeling beside her, easing her out of her blood-soaked trousers, and Taeela watching her, helping when she could. Nigel's father was sitting at one of the office desks making notes on a pad, with Nigel alone on the other side of the room, hunched into himself, shuddering and sighing.

Everybody else had found something to do. His eye was caught by a movement in the pool of light round the desk, his father's long-fingered hand combing the blond forelock out of his eyes and then picking up a pencil and writing two or three words and repeating the movement.

Something about the gesture…

Yes that's what it was, a gesture, a signal, to tell everyone, himself included, how deeply he was thinking, how urgent and important his notes were. Nigel knew he wasn't being fair, but he felt resentful. OK, his father had a lot on his mind, specially if he was right about what he'd told Nigel in the car park, but before starting on that couldn't he at least have asked Nigel how he was bearing up, said something to show he understood how utterly shattered he must be? Instead he'd plunged straight in, loading Nigel with a fresh lot of horrors, a whole new nightmare still to come.

The horrors withdrew into the darkness outside as Nigel thought about his father.

You don't think about your parents when you're small. They're just there, filling your life, too big to get your mind round. Slowly you begin to learn what they're like, compared to other people, but you don't judge them. They are what they are.

Until a few weeks ago Nigel would have said that his father had been a pretty good dad when he'd not been busy working or fishing or whatever. He'd taught Nigel how to do things, played games with him, read to him at bed-time if he was free, and so on. Nigel had just taken all that for granted till one weekend last term when he'd been staying with his sister Libby.

He'd been in the kitchen, drying up while she washed, relishing the feel of ordinary family life going on. He'd been missing that since Santiago.

On the spur of the moment he'd said, "Any chance we can all get together for a bit—you and Toby and Tim and Cath and Mum and Dad and me—next time they're home? Seven's a lucky number, you know."

Libby had sighed and shaken her head.

"Dad and I don't get on," she'd said. "I thought you knew."

"I didn't know it was still…I mean, now you're married and you've got a family of your own."

"Not unless he's changed, and he isn't going to. I'll still be just an add-on to his life, along with Toby and Tim now, not us with lives of our own. And now that he's got this precious ambassadorship… Nothing in the world is going to matter beside that…I'd better stop before I break something…I'm sorry, Bro. Raw spot. Anyway, Mum's lovely. I miss her."

"So do I. Thanks for telling me. I suppose."

He hadn't taken it all that seriously, then. Libby was just like that. But now he found himself seeing his father through her eyes.

Looking back, it struck him that his father had always chosen the games they'd played and read him the books that he himself had liked as a kid. He'd taught Nigel chess in Santiago, but really he just knew the rules and a few very simple things. Then he'd made the mistake of giving Nigel a book about the game, and Nigel had started beating him. He hadn't wanted to play after that. He didn't have time to read the book.

And of course Nigel had his father's own stupid name. It was difficult for him to be fair about that because he hated it so much, hated it almost as much as the baby name his father still insisted on calling him by. The same with the family likeness. If you looked in old albums at pictures of the two of them at the same age you couldn't tell them apart. The real difference was in what they thought about it. Nigel's father liked the way he looked. It had never before struck Nigel as odd that there should have been a mirror just inside the living room door of any house they'd lived in. Now he realised why.

So was it a good sign that Nigel hated the way he looked as much as he hated his name? Did it mean that in his heart of hearts he didn't want to be like his father, inside as well as outside? Like in the way they both hated rows, tried not to get involved, to keep their cool, to deal with anything like that just in their heads? He could dye his hair, of course, and dress like a slob, and change his name when he was old enough. That wasn't important, any of it. The real question was could he change the way he thought? And felt?

Next time something like tonight happened, if it did (please not!), would he be able to think about anything except getting himself out of it? The way he hadn't even noticed causing his mother to hurt her leg? Or his father hadn't really wanted to help carry the wounded guard? He was pretty sure of that now, looking back at the moment, though again he hadn't noticed it at the time. Too wrapped up in his private terror. But the moment the wounded guard had reached the woods his mother had stopped looking at her own leg and gone to help.

Why couldn't he be like that? He was her son as well. OK, he didn't look like her, the way Libby did and Cath didn't, but something of her had got to be there inside him, hidden away, secret even from himself.

I'll find it, he told himself. I'll bring it into the open. And next time…

No. No next time. Please.

When the meal was ready he ate without noticing. Taeela was sitting beside him, apparently as withdrawn into herself as he was. With an effort he roused himself try what his father had told him.

"Do you want to talk?" he muttered.

She shook her head.

After all that, the seating for the return journey worked out without Nigel or his father needing to do anything about it. Herr Fettler had found a mattress for the wounded guard to lie on. With the rear bench seats folded flat it fitted lengthwise along one side of a Humvee, leaving room for a couple of small individual seats to be unfolded from the other side.

"I will sit there and look after Annalin," said Taeela decisively. "It is too small for Lucy. She can go in front. Nigel can be with me."

Her father shrugged, his face expressionless, then whispered in her ear. Frowning, she climbed into her seat, and Nigel followed.

They headed off into the dark, with all the men in the President's car and Nigel the only male in the second one. They drove on sidelights only until they were over the ridge, when the President's car switched on its powerful headlights, allowing them to swoop down the curves of the new road to the valley beyond, and then on more joltingly along the road they'd come by.

One of the jolts caused something to brush against the back of Nigel's hand where it was dangling beside his seat. He felt around and touched Taeela's hand. She hadn't snatched it back into her lap, as any decent Dirzhani girl should have done. Instead she moved it to brush against his again.

He knew why, too. She wasn't breaking the rules for the fun of it, while she had the chance. Carefully as a pickpocket he found the edge of her hand and slid his fingers round it. Her fingers closed on his palm.

"Oh, Nigel," she whispered. "I was so scared."

"Me too. I threw up in the woods. Before you came."

"It is not the same for you. You are not ready. You don't expect it. But for me, all my life I get ready for it. I learn to shoot my gun. I learn how to fight a man who is attacking me, how to hit him with a knife, how to tear out his eye with my thumb, how to kick him with my knee. I learn how to jump from a window, how to walk with no sound, how to hide myself in a forest, how to leave no mark where I go—all this. I tell myself, when it happens, I'll be brave. I am ready.

"It happens, and I am not ready."

"There wasn't anything you could have done. A guy was taking pot-shots at us from the other side of the lake. None of the stuff you've been talking about would…"

"No, Nigel. I was not ready inside. I wasn't brave. I hid myself behind Nilzha. I wanted to scream, to run…"

"Me too."

"It is different for you," she said. "You do not need to be ready. England is a safe place."

She shifted her hand in his, but didn't let go. Fat lot of help he'd been, he thought. There must have been something he could have said. Too late now.

They drove on through dark woods, through an unlit village, up over a pass, visible only by the mountainous skyline seen through the opposite window against ten thousand stars.

Taeela's hand moved—squirmed—in his, and he discovered how tightly he'd been holding it.

"Sorry," he murmured, relaxing his grip. "Thinking too hard."

"Thinking is hard," she said. "These thinkings."

"Listen. I want to tell you something. When we were coming along the walkway my guard had to grab hold of me to stop me bolting. That's how bad it was. And we got into the trees and I turned round and saw you coming along behind us and I thought you were terrific. You were moving like a princess. No, listen. You felt like that inside because you couldn't do any of the things you'd been taught, but you didn't panic like I did. Suppose you'd needed to do some of that stuff, you'd have done it. And you'd have got it right. There was this grizzled old guy in a war movie I saw once talking about fighting to a rookie. 'If you aren't scared inside,' he said, 'you aren't going to live long.' Makes sense to me."

She nodded slowly, thinking about it.

They sat in silence, still holding hands, for an hour or more, until the cars drew to a halt and switched off their headlights. One of the guards got out of the leading car and disappeared. Nothing but forested darkness showed in the windows opposite, but twisting his head round Nigel caught glimpses of moonlit water beyond the trees. The President came back and opened the front passenger door.

"We are almost home," he said, "and no later than we would have been if we had stayed to watch the fish-owls uninterrupted. It will be difficult for you, but will you try to talk and act as if nothing unexpected had occurred at Lake Vamar? It is only natural that you should seem too tired for much conversation."

They waited till the guard came back and then drove on.

The windows of the hunting lodge were ablaze with lights.

Servants came down the lit steps to greet them and take their baggage up to their rooms, all indeed behaving as if nothing unexpected had happened at Lake Vamar.

Nigel was woken by the telephone. Still druggy with the sleeping pill his mother had made him take, he was struggling to sit up when Drogo came in and brought the handset over to him.

"Uh?" he grunted.

It was his father.

"Niggles? Sleep all right? 'Fraid you're going to have to wake up and have some breakfast. We're leaving in an hour. They've managed to repair one of the helicopters. The President has arrangements to make for this ceremony on Thursday, so he's leaving for Dara-Dahn in that, any minute now. He's taking the injured pilot and the guard who got accidentally shot yesterday, with a medical team to look after them. No room for anyone else. So Taeela's coming with us by road. Company for you, eh? Get down as soon as you can, old man. Your room servant will pack for you."

He sounded smug as hell, as if he'd managed to arrange the whole thing himself. Nigel registered that officially now the guard had been shot by accident. There was going to be a lot of stuff like that.

Day 9

Came back to Dara Dahn. Took pretty well all day. Dead boring. Long way better than the journey up, though…

Taeela took charge when they came to board the Humvee.

"I will sit by Nigel, Lucy," she said. "So we can talk to each other."

"Wait a mo," said Nigel's father. "I'm not sure we can…"

"Nonsense, Nick," said Nigel's mother. "Provided this lady doesn't object."

Taeela laughed and spoke in Dirzhani to the guard, who grinned and covered her eyes with her hands, like the third wise monkey.

"Four to one," said Nigel's father. "But perhaps when we're getting to Dara…"

"Oh, for heaven's sake, Nick! The windows are one-way glass. And can't you see they need each other?"

(No he couldn't. She could. That was something Nigel was going to have to live with.)

They settled in, a male guard beside the driver in front, Nigel's parents behind them, then Nigel, Taeela and the female guard, and then the baggage right in the back. All the guards who were fit to travel and most of the medical team followed in two more cars.

The guard kept her promise by looking out of the window all the way. That was her job anyway, Nigel supposed. The bench seat was wide enough to leave plenty of room for Taeela and Nigel to sit with a bit of space between them, keeping the Dirzhani proprieties as best they could.

Taeela sat brooding for a while with her chin on her fist. There was a bruised look around her eyes that wasn't eye-shadow. Nigel's thoughts were still a jumble: stuff about the attack on the viewing-point at Lake Vamar; stuff about what sort of man the President really was; stuff about his own family, and himself, and whether he was as like his father inside as he was outside. At length Taeela turned to him and spoke in an almost-whisper.

"'I have after all been forced to choose, my queen.' What does this mean, Nigel?"

"Uh…Something your father said?" he said, ambushed, playing for time.

"At Lake Vamar. When I am getting into the car. He makes it a joke, like it is important… No, you must tell me."

"Suppose it's got to be something to do with that time I was showing you about the queen sacrifice," he said slowly. "What was best for you and what was best for Dirzhan, remember? Best for you to sit with me, maybe, but not best for Dirzhan, because people mightn't like it."

Even to him it didn't sound very convincing. She shook her head, dissatisfied, then turned and sat staring at the back of the seat in front of her. Nigel watched the landscape slide by, but barely noticed it.

Beside him Taeela sighed.

"It is hard being a khan, Nigel," she whispered shakily. "It is hard."

She'd worked it out for herself.

"Take it easy," he said. "I don't think it was like that—I really don't. I was pretty scared when Dad told me to watch out for something—as if I wasn't scared enough already— and try and fix it that you came in the car with us. But now I've had time to…

"Look, Taeela, maybe your dad thought about it, but he's got to think of everything. He'd've known it was a crazy risk. It'd've been bound to come out. And you'd've been shattered, wouldn't you? He'd know that too.

"So I think he'd already decided against it, and you saying you were going to come in the car with us let him turn it into a sort of joke. A joke with himself. He's like that."

She sat for a while, brooding, obviously deeply troubled. Perhaps, like him, this was the first time she had ever needed to think about what kind of a man her father was. It was worse for her, far worse.

"Yes," she whispered at last. "He must think about it, think for Dirzhan. It is hard being a khan, Nigel."

They stopped up in the mountains for a picnic lunch. The guards insisted on finding a place where they could park without the cars being visible for miles, but they let them eat out in the open, with a spectacular view over the next valley. Somebody must have stayed up all night preparing the meal, a dozen different kinds of finger food, beautifully packed, very Dirzhani. While they were eating, five large military helicopters clattered north through the enormous emptiness. As the sound faded Nigel realised that he had stopped eating to watch them go by, and then that the others had done the same.

"Those poor villagers," muttered his mother. "It wasn't their fault."

"No!" said Taeela, instantly furious. "They..."

She stopped herself and swallowed her face working.

"I'm sorry, Taeela," said Nigel's mother. "Perhaps I shouldn't have said that in front of you."

"I tell Nigel it is hard being a khan, Lucy. This is true."

"There's no way you can have power without problems," said Nigel's father, as if that solved anything.

They stopped again when they were almost home, with Dara Dahn and the river valley spread out below them. The driver took a handset from under the dashboard, keyed in a number, waited, spoke briefly, pressed the off button and passed the handset to Nigel's father. It rang almost at once.

"Hello. British ambassador speaking...Certainly, sir. We'd be delighted. No problem at all...Yes, we can arrange that. One moment. Khanazhana, your father would like to speak to you."

She almost snatched the handset from him, clapped it to her ear and spoke eagerly. Nigel could just hear the characteristically level tone of the reply. She answered pouting, teasing. He heard the name Fofo. A brief answer, a goodbye, and she rang off.

"I'm staying at your embassy tonight, Nigel," she chortled. "I'll see where you live."

She'd got her grammar back, he noticed. She'd managed to put her doubts aside. Things were OK now. She thought.

Before the car pulled up at the embassy steps Taeela rearranged her headscarf so that it covered the lower part of her face. Apart from that, it was almost a repeat of the previous evening: stressed out travellers, weary with much more than their journey, reaching at last a large, luxurious dwelling, to be greeted by servants who knew nothing of the dangers they'd been through, and who still mustn't be told; the late supper, the desultory, pointless chat; the silences; the glances. Even Taeela was subdued.

As soon as they'd eaten Nigel's father took his coffee up to his office to start drafting his report, so that he could call during the London working day. A few minutes later his mother said "It's been a long couple of days. I expect you two would like to get to bed. There's no problem keeping to the rules, Taeela. We've told your father that Nick's moving into one of the spare rooms for the night. That means you can sleep in his dressing room, which leads off my bedroom."

"You are very kind, Lucy," said Taeela.

"Got to keep Fofo happy," said Nigel.

Taeela managed a smile.

CHAPTER 9

Day 11

Another nothing-much day. Spent some of it sorting out that stuff you've just been reading, and talking about family stuff you don't want to know about, so I'm going to give myself a rest. Big day coming tomorrow, though. Tell you about it when it's over . . .

Nightmare woke Nigel early, with nowhere for his mind to go but the real nightmare stuff of the last four days. No point lying there letting it go on churning, so he got up, had a shower, dressed and went to look for a CD that might take his mind off it. He found Taeela at the living-room window in her dressing gown, staring out at Dara Dahn.

"Hi," he said. "Great view, isn't it?"

She turned, and he saw the bruised look around her eyes. But the eyes themselves sparkled.

"When I am Khan, I will have this for my house," she said. "In the morning I will ride down to the palace on one of my horses and rule over Dirzhan. Then in the afternoon I will come home to my children."

"Sounds good to me. How many kids?"

She thought about it.

"Three girls and one boy," she decided. "Not two boys, or

they'll fight who will be Khan when I am dead. I'll choose good strong young men to marry my daughters, and they will give me nineteen grandchildren. No. I change my mind. My oldest daughter will marry the son of the President of America. My second daughter will marry the son of the President of Russia, and my youngest daughter will be very, very beautiful – hot – so she will marry the son of your Prince William. They will give me nineteen grandchildren still."

"That'll keep the photographers busy. Is it OK for us to be alone together in here?"

She shrugged.

"Lucy was asleep. Her light was lit and her glasses were on her face."

"She must have had as bad a night as I did. You too, I guess."

"Before this I never sleep not in my own bed."

"Wow! Then we are honoured, like Dad said. Nobody's told me why."

Her tone changed.

"There are not enough guards in the palace. Some are hurt in the helicopter, some have gone to Vamar to question the villagers. So they must teach new guards."

The call came on the private line while they were having breakfast. Nigel's mother took it.

"Hello . . . Oh, good morning . . . I don't think any of us slept that well. It's a bit difficult to settle down after all that . . . Not at all. It's been a real pleasure having her. . . . Of course. She'll be ready . . . Yes, here she is."

Taeela was already hovering by her shoulder, but managed not to snatch when the telephone was handed to her. She chattered away in Dirzhani until her father cut her short and she rang off.

"After lunch I'll go home," she announced. "I must stay in this house. My father doesn't want that that I . . . want me to be seen. He's making a speech at eleven o'clock, on the television. I must watch that. I will tell you what he says."

The speech was all about tax breaks for farmers to help them increase food production, and how that meant prices in the shops would come down. Not a hint about what had happened at Lake Vamar. Just a lot of good news for your average Dirzhani, and the President showing that he had made it happen. When it was over Taeela chose a Doctor Who to watch. Nigel had already seen it and hated the Doctor's icky sidekick, so he slipped away to look for Rick. He found him fixing a leak in the downstairs toilet. Nigel had already worked out how to deal with the obvious question.

"Hi, lad. How are you doing? Interesting weekend?"

"Amazing. And then some."

"Don't worry. I ain't going to ask you any more. Do anything for you?"

"Nothing special. It's just a feeling. Has anything been happening—anything funny? Everybody seems a bit jumpy."

"Who's everybody?"

"Well, Dad mostly, I suppose."

"You'll 'ave to ask 'im. 'Part from that, your guess is as good as mine, Nigel . . . Better, likely."

The pause, the deliberate flatness of the last two words, gave them their meaning. Rick knew.

To make Taeela's visit as unobtrusive as possible they said goodbye to her in the living-room. She thanked Nigel's parents and shook hands with his father, but then hugged his mother as if she never wanted to let go. At last she turned to him.

"Nigel," she said.

"Bye, Taeela. Been great having you. See you soon."

She took the meaningless phrase straight.

"Tomorrow? It is the Chiefs' present-giving . . . How do I say that, Nick?"

"Hm. The Tribute of the Chieftains? That sounds sufficiently formal."

"That's still on!" said Nigel's mother. "In spite of everything?"

"Of course. Officially there's no reason to change it."

"Am I still supposed to come? What about Nigel?"

"If you can bear it. A show of confidence on our part would be appreciated."

"But you will come to me first, Nigel," said Taeela.

Before he could answer her glance shifted sideways and up.

"Please, Lucy," she said, speaking at first as if her world depended on it, but then deliberately overdoing it. "Please. My father shows me to the chieftains. Just now he tells me. I shall be so . . ."

She mimed her nervousness, comically appealing.

"I'll come if I possibly can," he said. "Promise."

"Well . . ." Nigel's mother began, but his father interrupted.

"Let's talk about it later. We're holding the Khanazhana up."

Taeela sighed, smiled, wrapped the long end of her headscarf round her face and led the way out onto the landing. They watched her departure from the head of the stairs. The front door was open and a man and a woman wearing ordinary Dirzhani dress were waiting just inside it, with Taeela's suitcase. They bowed their heads briefly to Taeela and the woman slid her right hand in under her jacket—there'd be a gun in there, Nigel guessed—and moved out onto the doorstep. Taeela waited until she had gazed left and right, then joined her. The man picked up the suitcase and followed, closing the door behind him.

Nigel heard his mother sigh, and turned to her.

"I'm sorry, darling," she said. "I'm not happy about you going to this tribute thing. About any of us going, really. Something's up they aren't . . ."

"Please, Mum. She really . . ."

"Not out there, Niggles," interrupted his father. "We'll talk about it in here."

Reluctantly he followed his mother back into the living-room. He hated family rows. His mother began as soon as he'd closed the door, talking not to him but to his father.

"Let's be clear about this, Nick. You've got to tell me what's going on. Something is. All this fuss. Look at how our guards acted on the way back from the lake, checking out the hunting lodge before they'd let us drive up to the front door. And then yesterday not letting us have our picnic where I wanted so they could get the cars out of sight. And the President wanting us to have Taeela here overnight."

"She said that was because they were short of guards at the palace," said Nigel. "A lot of them have gone up to Lake Vamar."

"I don't believe it," said his mother. "They wouldn't be acting like this if they thought what happened at Lake Vamar had just been some stroppy villager taking a pot-shot at the President. Something's up, and I don't like the feel of it. Is there any way we can get out of this tribute thing, for a start?"

"Let's sit down," said Nigel's father, and settled into his armchair, putting his finger-tips together in front of his chin, ready to start talking smoothly, reasonably, calmingly.

"First, let me say that I partially agree with you, darling. It seemed to me from the first that it was unlikely that your stroppy villager would have a night vision sight of sniper quality.

"On the other hand it is hard to see how anyone in Dara Dahn, bar a very few trusted members of the President's personal staff, could have known that the helicopter accident meant that there were not enough uninjured guards to patrol the far shore of the lake, and furthermore known the timing of his visit to the fish-owl project. We ourselves didn't know that until the Saturday."

"Somebody at the hunting lodge?" said Nigel's mother. "I bet some of them are locals. They might be in cahoots with the villagers."

"But not with anyone in Dara Dahn. From what we've seen of the system I would guarantee that all unauthorised communication between hunting lodge and palace is strictly monitored. What we are discussing is whether the events at Lake Vamar were orchestrated from Dara Dahn, with the implication that it would not be safe for you and/or Nigel to attend the ceremony tomorrow.

"In fact they make it safer, if anything. It is automatic under any regime that after a serious security breach temporary precautions are put in place. Hence the choice of a picnic site and Taeela's visit. Security at the palace tomorrow will be even tighter than usual, if that's possible.

"For myself, I have every intention of attending the ceremony, and would feel obliged to do so even if I thought it was riskier than I do. But if Nigel were to have a diplomatic illness and you stayed to look after him . . ."

"If you're going I'm going too. And I suppose Nigel can come and sit with us, where he's under our eye."

"No, Mum. I've got to go to Taeela first. I've pretty well promised. Please."

"I don't see why he shouldn't . . ."

"No, Nick. I see you've got to go because of your job, and it'll look almost as bad if I don't go too. That doesn't apply to Nigel, but if he absolutely insists on coming I won't say no, but I'm not letting him out of my sight."

"But, Mum . . ."

"I'm sorry, darling . . ."

"Mum! Please listen!"

"If I may intervene . . ." said Nigel's father.

"Wait, Nick," said his mother. "I want to hear what Nigel says."

Nigel took a deep breath, trying to pull himself together.

"Taeela's going to notice, Mum. And she's going to know why you didn't let me come. Because you didn't think it was safe. Mum, she's really scared."

"We were all scared, darling."

"You're not getting it, Mum. She *is* scared. It's over for us. It isn't for her, and it won't ever be. She told me about it in the car coming back from the lake. All we've got to do is go away somewhere and we'll be out of it. Like waking up from a nightmare. But it's real for her, ordinary. She's been waiting for something like Lake Vamar to happen all her life. She gets taught nightmare stuff like we get taught PE—how to gouge someone's eyes out, what's the best place to stick a knife into him, all that. She's got her own pistol she carries around. It isn't a toy. It's in case she has to use it.

"And then the thing happens and it's real and none of that's any use and she finds out what it's like to be really, really scared, and she's going to be in it for the rest of her life, trying to pretend it's ordinary all her life. Just now, just for a moment, when she was asking you to let me go and be with her before the tribute thingy, she let us see how it really, really mattered. And then she hammed it up, so as to hide it.

"No, wait. I haven't finished. There's never been anyone in her life before who really cared about her, cared about Taeela for herself, not just because she's the Khanazhana. Apart from Fohdrahko and her dad, but they don't count. But now there's you and me. We don't just like her, we care about her. She knows she can trust us. And now we're going to let her down. She's never going to trust anyone again.

"Suppose one day she's going to be Khan herself, which is what she wants, do you want her to be a khan like her dad, not trusting anyone, not letting anyone care for her, killing anyone who gets in her way, hanging villagers in their doorways, just because they had a hunting rifle in the house? That's what she meant when she said it was hard being a khan. She'd worked it out about her dad having to decide whether to have us bumped off on our way back from Lake Vamar, before we could tell anyone what had happened there."

"No! He wouldn't have . . . Nick! This has got to be nonsense!"

"I'm afraid not, darling. This is one of the realities of absolute power. One of the reasons for my being here, and wanting to stay here, is that I—we—can attempt to mitigate it. Have you any more to say, Niggles?"

"Yes. That's the bit about Taeela. This is about me. It's about how I feel. How I'm going to go on feeling for the rest of my life if I don't get it right this time. I didn't at Lake Vamar. OK, we were all scared about what happened, like you said, but I wasn't just scared. I lost it completely. I panicked. I couldn't think about anything else except me getting the hell out of there. Not anyone else. I hurt your leg, bolting for the door. I heard you yell. I didn't think about it. When we were running along the walkway I saw you were limping, but all I thought about it was that you were slowing me up. Same when I found you sitting by the path, looking to see how bad your leg was. It just didn't register.

"Same with Taeela. I never even thought about what it would be like for her, what she must be feeling. Least I could've done was wait for her under the trees, just to be there when she got to safety. I didn't. I ran away again. I'd actually lost it completely again on the walkway and tried to bolt, and my guard had to grab hold of me to make me stay put, and there she was running along beside her guard like she was doing it just for the exercise. I couldn't face her. It was only when we were going up to drag branches down for the stretcher and she told me how scared she'd been that I started to think about her at all.

"Think about me, Mum! Me inside. How'm I going to feel for the rest of my life if I don't go? Let her down again, worse than before? Start telling myself that I haven't got the guts—that's just how I am? Finish up being like that? Is that what you want for me?"

"I really do think it's much safer than you suppose, Lou," said Nigel's father. Neither of them paid any attention. Nigel's mother was staring at him, blinking. She wiped an eye with her finger. He could hear the croak in her voice when she spoke.

"I understand what you're telling me, darling. I really do. Suppose I still say you can't go, what will you do? Try and go anyway?"

"I don't know. You could lock me in my room, I suppose."

She actually managed a sort of laugh.

"And find you with a broken neck under your window? What do you think, Nick?"

"I agree with Nigel. There's no chance the President would have let his daughter go back if he thought she'd be safer here."

She sighed.

"All right," she said. "I'm still not happy about it, but if you really think it makes that much of a difference to you . . ."

"Oh, Mum!" he said. "I knew you'd get it!"

He was hugging her the way Taeela had done, as if he'd never let go, when his father spoilt it.

"I told you we should have had you negotiating over the dam contract instead of . . ."

Nigel let go and spun round.

"This isn't funny, Dad! It's been . . ."

He stopped himself just in time.

". . . been whatever hard for Mum to say yes, and she's still dead worried about it. It's nothing to do with the dam! It's between Mum and me, and she's being terrific about it!"

Nigel's father rose, smiling.

"It seems we have a rebellious teenager on our hands, my dear," he said mildly, and walked out, automatically checking in the mirror as he left.

Nigel's mother sighed.

"Try to remember there's a lot of good sides to him, darling," she said. "It's not his fault that he can't help being a bit detached. He had a tricky childhood—I'll tell you some time. Perhaps if he'd met a Taeela of his own when he was your age . . . From what you were telling me it sounds as if a door has opened for you which never opened for him. That's why I'm letting you go to the palace tomorrow. You understand?"

"Uh . . . Yes, Mum. Thanks. For telling me. I'll be careful."

"Only don't get so wrapped up in Taeela's feelings that you haven't any time for your father's."

"Do you want me to tell him I'm sorry?"

"If you think it's a good idea, darling. Is there anything you want to do this afternoon?"

"Only getting my blog sorted. I'm four days behind."

"Oh dear. You're not going to . . ."

"No, of course not. Just a bit about the birds up at the lodge, and the fish-owls, and some stuff I was talking to Taeela about. But I'm going to get the rest of it down on my memory stick, so it's there if I want it."

CHAPTER 10

Day 23, I make it now.

I've seen the British papers, so I guess that some of you'll know why I've dropped out again for a bit. Probably sounds exciting your end, but all I can tell you is that it's been really scary a lot of the time this end, and sick-makingly horrible some of it. At least now I don't have to leave stuff out like us crashing in the lake and getting shot at while we were watching the fish-owls. So here we go.

Day 12...

Nothing new happened in the night. Next morning's TV news said that the President and the British Ambassador had visited the site of the proposed dam at the Vamar gorge and showed them shaking hands in front of a stretch of water. It was an old picture, his mother said, and they'd faked in the background. Nigel found it unsettling, harmless in its way but still the President lying to his people, a whiff of the monster they were all pretending wasn't there–just what Nigel had been doing himself yesterday afternoon, faking it, blogging about Lake Vamar and the fish-owls as if none of the horrors before and after had happened at all.

He was sorting out the mess in his shoulder-bag when his mother came in with the portable phone in her hand.

"It's for you, darling," she said and gave it to him.

There was only one person it could be.

"Hi, Taeela," he said. "How's things?"

"Very good. Very safe. You…are coming this morning?"

"Mum and Dad will be coming down for the ceremony, but you said…"

"Eleven o'clock. We'll send a car so you can come early."

"OK."

"I have a surprise for you, Nigel. Goodbye. I'll see you."

There was an odd, almost hysterical, note in her laugh.

"Bye, Taeela," he said. "Take care. Thanks, Mum."

"That sounds all right," she said, taking the phone back. "What are you up to, darling?"

"Just dithering. I put some stuff in my bag to take to the hunting lodge, but the guards are going to search it. They don't let me take my knife in, but they give it back when I go."

She studied the pile on the bed as if it mattered. It was just the things that he carried around anyway, either from habit or simply while he was in Dirzhan—passport, iPad and mobile, the knife, a coil of tough cord, his travelling chess set, a little compass, hand torch, monocular for bird-watching, street map of Dara Dahn, Dirzhani dictionary and phrase-book, and a few embassy match folders with the royal arms on them, which Roger had given him as silly little presents for people.

"Oh, I'd take it all," she said. "If you haven't got something, you're bound to need it, but if you have, you won't. Like umbrellas."

Her laugh didn't ring true. She still thought it might matter this time.

Mr Dikhtar was waiting for him at the top of the palace steps and took him straight in, so he didn't need to show his pass. Two TV camera crews were setting up on one side of the Great Hall. There were new guards on the door to the private apartments. Nigel took his knife out of his bag and gave it to Mr Dikhtar. A guard patted a few of Nigel's pockets, peered into his bag and gave it back without taking anything out. So much for the extra security.

They waited for Mr Dikhtar to say something, but seemed to have gone into some kind of trance. He just stood there staring at the knife in his hand. His face was shiny with sweat, though it was much cooler in here than it had been out on the steps. After several seconds he seemed to wake up, looked at the knife as if he was seeing it for the first time, and gave it back to Nigel.

"I will see you later, Mr Rizhouell," he said, and opened the door for him, but didn't follow him through.

There was a longer pause than usual when Nigel knocked on the living-room door, and then a sound of sliding metal before it opened. But Fohdrahko met him with an untroubled smile. They exchanged bows and greetings.

"Khanazhan Nizhil."

"Hi, Fohdrahko. Good to see you."

Taeela was already standing a few feet from the door, posed as if he'd been going to take her photograph. She looked terrific, well worth photographing.

"Hi, there," he said.

She didn't answer, but simply stood there waiting. Behind him he heard the bolts of the door slide home.

He got it now. No wonder she looked terrific. She was wearing serious make-up. Her lips weren't really quite that full and red, the flush in her cheeks quite that peachy, her eyes quite that large, the lashes quite that long and dark. This was the surprise she'd been teasing him about.

"Wow!" he said.

"Hot?" she said.

"And then some."

What could she be up to? Good thing Fohdrahko was here. No. The camera crews in the hall. With relief he put two and two together.

"I don't suppose it's just for me," he said. "You're going to be on TV? When your dad presents you to the chieftains at this tribute thing?"

"This tribute thing!" she snarled. "It is not a thing, Nigel. It is an old, old custom, from before the Tsars, before the communists. Every year at the...eighth—yes, eighth—whole moon the chieftains of all the big families—how do you say this, many families all one big family?"

"Um...clans?"

"Yes, clans. The chieftains bring...brought gifts to the Khan to show him they were his friends. Then the Tsars came. They said, 'You can keep your khan, but you will give him only small gifts. Instead you will send taxes to Moscow.'

"It was the same with the communists. They killed the last khan. The chieftains hid in the mountains. The men who gathered the taxes sent only half to Moscow and stole half for themselves. When my father made himself Khan he said, 'The people will still pay taxes and no one will steal them. I will spend them for the people' So it was done.

"And now, Nigel, he says 'Let us have the Tribute of the Chieftains again. They will come to the palace at the eighth whole moon, but they will not bring tributes to the Khan. Instead, each man will tell the Khan what tribute he will give to Dirzhan. This man will build a school, and this man will build rooms for a hospital, and this man will make a road good, and so on. And they will bring me signs of their gifts to show to the people.'

"Today is the first time this is done. It will be in the grand hall. We will watch it this from the balcony."

"Cool."

"Wait. There is more. This is new. Yesterday only my father told me. When his speech is finished he will make a sign to me and I will come down the stairs and stand at his side. So the chieftains will see me and each one will say in his heart, 'This is the Khanazhana. One day my son will marry her.'"

"Wow! Big day for you. No wonder you're looking hot. I bet he isn't going to tell them that actually you're going to choose."

"Not yet."

"You won't forget to invite me to the wedding?"

"You will ride in on your white horse and carry me away?"

"I'll think about it. What shall we do now, while we're waiting?"

"Let's watch *El Cid.* The horses are great. And Dzharlton Heston is so funny."

Maybe he was, but Nigel didn't give himself much chance to find out. His mind was elsewhere. Little things bothered him. Mr Dikhtar's manner—was he just scared of the President's anger if something went wrong with the ceremony? Why hadn't he noticed the guard not doing a proper search? And that business with the knife…?

And why did Fohdrahko keep bolting the door? He'd never done that before. And these weren't just ordinary bolts, by the sound of them. They were like the bolts of a big safe. And why was he staying at his post by the doorway instead of coming to watch the film, as he usually did?

And the way Taeela herself was carrying on. It just wasn't like her. He'd have expected her to act dead cool before something like this. But then, who was he to say? It really must be pretty scary for her, the thought of coming down the stairway to face all those proud old men, all gazing at her, each of them judging her, each of them making the same calculation, Which of my sons?

And the President had only just sprung it on her. OK, she'd look great on TV, but he could have thought of that before. But suppose stuff was happening that meant he needed the chieftains on his side. He'd promised he'd never sacrifice her, but there'd be no harm in giving them the idea that he might. You'd feel differently about a queen sacrifice if you were the queen.

It was a relief when the telephone rang and Taeela leaped to answer it. The conversation couldn't have been briefer. She put the handset down and spoke to Fohdrahko, who rose from his stool, slid a section of panelling aside and reached into the cavity. With a quiet clunk the bolts withdrew. Nigel could feel Taeela's tension easing as she returned to the sofa and pretended to be watching the film. As the door opened he jumped up and turned to face it, but she stayed curled in her corner of the sofa, giggling away at Charlton Heston.

The President came in, bowing his head to get his hat through the doorway. His robe was a rich, dark purple, reaching almost to the floor and covered with swirls of glittering gold. The hat was all gold, embroidered with golden cord. It would have been like a cartoon wizard's hat, without a brim, but instead of rising to a point it curved over, so that the tassel at the tip dangled above his left shoulder. It ought to have looked ridiculously over-the-top, but it didn't with him wearing it. The effect was slightly spoilt by Taeela thumping into his chest and flinging her arms round him. He gave her a brief hug and pushed her away.

"Now, my dear, that is enough," he said. "If I had wanted a puppy rather than a daughter I could have bought one. I have a present for you."

It was a soft package wrapped in tissue and tied with a ribbon. Taeela took it, drew herself up and stooped into a deep, professional-looking curtsey before retiring to the sofa to open it.

"Wow! Now that really is cool, sir," said Nigel.

"I am glad it has your approval, Nigel. The dress is authentic, and was worn by the last four khans. Since the communists took over it has been in the museum, as have some of the robes the clan heads will be wearing. The remainder have been specially…"

He broke off and looked beyond Nigel.

"You approve, my dear?"

Nigel turned and saw that Taeela was once again standing in her all-set-for-the-cameraman pose, only she'd changed the dark green headscarf she'd been wearing before for a new one, deep purple, edged with gold, and with long golden tassels at either end. Again she stooped into her curtsey, straightened, and thumped once more into her father's chest.

"You must be more careful with it," he said. "The fabric is very delicate. It was worn by a Khanazhana a century before you were born.

"Now, take if off and give it to Fohdrahko. We have about ten minutes. Put your other scarf back on. When I leave, you and Nigel will come out onto the gallery and watch from there. It does not matter if you are seen. The Tribute will take about twenty minutes. I will then make a short speech. As soon as I start Nigel will stay where he is, but you will move back from the balcony and change headscarves. You will then come round the gallery to the head of the stair, keeping close to the inner wall so that you are not seen.

"At the end of my speech the chieftains will applaud. Count to twenty and then come down the stair to stand on my right side on the dais and curtsey to the chieftains. I will then formally present you to them. I have not told them this is going to happen. I intend it to be a *coup de théâtre*. Elderly men in grey western-style suits talking to each other do not make for exciting television. You agree, Nigel?"

"Uh…Oh, yes sir! It'll make great TV."

The President nodded and settled into an armchair, opened his folder and began to read. Nigel returned to the sofa and Charlton Heston. When the ten minutes were up the President rose without a word and Taeela, Nigel and Fohdrahko followed him out to the gallery. Taeela gave him another hug and he strode off along the arcade, keeping to the shadows by the inner wall. Only the top of his hat glittered in the blaze of the TV lighting from below.

Nigel leaned on the balustrade, screwing up his eyes against the glare. The stairway and the dais were lit like a stage set. The invited audience was seated in a double row on the far side, almost invisible beyond that central brightness. Nigel spotted the ash-blond blob of his father's hair in the front row. He waved, and the shape beside the blob waved back.

One of the cameras was filming a line of soldiers spaced out along the further side of the dais, wearing uniforms that wouldn't have been out of place in *El Cid*, orange turbans, dark green jackets and kilts, and sword-belts, and carrying short spears. A similar line stood opposite them.

In the centre of the hall the chieftains waited, ten of them in a curving row, facing the dais. Their robes were in the same style as the President's, but in different colours. Three of them had less grand versions of his hat, the rest a sort of floppy turban. Behind each of them in a second row stood a couple of men with a polished wooden box on a low table between them. They wore turbans, jackets and baggy trousers, and a sort of sash running down from shoulder to hip, like a sword-belt. Their sashes matched the robes of the chieftains in front of them, red and brown, black and orange, yellow and green, or whatever. Like football shirts. This must be the Premier League.

A few uniformed functionaries stood in one corner of the dais, opposite a band of musicians carrying strange brass instruments and drums. There was no one else at floor level, apart from the usual guards standing well out of camera shot by the main entrance and at various doorways around the hall. The other camera was filming about thirty women wearing handsome head-scarves who were crowded into three of the arches of the opposite gallery. The remaining arches were empty.

Nigel turned to speak to Taeela, but she was rapt in the spectacle, her lips parted, her cheeks flushed with excitement. Beyond her Fohdrahko was watching through the strip of pierced ornamental stonework that ran up beside the next pillar.

The seconds on Nigel's wristwatch slid towards noon. The band stirred and raised their instruments. A drum rattled. The brass burped and hooted through a fanfare. In the middle of it the President appeared at the top of the stairs. The chieftains and audience clapped enthusiastically as he came slowly down to the dais. They made an astonishing amount of sound. No, they didn't. There was canned applause coming from somewhere

He waited a full minute and then held up a hand for silence. One of the functionaries stepped forward, made a brief pronouncement, opened a scroll and called a name. The chieftain to the left of the line, a dignified bearded man, came forward, followed by one of his henchmen carrying his box. They climbed to the dais and halted. The chieftain placed his palms together, bowed his head and spoke in a low voice. The President held out his right hand, fully open, thumb upward. The chieftain took it between both of his, bowing again over the three hands, spoke a few words and let go. The henchman opened the box and offered it to the chieftain, who very solemnly took out a child's doll in a nurse's uniform—the sort of thing you might buy at a cheap market stall—and rotated slowly so that all the imaginary audience could see it, while deafening applause filled the Great Hall and died away. Finally the chieftain presented the doll to the President, who thanked him unsmiling and passed it to another functionary, who put it on a table at the back of the dais.

One after the other the remaining chieftains repeated the process. The next one contributed a neat model of a bridge, the next one what Nigel guessed was a well-head, the next one a model pylon, and so on. Some of the chieftains seemed happy enough in their fancy dress, others looked as if they were thought they were being forced to make fools of themselves in public. There was one tall, angry-looking man whose colours were black and brown, like a hornet, who looked as if he'd rather have spat in the President's eye than give him the model of a tree he had actually come with.

When the last one had done his stuff the President squared his shoulders, raised his head and spoke for a couple of minutes to the imaginary audience occupying the floor in front of him and the arcade above. The applause was thunderous. In the middle of it Taeela appeared at the top of the stairs.

The applause redoubled. Nigel heard the shots, coming from somewhere to his right along the gallery, but didn't at once recognise what they were. Nor did he see the President fall, because like everyone else in the hall he was watching Taeela start down the stairs, smiling, demure.

Three steps down she stopped. Her face changed. Only then did he look to see what she was staring at.

The President lay sprawled on the lowest stairs dais in his purple robe. His hat was underneath him. His face streamed with blood. Everyone was shouting and milling about. Some of the soldiers had dropped their spears and started to run. Nobody had turned off the canned applause. A group of real soldiers burst through a door under the far arcade, firing into the air as they came. Nigel darted behind a pillar and peered through the screen, then stood, transfixed, every muscle locked in place.

What happened next was all his old nightmares made real. The smashed and bloodied horror on the stairs came to life, heaved itself onto one elbow and with its other arm made an urgent gesture to Taeela. Go!

She was already half way down the stairs, but she halted, just caught herself from falling, lifted her skirts and raced back up. Behind her the horror collapsed into a heap of purple and gold and blood.

Nigel shuddered himself out of the trance of shock and turned to run for the doorway. The guard at the door half-raised his gun and gestured to him to stay where he was. Another guard was watching the chaos below from behind a pillar at the far corner of the gallery. Nigel didn't think he'd been there before.

He waited, his heart pounding, his throat working to swallow nothing. The guard growled something, gestured again with his gun, and strode past him. Carefully he turned his head to see if it was safe to make a dash for the door.

Taeela had just come careering round the corner. The guard moved forward, ignoring Fohdrahko in the shadows of his pillar, and raised his gun, shouting at her when she still came on. She heard him through the clamour and halted, staring, only a few paces from him, and started to raise her arms.

Fohdrahko moved with extraordinary speed, three lurching steps, with his right arm already swinging out for the strike. Nigel barely glimpsed the thin blade of his dagger before it was deep in the guard's neck. The guard collapsed. Fohdrahko, unable to halt the impetus of his attack, caught his foot on the falling body and would have tumbled on top of it if Taeela hadn't dashed forward and managed to hold him upright.

Nigel turned and raced for the door, barely mastering his panic flight in time to halt and wait ready to close it. The soldier he had seen at the other end of the gallery was running towards them shouting. He was only a few paces away when Taeela helped Fohdrahko stagger through the door and Nigel could slam it shut and shove the bolts home as the guard flung his weight against it.

He ran for the inner door and swung it shut, then waited while Fohdrahko, wheezing heavily and supporting himself against the door-jamb, opened the hidden panel and worked the mechanism that slid the big bolts home.

Taeela was over by an open drawer of the desk strapping a belt round her waist. She tapped at a keyboard that had appeared in the surface of the desk, and a section of the panelling beside the desk slid away, leaving a narrow opening with darkness beyond it. She stepped through, gesturing to Nigel to join her. He found himself in a narrow passage stretching away to left and right. Fohdrahko stumbled through behind him and closed the panel.

CHAPTER 11

Absolute darkness. The only sounds Taeela's steady panting, Fohdrahko's wheezing gasps, and the distant, battering thuds of the soldiers trying to break their way in from the gallery. Nigel groped in his bag.

"I've got a torch in here somewhere," he whispered.

"Wait," said Taeela. "Let Fofo pass. He knows the way in the dark. Then hold my scarf and follow me. Where is your hand?"

Huddling against the inner wall to let Fohdrahko squeeze by, Nigel shoved the torch into his pocket and felt for her fingers. She pushed the tasselled end of her headscarf into his grip and at once started to move away. From behind them came a splintering crash of the outer door giving way and then more, louder thuds as the soldiers started to batter at the inner door.

Taeela halted so suddenly that Nigel stumbled into her.

"Wait," she whispered. "Fofo makes the trap work. Give me your torch."

He switched it on and gave it to her. Fohdrahko had vanished, but they passed him as they hurried forward, standing in a narrow niche in the right hand wall, with his hand twisting something out of sight. Taeela slowed her pace, and he heard the soft mutter of her voice, counting, by the sound of it. A dozen paces further along she halted again and knelt. Nigel waited, quivering. The racket from the living-room entrance paused. A decisive voice gave orders.

Taeela opened the purse on her belt and took out a tool like the blade of a table knife with a backward-curving slot near the tip. She slid this into the crack between two of slabs in the wall, felt around with it until the slot engaged and levered downwards. A catch clicked. She rose and switched off the torch.

"We wait here," she whispered. "We are the bait for the trap."

With his heart slamming he stood in the pitch dark until the silence was broken a violent explosion from beyond the living-room, followed by men's shouts, nearer now, fading into uncertainty. The voice they'd heard before asked a question. Another, quieter, answered. Taeela gasped and started to say something, but her words were drowned by a crash from along the passage. Light streamed through the broken panelling. Armed men burst through the gap.

Nigel turned to run, but Taeela stayed where she was, blocking the way.

"No," she muttered. "They must see us."

She pushed past him, raised her arms in surrender and waited, silhouetted against the light from the broken panel. Nigel forced himself to copy her. His throat kept trying to swallow saliva that wasn't there. A torch was switched on, its beam blinding. A man called out in Dirzhani, his meaning obvious.

"Got them!"

Fohdrahko had been setting a trap. Taeela and Nigel were the bait. It had better work. Boot-steps thumped on the paving, nearer and nearer.

A man yelled. The beam of the torch blanked out as a blackness rose from the floor, filling the passage, except for a faint crack of light running round its edges. From beyond came more yells, some dwindling away downwards and snapping short.

Calls now, anxious, questioning. Only echoes returned, and the rustle of running water.

Mutterings. Footsteps receding. Two pairs, or perhaps three. Taeela switched the torch on and Fohdrahko emerged from his niche. Just beyond him a shallow pit had opened in the floor, where a whole segment of paving stones had swung up, like one arm of a see-saw, to fill the corridor from wall to wall, allowing the other arm to swing down as soon as the weight of the men advancing onto it had altered the balance, and tipped them down into the water far below.

Fohdrahko muttered briefly. Taeela translated.

"He has locked it. They cannot open it from that side. Nigel, did you hear...? No, we must go now. Let Fofo come by. You take the torch."

Unused adrenalin thundering through his bloodstream, Nigel watched her kneel again and pull on the gadget she'd inserted into the wall. Two of the stone slabs at the foot of the wall hinged apart. She helped the old man sit and hunker round until his feet were in the opening. He edged forward until he could grasp something out of sight and then, with Taeela's help and gasping with effort, slither himself further in, pull himself upright and disappear.

"Now you," she said.

The opening led into a shaft with a series of iron rungs let into in the opposite wall. Nigel slung the loop of the torch round his wrist and wriggled himself through, feet first. Above him the shaft vanished into darkness, but below him he could see Fohdrahko climbing slowly down, leaning his back against the wall behind him each time he needed to shift his grip. A catch clicked overhead as Taeela locked the slabs into place. There was a long wait, hanging in the dark shaft while Fohdrahko twisted himself half round and used a tool like Taeela's to open another pair of slabs. He rested, gasping, and struggled back up and out.

Nigel found him sitting slumped against the wall of a passage like the one above. His breath wheezed painfully in and out, and the shadows cast by the torch turned his face into a Halloween mask.

Taeela crawled out and swung the two slabs shut. She twisted round, still kneeling, and stared at Fohdrahko and asked a question. He muttered an answer. She shook her head and waited, frowning. He didn't move.

"He looks pretty well all in," said Nigel.

"He is so tired. His heart is not good. He says to leave him."

"Suppose we got him onto his feet. One each side. Then he could lean on me. I think there's just room."

She spoke to Fohdrahko, who nodded and managed a feeble smile. Nigel crouched on his right so that he could pull the old man's arm round his shoulders and waited for Taeela to get into place.

"One, two, three, and up," he counted.

He could almost have done it on his own. The eunuch felt as light as a dead leaf and quivered uncontrollably. His feebleness, his need of Nigel, pushed terror into the background. Their shoulders brushing the walls on either side, they crept along behind Taeela in the direction they had come from on the floor above, rounded the shaft down which their pursuers had fallen, and saw the passage stretching ahead of them into darkness.

Taeela kept the beam of the torch trained on the bottom of the right hand wall. Again he heard the mutter of counting. She stopped, knelt, and used her gadget to open two slabs that looked no different from all the others. They helped Fohdrahko kneel and crawl slowly through. Nigel followed and Taeela came last, pulling the slabs together and locking them firm.

At the sound of the solid masonry settling into place things changed. The desperation of flight receded like water flowing down a plug-hole. Nigel rose to his feet, gave a long, slow, sigh and looked around.

They were in a fair-sized room, except that the ceiling was low enough for him to be able to reach up and touch it with his fingertips. There were bright-patterned mats on the floor, two cots with gaudy bedspreads, chairs, a table, a cupboard with drawers, two shelves of books, and a washstand with basin and jug, and a mirror above it. Everything was simple and solid and old-fashioned, apart from a slick-looking PC console against the left-hand wall.

Three walls were whitewashed, but covered with large cartoonish outlines of rabbits painted in different colours, like a nursery frieze for a giant's baby. The fourth wall looked out over the river through the same stone lattice as the room above, with a small curtained area in the corner beside it.

Taeela paid no attention to any of this. She gestured to Nigel to help, and again they lifted Fohdrahko to his feet and walked him over to one of the cots and shuffled round until they could lower him to a sitting position. He made feeble efforts to rise as Taeela knelt and took off his sandals, then sighed and let her help him twist round and lie down.

She stood and spoke to him firmly, a nurse with her patient, and bent and kissed his forehead. He smiled and closed his eyes.

Now, at last, she loosed her hold on herself, relaxing the force of will that had kept her going, decisive and clear-headed in the face of horror and loss. Her shoulders sagged and the set of her jaw slackened and voice quivered.

"Oh, Nigel! Dudda is dead! He is dead! He is dead!" She croaked.

The appeal was intense, direct. Her misery and need were all there was. He lurched towards her and wrapped his arms clumsily round her. She collapsed sobbing onto his shoulder.

And he needed her as much as she needed him, someone to cling to, share it all with, the horror of what had been done, the dread and anxiety of what would happen next. His parents—what had happened to them? There'd been gunfire in the Great Hall, bullets, splinters of marble and lapis flying around…And Fohdrahko, the only one who could help, himself helpless…

"Oh, Nigel!"

"How…? Who…?"

He barely knew what he was asking. The words had just come. Something outside the nightmare.

Her sobs cut short. He felt her body stiffen.

"Avron," she whispered, easing herself away from him.

"Avron Dikhtar? What about him?"

"In my room. I knew his voice. He said where the men must break the wall. He knows where the place is. Perhaps one time we forgot to switch off the closed circuit. He does not know the numbers to open the door."

Yes! Nigel's mind snatched at the chance to think. Mr Dikhtar had been scared stiff that morning—he'd known this was going to happen. It had been a new guard on the door, who hadn't made much of a job of searching Nigel, but he'd been in the plot and tried to capture Taeela...And that morning Nigel had set the alarms off, Mr Dikhtar had been in control of security. He'd've known a lot of the President's guards were out of action. They were training new ones, Taeela had said. He could have picked them...

And the men who'd come storming into the Great Hall, they'd been soldiers...Someone high up in the army must be in the plot too...

And Lake Vamar. The plotters had already set things up there at so that when the time came they could make it look like some local hunter taking pot shots at the President when he next paid a visit. They didn't expect to nail him then, but it would allow them to send most of the loyal soldiers up there to crack down on the villagers. Then they'd move their own men into the palace and stage their coup. He'd taken the Ridgwells there on the spur of the moment, and they weren't really ready, but the helicopter crash had made it too good a chance to miss, and the Tribute ceremony gave them a perfect target, so they'd gone ahead.

Footsteps sounded on the floor above. Nigel froze, straining to listen. Three, no, four people coming into the room. Voices, questioning. Somebody already there, nearer the window, answering. A man giving orders, the words muffled, but the urgency and anger clear. The Dirzhani for "Yes, sir." Footsteps—two sets? Three?—hurrying out of the room.

Taeela was at the PC console waiting for the screen to settle. Nigel crept across and watched over her shoulder. Her fingers moved decisively on the keys, and he was looking down at an angle into her living room from high in the corner to the left of the door. He could see the area around the sofa and TV, the window and the whole of the right-hand wall including the desk, with the splintered panel beside it.

The room seemed to be empty, but after a moment or two a soldier hurried in carrying a tool-box, which he placed in front of the desk and opened. He knelt and tried the drawers, but they seemed to be locked, so he chose a tool and started to pry at the central one.

Three men emerged through the broken panel, a short, stout officer in a smart parade uniform with three stars on his shoulder tabs, another with only one, and a younger man with two bars.

"Colonel Sesslizh!" hissed Taeela. "Why, Nigel? Why? My father...Oh, it is horrible! I will..."

A single dull thud broke the silence. On the screen the soldier who had been trying to open the desk reeled back and fell. The three officers staggered into each other but kept their feet, stared for a moment at the desk, flung up arms to protect mouths and nostrils, and rushed off screen. The soldier rose to his knees and started to crawl away, but then collapsed and lay still.

"They are such fools!" snarled Taeela. "Of course there is a trap!"

Nigel stared at the empty room. The soldier lay where he had fallen, not moving. Some kind of gas, he guessed. They wouldn't be trying to get through this way, then, not for a bit. And what with that other trap in the passage above, they were going to be jumpy about trying to break through anywhere. That meant there might be time to wait till darkness, get out somehow, sneak back to the Embassy...Or perhaps his father could fix something. For him, anyway. What about Taeela? What would his father...?

"Can we see what's happening in the Great Hall?" he whispered.

Taeela started as if he'd woken her from a trance and pressed a couple of keys. A menu list in Dirzhani came up. More keys, and there was the Great Hall, seen looking down the stairs towards the entrance. A camera crew was on the dais photographing the President's body sprawled in his blood, his arm still reaching out in that final gesture, telling Taeela to go. This was almost the angle from which she must have seen it happen.

Her face was set, her mouth a hard slit.

"I will have their blood!" she muttered. "I will have their blood!"

She reached for the keyboard.

"No, please!" he said. "Can we see...?"

"Lucy and Nick? Look, they are there. I think they are not hurt."

She worked the mouse and brought up the view across the Great Hall. The audience were still in their chairs, watched by a line of soldiers, their guns held ready to use. Nigel's father was sitting stiffly upright, staring in front of him as if he were doing his best to ignore a foul smell. His left arm was round Nigel's mother, who was slumped against his shoulder with her head bowed so that only her dark frizz showed. Nigel ached to reach to her, to whisper somehow in her mind that he was not far away, watching, safe.

There was a commotion in the row behind them, where a couple of soldiers had forced their way between the seats and were trying to drag a man out, and he was resisting. From the gaps in the rows it looked as if he wasn't the first. At the end of the row stood an officer and a civilian. The civilian studied the list in his hand and pointed. This time the victim rose and came without a struggle, and a soldier led him away.

"Who's that chap with the list?" said Nigel.

"I do not know him. The man they take away is Mattu Mandli. He is mayor in Dara. You see the girl next where he sits. His daughter, Jannah. In my school.... You see enough, Nigel?"

"I suppose so. I wonder what's really happening...There must be someone in charge of it all."

"I look."

The monitor flickered through a series of scenes, different views of the Great Hall, one with soldiers guarding the men they'd extracted from the audience and some of the chiefs who'd come to declare their tributes; a room full of soldiers, weaponless, looking angry and dejected, sitting in rows on the floor, guarded by other soldiers, armed; palace servants standing around, frightened or excited or both; four men having what was clearly a serious argument...This might be it. One was the colonel with the hissy name who they'd seen in Taeela's living room, one was a tall, smooth-faced soldier, also with three stars on his shoulder-tabs, one was the angry-looking chieftain who'd brought a tree as his tribute, still in his black and orange robes, and the fourth was Mr Dikhtar. The argument was between the chieftain and the two soldiers. Mr Dikhtar was desperately trying to keep the peace. The other three ignored him until the chieftain turned on his heel and strode away, with Mr Dikhtar scuttling behind him. The two soldiers followed, making no attempt to catch up.

"That's the colonel again, isn't it?" said Nigel. "And Dikhtar, of course. Any idea who the other two are?"

"The chieftain, he is Adzhar Taerzha," Taeela growled. "He wants his son to marry me. Then he will be Khan. He is West Dirzh. The other soldier is Colonel Madzhalid. He is East Dirzh. Sesslizh too. Of course they fight him. I tell you, they are such fools! Let bad things happen to them! All of them! I curse them! I will drink their blood!"

She stared at the retreating backs, her chest heaving as the deep breaths came and went. She gave a violent shudder and turned to him.

"Nigel, I am hungry."

He looked at his watch. Twenty past one. Barely an hour since he'd watched Taeela start down the stairway. He shouldn't have been able to swallow a mouthful after what had happened, but he was famished.

"Is there anything to eat?"

"Of course. I will leave the screen on so you can you see what happens with Lucy and Nick."

There was a shelf of canned food in the cupboard, another with plates and mugs and cutlery, and a small fridge. While he carried their meal to the table and opened the cans she took some clothes out of a drawer and retired behind the curtain in the corner. Fohdrahko seemed to be peacefully asleep, on his back, with his lips parted, and snoring gently.

Taeela returned, now dressed in the sort of clothes Nigel had seen Lisa and Natalie wearing, and they settled cornerwise at the table, where he could watch the screen and she didn't have to, but close enough to whisper.

"What happens now?" he said. "Is there a way out?"

"Fofo will show us. He knows all these hidden ways. They are the secret of the eunuchs. They kill any other person they find here. If they bring a man in here they cover his eyes. The men who put the computer in this room, and all the other things, Fofo brought them here with their eyes covered.

"He is the last of the eunuchs. There will be no more. He makes new rules. He didn't cover my eyes, and he teaches me the secret ways. He drew the animals for me to keep me safe when I was small."

"He can't take us much further, can he? He looks pretty well done for."

"I will give him food when we have finished. He will not eat while we eat. Then he must sleep again. When it is dark we will go to your embassy."

"Trouble is, that's where they'll be expecting us to head for. Is there anywhere else we could go? Have you got any friends..."

"No friends...no friends..."

Her voice was as bleak as a sunless planet.

"People I know, a few," she went on. "They will be so afraid. I do not know what they will do... Nigel, I think it is best I stay here. I will hide with Fofo. He will not leave the palace. You must go alone. If they find you they will not hurt you. You are son of the British ambassador."

He wasn't even tempted.

"Not on your life," he said. "Besides, these guys—suppose they do pick me up, they're not going to tell anyone. They'll just beat me up till I've told them where you are and then chuck me in the river, like as not. Do you think it would be crazy to try and call the embassy on my mobile? It should work from here, and I've got a number that's safe that end."

"Not your mobile," she said. "My father tells me, use only this telephone. I'll show you."

"Hang on. Something's happening...Looks like they're taking your dad away. Do you want to...?"

She was already hurrying over to the console. He joined her and she slid her hand into his and gripped it tight. They watched a couple of soldiers spread a stretcher out on the dais, dump the body on it and carry it away, Another couple of men spread a bit of canvas over the blotch of blood where it had lain and weighted it in place with what looked like account books.

"It is the last time I see him," said Taeela.

For a long while she stood there, weeping silently. He himself could hardly see for tears. Then, not letting go of his hand, she wiped her eyes with her other sleeve, closed the picture, clicked on an icon and keyed in a code. A panel opened in the surface of the console, bringing a telephone up with it. He watched which keys she used as she restored the scene in the Great Hall on the monitor and returned to her meal.

He fetched the list of numbers out of his shoulder bag and checked the country code for the UK, keyed it in, followed by Hastings, end of World War One and Battle of Britain, all backwards, pausing between each date to make sure he'd got the next one right. Silence. UK ring-tone. Clicks and whistles. Dirzhani ring-tone. At last, a known voice.

"British Embassy."

Nigel pitched his own voice high, and a bit giggly.

"Uncle Roger?"

Brief silence.

"Himself. To which of my innumerable nieces have I the honour of speaking?"

"Gina, Uncle Roger. Is it OK to call now?"

"Seems like it, Nigel. What on earth's up? Where's your father? I thought it'd be him calling."

"They've shot the President. On the stairs. In front of everyone. They're holding them all captive in the Great Hall. Mum and Dad are there too. I can see them on CCTV."

"Good God!...Where are you?"

"Hiding. With my friend. We didn't see who shot him. Look, I'm desperate to tell Mum I'm OK. If there's anything you can do...Don't tell her anything else. Just I'm OK. We're going to try and get out when it's dark. Can we come to the embassy?"

"Better stay clear for the moment. The military have just shown up, front and back, not letting anyone in or out. For our own safety, they say, because of some kind of disturbance. I take it some of them are behind this."

"Lots of them. We saw a guy called Colonel Sess something..."

"Sesslizh?"

"That's right. We've just seen him on CCTV with another guy called General Madzh something having a row with a chieftain called Adzhar Taerzha...something like that—they're different sorts of Dirzh and they don't get on—anyway, he was in it too, and Avron Dikhtar—he was one of the President's secretaries…"

He ran out of steam.

"Right," said Roger. "That's all very helpful. Look, we'd better cut this short, so I can call the FO back home. It seems to me the sooner this gets out into the world the more chance there is these thugs will behave themselves, and decide they'd better let your parents go. Meanwhile I'd strongly advise you to lie low for a bit, if you think you're safe where you are. There'll likely be rioting when the word gets out. The old boy was a Varak. There are a lot of Varaki in Dara, around the market area. They won't like this at all. It's going to be pretty hairy out there for a while. There'll be a curfew as soon as it's dark. Streets full of soldiers. Anyway, give it a couple of hours and call again if you can. All right?"

"I suppose so."

"Good luck then. Bye."

CHAPTER 12

Nigel put the telephone down and stood staring blankly at the screen. Nothing much seemed to be happening, though soldiers bustled to and fro like ants round a nest—no way of knowing what their scurryings meant. The captive bigwigs fidgeted in their chairs.

He went back to the table. His food was still on his plate. He didn't want it. Without thinking he reached across the table and Taeela took his hand.

"I am wrong, Nigel," she whispered. "I have four friends. Two are in this room. Two are there."

She nodded towards the screen.

"Who did you talk to, Nigel?"

"Roger, at the embassy. He says we're better off staying here. We can't go to the embassy—they're watching it. Besides, there'll be a curfew, soldiers everywhere. And he thinks there'll be rioting as soon as it gets around what's happened. Shooting and tear gas and that sort of stuff. I don't know. The longer we give them the more chance they'll have to get organised and find us."

"We ask Fofo. Soon I will wake him. Eat, Nigel. You must be strong."

"If you say so."

He began to pick listlessly at his food with his free hand,

watching the monitor screen while he chewed. He had almost emptied his plate when Mr Dikhtar showed up and spoke to Nigel's father and mother, and then worked along the front row of the audience, doing the same. He gestured to them and they rose and followed him sideways across the Great Hall and out of sight.

Reluctant to bother Taeela, Nigel went to the console and keyed in the CCTV Index code she had used. He worked through it and found his parents sitting with the other chosen bigwigs while Mr Dikhtar introduced Adzhar Taerzha and the smooth-faced colonel, who both made speeches while Mr Dikhtar translated.

It was desperately frustrating to watch. The only time anything happened that Nigel understood was when his father asked a question, his mother came suddenly alert, and the colonel answered, making soothing gestures with his hands as he spoke. They were doing their best to find Nigel (true). They'd make sure he wasn't hurt (maybe). When they'd finished talking the colonel and Adzhar Taerzha shook hands, pretending to like each other fine, and left. Time passed. Nothing new happened.

Restless, he gave up watching and explored the room. The rest of the cupboard contained clothes, packages, boxes, files, a tool-set and so on, The curtain in the corner hid a seat with a hole in it, leading down to a dark shaft from which rose a faint whiff of river-water. Through the window he could see army vehicles moving along the embankment road on the other side of the river. Tanks guarded that end of the bridges either side of the palace.

Taeela had cleared away the remains of her lunch and was sitting brooding at the table. Beside her was a mug of water and a bowl with morsels of food chopped small. It didn't look as if she wanted to talk, so Nigel got out his travelling chess set and experimented with variations of the French defence while he finished eating. Unexpectedly, he found one which actually led somewhere interesting, and lost himself in it for half an hour.

"Now I wake Fofo," said Taeela.

She picked up the bowl and mug and went over to the cot. The old man woke at a touch, and immediately tried to rise. She helped him to his feet and then over to the curtained corner, waited and brought him back. He tried to protest when she told him to sit on the cot, but gave in and waited, smiling, while she piled pillows and cushions against the headboard, and eased him back on them. He settled down with a sigh and allowed her to feed him morsel by morsel, and to steady the mug for him while he drank.

When he'd cleared the bowl he lay still, his good eye bright and interested while she talked, finishing with a question. He answered slowly. She protested earnestly. He shook his head and answered more briefly, then closed his eyes and fell asleep. She returned to the table, shaking her head.

"Bad?" said Nigel.

"Fofo says we must go, when it is dark, today. He will show me how we do this. These traitors are not ready, not—like you say—organised. They will be very busy everywhere doing other stuff. Perhaps they will not see us, and we will go away from Dara Dahn to Sodalka, where the chieftain is my father's cousin, Baladzhin. He is an enemy of Adzhar Taerzha. I don't want this. Baladzhin wants to marry me to his son. I tell…told Fofo we don't go before he is strong again. He says he will not come. He will stay here and spy on our enemies, but there is a good man who will come with us.

"What do I do, Nigel? I do not wish to leave Fofo. There is no place I can go, so I stay here. If these traitors find me, I kill myself."

She would, too. He shook his head and took her hand.

"Don't let's think that far," he said. "Let's get absolutely ready to go, in case we have to get out in a hurry, and then let's wait and see. The embassy's out. They've got soldiers watching it front and back. And it's not going to be that easy getting anywhere in Dahn, because it means crossing the river, and they've got the bridges guarded, by the look of it. Anyway, Roger told me to call again soon. I'll ask him if he can think of anywhere to go in Dara."

They got everything ready they could think of. Fohdrahko woke, obviously stronger, ate a little more, then showed them the entrance to a hidden passage on the other side of the room. They practised leaving, and stacked everything ready in it—a large-pocketed sleeveless military-looking jacket for Taeela, a dahl to go over it, and a small embroidered duffel-bag of the sort Nigel had seen women carrying in Dahn; a dahl for Nigel, plus his shoulder-bag, stuffed to bursting; and a man's jacket that Fohdrahko insisted on taking.

That done, Nigel called the embassy again, but Roger said he didn't know anywhere they could safely hide in Dara, and anyway he was still strongly against their leaving the palace unless they had to. Somebody had called from there, he said, and told him that the ambassador and his family were staying there for their own safety because there was a minor disturbance in Dahn; but they would be coming home as soon as it was under control. Nothing about the President being dead, or Nigel missing. When Roger had asked to speak to the ambassador the line had gone dead. Nigel was actually watching his parents on the monitor as he spoke. Food had been brought to the room, but his mother didn't seem to be eating anything. She had a book with her, of course, and was reading..

Time crept past. Ten minutes seemed a whole hour. And they still couldn't be sure whether they were staying or going.

Their minds were made up for them as dusk gathered over the roofs of Dahn. Nigel and Taeela were at the window taking turns to use his monocular to watch what was happening at the far end of the bridges. At least whoever had spoken to Roger had told him one bit of the truth. There was a disturbance all right. Three more tanks and a lot of soldiers had arrived to confront a mass of people who had swarmed down from the crooked little streets above the river and were trying to force their way onto the bridges. Beneath them the fishing fleet was heading out for the lake just as if this had been a day like any other day. It was getting too dark to see when footsteps sounded on the floor above.

They froze, listening, then crossed silently to the console. Taeela adjusted the monitor and they were looking down into her living room. Colonel Sesslizh was there, with a junior officer and two men in western dress.

"Russians," whispered Taeela. "What do they do?"

One of them started to plug cables into sockets on the electronic case he'd been carrying. The other took a gadget like a metal-detector, put on a pair of headphones, lowered the business end almost to floor level and waited while the other man adjusted controls in the case. Then he began to work to and fro across the room as if he were looking for buried treasure. They could follow the sound of his footsteps as he moved to and fro.

"What does he do?" said Taeela again.

"Looks like some kind of heat-seeking…Wait…I think he's found Fohdrahko!"

The footsteps had stopped roughly over the cot, and on the monitor Nigel could see the operator moving his gadget probingly to and fro.

Taeela frowned a moment, thinking, tapped in a code and closed down.

"We go," she said decisively, and helped Fohdrahko to his feet.

"Hold it!" said Nigel. "Don't go straight there. They'll know where to look when they get in. Take him across to where we came in, so they think we've gone back that way. Then round and back to our bolt-hole. We'll sort ourselves out inside the passage."

Taeela nodded and led Fohdrahko across the room, explaining to him as they went. Nigel nipped over to join them at the other entrance, and then took some of the old man's weight as they moved as quickly as they could along by the wall, over in front of the window and back to the bolt-hole.

While Taeela and Fohdrahko were crawling through he listened anxiously to the movement of the footsteps. It seemed to have worked. The searcher had followed them to the far wall and lost them there. With luck when their pursuers found their way in they'd waste time exploring those passages. Taeela was closing the entrance slabs well before the searcher's footsteps reached them.

"You have this now," she said, handing him the key. "I go first with Fofo, to be helping him, and so he can tell me stuff. I use his key. You come behind and close the holes. And you pull this after us, so you wipe away our feet marks. All right?"

"This" was a roll of soft cloth wrapped several times round a pole almost the width of the passage, weighted, and with a loop of cord tied to either end. Looking where they had been standing he could see the scufflings of their movements on the dusty paving.

"I get it," he said.

She muttered to Fohdrahko, switched off her torch and together they moved away into the darkness. He fitted the roll across the passage by feel and followed, dragging it behind him, with his left hand held forward to brush the inner wall and guide him. The darkness wasn't as absolute as it had seemed. The black shapes of the other two disappeared into a pale gleam from the left. Beyond the corner lay a long passage stretching across the front of the building, lit here and there by the last of daylight coming through small openings in the fancy stonework of the facade.

They halted by the nearest one to sort out their loads. Nigel folded his dahl over his shoulder-bag and Taeela put on her sleeveless jacket, with her dahl slung through the cords of her duffel bag, then draped the jacket Fohdrahko had chosen over his shoulders and knotted its sleeves under his chin.

They moved slowly on. At one point Fohdrahko stooped to peer through an opening in the inner wall. Nigel, when he reached it, did so too and found himself looking down into the Great Hall. The last of the audience who had come to watch the Tribute ceremony were being led away. Two women were kneeling on the stairs with buckets beside them, scrubbing at the area where the President's body had lain. Two officers came down the stairs. They didn't even glance at the place.

There was something about the scene…

Nigel's skin crawled as he grasped for the first time how creepy these passages were. How often through the centuries had the unseen watchers stood here, spying on the scene below? All now dead and forgotten, but still their spirits seemed to breathe from the chill masonry.

He shook himself out of the daze and hurried after the others. By the time he reached them Taeela had unlocked another pair of slabs, but instead of crawling through the opening, Fohdrahko took the cloth-roll from him and dragged it off along the passage, leaving behind it a smooth layer of dust that looked as if it hadn't been disturbed for years.

"He works another trap," whispered Taeela.

They waited until the old man came back and crawled through the opening. Taeela followed. Nigel crawled in backwards, using the cloth-roll to smooth out the dust at the entrance. He closed and locked the slabs and helped Taeela lift Fohdrahko to his feet. Already visibly tiring again, the old man tottered ahead into the darkness. Taeela followed close behind, holding her torch pointed to shine just in front of the dragging feet. Nigel came last, still hauling the cloth-roll behind him.

This passage was different. Instead of a vertical wall on the left, the torchlight showed the base of an arched surface curving away into a wider darkness. Light glimmered a little further ahead. When he reached it Nigel found it came from a spy-hole looking down through the ceiling of a meeting room, with chairs arranged around a large table, all lit by the afterglow of sunset coming through unseen windows.

He caught up with the others as they turned a corner. Now the passage, pitch dark, ran between two vertical walls, as narrow as before. A little way along it Fohdrahko halted, leaned his back against the wall and slid himself down into a sitting position.

"He must rest," whispered Taeela. "It is a long way to climb down. We practise this three times. Fofo says I must know to do it alone."

She took a wrapped bar out of one of her bulging pockets, broke off a piece and handed it to Fohdrahko, then another for herself and offered the rest to Nigel. It was some kind of energy food, dates and grain and honey. She switched off her torch and he settled beside her and nibbled slowly in the dark, thinking about the women working at the blood-stained stairs, and that large life, that overwhelming personal presence, gone, its last traces being scrubbed away while the little lives around it carried on.

He himself was one of those lives. The horror of the event, the near-panic of their escape, the long, tense afternoon, the worry about his parents—for the moment all that seemed to have happened to someone else. He'd had as much as he could cope with. That bit of him was numb. Just another little life.

And this wasn't the first time. Again and again blood, the blood of khans perhaps, must have stained those stairs. The spy-hole he had looked through had been splayed like an arrow-slit in a castle, and the hole itself, hidden among the ornamental curlicues of the Great Hall, had been large enough for a musket to be aimed through...How many, many times through the long generations of khans had their eunuchs used these secret ways to spy on their masters' enemies, or steal from them, or poison them? It was almost as if their ghosts were there among the shadows beyond the torchlight, whispering too faintly for living ears to hear, telling him that the splendid building he had seen from across the river, or standing in the Great Hall, was only an outer shell. These hidden ways were the veins of the creature. This was where it lived its mysterious life. He shivered at the thought, not with fear but with a kind of excitement.

The mood was broken by a mutter from Fohdrahko. Taeela answered and they started to talk, the old man telling her things and she asking questions. Nigel became restless with anxiety. Every minute that went by was another minute in which the soldiers might get on their trail. The glimmer of a spy-hole showed in the darkness ahead, so for something to do he rose and felt his way along to it.

Once again he found himself looking out across the Great Hall, this time from the side. There was more to see from this angle, men scurrying around, one stopping to ask something, another answering with a shrug, and both rushing off. It didn't look as if anyone was in control enough to organise a proper search. He watched for a while, then returned to the others, spread his dahl out on the floor and lay down it, using the bag as a pillow and set out an imaginary game in his mind. Taeela woke him almost two hours later.

"We go now," she whispered. "Leave the floor-sweep in the shaft."

By the time he'd sorted himself out she was opening another entrance. Slowly Fohdrahko hunkered himself round and worked his legs into the gap. One at each shoulder, Taeela and Nigel eased him forward onto the rungs. They watched him sink slowly out of sight. Taeela switched off her torch and followed.

Nigel closed the entrance slabs by feel and tied the cord of the cloth-roll round a rung, leaving it hanging. The descent seemed to go on for ever, with pauses while Fohdrahko rested and the only sound in the dark shaft the weary rasp of his breath. At last he reached the bottom, Taeela switched on her torch, and Nigel could see him huddled against one wall to let her crouch beside him and unlock another pair of slabs. As she swung them outward a draught of reeking air blew up the shaft, bringing with it the mutter of fast-moving water.

They came out into a low brick tunnel, with a narrow walkway running along beside a stinking stream, the clean clear water from the hills carrying the filth of Dara away. The walkway was too narrow for either of them to help Fohdrahko but he refused to rest. Without closing the entrance slabs he led them upstream until they reached an iron-studded door set back a metre or so into the wall, leaving a small platform between it and the water. Here he stopped and with a shaking hand indicated a crack in the brickwork.

Taeela levered out a loose brick, felt into the cavity behind it and brought out several large keys on an iron key-ring. The door opened on well-oiled hinges, without creak or groan. Beyond lay a narrow passage with an iron-barred gate at the other end lit by a weak light from somewhere out of sight.

Taeela switched off the torch and unlocked the gate. Faint stirrings came from somewhere near by, and what sounded like a moan of pain. Beyond that the voices of a man arguing with a woman. Fohdrahko grunted and Taeela eased the gate open. They stole out into a wide, low-ceilinged corridor running right and left, with a series of closed doors down either side, each with a small barred window in it, head high to an adult. The air stank of people and sweat and dirt. Another place of ghosts. The ancient dungeons of the khans, where they had kept their enemies.

And still did. The lucky ones.

Now there was room to help Fohdrahko. One each side of him, taking most of his weight, they crept along between the cells, allowing him to crouch out of sight below the level of the windows. Beyond another corner at the end of the corridor the argument raged on. Was that Dirzhani they were talking…? Oh, of course. The gaolers must be watching a Russian soap.

Fohdrahko stopped at one of the doors and whispered to Taeela. She let him choose a key and then shone the torch onto his face while he straightened and looked through the window with his finger to his lips. Nigel heard the beginnings of a shout stifled back into a gasp, then rapid movements as Taeela unlocked the door and pushed it open.

The man in the doorway stared for a moment and fell to his knees, sobbing. He was pale and filthy, wearing only a collarless shirt and rough trousers. Taeela hissed at him but he didn't seem to hear her, just knelt there, gasping and sobbing. She took him by the shoulder and shook him, forcing him to pull himself together and stand. Grabbing a fold of his shirt she tugged him out and stood him where Fohdrahko could put his arm round his shoulders.

Finally he seemed to get what was expected of him. He clasped Fohdrahko's wrist, shrugged himself sideways to take his weight, and followed Taeela back the way they had come. While she locked the gate they squeezed along the narrow passage, and out onto the platform above the reeking stream.

Taeela locked the door and put the key-ring back in its hiding place, but instead of moving on Fohdrahko muttered and the man altered his grip so that he could lower him gently to the ground. Taeela crouched beside him with her arm round his shoulders, while Nigel and the man stood and listened to the wheezing rattle of the tired old lungs dragging at the stinking air. He's done for, Nigel thought. There's no way he's going any farther. We'll be in trouble without him. This other guy doesn't look much use. A bit of human wastage picked out of the gutter.

Yes. With a shudder he realised that this was what the passage they had just come through, and the little platform on which he was now standing, was for—part of the secret life of the building above him. This was where it had got rid of its own kind of waste, the dead enemies of those ancient khans, to be carried away down river and thrown into the lake for the fish to feed on.

Fohdrahko's breathing eased. He squared his shoulders and sat upright, then spoke in a stronger voice. Taeela eased the jacket out from behind him and handed it to Nigel. Fohdrahko drew his knife out of his surcoat and spoke again. The man knelt beside him facing Taeela, bared his arm, chose a place just above the wrist where the veins ran close to the surface, took the knife and carefully slid its point under the skin and gave it back to Fohdrahko. He pinched a fold of flesh between finger and thumb and squeezed out the blood.

All the time the foul stream whispered by.

Fohdrahko spoke again and Taeela rose to her feet. The man, still kneeling, offered her his arm. She took it by the wrist, rubbed her other thumb into the blood and placed it firmly against the man's forehead, leaving a red blotch like a fuzzy caste-mark. Fohdrahko spoke a few words, more slowly, so that she could repeat them to the man. She took the jacket, came round and put it round his shoulders. Still following Fohdrahko's instructions, she took an energy bar from her pocket, broke off a corner and put it between the man's lips, waited for him to swallow and offered him her left hand. He held it between both of his and solemnly repeated several sentences after Fohdrahko. She let go and the man pulled his sleeve down and rose to his feet.

"Nigel, this is Rahdan," said Taeela. "He will help us."

"Hi, Rahdan," said Nigel, holding up a hand in greeting. "Good to meet you. I'm Nigel."

Rahdan seemed to notice him for the first time. He stared. His mouth fell open, he began to say something and then burst into a guffaw of laughter, shockingly loud in that place of whispers and secrets, almost the first real sound they'd heard since the clamour of gunfire in the Great Hall.

Taeela snarled at him and he cut the laughter short with an apologetic gesture, a shrug and a sidelong glance. The glance forced recognition. This was the guard who'd let Nigel into the back entrance of the palace that day and then kept him waiting until he'd tried to use the lift on his own. Rahdan had no reason to think kindly of him.

Taeela was watching him.

"Are you sure he's all right?" he said. "This is the chap who…"

"Nigel, I know this. He is the son of the daughter of the cousin of the husband of Fofo's sister, and because of this my father gave him a place in the guard. Then he brought shame on the family by what he did to you. It was right that he should be punished. Fofo said this too. It was for thirty days only.

"Now all that is finished, changed. My father is dead. I am the Khanazhana. I set him free. I put a coat on his back. I put food in his mouth. I put my mark on his forehead. He swears to me the blood…swearing…?

"Oath?"

"…the blood oath. He is my man for one year, to live and to die."

"Sounds good to me. Hi again, then, Rahdan. Hope we have better luck with each other this time."

Rahdan returned his greeting with a gesture and an uncertain smile but didn't say anything.

"What happens now?" said Nigel. "He can't be up to much after what he's been through. Do you think he can carry Fofo back up the shaft? There's some of that bar left, isn't there? That might help."

She nodded and gave the bar to Rahdan, who eyed it doubtfully but then chewed at it with gusto.

"I talk to Fofo," she said, and did so, crouching beside him, taking his spidery fingers between her small plump hands, cajoling and pleading. He listened, smiling peacefully but shaking his head from time to time.

When he answered he didn't seem to be arguing with her, but telling her stuff she needed to know. She replied with little grunts of understanding. At one point he reached into his surcoat and drew out a package of what looked like two thin old sheets of leather with some folded paper between them, tied round with a faded ribbon. Taeela took it and slid it into a pocket.

When he'd finished she leaned across and hugged him, leaving a blotch of tear-streaked eye-shadow on his cheek when she withdrew. He smiled and patted her hand, then heaved himself over onto his knees and crawled purposefully along the walkway towards the shaft with Taeela lighting his way with her torch. Nigel gestured to Rahdan to wait before they followed. This was something private between the two of them.

Fohdrahko crawled straight into the shaft when he reached it and Taeela stopped half way in. They whispered briefly and she withdrew, rose and stood aside.

"You close the doors, Nigel," she muttered. "This I cannot do to him."

He crouched and saw Fohdrahko sitting against the wall at the back of the shaft with his knees drawn up and his lit torch beside him.

"Goodbye, Fofo," he said. "Thanks for everything."

Fohdrahko smiled, whispered something and raised his hand in farewell. Weeping himself now, Nigel swung the two slabs gently together and rose. He wiped his eyes on his sleeve, felt in his bag for his torch and switched it on. Without a word Taeela led them along beside the reeking water.

The tunnel curved left and right and then was barred by a heavy iron grating. Noises came from beyond it, audible above the rush of the stream, a police siren piercing the surf-like rumble of an angry crowd. A burst of gunfire stilled it for a moment, then it rose to a roar.

Shading her torch with her free hand she searched a section of the brickwork, found the place she wanted and switched off her torch. He did the same. He heard the grate of a brick being removed, the clink of a key ring, the dull double click of a big lock. By the time a gate in the grating swung open his eyes had adjusted and the darkness beyond it was no longer absolute.

Taeela waited for them to follow her through, closed and locked the grating and put the key in her pocket. A dozen paces on they were standing under the first arch of the fancy bridge.

On either side two more massive iron gratings reached from pillar to pillar, closing off the whole section under the arch, the upstream one with a bank of driftwood piled against it. Between their bars Nigel could see the moonlit roofs of Dahn climbing the hill, and the river itself with the lights of the embankment reflected from the greasy water.

At the light touch of Taeela's hand he felt for it and held it.

"My father is dead," she whispered. "Fofo is dying…"

"He may still be all right. When he's had a bit of a rest…"

"No. He gave me his map of the secret passages. That means it is finished for him. He has cut his wrists. When eunuchs cannot serve their masters more…any more…they cut their wrists. It is how eunuchs die."

She let go of his hand and drew herself up.

"Now we go," she said, and led the way back into the tunnel.

CHAPTER 13

Using the bars of the grating for hand-holds and footholds they crossed the stream to a ledge like the one they'd been on, and Taeela led the way out under the bridge and round the corner to where the next grating barred the archway. She knelt and Nigel held and shaded the torch while she searched the masonry beside it and found the slot, but it took several trials to get the key to engage. The catch clicked, but the iron had rusted and it needed Rahdan's strength to swing a rectangular section of the bars outwards, leaving an opening large enough for a man to crawl through.

The uproar from the bridge rose as they emerged from the sheltering archway. Ahead the ledge seemed to end at the wall of a large building. Taeela disappeared into its moon-shadow and Nigel groped his way after her. Keys clinked, followed by the scrape of a lock, and the creak of hinges, and he found himself looking up a narrow slot, visible only by the strip of night sky above it, between the blank wall of the building and the approach to the bridge. Half way along it Taeela halted.

"Now you must wear your dahl and be a girl, Nigel," she whispered. "Fohdrahko tells me the boats bring in the fish to a near place. A man is there, waiting for them to come. Rahdan will say to him we are afraid to go over the bridge, so he we will pay him thirty dzhin to row us across the river. I have only big money."

"I've got thirty, I think."

It sounded a bit iffy, but it went fine. Beyond the door at the top of the alley a narrow, dark street ran left and right. Their noses led them to the fish quay, a few turnings on along it, and then, by the sweet reek of whatever it was he was smoking, to the man in charge in a shed close to the water's edge. Rahdan was in his element bargaining for the crossing, no longer the blubbering wreck who had crept out of his cell, but the big, manly man, protecting his timid little females from the trouble on the bridge.

It was a warm, still night. Nigel was streaming with sweat under his heavy dahl. His incongruous European sneakers poked out below, so he kept behind Taeela until they settled into the boat and he could hide them under her duffel-bag. She sat silent beside him, staring straight ahead, dry-eyed.

The boatman rowed upstream for a while, keeping in the shadow of the buildings that lined the shore, and then slantwise across the dark, silky water. Once they were well under way Nigel counted the money out and passed it to Rahdan. They were half way across when the racket on the bridge was interrupted by a heavy boom. A moment of silence, then uproar. Yells, screams and another boom. Tank gun, he guessed.

The boatman hesitated and rowed on, urgently now. The gunwale grated on a stone wharf, the boatman grabbed at a ring and muttered whatever was Dirzhani for "Get on with it." Rahdan was gave him the money and they scrambled out. He pushed off and rowed away without bothering to count it.

Stone steps led up to the avenue that ran along the embankment. People were already streaming past, away from the bridge. Taeela asked Rahdan a question, but he shrugged and spread his hands, miming ignorance.

"I know somewhere we can try," said Nigel. "Up near the market. I think I can find it. I've got a street map."

Another boom reverberated, nearer now. Then another, and another. The fugitives broke into a run. Rahdan turned to follow, but Taeela snapped at him and grabbed his hand.

"Where, Nigel, where?"

He pointed across the road and to the right, then, playing his part as a girl, took Taeela's other hand. Linked together, they fought their way through the torrent of people and back towards the bridge. The first alley on the left was jammed solid. They struggled on. In the reflected floodlighting of a grand building close ahead they could see the tops of the approaching tanks. Again Rahdan hesitated, but Taeela dragged him into the driveway of the building and ducked behind the low wall that separated it from the roadway.

The curve of the drive had left room for a bed of ornamental shrubs, letting them crawl right in under the rough tunnel between their lower branches and the wall and lie there while the tanks rumbled past. Some soldiers came scrunching along the gravel of the driveway and took a whack or two at the bushes as if they were trying to drive birds out, but didn't do any serious poking around. They moved on, grumbling about something as they went. Nigel let out the breath he wasn't aware he'd been holding. Now desperately hot, he clawed the hood of his dahl off and lay there, panting like a dog.

Fresh shouts arose from behind them. An ambulance went past with blue lights flashing and sirens squealing. Then silence.

"They have gone," said Taeela, starting to get to her knees.

"Wait a mo," said Nigel. "I'd better check where we're going."

He wriggled himself over to a patch of brighter light coming through a gap in the branches and got out his street map. There was the palace; that was the fancy bridge; that must be the fish-quay; they'd crossed the river on a slant, so that must be the wharf where they'd landed. The map was for tourists, so he didn't have to try and read Dirzhani script.

"We want Galadny Sixteenth Street," he said. "Whatever that

means. There can't be that many Galadnys."

"August sixteenth," said Taeela bleakly. "My birthday. Last year my father gives…gave it to me."

He didn't know what to say. How do you mourn for a monster? A monster who happened to be nice to you, and named streets after his daughter's birthday, but who kept ordinary people who'd got it wrong somehow in a place like the one where they'd found Rahdan?

"Perhaps it is a sign," said Taeela in the same dead voice. "I think we go now."

On hands and knees she led them to the far end of the bed, where the driveway curved back into the avenue. She peered round the gatepost and beckoned them on. The avenue was deserted. Galadny Sixteenth was a well-lit modern street climbing the hill, part of a simple grid pattern, so all they had to do for the moment was make a series of right-and-lefts up towards the old city. The soldiers must already have swept these streets clear and moved on, apart from a place below a crossroads where some of them had cornered a couple of men breaking the curfew and were hammering them with their gun butts. Luckily they were too busy with that to notice three more curfew-breakers dashing across the street higher up the slope.

The change to the old city was as sharp as moving from open fields into ancient woodland. The narrow lanes wound every which way. The occasional street lamps cast only small pools of light. Nigel used them to check the map as briefly as he could. A few other people scuttled through the shadows

He remembered that Rick lived in a street off the one that ran directly up from the fancy bridge—the Iskan Bridge, according to the map, so the street was Novodzhan. It was a main thoroughfare, likely to be better lit and patrolled than elsewhere, so they didn't want to be in it longer than they needed to find the big poster of the President with the ibex.

Well down from that point they struck Digvan Ildzhu, narrow

and dark and twisty, climbing the slope only a variable block away from Novodzhan. From then on it was just a matter of working their way uphill and looking down every opening for the poster. They reached it sooner than he expected, where the twists of the two streets brought them only a dozen houses apart. If they'd come much later the poster wouldn't have been there. A soldier at the top of a ladder had started to tear it down. A couple more lounged at the bottom, one of whom happened to be looking along the side street when Nigel and the others darted across. Almost the only lamp in Digvan Ildzhu lit the junction.

The soldier shouted and started to run, unslinging his gun as he came. They hared up the slope, turned into the first possible opening, right again, and into the small courtyard with the curious old tree, its bare, twisting branches now silhouetted against the night sky.

"This way," Nigel panted and ducked under the archway into the courtyard behind Rick's house. The door was unlocked, so Rick must still be stuck in the embassy. He led them in and locked it behind them.

They stood and listened in the dimness of the hallway. There was light coming from the top of the stairs, and the drone of a TV newsreader.

"I'll call if it's safe to come up," he whispered, and pulled the hood of his dahl back.

As he climbed the stairs he realized for the first time how exhausted he was. His legs seemed barely able to do their job. He dragged himself up by the banister. Please, please let Janey understand, or at least let them rest here for a couple of hours before she threw them out. His normally pale face must be scarlet. She'd have to recognize him by his hair.

"Janey," he called just loud enough to be heard above the TV.

In an instant she was on the landing with the girls in the doorway behind her. She halted and stared.

"Nidzhell! Where's Rick? I been calling and calling but their phone ain't working."

"In the embassy, I think. They aren't letting anyone in or out. We can't go there. We were hoping…"

"But your dad— he's the ambassador!"

"He's still in the palace. So's Mum. We got out by, er, back ways. That's why I'm dressed like this."

She stood there, taking it in.

"It's true, then," she said at last. "He's dead."

"We saw it happen. Look, Janey, we were wondering…"

"Who's we? You got someone with you? British, I suppose?"

"No, Dirzhani. A man and a girl. Can I bring them up? We need your help."

"Suppose you better."

He turned and called softly, and Taeela appeared on the stairs, followed by Rahdan. Janey moved back to the doorway and stopped there, clearly with no intention of allowing anyone any further for the moment. Nigel stood aside to make room for the other two on the landing. Taeela looked OK in her dahl, the sort of girl Janey might approve of, but Rahdan was another matter. Even his new jacket was smeared with dirt from crawling under the bushes. The rest of his clothes were filthy and torn, and his face haggard under his beard—like a druggie begging in a gutter. In the close quarters of the landing he stank.

Nigel couldn't think where to begin. His mind didn't seem to be working. He turned to Taeela. "You better explain," he said. "This is Rick's wife, Janey Constantine. You'll have to explain to her about Rahdan…"

Taking her time about it, Taeela moved to the centre of the landing, unhooked her veil and pulled her hood back. She looked at least as exhausted as he felt, and she had been through far worse, but you wouldn't have known it from the way she held herself. There couldn't have been more than a dozen people in Dirzhan who wouldn't have recognized her.

There were gasps from Lisa and Natalie. Janey's face changed.

She started to make an involuntary movement with her hands but changed it to a gesture of welcome, bowed her head stiffly and said something in Dirzhani.

Taeela answered in a low, even voice, obviously picking her words. Nigel heard Rahdan's name. When she finished Janey stood aside, gesturing to her to come through into the room. Nigel followed, but Janey stopped Rahdan in the doorway. She introduced the girls, who both managed curtseys of a sort, and led him away, leaving Nigel alone with the three girls. Dirzhani proprieties seemed not to apply in a crisis.

They stood there for bit, Lisa and Natalie looking at their feet and Taeela and Nigel waiting for them to say something.

"Can we sit down," said Nigel at last. "We're dead beat."

"Uh…uh…" said Lisa. "Puh…please sit down, your…uh…"

"Great," said Nigel, and proceeded to get into a tangle unhooking his dahl. By the time he'd sorted it out Taeela was sitting stiffly upright in one of the easy chairs and Natalie and Lisa were still where they'd been, looking unhappily to and fro between him and Taeela and the door, but refusing to catch his eye, obviously wishing they were anywhere else in the world. He flopped into a chair, acting as relaxed as he could.

"Do you think you could find us something to eat?" he said.

"If your mother wouldn't mind," he added, as they dashed for the door.

Taeela hadn't moved, but was still sitting bolt upright, staring at nothing. Wearily he heaved himself out of his chair, perched on the arm of hers and put his arm round her shoulders. She didn't respond.

"Come on, Taeela," he whispered. "Stop beating up on yourself. You've been effing marvellous. Your dad would be proud of you. But you've still got stuff to do, stuff he'd want you to do. You've got to ease up, instead of wearing yourself out. Top of that, you're scaring the girls out of their wits. You need them. They're going to help us. Now come on, curl up the way you do, come on, you can do it…"

Still coaxing her as if he'd been talking to a small child he let go of her shoulders, leaned forward, grasped her ankle and made as if to lift it up onto the chair. At last she produced the ghost of a smile and gave in, twisting round and curling herself up in the corner of the chair the way she used to do on her sofa.

"That's more like it," he whispered. "They're bringing us something to eat. I'll go and see how they're doing."

He headed for the sound of bustle, along past the stairs towards the back of the house, past a room where Janey was laying out clothes on a bed, and another where Rahdan was taking a shower, by the sound of it. He found Lisa and Natalie arguing in whispers as they loaded a couple of trays out of a gleaming fridge As soon as they realised he was in the room they stopped and stared at him as if he'd been a burglar.

"That's great," he said. "Look, try and ease off a bit with Taeela, like you did with me that time. Forget about her being the Khanazhana. Suppose one of the kids at your school had seen her dad gunned down in front of her eyes, and then she'd been hunted like a rat through Dara Dahn, and she'd got somewhere where she can rest for a bit and pull herself together…

"See what I mean? She wouldn't want people staring at her like she was some kind of freak would she? She'd…"

He saw the girls eyes move, and turned. Janey was standing in the doorway, her face unreadable.

"I…I was just trying to explain…I hope that's all right."

She nodded.

"What she want to do?" she said.

"Head north, I suppose. She's a Varaki. We haven't had time to talk about it. When we've had a rest and something to eat…"

She nodded again and held up a hand to stop him.

"We come too," she said. "Rick telling me, something bad happen, like today, we clear out. Find a man who go with us, he says. This guy Rahdan, he OK, you thinking?"

Nigel started to try to explain. Janey cut him short.

"Khanazhana telling me," she said. "I ask, is he brave man?"

"He's done OK so far."

Janey nodded, unimpressed, and picked up one of the trays. They found Taeela already asleep. She woke when they'd almost finished eating, had a few mouthfuls, and let Janey take her off to her bed.

Nigel felt that he had barely closed his eyes when Janey was shaking him awake. He was curled up in the two easy chairs pushed end to end in the living room. Rahdan was sitting up yawning on the floor beside him. Taeela had slept in the spare room and Janey and the girls in their own beds—if Janey had gone to bed at all, he later realised; she must have been up most of the short night getting stuff ready.

They'd talked it through over supper, so there was a lighter dahl for him, one of Lisa's jackets and a skirt of Janey's long enough to hide his feet. He'd enough of a suntan to pass for a local, with a pair of sunglasses to hide his blue, northern eyes. Rahdan was wearing some of Rick's clothes—a bit too small for him but looking like any other Dirzhani. Taeela looked as though she'd hardly slept at all, but you'd still have known she was a princess.

There were knapsacks or shoulder-bags already packed for all of them. Breakfast was cold, apart from hot chocolate. Last thing before they left Nigel called the embassy. His father's voice answered, furry with sleep.

"Ambassador speaking."

"Hi, Uncle Nick. Is Nigel there? This is Timmy."

There was a kind of echo on the line.

"My dear Timothy, have you any idea what time it is here?"

"Oh, I'm terribly sorry. Did I wake you up? Could you just give him a message, then? He'll know what it means. It's about Rover."

"Some kind of dog?"

"There's this guy who looks after him who told us to go to the country. Wales, somewhere. We're all going. Could you tell him?"

"I'll do my best. All well with you?"

"We're fine, Uncle Nick. Got to go now. Best love to Aunt Lucy."

"Will do. Next time please call at a more sensible hour."

"I'm terribly sorry. Bye."

"Good bye, Timmy. And good luck."

He put the phone down. It had been contact of a sort, but pitifully little. The others were staring at him, baffled.

The stars were fading between the branches of the twisted tree when they crept out into the courtyard. They waited while Janey checked the street outside, then followed her across Digvan Ildzhu into the maze beyond. The route she took would have been difficult even with a map, but she knew it as a rabbit knows its warren. They saw no patrols as they worked their way north.

The old city ended as suddenly as it had begun, at the ring-road the palace drivers used to ferry Nigel back to the embassy. They crouched behind a hoarding to let a patrol car go slowly past, then dashed across. This was a different kind of maze, one that he was familiar with from the shanty towns of South America, with open sewers running in the streets, and houses built any old how out of corrugated iron and odd bits of planking. These were the homes of people who'd come to the city looking for a better life, and not found it.

Taeela stared around.

"Those murdering fools!" she muttered. "My father had good plans for all these places, after the dam is built and the money comes. Now...They will not do it. They will steal the money for themselves. Murderers! Robbers! Soon you will see, Nigel."

"See what?" he said. "You've lost me."

"The Garden of the Khans. You will be seeing it. It was beautiful long ago, but the communists stole it for their pigs. My father made it beautiful again for his people."

"We can get out of Dahn through it? They won't be guarding it?"

"We will see."

There was almost no one about so early, and they picked their way through the empty streets and came out into what might one day become a handsome avenue, though its trees were still little more than saplings, and the houses either side of it had been bulldozed flat but their replacements not yet built. The vista to the left stretched away down over Dara to the mountains beyond, but to the right it ended only a hundred yards off with a huge bronze statue of the President in front of a green slope dotted with young trees. A soldier was leaning against the plinth of the statue, smoking, with his gun propped beside him.

Janey gestured and they drew back out of sight, except for Rahdan, who stayed where he was for a while, stroking his chin and studying the man, before he joined them to talk with Taeela and Janey. Lisa muttered an explanation.

"Talked about it last night, case something like this come up. He's going to make out they're wife-dealers, him and Ma. Happened in the old days, despite it weren't legal. Guys got hold of kids from areas like we just been through, families glad to have 'em off their hands, and sold 'em on to guys out in the sticks. Only took a few dzhin to make the cops look the other way. The Khan put a stop to it. Hanged anyone he caught, and the cops what took the money along of 'em.

"Rahdan's going to make out he's starting up again, now the Khan's dead. Says there's an old guy in his village used to do it this way so's not to have to pay the cops. We're the wives. You too, Nigel, and we ain't happy about it, right?"

"It sounds pretty hairy to me," said Nigel.

"Me too, but Rahdan, he's been a soldier. He says it'll work. All set, Ma? We going to try it?"

"I talk with the guy. I decide then," said Janey.

"Do you need any money?" said Nigel.

"I got enough. Sorting it out after," said Janey and walked confidently away.

A few minutes later four sobbing girls were herded along the unfinished avenue roped wrist to wrist in pairs with Janey's washing line, followed by Rahdan with the other end of the rope wound round his hand and one of her kitchen knives in his belt. When Natalie stretched out a pleading arm to the soldier he turned away.

Once inside the park they hurried away to the left and worked their way round it, looking for a gap in the fence. Behind them the mountain peaks glittered under the rising sun, but the distances were already becoming vague as the heat haze rose. It was going to be another roasting day.

CHAPTER 14

It was mid-morning, hot and still, by the time they reached the main road north. Nigel had stripped down to shirt and trousers but was sweating under his dahl. They settled to rest in the shade of a few scrawny trees, drinking sparingly from their water-bottles and watching the traffic stream by—cars, trucks and pick-ups crammed with passengers; the occasional group of sweating cyclists; mules under mountains of baggage or with two or even three riders; a camel, once, with four perched on it somehow—all fleeing from the chaos in Dara Dahn.

An empty truck came past going the other way. Rahdan raised an optimistic thumb pointing north. Astonishingly the truck pulled over and a man got out and came across. The haggling—Janey, Rahdan and the man—lasted several minutes before Janey gave him some money, the man waved and the truck drove on without him.

"Gone for collect another lot," muttered Janey. "I give him twenty dzhin so he stop for us when he coming back, then a hundred sixty if he take us to Podoghal. Varaki town, one fifty kilometres. OK?"

"Thirty dzhin a head?" said Nigel. "That sounds cheap, time like this."

"Is cheap," said Janey. "Not much trusting him, case he

making a run for it when truck coming back, all full. Taking our twenty dzhin, leaving us here. I tell Rahdan keep an eye at him."

Nigel didn't like the look of the man either. He smiled too much as he chatted to Rahdan, and when he was offered a drink of their precious water he downed more than half the bottle. But half an hour later the truck stopped as arranged, and there was just about room on it for six more passengers once Janey had paid the rest of their fare.

For thirty miles or so they ground north along a winding valley, sitting on their bags or perching on the sideboard of the truck, with endless gear changes as the traffic accelerated and slowed. The packed mass of bodies generated its own heat, and the wind of their passage, laden with the exhaust of labouring old engines, gave them no relief.

News and rumours were passed to and fro. Seventeen, no, twenty-four, no, eleven, no, fifty-eight people had been killed when the tanks had fired into the crowd at Iskan Bridge. The soldiers who had stormed the TV station had been dressed in Dirzhaki uniforms but had given their orders in Russian. The Khanazhana had been captured and would be forced to marry the son of Adzhar Taerzha. It was an American plot to prevent Dirzhan becoming an Islamic state. No, it was an al-Quaida plot to make it an Islamic state…

On a hill no steeper than several they'd climbed the engine started to falter. They staggered on with the stinking cloud of their exhaust billowing over the traffic behind, down again and along a level with it sounding increasingly unhappy, until they left the main convoy, turned off along a side road and reversed into a track beside a peach orchard, where they stopped in a cloud of their own smoke.

The driver and another man got out and raised the engine-cover, while the man who had stayed with them came round and talked to the passengers, gesturing towards the orchard as he did so. The shade under the trees looked extremely inviting, and even before he'd finished speaking the passengers were climbing down, leaving their belongings behind and heading for the trees.

Janey said something as she picked up her bag. Rahdan demurred. She answered and he hefted his knapsack.

"We're taking our stuff," said Natalie. "The guy said not to, but Ma dun't trust him."

Behind the concealment of his sunglasses Nigel watched the man as they filed by him. He nodded at Janey, apparently accepting their decision, but as soon as she was past his expression changed to a sort of contemptuous smirk.

"She's right," he muttered. "Did you see his face, Lisa?"

"Engine was sick all right."

"It's old enough to have a hand throttle. There were trucks like that in Santiago. You've only got to pull the throttle out and that's what happens."

"Hear that, Ma? What are we…?"

She didn't have time to complete the sentence. The truck's starter grunted twice, the engine caught, coughed, caught again and steadied. The passengers had hardly begun to get to their feet when the men slammed the engine cover shut and scrambled aboard the already moving truck. The passengers rushed out. One who was quick enough to grab the tail-gate clung on till a stamp on his hands forced him to drop. The truck disappeared round the corner with the men waving mocking farewells.

Some of the abandoned passengers continued their rush, screaming their outrage, but gave up one by one and waited for their family group and then trooped miserably back to the main road in the unlikely hope of thumbing another lift. Having got last out of the truck Nigel and the others had gone further along the track to find a resting place, so had been in a better position to see that pursuit was hopeless. All they could do was stand with their bags in their hands and watch it happen.

"Let's have a look at Rick's map," said Nigel. "See where this road goes. There might be a village…"

He saw Janey's face change and her eyes look past him, over his shoulder. A man had appeared at the corner of the orchard, clearly not a soldier, but with an AK held in front of him, ready to use. He snarled an order. Rahdan, Janey and the girls raised their hands. Nigel was about to follow suit when he realised that Taeela on his left hadn't moved. He hesitated and copied her.

A voice behind them snapped the same command. Again Taeela didn't move, but Nigel glanced round. This man's AK was slung over his shoulder, but a heavy truncheon was dangling from his wrist. Nigel forced himself to turn away and stand, readying himself for the blow, but then watching, unable to move or cry out, as the first man walked towards Rahdan, raising his gun as he came. Rahdan backed away. The man's thumb moved on the safety catch.

Close behind him the second man, nearer now, growled the order again. Something inside Nigel broke, the same kind of total loss of control that he'd experienced at Lake Vamar, but this time exploding not into panic but rage. He hit the first man in a clumsy rugby tackle, catching him a solid thunk, and then somehow clinging on for a couple of seconds until the gun butt hammered against his shoulder. As he staggered and fell he heard the bark of a single shot, quickly repeated. He was starting to get to his feet and run when a massive weight thumped across him, pinning him face down. Twisting his head he saw Taeela, sideways on to him, raise her pistol two handed, take aim and fire, again twice, and then step aside as the man with the truncheon charged past her and collapsed.

Half stunned, he struggled up from under the thing that had fallen on him and found himself staring down at the body of the man who'd been about to shoot Rahdan. Taeela was standing where he had seen her, with her head bowed and her lowered pistol still clasped between her hands. Janey, Rahdan and the girls were just beside him, staring at her.

"Wha…what…?" he said.

"She shot 'em," said Janey. "It was them or us. Good riddance."

"I killed two men, Nigel," said Taeela, dragging the words out. "I killed two men."

"Uh…Like Janey says, it was them or us."

"Yes. But I killed two men. They were my people."

Slowly, as if the air were as dense as water, she slid the safety catch on her pistol down, fished a small cardboard box out from somewhere under her dahl, tipped four rounds into the palm of her hand, fed them into the magazine and slid pistol and box back under the dahl. Every movement seemed to quiver with the horror of what she had been forced to do, this new, huge shock on top of yesterday's tragedies and terrors. Hardly noticing what he was doing or how his shoulder hurt Nigel moved beside her and put his good arm round her shoulders. He stared at the bodies, hypnotised. Two more deaths. The guard in the shadowy gallery above the Great Hall. The President in the glare of lights on the stairs. The men who'd fallen into the trap Fohdrahko had set. These two now in the clear hill air. Yes, they had been vile, the President a monster, the guards, who knows? How many more before the nightmare was over?

Beside him Taeela straightened, drew a long breath and let it go, and eased herself away from him.

"Natalie sees something," she muttered.

The others had moved up the rough track beside the orchard and were looking down at its surface. Rahdan had one of the dead men's AKs slung over his shoulder. Nigel disentangled the other from its owner's body and followed Taeela over.

"Natalie spotted it," said Janey. "Been some sort o' truck 'long here, looks like. Not come back, neither."

"It" was a single tyre-track crossing a patch of bare earth where a puddle had formed in the rains but had now evaporated. The surrounding surface was already dry, but in the track itself it was soft. Moisture glistened in the individual tread-marks.

Rahdan unslung his gun. Taeela took her pistol out of her dahl. Nigel put his thumb ready by the safety catch of his AK. His shoulder was getting increasingly sore. Without discussion they stole up the track. Here and there the tread-marks showed again, and then more plainly where they turned round the corner of the orchard. A shabby, medium-sized brown van was parked beside the trees about twenty yards further on.

Rahdan took control, gesturing where he wanted everyone to go—himself directly opposite the rear doors with his AK raised to his shoulder, Taeela and Nigel facing each other a few paces either side of the van, Janey to open the doors and Natalie and Lisa watching their rear.

Janey tried the doors, but they were locked. She held up her hand for silence and called softly, a question. Distinct thumping noises came from inside the van. She called again, reassuringly, this time. The thumpings stopped. She tried both cab doors, but they were locked too.

Rahdan said something and hurried off.

"Gone to look in the guys' pockets," said Lisa.

They waited, twanging, till he returned and gave a key-ring to Janey. The doors opened with the first one she tried. Nigel heard a steady scuffling and saw Janey, who had started to climb up, shift her position to reach in. Two girls emerged, roped together back to back at the wrists. Janey helped them to the ground and cut them free with Rahdan's knife. One was about Natalie's age, the other a couple of years younger.

They stood for a moment staring at their rescuers, then without a word turned and ran round the van and along the side of the orchard. They stopped, stared, screamed and dashed out of sight. The screams became wails.

"I better go," said Janey. "You lot waiting here."

They watched her follow the two girls and duck in under the trees. The wailing died, became a few sobbing words in answer to Janey's voice, and broke out again. The pattern repeated itself several times before it reverted to agonised wailing as Janey came back, grim-faced, and told them in Dirzhani what she'd seen, finishing with a question addressed to Rahdan.

He didn't answer, but looked at Taeela.

"I will talk to them," she said.

Janey made as if to protest, and stopped herself. They watched Taeela strip off her dahl and pocketed jacket, and walk away bare-headed.

"Their mum and dad. Shot in the back of their heads," muttered Lisa. "Girls don't want to leave 'em. Would've happened to us, but for you two."

Nigel blinked. Him? He put it aside and turned to Janey.

"Listen," he said urgently. "We've got to get out of here before that other lot come back. We can't hang about. They may pick up another load before they reach Dara Dahn. We can't leave those girls here. If they won't leave their Mum and Dad's bodies I know what Taeela will say. We've got to take them too. No, Janey, listen. She saw her own dad killed in front of her eyes yesterday. She saw men come and take his body away like a dead animal to dump it somewhere. She'll never know where. She knows what it's like.

"If we can't take them she'll stay with them, and so will I and so will Rahdan. He's sworn the blood oath, remember. Maybe we can ambush the men when they come back, and take their truck..."

He ran out of steam.

The silence was broken by the twitter of a mobile's ring-tone down on the track. They froze.

"That's the other lot checking these two have got us OK," said Nigel. "They'll be slower coming back in that traffic, but..."

"OK, let's get on with it," said Janey. "You lot clear out. We'll deal with this, Rahdan and me."

Back on the track Natalie kept a look-out while Lisa got their baggage ready for loading and found the road map. Rahdan had been through some of one man's pockets, pulling stuff out and leaving it scattered around until he found the keys. Nigel, outraged by the sheer wickedness of what the dead men had done, put his horrors aside and finished the job. The mobile was lying by the track, but twittered again while he was working. The wailing had stopped and from beyond the orchard came the comforting sound of the van being reversed up to where the murdered parents lay.

The mobile didn't appear to have a licence. It must be illegal. He stuffed it into his bag, plus a couple of loaded AK magazines, matches and fags for Rahdan, and both wallets, one bulging with dzhin notes, and threw the rest away. Then with Lisa's help he rolled the two bodies off the track. She did the job untroubled, and when they'd dealt with the second one she gave it a kick.

"Scum," she said, and went to join Natalie. Nigel settled down to look at the map.

It was a single large sheet but well detailed. Most of the place names were in Dirzhani script, but the larger towns were bilingual. They'd passed a couple of small towns on the way north, and turned off this road soon after the second one. It appeared to lead to a village a few miles on and then ramble away eastward, but at the village a smaller road branched northwards and after a while turned west to rejoin the road to Podoghal.

At that point he heard the van start up, and was folding the map when it came lurching round the corner of the orchard. Janey got out of the cab and opened the rear doors.

The two girls were huddled together in the far corner beside a battered suitcase and what could only be their parents' bodies, covered with a piece of tarpaulin. Taeela was sitting opposite them resting her chin on her hands; their own baggage was stacked beside her. There were a couple of large jerry-cans strapped either side of the doors.

"Wait," said Nigel, as Janey started to climb in. "Don't you want to go in front? I've found where we are on the map. I'll show you."

"No good with maps," she said. "You go front."

"You'll have to show me where we're going. I can't read most of the names."

"Cousin to my mother living in Sodalka. Is to west from Podoghal, sixty, seventy kilometre."

Sodalka? The place Fohdrahko had wanted Taeela to go, and she didn't?

"Sodalka is OK," said Taeela without looking round. "We must go, Nigel."

The map was difficult to manage one-handed. His shoulder, after the initial blast of pain, had just felt badly bruised, but now it began to hurt every time he moved his left arm. Sodalka had its name printed in both scripts, and was roughly where Janey had said. The route he'd traced would do as far as he'd got, so at the village he raised a warning hand to where Rahdan could see it and pointed ahead and left.

They started to climb, gently at first, following the twists and turns of a fair-sized stream, still a foaming cataract in places after the rains. The road surface was riddled with potholes. In bottom gear they jolted up a series of hairpins, through scraggy woodland and out onto a bleak, rock-strewn slope. By the time they reached the top of the pass the engine was sounding increasingly unhappy. At the first possible place Rahdan pulled off the road, climbed out and raised the engine cover. The heat that rose from it wavered in the cooler upland air.

"That's more like it," said Lisa as she climbed out of the back of the van. She wasn't wearing her dahl and had stripped off what clothes she could but was still flushed and streaming with sweat. So were the others.

They gathered at the roadside and looked around. The two orphans, haggard with heat and grief, clung like nervous puppies to Taeela's side. It was a typical mountain pass, a broad saddle between two bare slopes that rose more and more steeply towards the separate summits, neither high enough to have kept a covering of snow at this time of year. Behind them they could see all the way down the road to where the first set of hairpins emerged from the trees.

"Not much of water left," said Janey. "Been a right oven in there. Maybe we find a stream."

"Rahdan's going to need some too," said Nigel. "We must pretty well have boiled the radiator dry, climbing that last bit. That looks like it might be a stream, that greener bit. Water should be pretty good, right up here, after the rain. Why don't you lot go and have a look? I'll keep a look-out. Someone in that village could've seen us turn off and told them."

"If you saying so," said Janey.

They collected the empty water bottles out of the back of the van, and after a brief conversation with Rahdan she and the five girls trooped off. Nigel got his AK out of the cab, though he doubted he'd be able to use it with his shoulder the way it was, climbed up to a boulder high enough to stop him showing above the skyline, and settled down to watch the road and try to put his nightmares aside and come to terms with what had happened back at the orchard.

Between them he and Taeela had killed two men. OK, his part in the killing had had been pretty well pure chance, but he didn't think Taeela could have done it without him. He'd taken both men completely by surprise. They'd never expected a girl to react like that, let alone bang into the man the way he had; and they hadn't wanted to shoot him because if he was a girl he was worth money. The other guy would have been watching it happen, and that had given Taeela her chance to get her pistol out.

He thought about it, massaging his shoulder. Yes, killing someone was a big deal. It would have been easier to cope with if he'd done it on purpose, because then it would have been the right thing to do. Otherwise Janey and Rahdan would be dead, and Lisa and Natalie would be trussed up like the other two, to be taken away and sold to some bastard, and Taeela auctioned off to the highest bidder, while he himself was either dead or held for ransom.

It must have looked that way. Lisa had just pretty well told him she thought he'd deliberately charged into the man, and Janey not so clearly, the way she'd accepted it when he'd suggested they might go and look for water. She hadn't been like that before.

That wasn't enough. It was pure accident he'd managed to help kill both men, so their wickedness was no excuse. They'd been living, breathing creatures, and now they were dead meat lying by the track. Only in his dreams they would wake and search for him. He shuddered, pulled himself together and craned round the rock to see how Rahdan was doing.

He'd changed his mind about Rahdan. His picture of him had been coloured by their first meeting, when he'd seemed just a swaggering careless slob; and then by the cringing wreck who'd crawled out of his prison cell. Nigel had told Janey he'd done OK as they'd found their way up through Dara, but that was only because Taeela had made him. But since then he'd done more than OK, taken charge of things when they'd found the van, driven it sensibly. He obviously knew how to handle a gun. And now he'd found some tools in the van and was up on the roof of the cab sawing an air-vent into the rear section.

Time passed. Rahdan stopped sawing and scrambled down just as Janey arrived with a couple of refilled water-bottles. By the time Nigel joined them Janey was having some kind of an argument with him while he topped up the radiator. He shook his head and made a despairing gesture towards Nigel. Janey frowned, pursed her lips and turned.

"We going bury these kids' mum and dad here, Nidzhell," she explained. "We find very good place. Making it OK by them, telling them Rahdan will say one prayer. He's being stupid on this, scared. Isn't religious, don't know what he say. Maybe you do it for them. Much better it's a man."

"Oh Lord. I suppose so. Have we got time? Somebody better keep a look-out still. How do Moslem prayers start? 'In the name of Allah, the something, the something,' isn't it?"

"'All*ah*,'" she corrected him. "Yes, 'Allah who is, er, judge, who is kind.'"

"Oh yes, of course. 'The just, the merciful,' isn't it?"

"You do it, then, Nidzhell?"

"Do my best. I'll need to think what to say. Rahdan's getting a bit of air into the back for you, and he'll want to top up the petrol and stuff. I'll go ahead and try and work something out. Somebody'd better keep an eye out down the pass as long as possible."

"OK. I do that till you send Lisa and Natalie back. Then I come help Rahdan lifting bodies."

He walked slowly along the road trying to remember that what had happened at Uncle Ted's funeral. Usually he tried not to think about it. His godfather Ted Finching was the first ambassador his father had served under. Typical of his father to pick someone like that, and to insist on their coming home for the funeral when he'd been killed in a motorway pile-up, and on Nigel going to it with them. He'd been only seven, and he couldn't remember anything much about the church service, except that it had been boring. But he'd remember the bit at the graveside all his life.

Lady Finching had Alzheimer's and hadn't a clue what was going on. As she stood by the open grave, a tall pale, bewildered old woman all in black, she kept looking over her shoulder to see where Uncle Ted had got to, while her son beside her tried to calm her down. Then, as the first handful of soil rattled onto the lid of the coffin—"Earth to earth, dust to dust, and the spirit…"—understanding had suddenly broken through and she'd started to scream and pulled herself away from her son and thrown herself down into the grave. Somehow she hadn't hurt herself, but had clawed herself upright and then just stood there, clinging onto the edge of the grave, screaming. He never saw how they got her out because he'd started screaming too and his mother had taken him away and hugged him close and explained about Alzheimer's and stuff to him until he'd calmed down. That was how he'd always remembered it. It was what everyone else had seen. But now…

He stopped in his tracks. He'd reached the top of the pass. Ahead of him the foothills stretched away, ridge beyond ridge. He saw none of that. Two scenes filled his mind, two images that were somehow the same image. Only yesterday he'd seen the shattered body of the President on the stairs of the great hall rear itself up out of the pit of death in a last desperate gesture to the one person he'd loved. And long before, in an English churchyard, he'd seen the smashed body of Uncle Ted claw its way out of a hole in the ground, the grey, distorted face, the wide mouth screaming.

That was where the nightmares began.

"Earth to earth, dust to dust…"

Over and over his lips repeated the words, laying the ghosts, thinning the nightmares until they faded into the warm hill air and he woke from his trance and walked on.

The good place Janey had talked about was a little way up the stream, where a couple of boulders had embedded themselves parallel to a huge sheer-sided slab of rock, leaving a narrow strip of clear ground between them. The girls were fetching loose rocks brought down by the stream and piling them into the gap between the boulders. Nigel sent Natalie and Lisa back to keep watch and did what he could one-handed until Janey and Rahdan arrived with the truck.

"Good," said Taeela. "I will take Halli and Sulva to look for flowers, so they do not watch while you carry their mum and dad up. You make them look nice, then you wave to me. Rahdan will say prayers for them, and then we cover them over."

"He doesn't want to. He says he isn't religious, but I guess he's afraid of messing up in front of everybody. Janey asked me, but you'll have to translate. I think they'd like that anyway. Do you know all their names? I'll just say 'father,' 'mother' and so on and you can put the names in."

"Yes, this is better. I'll tell them who you are, Nigel. They'll like that."

They used the tarpaulin to bring the bodies up from the van, Rahdan taking the weight of the head and shoulders and Janey the lighter end, with Nigel, still one-handed, taking a corner beside her. They'd been shot in the back of the head, so there wasn't a lot of blood, but it was gruesome all the same. They looked so dead.

They spread one side of the tarpaulin out between the wall and the slab, laid the bodies on it and folded the other half beside them. While Janey cleaned their faces and tidied them as best she could Nigel checked the position of Mecca with his compass, then used a screwdriver from his knife to loosen a patch of soil beside the grave. When the others were ready he climbed onto the slab and waved to Taeela to bring the girls back.

There weren't many flowers pick at this time of year, but they'd made two little sheaves of some kind of reed with pretty golden seed-heads. Side by side, kneeling on one of the boulders, the girls leaned over and placed one on each of their parents, then went round and stood at the foot of the grave weeping silently. Janey and Rahdan folded the other half of the tarpaulin over the bodies.

Nigel faced west and counted five.

"In the name of Allah, the just, the merciful," he said, and waited for Taeela to translate. "We've brought the bodies of—father's name…and mother's—here to bury them. Please look after them, Allah…and take their souls into your paradise…so that their daughters—girls' names now—can meet them there one day…"

He bent, scooped up some of the loosened earth, and sprinkled it over the two bodies. He was so choked he could hardly get the words out.

"Dust to dust…earth to earth…and the spirits to…Allah who gave them."

He bowed his head, trying to master his tears. He realised he was weeping for Lady Finching as much as he was for the murdered mother and father. It was as if there was one unchanging pool of grief below the scurrying surface of things, and they were all three there.

He moved aside to watch Taeela and the two girls place the first rocks on the tarpaulin. Covering it right over with enough rocks to keep scavengers out was going to take a while.

"I'm not going to be much use here," he muttered to Janey. "I'd better go back and keep a look-out, and Lisa and Natalie can come and help you. I'll give it half an hour."

"Your shoulder is bad?"

"Pretty sore. I can't do much with that arm."

"When you come back I make you a…"

She gestured, not knowing the word.

"A sling. That'd be great."

CHAPTER 15

It was in fact getting on an hour before they finally left the pass. Nigel watched the last rocks being added to the pile while Janey adjusted his sling, adapted from a headscarf. The sun was well down the western sky, and beneath it the mountains of Dirzhan stretched away into the distance. It wasn't a bad place to be buried, he thought. He fetched the map out of the van and marked the place with a cross, in case there was ever a chance for the children to give their parents a proper Muslim funeral.

They drove on for a while through featureless upland, passed a couple of shabby hamlets and turned west, then down through a series of hairpins into a wooded valley. In the fading light they found a place where they could get off the road far enough to hide the van among the trees.

They shared out the food that Janey had brought, and after they'd eaten she made Nigel strip off his shirt and probed around on his shoulder with firm, efficient fingers.

"Caught you a right wallop, didn't he?" she said. "No wonder you feeling it. Too swoll up for telling if anything's broke. You must be moving it sometimes, little, little. Like this. I bring paracetamol."

"Oh, that'd be great."

Sorting himself out to sleep, Nigel found the stuff he'd taken from the two thugs. He gave the fags to Rahdan and showed Taeela the wallets.

"Good," she said, leafing through them. "The money will be for Halli and Sulva. And I will find who these men are, and the men in their gang, and they will be punished."

"One day."

"Yes, Nigel. One day."

Lisa had managed to sleep a bit in the van, so she kept first watch. Janey and the girls bedded down in the back, Nigel on the bench seat in the cab, and Rahdan on the ground beside it. The paracetamol did its work and he was deep under when Lisa came to wake him.

He sat up, wrapped his blanket round him and gingerly started to ease his shoulder the way Janey had shown him, until a bit of his dream came back to him and he was gazing down into dark, moonlit water. A pale shape wavered up out of the depths, vague at first but then becoming a face, a face with its mouth wide open, Lady Finching's face, screaming. The pool of grief.

He jerked himself fully awake, startled by having dropped off again so instantly, and tried to force his mind to think about stuff that mattered. With a bit of luck they'd reach Sodalka tomorrow, and Taeela would be recognised and they'd be taken to some tribal bigwig. It struck him that as soon as the others found someone to talk to they'd start telling them what had happened by the peach orchard.

Bad idea. It might play OK in Dirzhan if it didn't land Taeela with some sort of blood feud on her hands, but not back home. There'd be headlines you could read across a football pitch.

KILLER PRINCESS!!!

So nothing like that had happened by the peach orchard or anywhere else. The van was Rahdan's and they'd hired him to take them to Sodalka. On the way they'd picked up this couple of kids whose parents had been robbed and murdered. Taeela'd have to explain to Rahdan and the kids anyway, so she could make sure they all said the same thing and stuck to it.

That was as far as he got before Lady Finching's screaming face was swimming up towards him out of the darkness again and he woke with a start. It wouldn't be the last time, either, if he stayed in the cab. Blearily he clambered out and started to walk around.

It was a warm, clear night with barely enough breeze to rustle a leaf. He'd have heard a car on the road a mile away. None came. Still, it was best if someone was on the watch. It meant the others could sleep easier.

Time crawled by. He tried to make plans for tomorrow, how he was going to call the embassy again, and what to say. Supposing all went well at Sodalka and Taeela was in safe hands and so on, what next? Try to get some kind of a lift out to Kyrgyzstan, maybe. Or perhaps…

His mind kept straying back into the dream. He lost count how many times he stumbled and almost fell because he'd actually fallen asleep until the stumble woke him. Again and again he flicked on his torch to peer at his watch until at last the second hour was up. He shook Rahdan awake, climbed into the cab, took another paracetamol and was asleep as soon as he lay down. He woke in bright daylight with his arm too stiff and sore to move.

The dawn mist was lifting from the valley when they left, churned up through the usual hairpins to the saddle of a pass, and then down to the main road from Dara Dahn to Podoghal. The refugees were still streaming north, but Nigel signalled to Rahdan to turn the other way and switched on the thugs' mobile. Surprisingly he was getting a signal, so after a couple of miles he told him to pull off the road. While the others took the chance to stretch their legs he crossed the road, climbed out of sight and called the secure number. No piano was playing when at last the answer came.

"Embassy."

"¿Estoy hablando con el embajador británico en Dirzhan?"

"Habla el embajador Ridgwell."

"¿No lo molesto en este momento, embajador?"

"That sounds fine, Niggles. If we get interrupted ring off at once and don't use that telephone again."

"It's a spare mobile, Dad. I'll bash it with a rock as soon as we're done. Is Mum there?"

"Hovering at my elbow. Anything I need to know first?"

"Only I'm way outside Dara Dahn now. We've got transport. Tell Rick Janey and the kids are OK. We're hoping to get somewhere safe this evening. What do you want me to do then? I thought I might be able to get to Kyrgyzstan, if you want me to."

"Not unless you can fly. If you think you're safe where you are, I'd stay put until the dust settles a bit more. Just don't let anyone think you're representing the British government."

"Got it, Dad. I'll be careful."

"Fine. Good luck, Nigel. Here's your mother."

"Darling? Are you…oh, don't be silly, woman!"

"Hi, Mum. I'm fine. I got a bit if a bang on my shoulder so I've got my arm in a sling, but we don't think anything's broken. Don't worry – it's not a big deal, Mum, compared with a lot of stuff going on."

"Those horrible men! Doing it in front of our eyes, too! As if they didn't give…you know what!"

"I guess one big monster was better than a lot of little ones, Mum."

"I don't…"

The piano started to tinkle in the background. In his haste ring off he got tangled with his sling and dropped the mobile, so he stamped on it with all his force and tossed it into a patch of scrub, then walked back down to the road feeling very alone, very vulnerable.

At least he'd got through and talked to them both this time.

And if the colonels' security lot were up to locating where he'd called from they'd think he'd been heading north to Podoghal. That was why he'd crossed the road.

They turned west at a small town three or four miles further on, stopping on its outskirts to buy a refill of petrol for six times what it would have cost a week ago. Then on up into the mountains, threading their way through a network of valleys and passes and the occasional ramshackle village, with not a signpost anywhere, no guide but the map and Nigel's compass. Luckily there weren't that many choices and most of them were obvious.

In the late afternoon their road ran along the shore of a small mountain lake dominated by a wonderful wooden building, like a Hollywood palace. There wasn't a sign of life anywhere. He signalled to Rahdan to stop and went round and opened the rear doors.

"Time for a break," he said. "Look, Taeela. I think this might be Forghal. You remember, where…"

"I remember," she said. She climbed out, glanced at the map and stared round.

"I shall not come here again," she said.

"Oh, sorry. That was stupid of me. Do you want to move on?"

"Rahdan must rest. Come with me, Nigel."

They walked in silence along beside the water, with the rescued girls trailing behind them hand in hand. Fish rose here and there. A raucous gang of birds flew overhead, mobbing a hawk. A family of small ducks were diving for something by a reed-bed. The adults were black, with scarlet trimmings, the sort of thing you see in an ornamental park, but obviously wild here. After about ten minutes they turned and went back to the van.

"I think it's a bit over an hour to Sodalka," he said as they reached it.

"Good. I will come in front with you now. Wait for me."

She fetched an ornate little bag out of the rear compartment and took the two girls down to the water's edge, where she gave one of them the bag and the other one a hand-mirror to hold for her while she cleaned off the remains of her make-up and put on fresh, as carefully as if she'd been about to appear for a formal photo. OK, perhaps the girls were a bit of a help. But that wasn't why she'd done it. It was because it allowed them to put their tragedy aside for the moment and absorb themselves in their roles as the Khanazhana's hand-maidens.

He waited at the door of the cab while she coaxed the girls into the rear compartment without her.

"D'you mind going in the middle?" he said. "It'd help if you hold that side of the map for me, which'd make life a lot easier."

She climbed in, saying something to Rahdan as she settled into place. He grunted, obviously pleased.

Nigel opened the map and spread it out between them. Much better than fiddling about one-handed. She seemed to guess his thought.

"Your shoulder hurts, Nigel?"

"It's not too bad provided I don't jerk it around. The sling's a help, and so's whatever it is Janey's been doing."

"When we get to Sodalka we will find you a knowing woman."

"You don't have to bother about me. I'm OK, and you've got your hands full with Halli and Sulva. You're being totally amazing with them."

"They are my sisters, Nigel. We are...orphans together. They are my family..."

He waited for her to say more. He could feel the thought shaping itself.

"Nigel, they are Dirzhan."

He didn't get it for a moment. Of course they were. No... She'd said Dirzhan, not Dirzhaki. The country itself.

She meant it too. He realised that in her eyes she was all that stood between the possibility of any kind of sensible life for ordinary Dirzhaki, Dirzhaki like Halli and Sulva, and the sort of thing they'd seen in the last two days, coup after coup, tribe against tribe, tanks firing on unarmed crowds, bloody banditry on the roads, open corruption everywhere, chaos.

Crazy kid, he thought. But wonderful. He wasn't going to Kyrgyzstan or anywhere else. He was sticking with her. And by her.

The pass above Forghal started like all the others they'd climbed, but once over the crest they were in a different world. Below them a vast brown plain reached away westward, hazy with heat under the low sun. The range they were on stretched out of sight to left and right. At its feet the road to Sodalka snaked north. There was very little traffic on it; any refugees from Dara Dahn would have come by Podoghal.

"Nearly there. We can get rid of this now," Nigel said, and started to fold up the map. She took over, patted it flat and gave it back to him.

"Now I come by the door," she said, pulling herself up to let him edge along the bench seat behind her. Once in place she spent a little while craning sideways to peer in the wing mirror and adjust her headscarf, then sat bolt upright, staring ahead. Her lips moved as she rehearsed inaudible sentences.

The main road, once they reached it, ran smoothly along, giving them occasional glimpses of Sodalka itself, an old walled city draped over the foot of a mountain spur protruding into the plain. In the bronzy sidelong light it looked like a city on the cover of a fantasy novel. They rounded the base of the last rocky ridge and were faced by a road-block.

The barrier, a heavy wooden beam, weighted and pivoted at one end so that it could be tilted up, was guarded by five bearded men, armed with AKs. Rahdan braked, but Taeela spoke calmly to him and he drove slowly on. A few yards short of the barrier he braked again and climbed out. Somebody shouted an order and the AKs levelled. He raised his arms above his head and marched round the front of the van to Taeela's door, still with his arms above his head and with the gun-barrels following him all the way.

With an anxious glance towards the guns he opened the door with his left hand and at the same time lowered his raised right arm into a salute and helped Taeela climb down. She thanked him regally and walked confidently towards the guns.

The barrels dropped. The men stared. One of them moved aside, took out a mobile and called a number. Another leaned on the weight to raise the barrier for her. Rahdan climbed into the cab, started the engine and drove slowly past where Taeela was now touching hands with one of the men, then pulled off the road and climbed down. Nigel stayed put and watched what was happening in his wing-mirror. It wouldn't do his father much good if it got around that the British ambassador's son was holed up in a rebel stronghold.

A car drove up from the south and was casually waved through. Janey and the others had got out to watch. The man with the mobile signed off and hurried across to talk to Taeela, then accompanied her towards the van. Nigel opened the door and moved to the middle of the seat to make room for her, but she beckoned him out.

"We go in the back now, Nigel," she said. "He will take us to Chief Baladzhin."

He put on his cap and pulled it down to cover as much of his hair as he could, then slipped out the other side and round to the back while everyone else was still watching her, and waited for the others to join him in the stifling dimness of the rear compartment. Halli and Sulva crouched behind Taeela, staring at Nigel over her shoulders as if he were some great wild predator and she were the lion-tamer keeping him at bay.

"Baladzhin's this guy who wants you to marry his son, right?" he said as the van started to move.

"There are fourteen chieftains of the Varaki, Nigel. He is only one. Two others are here, and five come tomorrow. They will talk about what they will do, how they will fight the Dirzh."

"Can they do that? I mean, the army've got all…"

"There are many Varaki in the army. But I don't want fighting like this, Nigel. Aeroplanes, tanks, big guns. It is stupid, stupid."

"Yes, of course it is, but…"

"They'll drop their bombs on my Varaki. They'll kill many hundreds who do not fight, men, women, children. They think the Varaki are nothing. Then the Dirzh will fight each other, East Dirzh and West Dirzh…Many, many times my father said this to me. It was his nightmare. I must stop them. How do I do it, Nigel? Think!"

"Oh, Lord. I don't…"

"Think, Nigel!"

"OK."

They started to climb, more and more slowly. Nigel could smell the sweet reek of Dirzhani market stalls and hear the cries of the stall-holders and voices of people jostling past. Sounds and odours faded out and they drew to a halt.

"Look," he muttered hurriedly. "Don't make a big thing of me being the ambassador's son. I mustn't get Dad involved in this. We don't want those bastards telling people he's on your side. Of course he is, but…"

"OK. You're right. You must have a new name. Quick!"

"Um. Nick Riddle? Hope that's easier than Ridgwell."

They climbed out into a square that looked as if it had been purpose-built for tourists, though there weren't any around. On one side was a mosque with three golden domes and a spindly minaret. The building opposite looked like a way-over-the-top little fortress, dark red brick with the muzzles of bronze cannon, green with age, poking between the fancy battlements. At the centre was a gate tower, with a wide double gate and an inner courtyard beyond.

A reception committee was waiting under the archway, three

bearded men, all with that look as if they expected you to know that they were someone who mattered. A group of lesser mortals stood behind them, some of them wearing coloured shoulder-sashes to show which clan they belonged to.

The man at the centre of the group, shorter and fatter than the other two, stepped forward to meet them. Taeela offered him her hand, palm down, and he took it between both of his, bowed briefly over it, muttering what had to be some kind of ritual greeting, and straightened with red lips smiling amid his beard.

He glanced briefly at Nigel, then back to Taeela, and then after at least a couple of seconds, back to Nigel. A stare this time. Taeela did the Dirzhani bit of the introduction first.

"And this is my cousin, the Chief Baladzhin," she said. "He was a very good friend of my father."

"Honoured to meet you, sir," said Nigel and shook hands.

"I spik not good English," said Chief Baladzhin. "My son spik good. He is two year in Ogzhvord – Bahliohl Colledzh. You know?"

"I should think I do, sir. My dad – my father – was at Balliol."

Chief Baladzhin's mouth opened, but his English deserted him in his amazement. He swung round with a delighted bellow and clapped his hands above his head. A plump young man wearing heavy horn-rimmed spectacles came forward, did the greeting thing with Taeela and held out his hand to Nigel.

"Hi," he said. "Welcome to Sodalka. I'm Mizhael Baladzhin. That's Mike in English."

He was less impressively bearded than his father but with the same enthusiastic manner and glance. The words seemed to tumble out of him. A bit under thirty, Nigel guessed—difficult because of the beard. He spoke English easily, but with a bit of an accent, rather like the President.

"Hi," said Nigel. "I'm Nige…Nick Riddle. You can tell your father his English is a lot better than my Dirzhani."

"We'll have to do something about that. How come you've got

mixed up in this mess?"

"Er...My dad's..."

"Hold it. You're wanted."

In the nick of time, too. Nigel took the chance to think his story through while he was standing around after being introduced to the other two chieftains. Mizhael Baladzhin joined him as the whole group started to move in under the archway, Rahdan tagging along behind Taeela with his AK slung over his shoulder, and Janey and the girls following, all five with their head-scarves folded to cover the lower half of their faces.

"She's pretty impressive," said Mizhael. "Twelve, isn't she?"

"Taeela? She's thirteen next month. She's amazing."

"You can say that again. All sorts of stories going around. She's holed up in the palace. She's dead. Adzhar Taerzha's got her, going to marry her off to one of his lads. Ditto with a couple of the East Dirzh lot. She's hiding in the British embassy. And then she shows up here unannounced in a battered old rust-bucket with her own bodyguard and bidzhaya and vinaili..."

"Uh?"

"Sorry. Chaperone, I suppose, and, um, well, ladies-in-waiting, kind of, except they're usually kids even when she's grown up... and Dad and the others are treating her pretty well like that's what she was. What's happened with your arm?"

"A guy bashed it with an AK."

"Ouch. Been like that, has it?"

"Some of it. Taeela says I've got to see a knowing woman, whatever that is."

"If that's what you want. Alinu's damn good, but we've got a decent little hospital if you'd rather."

Tempting, but the first thing was to get out of sight. All eyes were on Taeela, but that didn't stop Nigel feeling desperately exposed, gossip-worthy, like a streaker at a Test Match. It would be worse at a hospital.

"Let's try the knowing woman," he said. "What happens now?"

"We were just sitting around talking about it all when you lot showed up. I guess we'll let the Khanazhana settle in to her quarters and give her a bit of time to sort herself out—you can hole up with me—and…Trouble, Nick?"

"I can't go…?"

"Go along with the Khanazhana? She'll be in the women's quarters. Dad acts pretty laid-back, but he runs a very orthodox establishment. I get a special dispensation, mind you. You'll see. This way."

The procession broke up in the courtyard, a space of fountains and flowers and shade trees, surrounded by an elaborate arcade. The main body continued straight ahead, Chief Baladzhin took Taeela, Janey and the others to the right and Mizhael led Nigel towards the single large door under the arcade on the left, which he opened and stood aside with a welcoming gesture. Nigel hesitated, turned and saw almost exactly the same thing happening at the door opposite, Chief Baladzhin making the gesture and Taeela turning. Her mouth was hidden by her headscarf so she couldn't answer his smile, but they each raised a farewell hand and turned away.

CHAPTER 16

They crossed a dark entrance hall, climbed two flights of stairs and stopped at a pair of double doors. Mizhael drew a large key from under his robe, unlocked them and pushed one leaf open, locking it behind him once they were through.

"Dog-dog!" he shouted.

There was a cry of delight, a charge of feet, and a small boy came scampering out through an open door and into Mizhael's arms. Mizhael swung him around a couple of times and held him up to present him to Nigel. "This is my friend, Nick, Dog-dog," said Mizhael. "And this is my son Doglu—Douglas to you. And this is my lovely wife, Lily-Jo."

Nigel turned and saw a small slim woman watching them from a doorway, quietly smiling. She was no taller than he was, with jet black hair and a light brown oriental-looking face, with huge-lensed spectacles. Her flowered blouse and white slacks would have looked OK almost anywhere in the world.

"I'll leave you to their tender mercies for a bit," said Mizhael. "You must be dead beat. Why don't you have a bit of a lie-down while I go and try to stop these crazy old men from marching on Dara Dahn?"

"That's fine…" Nigel started, then registered what Mizhael had just said.

"No, wait!" he said urgently.

Mizhael turned in the doorway, eyebrows raised.

"Look, you've got to talk to Taeela. She's desperate to stop that happening."

"Is she now?" said Mizhael speaking slowly for the first time. "She has a plan?"

"Not yet, but…"

"No time now. I'll fix for you to sit next to me at dinner. The Khanazhana has shown up unexpectedly, darling. Nick's an English friend of hers. Explain our set-up here to him—he's obviously baffled. I'll get them to send old Alinu up to him—he's had a bash on his shoulder. Then he'd better have a bit of a rest. I'll be back in half an hour. Love you. Bye. Go to Mummy, Dog-dog, that's a good boy. Be nice to my friend Nick."

He closed the door. The key clacked in the lock. Nigel turned to his hostess. She was no longer smiling.

"The Khanazhana is here?" she said, very softly, with a slight lisp. "In Sodalka?"

"That's right. We've just arrived. You've heard what happened to the President."

"Sure. Why does she come here?"

"She had to come somewhere. The soldiers were hunting for us in the palace. The old man who used to look after her told her to come here because your father-in-law was some kind of cousin. She didn't really want to…"

Nigel hesitated. He'd already got himself in deeper than he'd meant to, and the intensity of her gaze was unsettling. The child clung to her leg, staring at Nigel, sensing something was wrong.

"Yes?" she said. "She did not want to come to Sodalka? Why is that?…Tell me, please. It is important."

"Well, er, I think maybe she was afraid your father-in-law might try to make her marry one of his sons."

"My father-in-law has one son only."

"Oh, but…"

"You are right. This is what my father-in-law wishes. A man may take more than one wife in Dirzhan. We have an apartment in Singapore. He says the Khanazhana will be Mizhael's chief wife and they will live in Dirzhan, and I will be his second wife and he will come sometimes to visit me in Singapore. I will not accept this. It is difficult for Mizhael. I cannot tell you…"

"Oh…well…if it's any help, Taeela—the Khanazhana—told me she isn't going to marry him if she can possibly help it."

He watched her relax, but doubtfully. She managed a smile and picked the child up.

"Now you had better rest before Alinu comes," she said, rapping her knuckles against a small gong on the table by the door. "Darzha will show you your room. I don't go through this door unveiled and unaccompanied. There is another door, and if I want to go out I put on boy's clothes and use that and tell people I am my brother. It is ridiculous. Everyone knows who I am but they keep the pretence up because I'm a foreigner and one day Mizhael will marry a proper Dirzhani wife and I will go and live in Singapore and they will be rid of me."

She spoke with the same soft lisp as before, but with steadily increasing bitterness, paying no attention to the stout middle-aged woman who had appeared through another door and was standing watching them.

"You must miss Singapore," he said, because he had to say something.

"Yes, of course. But I love him, you see. That's what makes it so difficult."

She turned and spoke in what sounded like rather stumbling Dirzhani to the woman, who nodded, drew a key from the pocket of her house coat, unlocked the door and beckoned to Nigel.

"See you," he said to Lily-Jo. "Do you want me to tell Taeela about you?"

She shrugged and turned away.

Nigel's room was a fair size, with a high ornamental ceiling and three narrow barred windows looking out at a blank wall. It was clean, and could once have been rather grand, but obviously hadn't been decorated for years. There were a few strange-shaped bits of dark old furniture and a large old iron bed with brass knobs and something like an outsize pillow for a mattress.

He was lying on this, painfully trying to ease his shoulder, which had stiffened horribly in its sling, when he heard a scratching at the door. It opened before he could call out and man wearing a brown and green shoulder-sash—the Baladzhin colours, presumably—came in with his shoulder-bag, followed by two veiled women. The older one wore opaque black-lensed spectacles and grasped the shoulder of the younger one as she moved; she too, Nigel realised, must be at least half blind, to judge by the thickness of her lenses.

The man put the shoulder-bag down and asked Nigel a question.

"I'm fine, thanks," he said, waving his good hand to show what he meant. The man nodded and left.

"Alinu. Veela," said the younger woman, pointing first at her companion and then herself. "She my auntie. She make your shouldzha good."

"That'd be great," said Nigel. "Do you want me to take my shirt off?"

"Please to," said Veela.

She helped him ease it off, led Alinu to the bedside and guided her hands to his chest. They explored gently. He could feel the tips of the fingernails at the edges of the gently probing pads. It was as if a couple of crabs were scuttling around on him.

Alinu withdrew her hands and Veela took over, feeling rather more hesitantly, while her aunt muttered in her ear. Teacher and pupil, he guessed. The family secrets being passed on. Then, in turn, they sniffed all over the left side of his chest. If they'd been dogs, he thought, they'd have been wagging their tails with excitement.

"To turn," said Veela, gesturing the motion. "I help?"

"I can manage," he said, and rolled himself awkwardly onto his front. They went through the whole process again and turned him back over.

After a brief discussion Veela unslung her shoulder-bag and rootled around, eventually bringing out a small clay flask which she handed to Alinu. She then made him sit, rearranged his pillows to prop him up, laid him back, and placed her hands firmly either side of his head.

"Not to move," she said.

Alinu groped her way forward and found his body. She checked the position of his nose, held the flask below it and removed the stopper.

The reek leapt out like a tiger, fierce as pain. Instinctively he tried to jerk his head away, but Veela held it firm until Alinu stoppered the bottle and it was over. His head rang, his lungs gulped air, his eyes streamed.

"Wha…Wha…Wha…?" he protested and tried to get up. Effortlessly Veela pushed him back. His muscles were jelly, his bones weightless. He seemed to have no strength at all. Both women laughed so cheerfully at his feebleness that he managed to smile dopily through his tears.

They began to work together, Veela moving his arm to and fro according to Alinu's instructions, while Alinu poked and squeezed and prodded. It should have been unbearably painful, and yes, the pain was there if he chose to think about it, but it was somewhere outside him. The only reality was the after-smell of that odour, which rapidly eased until he found himself dragging in great lungfuls of air and feeling enormously alive inside the weirdly enfeebled body. The women were still at their work when he fell asleep.

He woke with a shock, unable to think where he was. The whole of the last three days could have been a dream.

"How's the shoulder," said a voice.

"Oh…? Ungh…?"

"Knocked you out, did she?"

He opened his eyes. Mizhael Baladzhin was at his bedside. The two women were gone. It was almost dark outside the window. Gingerly he shifted his arm an inch, and then several inches, feeling only a mild twinge where before there had been wincing pain. The flesh round the joint was sweetly tender to the touch, like a mild bruise, but that was all.

"That's amazing," he said. "That stuff she made me smell…"

"Gave you darm, did she? You're honoured. Worth its weight in gold. Distilled from a fungus. You'll feel two hundred percent for a few hours and then you'll flake right out. Only the chosen women in her family know the recipe, and then it takes a hundred years to reach full potency.

"Right, are you ready for a bit of a shock? I'm later than I said because I've been doing a search on the Balliol website. Can't find any Riddles anywhere near the right age. On the other hand there's a Nigel Ridgwell, '82 to '86, currently Her Majesty's Ambassador to Dirzhan."

"Oh."

"Don't worry—I'm not proposing to tell anyone about this. Lily-Jo, maybe. It'd be bound to get out, and we don't want the Dirzh telling the Russians the British are interfering in our internal affairs. I doubt anyone except my dad has paid much attention to you so far—they were all too busy staring at the Khanazhana. But your father's been on TV once or twice, and he's an exotic figure here in Dirzhan. If you go swanning around with your blond hair and your blue eyes someone's going to put two and two together.

"I've brought you some clothes. They're Lily-Jo's, for when she has one of her outings—she tell you about that?—so they should about fit. Dad dines formal so you'll be wearing a turban…"

"Provided it isn't a dahl. I've got some sun-glasses."

"Great. Can you do an American accent?"

"Um. I'd make a mess of it. What I thought was, Dad's here working on the dam project. He met the President and told him I was coming out and the President asked if I could spend a bit of time with the Khanazhana to help with her English. I was doing that when he got shot and I escaped with her."

"That's fine. Then not to bother with the sun-glasses. Yanks wear sun-glasses. Brits have blue eyes. Known facts in Dirzhan. I'll give you five minutes to dress. I'll do the turban for you."

He bustled out. Nigel stayed where he was, thinking with the dreamy clarity of the darm-trance about Mizhael Baladzhin. Lily-Jo and the Balliol website; Alinu and Darzha. A computer nerd and a Dirzhani princeling. One foot in the age of the internet, and the other still in the Middle Ages.

Nigel liked him, liked the way he talked to him, not just friendly-adult, but as if there wasn't any age gap at all. As if age simply didn't matter. As if dishing the colonels had been a video game they were playing. "Dishing," "swanning around," weird. It could have been Nigel's father talking...

He pulled himself together and started to put on Lily-Jo's clothes, dark brown baggy trousers, fastening at the ankles, and a knee-length embroidered jacket. There weren't any buttons, just laces and loops to thread them through. He was sorting out the ankle fastenings when Mizhael came back.

"How are you doing? I've found you some sandals might do. Let's have a go at your turban. We can get your hair dyed tomorrow—it'll wash out—so you won't have to bother with this. There. Suits you. Lawrence of Dirzhan. Need a hand with your sling? Well done. Time to get down."

"Will Taeela be there?"

"Up in the gallery with the ladies, I'm afraid. This is Sodalka, Nick. Tell you what—I'll send a note up inviting her to come and meet Lily-Jo after. She can bring her bidzhaya. Ready? Let's go."

Dinner was in a much smaller and less ornate version of the Great Hall at the palace, without the staircase, and arcaded across only one end, with the arches above filled with a pierced screen. The meal had already started when Mizhael and Nigel arrived. Nigel copied Mizhael as they halted at the entrance, placed their palms together and bowed to Chief Baladzhin, immediately opposite them. Still chewing vigorously, he raised a welcoming hand and waved it vaguely towards his right, then turned to listen to the chieftain seated on his left, who had continued speaking volubly throughout. Thirty or forty men were sitting around in a rough rectangle, some cross-legged on cushions on the floor, some half-lounging on thick-padded divans, one or two on ordinary upright chairs. The centre of the space was cluttered with low tables and tiered cake-stands carrying plates of typical Dirzhani finger-food. Attendants wandered around with dishes and pitchers. It looked more like a grand indoor picnic than a formal dinner.

"Chap spouting at Dad is Ahkuvo Ahkhan," muttered Mizhael as he led the way across the room. "Chief hot-head. Looks like we're sitting next to Dad's cousin Zhiordzhio – the guy with the foxy look. Speaks a bit of English. Crony of Ahkhan's. Probably try and pump you about the Khanazhana."

"Honestly, I hardly know her," said Nigel earnestly. "Her dad just got me in to talk to her about books and stuff. My dad warned me to keep off politics. Like I told you, I just happened to be there when there was this coup and I tagged along with her because I hadn't got anywhere else to go."

Mizhael laughed.

"You'll do," he said.

Zhiordzhio Baladzhin was a haggard-looking elderly man with a slight squint in his bloodshot eyes. Thin lips smiled briefly in the tatty grey beard and he beckoned Nigel into the space beside him on the divan. Attendants appeared with food, and a drinks trolley. Mr Baladzhin didn't wait for Nigel to choose.

"Mizhtair…Uh. Is good you come to Dirzhan."

"I could have picked a better time, sir. It's been pretty scary."

"Yes, yes. But you safe now in Sodalka. You hurting your arm?"

"A man hit it with a gun. There were these two guys trying to rob us, but Rahdan—the Khanazhana's bodyguard—he dealt with them. That was one of the scary bits."

Mr Baladzhin shrugged. It wasn't what he wanted to talk about.

"You are friend to the Khanazhana?" he said.

"Not really, sir. I've visited her just a few times to help her with her English. My father met the President, you see, and he asked if…"

Nigel spun the story out, speaking slowly and clearly, keeping it as boring as he could. He didn't mention the visit to the hunting lodge. Mr Baladzhin nodded every now and then, but his eyes kept roving round the room. He didn't say anything till Nigel got onto the Tribute of the Chieftains.

"You see this? With you own eyes?" he said, looking directly at Nigel for the first time.

"Yes, sir," said Nigel. "I was up in the gallery…"

No way could he keep the death of the President boring. He didn't try. Mr Baladzhin listened intently.

"Who did shot him?" he said suddenly. "You seeing who did shot him?"

"No, sir. Everyone was cheering the Khanazhana coming down the stairs. I think the shots came from somewhere up in the gallery on my right. It might have been one of the guards. They weren't the President's usual lot."

"Dirzh," said Mr Baladzhin, spitting the word out. "And the chievetans—what?"

"I didn't see then, sir. We were too busy running away and hiding. But later on we saw soldiers taking some of the chieftains away along with some other important people."

"Chievetans—how many?"

"Oh, six? Seven, maybe."

"Seven. Seven Varaki chievetans go to this tribute. The Dirzh keep them for balukiri."

"Hostages?"

"Hozhtadzhes. So. Where they taking them?"

"Another room in the palace, I think. That's all I saw, sir. The soldiers were hunting for the Khanazhana. We were hiding until we could get out."

Mr Baladzhin stared furiously at him for several seconds.

"Dirzh!" he spat again, and turned to the man on his other side. Mizhael was now talking to the man on his right, so Nigel relaxed and settled down to eat what Mizhael had chosen for him. Taeela had asked him to think. Fat chance anyone would listen to him, but it was something to do.

She was who and what she was, so you could rule out the sensible ambassador-type answers, peace deals with the murderers, power-sharing arrangements and so on. You could rule out the crazy ones too, Dirzh against Dirzh, cities reduced to smoking rubble, farms deserted, tens of thousands half-starving in refugee camps.

Anyway, none of that was what she'd asked him. Fohdrahko had given her a map of the passages. She'd kept the vital keys. So how could she use them? It was a day-dream only, a shoot-'em-up video game without the kit.

No, not a day-dream. A darm-dream. He felt he could remember every instant of their escape from the palace, every step through the passages, every rung of the shafts, every breath he had drawn, every beat of his heart…

The trance was broken by Mizhael's voice.

"I guess you like Dirzhani food then. Want any more?"

Nigel stared at his empty plate, vaguely aware of the series of tastes that had been in his mouth.

"Uh…Oh, yes. I like it a lot. No, thanks. I'm fine."

"Sorry to desert you. You seemed to be managing OK with Uncle Zhiordzhio. Maybe I should've sat between you, but he'd've just talked across me. Tricky old boy. He thought he was all lined up to be chieftain, but the tribal seniors didn't like the way he took it for granted and chose Dad instead. I reckon he's trying to get us into a fight with the Dirzh, and if it works out—which it won't—he'll take the credit and if it doesn't he'll say it was all Dad's fault and it's time he took over. Tell him anything useful?"

"I don't think so. He was mainly interested in the hostages. The other Varaki chieftains."

"Yeah. It's getting to look like that. We haven't heard from them as far as I know. Those stupid bastards. They're playing into Uncle Zhiordzhio's hands. If they wanted to stir the Varaki up they couldn't have done better.

"Trouble is, Nick, Dad listens to Uncle Zhiordzhio. Tell you the truth, Dad's a bit of guvla. 'Cushion' in English, but in Dirzhani it's used for the kind of guy who's easy to persuade. Carries the impression of the last arse that sat on him, right? If we're going to do anything to stop Uncle Zhiordzhio we're going to have to come up a better suggestion damn soon. You said the Khanazhana had a plan."

"Well. Sort of. I haven't told you how we got out of the palace. It's full of secret passages. There was this old guy who looked after Taeela…"

Mizhael listened intently, nibbling at the knuckle of his thumb, while Nigel told him, low-voiced, what had happened from the moment the shot was fired to their crossing the river. He didn't smile or look away. When a servant came up and offered them more food he waved him away.

Nigel finished and waited while Mizhael studied his nibbled thumb.

"You've seen this map?" he said at last.

"Only the outside. It looked really old but it should be pretty accurate. Fohdrahko wouldn't have given it to Taeela if he thought it wasn't any use."

"The guys who were after you got into part of the system. They may have explored it all by now."

"I don't know. It isn't easy. There's a lot of booby traps. The eunuchs didn't like outsiders using the passages."

Mizhael's expression changed completely. He glanced sideways at Nigel like a teasing child and grinned.

"Lily-Jo tell you why I make her come here when she'd much rather we stayed in Singapore?" he said. "I run a little company there, developing computer games. Some guy comes up with an idea for a game but he doesn't know where to go with it, so he brings it to us and we work it up till we can try it on one of the big players. Right? Takes a lot of expensive kit to do it properly and you'll be lucky if you get a bite one time in twenty, so it can be a while before you see a return on your money, if you ever do. Dad's putting up the cash to get us started and keep us going till then, but part of the deal is I spend half the year here. I could leave Lily-Jo in Singapore, but she won't have it and nor will I. You a games freak?"

"Only chess."

"I'm impressed. Pity you didn't get on with Uncle Zhiordzhio. Challenged for the national championship once. He'd have given you a game. I guess you don't dream about playing chess for real, though. That's what games freaks do, most of us. If you'd come to me with what you've told me as an idea for a game I'd've turned you down. Way too old hat. But to play it for real…

"Let's go back a bit. Before we can use the passages we've got to get there. Forty armed men, say. We could sneak them into the city, one or two at a time, but not if they're carrying guns. There'll be searches on all the gates. And we'd still have to get them into the palace. You've thought of that?"

"Do you know about the fishing boats? They go out in the evening when the fish are rising and come back and unload them at the fish quay. Just the other side of the Iskan bridge from the palace. It must've been about ten-something when we got there, and they hadn't come back yet. Some of the boats belong to one of Janey's neighbours. I thought if you paid him enough he could pick you up somewhere on the lake…"

"Uh huh. I'll look into it. Anything else?"

"Rahdan used to be in the palace guard. He'll know stuff about how they do things. I thought—we'd have to ask him about this—I thought…"

"Hold it. Dad's going to make a speech. I'll just…"

And he was gone, picking his way rapidly round behind the diners and reaching his father when he was already on his feet, waiting for the chatter and bustle to die down. He turned to listen to Mizhael, frowned, shrugged, turned back to the room and started to speak while Mizhael came quietly back.

"Didn't want him saying anything about you," he whispered. "He's totally wound up. He's got something up his sleeve."

Even not understanding a word of Dirzhani Nigel could tell it was true. It looked like everyone else in the room could too. They listened in expectant silence, apart from occasional murmurs of agreement, and an angry rumble at the name of Adzhar Taerzha. On Nigel's left Zhiordzhio Baladzhin was nodding vigorously. Chief Baladzhin worked up to a climax, turned to his left and flung out an arm like a TV host welcoming a star guest. A door beneath the gallery opened, and Taeela came in, unveiled, but wearing deep mourning, black from head to toe, with almost no make-up. She was followed by what had to be Janey, unrecognisable in a black dahl with the purple shoulder sash of a khan's attendant.

After the first hush of astonishment the clapping broke out. The attendants joined in. Chief Baladzhin bustled to meet Taeela. The applause only died away as he led her round the room, introducing her to everybody there, followed by Janey a pace or two behind her. She touched hands with them all, said a few words now and then and passed on, just like you see the British royal family doing when they're launching a submarine or something.

Mizhael and Nigel rose together as she reached them, almost

last in the room. She touched hands with Mizhael, but said nothing for several seconds, simply looking at him. Nigel could see her face but not his. What were they thinking, these two people who were booked to marry each other and didn't want to? She spoke briefly, smiled at his answer and moved on to Nigel.

Regally she eyed him up and down.

"Wow! You look really, really hot in that gear, Mr Riddle," she said softly.

"Better not tell Janey you think so."

Her lips twitched and straightened, and she moved on to Mr Baladzhin. He'd been fidgeting with excitement ever since she'd come in, and now he couldn't wait for her to speak. A flood of words burst out of him, a public speech, meant to be heard by everyone there. Taeela nodded gravely, and flicked a glance at Nigel. He answered with what he hoped was a warning look.

She listened a little longer to the tirade, then tried to stop it by holding up her hand. He paid no attention. She turned to Chief Baladzhin for help, her face tragic, on the verge of tears. Chief Baladzhin said something. Mr Baladzhin ignored him. Chief Baladzhin took Taeela's arm and started to lead her away. Mr Baladzhin tried to follow, still ranting. Mizhael lunged across and grabbed his wrist. Mr Baladzhin tried to shake him off. An attendant joined in, and together they forced Mr Baladzhin back onto his seat. He sat there muttering while Taeela and Chief Baladzhin finished their circuit.

"That's lost him a few friends with luck," Mizhael whispered as he returned, panting slightly, to his place.

Their tour done, Taeela and Chief Baladzhin held a brief discussion. He stood aside; she turned to face the room and waited for silence, then spoke a few sentences in a clear, sad voice. The clapping that broke out as she left was quieter, respectful of her sorrow, but continued for some time after she'd gone.

CHAPTER 17

"Hearts and minds!" said Mizhael. "Apart from Uncle Zhiordzhio, of course. Probably just as well. I'd rather have him as an enemy than a friend. Only what's she going to be like when she's twenty?"

They were sitting in Mizhael and Lily-Jo's living-room waiting for Taeela, Nigel now very conscious of the long day it had been and how late it was. The darm had left his bloodstream and his body yearned for his bed.

He was back in his own clothes. Mizhael was wearing dark green slacks and a top half a bit like a Hawaiian shirt, only clearly Dirzhani. Lily-Jo had got Doglu up to say hello to his father and was putting him back to bed.

"She wasn't faking it," said Nigel. "Her dad was the only person who mattered to her in the whole world, him and Fohdrahko, and they're both dead. She covers up what she's feeling, mostly. She just let them see it."

"I guess you're right. Lot more impressive that way. Hope she can lay on a repeat performance when the rest of the chieftains show up tomorrow. Going to be touch and go. We're a patriarchal bunch up here for a start, and the notion that a twelve-year-old girl might have any more to say for herself than a pet dog is pretty foreign to us. Top of that a couple of them are cronies of Uncle Zhiordzhio's, and they'll all have it in for one lot of Dirzh or the other…"

He broke off at the click of the key in the outer door and reached the inner door in time to let Taeela and Janey in. Lily-Jo arrived a moment later, cradling the sleeping Doglu. She'd changed into a soft golden housecoat, and looked, Nigel thought, terrific. Mizhael's wife, with his son in her arms.

Among other things that meant she couldn't shake Taeela's hand when Mizhael introduced them, but she acknowledged her presence with the smallest possible bow. For several seconds they stood looking at each other in silence.

"I grieve for your loss," said Lily-Jo. "You may come in to our home, but I cannot for myself give you a welcome. My husband's father plans for you to marry my husband."

"Nobody chooses who I will marry," said Taeela, equally stiffly.

"That's all right then," said Mizhael, totally ignoring the chill in the air. "Hell, I'm happily married already. Why change?"

For once Taeela was taken aback. She turned and stared at him and broke into laughter, her old self for the moment. Mizhael joined in with the Baladzhin guffaw. Lily-Jo relaxed more slowly but had managed a smile by the time they stopped laughing.

"Then of course you're welcome," she said. "Why don't you sit down? I'll just put Doglu to bed."

They sat. Nigel broke the silence she left behind her.

"Hi, Taeela. How are you doing? I'm dead. You've got to be too."

"I'm tired. I try not to be dead. Your arm is better?"

"They've got a knowing woman here. Alinu. She's really amazing. But look, Mike's got to talk to you before these chieftains get here tomorrow. He's OK. He's dead set against fighting. But he says you're going to have a job persuading the chieftains. Mr Baladzhin—Zhiordzhio, the guy who started yelling at you—he'll try and stir things up. A couple of them are mates of his."

She nodded and turned to Mizhael.

"Your father? What does he think?"

"That's part of the problem. Trouble is he's a guvla, know what I mean? And of course, he's not diradzh—that's senior chief, Nick. Paramount, I suppose. Urvdahn Idzhak's diradzh, and the bastards have got him in Dara Dahn. My ma can usually make Dad see sense, but she won't be there tomorrow, and Dad'll likely have committed himself before she can get at him. If that happens, she'll have to get him to play for time. You've met her?"

"I think she does not approve of me. To show my face. To speak how I did to the men."

"Yeah, she's pretty old-fashioned. She doesn't stand any nonsense from Dad, mind you. Anyway, Nick and I've been talking about how we might get our blow in first. That's what I mean about playing for time. He says you're thinking along the same lines, right?"

"Yes. I will do it. I have a secret way into the palace. I will find good men. How many?"

"Twenty, minimum. With weapons and supplies. It's not just a question of getting them into the palace. You've got to get them into Dara Dahn first. Nick's got an idea about that. Nick, when you've stopped yawning?"

"You tell them," said Nigel. The two or three little organising notions he had had under the influence of the darm were swamped by the huge tangle of the unknowable. The whole idea was crazy. Vaguely he was aware of Lily-Jo coming back and settling quietly onto the sofa beside Mizhael, and seeming to be listening just as intently as Taeela.

Taeela must have read his mood.

"It will work, Nigel," she said.

Involuntarily he shook his head. She thought it would work because she willed it to work. But the world isn't like that.

"It will work, Nigel," she insisted.

"I think it might," said Mizhael. "We'd have to get it just

right, but…"

"We?" said Lily-Jo. "You are not doing this, Mike. This isn't one of your games. Don't be stupid. This is real. Anyway, you hate guns. Khanazhana, you don't want him. He wouldn't be any use. He never takes any exercise. He can't run. He can't do the tough stuff. OK, Mike, you can be the back-room boy, get it all ready, deal with the guys who're going to do it if you can find anyone that stupid, but you're staying right here."

Mizhael laughed.

"Another one who doesn't take any nonsense from her husband," he said. "We do pick 'em."

"She is right, Mizhael," said Taeela. "We cannot take many men. I thought only a few, but I didn't think of the fishing boats. We can take more in them. Your friend will do this, Dzhanayah?"

Janey shook her head doubtfully

"Perhaps I write to him letter," said Janey. "Rick is good friend for Nardu. Lend him money for buying one boat. But this is big ask. Rick is friend for him, not you."

"We'll find somebody," said Taeela. "If we pay them enough… Anyway, somehow we will get there."

"You're planning on going yourself?" said Mizhael. "That's even crazier…"

"I must go," said Taeela. "I know the passages—not all of them, there are so many. They are very dangerous, full of traps. The through-ways are hidden. Nigel can tell you. I must show the men how to find them."

"Isn't all that in your map?"

"I can't tell. The passages that I do know, even. The map is very old, very difficult. I can't read the writing. Look."

Carefully she drew Fohdrahko's map out from under her clothing, unfolded it and spread it out on the coffee table. Nigel stared at it in dismay. It was hand-drawn onto what he thought might once have been be very fine white linen but had now gone brown, and crumbly at the folds. It showed all four storeys of the palace. At least, there were four separate plans, plus a couple of smaller ones, but they weren't anything like an architect's floor-plan, just a lot of fine spidery lines wriggling to and fro round small, shapeless spaces filled with neat patches of tiny writing, Dirzhani he assumed, but not in any letters he could read. Where was the Great Hall, for heaven's sake? It should have been obvious on at least three of the four storeys, but it wasn't on any of them. It was like trying to read a book in a dream. The details seemed to waver, change…

"Hell, it's in old script," said Mizhael's voice, somewhere in the distance. "Those aren't letters, they're syllables. There are about nine hundred of them. We'll have to ask Doctor Ghulidzh. Dad's librarian. He should be able to read old script."

Again a voice woke him, a woman this time.

"Time to wake up, Nick, if you're going to have any breakfast."

Who…? Where…? The daylight seemed blinding. But he'd heard that soft lisp before.

He dragged his eyes open. Lily-Jo was standing over his bed. He had no idea how he'd got here. Darzha, the Baladzhins' servant, was watching from just inside the door. He peered at his wrist-watch. Half past nine.

"You've got an hour," said Lily-Jo. "The Khanazhana wants you for when she meets the chieftains. Something about being a witness. Mike says to wear my clothes again, but you'd better come and have breakfast in your bedclothes. Here's a bath robe."

"OK, thanks. Give me five mins."

The bath robe matched the pyjamas, dark blue with a pattern of yellow lilies. Breakfast was fresh orange juice, a poached egg, toast and wild honey from the mountains.

"Mike gets it on Sundays, provided he's kept his weight." said Lily-Jo. "One ounce over and it's crisp-bread."

"It's great," said Nigel. "Just like home."

"How are you feeling?"

"Fine. Better than fine."

It was true. His shoulder had been pretty stiff when he'd woken and was still bruise-sore if he prodded it, but he'd managed to ease it without pain, and apart from that he felt as well as he'd ever felt in his life, alive, interested, confident that he could cope. There were only two things wrong with his world. His parents would be worried stiff about him—he needed to talk to them. And he wasn't seeing enough of Taeela.

He'd hardly started eating when Mizhael came bustling in.

"You're up? Great. Slept OK? Any problems, apart from Lily-Jo's taste in nightwear?"

"My taste!" said Lily-Jo. "Men have so little imagination. I am given lilies. Doglu gets dogs."

"Could be worse," said Mizhael. "You might have been Camilla. Yes, Nick?"

"Is there a secure line out of here? I want to tell Mum and Dad I'm still OK. There was one in the palace, like I told you, and the embassy line's OK, and it's fixed to tell you if anyone's listening. Whenever I tried after the palace someone always was. I had to talk in code, sort of, or Spanish. But even if I do that now they'll still be able to work out where I am, and they'll guess Taeela's here too, and they'll come and try and get her."

"Day or two and they'll know anyway, after yesterday. No way you can keep something like that quiet, not in Dirzhan. Got to think about that, before they come and bomb us flat. Anyway I can do a phone-line for you. Have to be this afternoon. You've got a date with the chieftains this morning. The Khanazhana says she needs you for a witness. Know what that's about?"

"I think so."

"Great. After the chieftains, will you see if you can make sense of that plan of the passages? Doctor Ghulidzh can read old script. Doesn't speak much English, I'm afraid. Point is, you've seen them..."

"Only that once. I'll give it a go if you like, but Taeela…"

"She's going to have her hands full helping Dad keep the chieftains in check. My Ma's been talking to Dad. Laid down the law a bit. He's going to play for time, negotiate about returning the Khanazhana in exchange for…"

"No!"

"Her own idea. Not going to do it, of course, but it'll hold the bombers off for a week or two…Tell you later. We've got to get on."

The chieftains were meeting in the room where they had dined the night before. It was already crowded—fifty or sixty men, Nigel guessed. Most of the furnishings had been cleared back against the walls, apart from a semi-circle of low seats beneath the gallery, where the seven chieftains sat, each with a group of men standing behind him, wearing the different coloured shoulder-sashes of their clans. You could have knitted a romper suit for a camel out of their beards. Zhiordzhio Baladzhin was in the group behind Chief Baladzhin, still looking flushed and furious.

One of the chieftains was on his feet, thumping his fist into his palm as he made his points. Each time he did so mutters of agreement rose from among the watchers. The strong bearded faces were easy to read, some fierce, confident, spoiling for the fight, some scowling disapproval, or anxious and uncertain. There was a bit of applause when the speaker sat down, and Zhiordzhio Baladzhin elbowed his way across to pat him on the shoulder.

By the time he got back to his place another chieftain was speaking, making much less of a meal of it. Mizhael whispered the gist of it. Did they want Sodalka bombed flat? Where were their anti-tank guns? And so on. Some of his audience looked ostentatiously at their watches, yawned and muttered among themselves, others nodded and murmured agreement. He too got a bit of applause when he sat down, not as loud as the first speaker, but from just as many people, Nigel thought.

Two of the chieftains must already have had their say before Mizhael and Nigel arrived, because only three more followed. The first was another hawk, the second wanted to get the hostages back and then decide what to do, and the third was a little old man who'd been sitting out of sight behind Chief Baladzhin and needed to be helped to his feet.

"My ma's uncle Doglu," whispered Mizhael. "Dog-dog's named for him. Dad doesn't get to speak because he's in the chair, so Uncle Doglu speaks for the clan. They'll listen to him. He's a good guy. I've been talking to him."

Despite his frail appearance, Doglu Baladzhin spoke in a slow, firm voice, pausing to gather his strength before each sentence, which gave Mizhael time to translate. His audience listened in respectful silence.

"He's saying we may have to fight in the end, but we aren't ready," whispered Mizhael. "Got to play for time, protest and so on—send delegation to negotiate about the hostages, etcetera—meanwhile, got know more, find out who was behind the coup, paid for it—what the bastards intend to do next, how widely army supports them, etcetera…Ah, this is it. They must meet the Khanazhana— listen to what she says—forget that she's a kid, a girl. Knew her father's mind—saw him killed at her feet—watched his murderers from hiding-places—knew their names—got a lot to tell us…There's two or three of the chieftains very old fashioned. Aren't going to like that…Told you so…"

Two of the chieftains were their feet with their right arms held out rigid in front of them. Doglu Baladzhin stopped speaking.

"Points of order," whispered Mizhael.

Chief Baladzhin asked a question and looked along the line of chieftains. One of them half stood, but sat back down as the mutter rose to a rumble.

"All of 'em want to take a look at her," whispered Mizhael. "Doesn't matter which side they're on."

Doglu Baladzhin said a few more words and sat down. An

attendant went to the corner beneath the gallery and spoke to someone there. The room waited in silence until Taeela came sedately in, unveiled, followed by Janey, and this time Rahdan, wearing a smart uniform with a purple shoulder sash.

It was almost a repeat of last night's entrance. The clapping began at once, and continued, louder and louder, as Chief Baladzhin went to meet her and lead her along the line of chieftains, introducing them in turn. They rose and bowed as she came, and she seemed to have something different to say to each of them. One of the hawks tried to patronise her, smiling as he might have done at a too-clever child. The chieftain on his left, near enough to hear her reply, suppressed a different sort of smile as she moved on.

Finally Chief Baladzhin led her back to the centre of the semi-circle, and signed to the chieftains to sit. She turned and faced the room, waited for silence, drew a breath and started to speak.

"She wants to tell us how her father died," whispered Mizhael. "She says…"

The man next to them turned and frowned.

"Don't bother," whispered Nigel. "I was there. I saw it happen."

In fact he barely needed the translation. Taeela told the story slowly, in a clear, level tone, and he lived it through as she spoke. Only near the end, when he could almost see her coming down the great stairs, her voice faltered for the first time. She paused, swallowed, drew breath and carried on as before. The shots. The President's collapse. His final, desperate gesture to her to run, and it was over.

Nobody spoke or moved until Taeela turned towards Nigel. As far as he could tell she hadn't once glanced his way since she'd come in, but she knew where he was standing. Perhaps she'd picked him out through the gallery screen while the chieftains were speaking. She waved him over.

"You'd better come too," he whispered as he started towards her.

He could feel the pressure of everyone's attention, all those eyes on them as they crossed the room. Close up, he could see the strain in her face.

"You wanted me for a witness, Lily-Jo said," he muttered.

"You remember what my father told me, Nigel?"

"Yes, of course."

"Today I sacrifice my queen."

He stared at her, hearing the sadness in her voice and half-guessing what she meant.

"Oh…Well…Good luck," he managed.

"Thank you," she said. "Please tell him what I say, Mizhael."

"Right , . ."

The two of them moved aside to give everyone a clear view as she started to speak again, louder and slower, as though she was speaking to a much larger audience. Nigel forced himself to listen to Mizhael's whisper.

"She must avenge her father's death—they'll all go along with that, whichever side they're on. But not by fighting a war, Dirzhaki against Dirzhaki. Her father told her again and again she mustn't let that happen. He said if there is war the Russians and the Americans will make it an excuse to butt in. It's the men who killed him she's after, and the men who gave the orders, Adzhar Taerzha, Colonel Sesslizh, Colonel Madzhalid, Avron Dikhtar, men like that; and also the men who paid them.

"She can't do this alone. She needs help. So she makes the chieftains an offer. One day she must have a husband. She will choose him herself. No one will do it for her. Her father promised her this. He gave her the word of the Khan. Now she gives her word that she will choose her husband from the clan that gives her most help in avenging her father's death. This is the word of the Khan. Let them all be witnesses."

There was a moment of astonished silence, and then the hubbub broke erupted. For a good five minutes the meeting was completely out of control. The chieftains and their supporters were on their feet and gathered round chief Baladzhin like footballers round the ref after a red card; and crowd trouble was brewing down at the other end of the room, faces vivid with anger and excitement and bewilderment.

Nigel ignored the uproar, shutting it out, retreating into himself. He'd known all along that something like this was bound to happen. It had been inevitable from the moment her father died. She had as good as told him at Forghal, saying what she felt about the girls they had rescued at the peach orchard. When they had waved to each other across the courtyard before being taken to their separate quarters, they had been saying goodbye. The sadness in her voice had been for both of them, for their less-than-a-fortnight's friendship that couldn't be the same again. A few days ago he'd been a year or so older than she was, no real difference at all. Now she was years older than him.

"Trouble, Nick?" said Mizhael.

"Uh…Sorry," he said. "I suppose I'd guessed she'd say something like that, only I didn't realise it would be this big a deal."

"It's huge! Not the vengeance thing. But a daughter of the Khan! I've got five Khanazhanas in my family tree, going back six hundred years. There's been blood spilt over them, time and again, clan against clan, but she's the first on offer getting on a century. Girls didn't get much of a say, mind you. No nonsense about marrying for love. She's got that bit right. Question is, will they wear this Word-of-the-Khan business? They don't want their daughters getting ideas. Elder brother's her guardian now, I guess, but he's in Moscow, right, Russianised to the teeth, do what Moscow tells him. They won't want that, either. Depends on you, I guess. Whether you can make it stick the old boy said what she says he did. And meant it."

"What happens?"

"You make a statement. Then anyone who wants to can ask you questions, try to prove you're lying. Doesn't have to be anything important, provided it's got something to do with your statement. One detail untrue, and your statement's no good. In the old days you could challenge them to a fight to the death if they wouldn't accept your answer, or have a champion do it for you, but I don't guess it'll come to that."

"Have I got to tell them my real name?"

"Um. Tricky. Guess you'd better. Your name's a mouthful for Dirzhaki. Just say it quick as you can, and maybe they won't get it."

Slowly the clamour died down. The chieftains went back to their places. Taeela, still standing impassively where she'd been while the uproar raged round her, motioned to Nigel and Mizhael to join her. The three of them took their places in a row with Nigel in the middle, facing sideways across the room on Chief Baladzhin's right, and waited for silence. Doglu Baladzhin tottered out from behind the chieftains. Somebody brought a chair so that he could stand facing them, resting his hands on the chair-back. Chief Baladzhin rose and made a brief pronouncement and sat down again.

Doglu Baladzhin asked a question.

"Your name?" said Mizhael.

"Nigelridgwell," he said, slurring the syllables.

"You are an English boy? How is it that you are a witness to the word of the Khan?"

"My father's living in Dara Dahn, negotiating on the Vamar dam project. I came out to visit him and my mother during the school holidays. When he met the President-Khan, the President-Khan asked…"

Pausing now and then for Mizhael to translate, Nigel sketched in what had happened those first two mornings: playing chess with the President to see if he was good enough to teach Taeela the game, and managing to bring off a queen sacrifice against him; then starting to teach Taeela next morning; forking her knight and rook; Taeela wanting to keep the knight; him explaining why it was better to keep the rook, and that she mustn't mind sacrificing pieces if it was worth while, even the queen sometimes; then setting up the position in his game against the President to show her, and the President coming in.

He slowed down for the actual conversation leading up to the promise, repeating it word for word as far as he could…

"'You don't choose,'" she said. "'You ask me who I want to marry, and then I choose. Am I right?'"

"He tried to get out of it, saying it was time for me to go home, but she wouldn't let him. She wasn't joking any more. Neither was he. They were both dead serious. He thought about it for a bit.

"Then he said, 'Yes, you're right. I don't sacrifice my queen, even if it means losing the game.'

"'Word of the Khan?' she asked him.

"He thought about it again and then he gave her his hand and she put her hands round it.

"'Word of the Khan, Taeela.' he said

"'It is spoken, Khan,' she said, and then she told me I was her witness.

"That's how it happened."

Mizhael translated.

"That sounds pretty watertight," he said as the mutterings ran round the room.

Doglu Baladzhin held up his hand for silence, turned to the room and asked a question.

"Anyone want to contest the statement?" muttered Mizhael. "Oh God! Bloody Zhiordzhio!"

The shout had come from their left, behind the row of chieftains. Nigel turned and saw Zhiordzhio Baladzhin pushing his way through. He stalked forward and stationed himself beside old Doglu, directly facing Nigel. He was smiling, and his voice when he spoke wasn't particularly aggressive, only a bit patronising. He looked at Doglu, who nodded to him to go ahead.

Mizhael translated his questions.

"How old are you?"

"Thirteen."

"You played chess against the President-Khan. For how long?"

"Oh, about forty minutes. Then a call came through for him and we had to stop."

"What advantage did he give you?"

"He didn't. He offered me a piece but I didn't take it."

Zhiordzhio's eyebrows went up. He stared at Nigel, then nodded.

"What else was he doing while you played? Reading? Dictating?"

"Just eating. He said he wanted to play seriously. He was really trying to beat me, if that's what you're asking."

"He was about to beat you when you were interrupted?"

"No," he said. "He'd got an attack building up. If I hadn't spotted the queen sacrifice it'd have been a near thing, but I think I could have held it off."

Zhiordzhio swung abruptly away and spoke to the room in a bored, sneering voice.

"The bastard," said Mizhael. "He says you're lying. What you've told us is just a childish fantasy. The President was a strong player. You're a child. If he'd being playing seriously he'd have beaten you in twelve moves."

"Twelve moves! That's stupid! Look, tell him I bet him a hundred dzhin he can't beat me in twenty."

"Are you sure? He used to be pretty good."

"Yes."

"Make it three hundred. That's a serious bet. I'll stake you."

"OK...No, wait. I'm allowed to challenge him, right? Don't worry. It'll just be to a game of chess. If he beats me in twenty moves..."

Mizhael grinned, and rubbed his hands together.

"Right," he said. "They're going to love this."

He turned to the room and announced the first part of the challenge in a formal voice, waited for the gasp of astonishment and added the second part.

A moment of startled silence, and then somebody laughed. Deep male voices boomed and bayed, Chief Baladzhin as loud as any. Zhiordzhio grabbed Doglu Baladzhin's arm to protest, but Doglu cackled in his face. Nigel turned to Taeela. She nodded, unsmiling.

"I threw in the bet," said Mizhael. "He'll lose a lot a face if he turns it down. What's he up to now?"

Zhiordzhio had given up on Doglu and taken his protest to Chief Baladzhin. The chieftains gathered round. Mizhael shifted across to listen.

"You will beat him, Nigel?" said Taeela quietly.

"Not a hope, if he's as good as Mike says and if he keeps his cool. But I should be able to hold him off for twenty moves."

"You will beat him," she repeated confidently.

"Look, you can't have everything. I'm not even going to try for it, or I mightn't make twenty. You want to risk everything for that? Getting to twenty will be beating him, Taeela. Bet you that's what your dad would've told you."

It wasn't fair, but it did the trick. She nodded gravely and turned away.

Slowly the room quietened. The chieftains went back to their places, Zhiordzhio Baladzhin stood aside, muttering irritably, Mizhael returned.

"Couple of 'em wanted to postpone it till the serious stuff was finished," he said. "Rest said let's get it over. Won't get anywhere till then. They're taking bets on it already, which move he'll get you on."

"We'll need a referee. He'll try and put me off or something."

It took about ten minutes to get set up. By then servants were going round with drinks and snacks. The table was in the middle of the room with a stool either side. Almost everybody gathered round to watch the game. Zhiordzhio had objected to Mizhael translating, saying he'd help Nigel, so a jolly-looking man with a thick Dirzhani-American accent was doing it instead. The referee was older, with a serious face and keen bright eyes. There'd been a bit of argy-bargy about how quickly they played. Zhiordzhio wanted ten seconds a move, saying he didn't want to waste everyone's time, but the referee had said that wasn't fair and they'd settled for a minute.

The referee hid a pawn in each fist. Zhiordzhio got to choose, because Nigel had issued the challenge. White, worse luck. He stared contemptuously at Nigel for several seconds then plonked himself down and without waiting for Nigel to sit banged out his queen's pawn. Nigel did the same, but next move pushed his king's pawn only one square, supporting the other one.

"Stupid boy," muttered Zhiordzhio in English, and took Nigel's queen's pawn. Nigel took back.

"Stupid," said Zhiordzhio.

Before Nigel could protest the referee spoke to Zhiordzhio. He scowled, but didn't do it again. He didn't really need to. He was dismayingly good, and he kept his cool. He didn't give Nigel any extra time to think, but moved almost at once, not rushing into an all-out onslaught but getting his pieces out, forcing another pawn exchange, opening up the position which Nigel was doing his best to keep closed, not giving him a chance to form a plan of his own, but keeping him busy countering each move, and steadily getting the upper hand.

The attack came on the sixteenth move with a knight sacrifice. Nigel stared at the board for almost his full minute. Mate in three...In any ordinary game he'd have resigned. His queen was out of position after the knight sacrifice with no time to bring it back. He used it to take one of the three pawns guarding Zhiordzhio's king. Check. Zhiordzhio could move the king out of check, but then the queen would check it again, and that would be two moves gone, so he was forced to use his king to take the queen. That brought it into the open.

Seventeen.

Nigel checked it again with his second bishop. To capture that Zhiordzhio would have to take a knight out of his attack, so he retreated his king.

Eighteen.

Moving the bishop meant that Nigel could now bring it down onto his back rank, completely unprotected, a fragile barrier, an obstacle which it would take Zhiordzhio only a move to brush aside.

So it was still mate in three. There were two moves left.

Zhiordzhio used up his minute staring at the board and swept the pieces onto the floor.

"You play like idiot!" he yelled. "How I play idiot? Five moves you been dead! Dead!"

He jumped out of his seat, stamped on the pieces and lurched towards Nigel. The interpreter stuck out a leg and he fell sprawling. Nigel paid no attention. He stayed where he was, slumped forward on his stool, staring at the backs of his hands, shuddering with the release of tension.

CHAPTER 18

The stranger looked a year or two older than Nigel; skin brown with summer, pale blue eyes, strong dark brows, dark eyelashes and short black hair. Nigel closed his left eye and the stranger's right eye closed.

It was the eyebrows that made the most difference. The fine blond hairs that used almost to fade into the pale northern skin now boldly asserted themselves, seeming to change the shape of his head. You saw them, rather than the uncertain mouth and jaw-line.

Yes, he thought. One day, perhaps…Though Dad would really mind. Mum too, probably.

The barber, a skinny little man with a permanent shake in his hands, who had muttered quietly to himself in Dirzhani all the time he was fussing over his work, removed the mirror and looked at him anxiously.

"That's great!" said Nigel. "Thank you very much."

The barber produced a gratified smile, bowed and backed away.

"Your own mother wouldn't know you," said Mizhael, who had come in a few minutes earlier, obviously bursting with news. "I'll settle with this chap. Should've had three hundred dzhin to bring you. Zhiordzhio's refusing to pay up. Says your last few moves don't count, weren't chess. Referee ruled in your favour but Zhiordzhio still won't have it. Dad's mad at him. I'll give you the money, get it out of him later."

"I don't want it. I didn't cheat, but I didn't play fair. He's right. What I did wasn't chess. You can give it to Halli and Sulva if you like."

"Uh?"

"Those kids we picked up on the way here. For their dowries or something."

"Right. Wanted to ask you about them anyway. One of 'em told my niece it wasn't the bodyguard dealt with the thugs who'd kidnapped them. It was you and the Khanazhana."

"Hell! I told them…! And they weren't even there! They didn't see it happen!"

"They'd heard the bidzhaya and the bodyguard talking about it. It's a problem?"

Nigel explained.

"Got you," said Mizhael. "Other way round here, though. Sort of thing we go for big. Great propaganda. Khanazhana not just a crazy kid, but putting herself on the line to look after her people. And these guys we're hoping to get to go back into the palace with her, they'll be impressed."

"Well, for God's sake leave me out of it or Dad will be really in the shit. I didn't do that much anyway."

"Bit more than that by what I hear, but suits me. We don't want the bastards telling everyone we're in the pocket of the Brits or anyone else. We'll write you out of it.

"There's just one thing. We've got a problem. That map the Khanazhana brought. Doctor Ghulidzh, Dad's librarian, he's got a cold. Daughter won't let him out of the house."

"I could go round."

"Doesn't want that either. He's getting on, and he's got a weak chest. Best she can do is let him read the old script to her and she'll transcribe it into modern. Lily-Jo's enlarged the Khanazhana's map onto separate sheets and we've sent a set round to him. Won't be that quick even like that. Limit to what the daughter will let him do. Trouble is, Khanazhana's not going to get anyone to come aboard with her if she hasn't got a plan of the passages they can use. Whole notion's crazy enough as it is. Without that..."

He spread his hand in a gesture of despair.

Nigel hesitated. If Taeela couldn't get anyone to go with her then the whole idiot scheme would be off. Except that it wouldn't. She'd go on her own if she had to. Or with just Rahdan.

"OK, I'll give it a go," he said. "It looked pretty hopeless."

"Good egg. At least you've been there. If you can locate the bit you were in, that might be a start. I've got blow-ups of the map for you, of course, and Lily-Jo's pulled an outline of the palace off Google Earth, which'll give you a framework. I'll set you up in the library where you'll be able to spread stuff out. Not much chance you'll be disturbed in there. If you need me, it's seven-three on the house phone."

The library was a tall, well lit room with several bays of shelves down either side, carrying row on row of huge old leather-bound books, none of which looked as if it had been opened for a century. The central bays were wide enough to leave room for two fair-sized tables with a few stools either side.

Nigel perched on a stool and spread the various sheets out on the table. Google Earth showed the palace as a simple rectangle, two squares fitted together, with the main block, including the Great Hall, fronting the river and the courtyard block behind. None of the plans on Fohdrahko's map were anything like the right shape to fit into it. Instead they were the shape of the pages of the map itself, with a series of parallel lines running up the page, curving back at the top and running down, only to curve back up at the bottom. The whole thing was sprinkled with what must be letters of old script, sometimes a short line of writing, but mostly just single letters a bit like Egyptian hieroglyphics, some of them with circles round them.

He chose a page at random and studied it more closely. Sometimes a line branched and ran on parallel to itself for a bit, but then one of the branches stopped short before the end of the page while the other one ran on. A main passage, with a short one branching off? But not so close to it, surely…

No, of course not. It wasn't that kind of a map. It was a route map, the sort Toby drew for Libby when she was driving anywhere she didn't know, a single line for the road she had to follow with anything she needed to know, turnings, side roads, roundabouts and which exit to take, marked along it.

Yes! A route map of the passages. The passages and nothing else. Not the Great Hall. Not any of the other rooms and corridors and stairs. Not the outer shell of the palace, even. It didn't have to fit into that. All it had to do was fit into the page. And the bits of old script were the need-to-knows—spy-holes, hidden entrances, shafts, drop-traps…

His eye was caught by a kink in one of the lines, a place where it turned a millimetre off course and then sharply back. A place where the real passage, the passage hidden in the walls of the palace, turned a corner.

Near it was a tiny picture. Not a bit of old script, which he'd taken it for at first, but a careful drawing of a tufted duck. Unmistakable. He blinked, stared, and saw that there were birds and animals all over the sheet, a swallow, a horse, a fox, a pig, an eagle…

What the…?

He looked at the other sheets. Two were like the first one, animals all over the place. One had fewer animals but made up for it with a much more complicated set of lines. That would be the level below the Great Hall, where there was space for a lot more rooms. One was simpler, with fewer lines and only two or three animals. That must be the hidden level. The top half of the final sheet was filled by a few simple lines running to and fro across the page. No pictures. Just one shaft with an entrance, and two grid symbols he hadn't seen anywhere else. The dungeons. And below that a patch of writing on one side of the page and on the other a column of single symbols with two or three words beside them. Nigel recognised at once what he was looking at. Not single syllables, but a list of map-symbols and their meanings. The need-to-knows.

So what did they need to know, the people the map was meant for? The hidden entrances, spy-holes, shafts, drop-traps and so on. And there they were, tiny icons, obvious the moment you knew how to read them; a square with a line down the middle—two entrance slabs; oval with pointy ends—he drew a dot into the middle of one and it became an eye—spy-hole; square with three lines across it—rungs in a shaft; square with slant line across and a thicker line running down from its centre—see-saw—drop-trap; those grids—the iron gratings that sealed off the tunnel through which they'd escaped; and two he didn't recognise, a couple of horizontal lines a little way apart, and two columns of shorter horizontal lines (more rungs?) joined at the top by the same pair of lines.

So far so good, but not good enough. You were creeping along this pitch dark passage with nothing but a blank wall either side, apart from one place where a spy-hole let in a glimmer of light. Somewhere in that wall was a place where the mortar would give way and let you insert a key like Taeela's and unlock the entrance marked on the map. She hadn't gone poking around. She'd known exactly where to find the shaft.

He'd heard the mutter of her voice, counting. She'd needed his torch…

Memory shaped the image in his mind, Taeela's figure, black against the glow of the torch, the endless line of identical slabs at the foot of the wall fading away into darkness…There was only one thing she could be counting. The slabs themselves.

He chose a line and followed it along. The same pattern

repeated itself the whole way. First one of the map symbols, a spy-hole, say, then a letter in a circle, then an entrance, another circled letter, a corner, a circled letter…

The circled letters weren't letters, they were numbers. Numbers of slabs between one point and the next.

Got it!

He straightened, stretched his arms wide, threw his head back and breathed a deep, exultant breath. The sunlight that had shone slantwise on the table now streamed across him. He'd been sitting on his stool, barely moving, for over an hour. The muezzin was calling the faithful to prayer from the minaret across the square.

What next? Try and draw some of the passages out as they actually were. The only part of the palace he knew enough about was the bit around the room where they'd spent that awful, endless afternoon surrounded by the guardian rabbits that Fohdrahko had drawn for Taeela when she was a small child. The hidden level was the simplest sheet anyway.

There were only three animals on it. The one in the bottom left-hand corner was a rabbit. No it wasn't. The tiny, delicate drawing was a hare. Not guardian rabbits—guardian hares. That had been the Hare Room. The rooms—at least the ones that mattered—were named after animals. Wherever there was an animal there was a room.

To the left of the hare a passage led to the shaft by which they'd reached it. Just below the hare was the entrance to the room. A little box beside it represented the room itself and a dotted line across the box led to another entrance and the passage beyond. At this point the line on the map curved back up the page, but there was the corner they'd turned into the long stretch across the front of the Great Hall.

By the time Mizhael came to fetch him he had the ground plan of the whole of that corner of the hidden level sketched out clearly enough to show how Fohdrahko's map worked. But that was only the easy bit, the stuff he'd seen. Just a tiny part of the immense, haunted labyrinth. And it was only the passages. What about the honeycomb of rooms the other side of the spy-holes? The assault party would need to know about them. He'd seen the Great Hall and Taeela's living room and the lobby outside it and part of the President's offices, and that was all. Maybe he could work out some of the rest of it from the measurements of the passages once he and Lily-Jo had got them sorted, but it would take for ever. He'd have to ask Taeela. She'd lived there most of her life. And Rahdan would know about the bits the guards used...

"Never mind about that—it's a great start," said Mizhael. "Show Lily-Jo. You played *Monsters of the Maze*? She was working on that when I met her. I tell her she's wasted cooking noodles. Lunch now, anyway, and then we'll go and make your phone call."

Lily-Jo had done them Chinese food, and it was pretty good, but Nigel was too brain-dead to feel hungry. Fortunately Doglu had decided that black hair wasn't scary, the way blond was, so Nigel and Mizhael kept him amused by hiding toys for him to find while Lily-Jo took what Nigel had done away to scan it section by section onto her computer.

After lunch Mizhael got a great big beast of a quad bike out of the garages at the back of the palace and clipped a large black case with an odd bulge in the lid onto the rack behind the rear seat. They roared up through the narrow streets to a turreted gateway, and out onto the ridge above Sodalka. The road was little more than a steep track along the southern flank of the ridge, with terraced fields and orchards below it, but only a boulder-and-scrub-strewn slope above. After a mile or so they turned off and threaded their way up a slope almost as steep as a roof, stopping at a small natural platform at the crest of the ridge. Sodalka's russet tiles and green or gold domes and leafy courtyards were beneath them on their left. Only a few modern-looking buildings lay outside the ancient walls, lining the main road south. Beyond the city the limitless mottled plain reached away westward.

"Pretty, uh?" said Mizhael. "Doesn't bear thinking what a bomb or two might do to it. I'll be a few minutes setting up."

Nigel took some photos for his blog, if ever he got back to it, then looked for birds. A dust cloud emerged from behind the next ridge and began to circle towards the city. The dark shape or shapes that produced it came and went in the swirling dust, but resolved through his monocular into about a dozen horsemen, one of them holding a little red and black pennon.

"You've got visitors," he said

"That's the Akhlavals," said Mizhael, glancing up. "They're a primitive lot. They've got perfectly good jeeps, but they're putting on a show for the Khanazhana. There's a couple of chaps there might come in on things."

"You're going to tell them what we're trying to do?"

"Those two, maybe, in a day or two. Most of 'em we're taking the line that the Khanazhana's offer is just a crazy kid's idea, and we're going to use her to negotiate for what we can get, our own people back, for a start, and then some kind of a constitution plus a say in what's in it, etcetera, etcetera.

"Same time we're getting in touch with some of the Varaki units in the army. Akhlaval's brother's a colonel, and there's plenty of others going to be pretty disaffected—we've got to do stuff like that or the bastards in DD'll get suspicious…Nearly there…"

While he was talking Mizhael had connected various leads from the case to a small satellite dish on a folding tripod, and others to the battery of the quad bike. He used a compass to align the dish, aiming it horizontally out across the plain. When he was satisfied he put on a pair of headphones and twiddled control knobs, then made a brief test call on an ordinary handset, rang off and gave the handset to Nigel.

"Set this up for business purposes," he said. "There's a mast out there, sixty kilometres over the border. We've got our own mast, but everything's monitored. You should be safe with this."

Nigel dialled carefully and waited through the clicks and beeps and silences. At last his father answered.

"British Embassy in Dirzhan. Ambassador speaking."

"Hi, Dad."

"Nigel! You appear to be in Kyrgyzstan."

"Oh…it just looks like that, I suppose. Can't explain."

"Never mind. There's a rumour that the Khanazhana's in Sodalka."

"Um…"

"No, better not tell me. I'm afraid your mother's out. My fault. I pretty well forced her to get out of the embassy for a bit, while the curfew was lifted."

"Hell! Hang on. Mike, any chance we do this again tomorrow? Mum's out…. Same time?…Did you get that, Dad?"

"That should be all right. I take it you're safe with friends for the moment."

"Yes, we're all fine. Will you tell Rick?"

"Ah…His family's still with you, then? I'm afraid I've got some disturbing news for you to pass on to them. Tell me, that first call you made to us—you did it from his house?"

"Yes."

"That explains it then. Yesterday the authorities lifted some of their emergency measures and Rick went down to check on his house and hasn't come back. The authorities claim to be making every effort to find him, but we've reason to believe they've got him and are planning to charge him with helping the Khanazhana to escape. They'll claim he doesn't have diplomatic immunity because he's got Dirzhani citizenship."

"Bastards! Yes, I'll tell Janey. Does that mean they've got everything under control?"

"By no means. There's still a night curfew in Dara Dahn, road blocks, foot patrols, house searches and so on. My impression is that their hold is pretty precarious, with most of the army still sitting on the fence. There's rumours of a mutiny in the barracks at Dorvadu and unrest elsewhere. I and my diplomatic colleagues are pressing them to draw up a provisional constitution leading to the introduction of democratic government. Can you give me any kind of a line on Varaki reactions?"

"They're hopping mad. The Dirzh lot are still holding seven of their chieftains hostage in Dara Dahn. Some of them are all set for a fight, which they'd lose. But most of them know that, so they want to try and sort things out, get their hostages back, have a say in the constitution, all that."

"Useful as far as it goes. I have deliberately not asked you about the Khanazhana. I'll leave it to you to tell me what you can, when you can."

"Well…Hang on…"

He'd turned in response to a touch on his elbow. Mizhael made an urgent gesture for him to ring off and pointed south. Three large helicopters had appeared, two or three miles away.

"Sorry, Dad," he said. "Something's happening."

"All right. I'll tell your mother you're safe and well, and will call tomorrow."

"Thanks, Dad."

"Good luck, Niggles."

He signed off. Mizhael was already starting to dismantle his equipment. Nigel gave him the handset and watched the approaching helicopters. They had almost reached the walls of Sodalka when they swung out over the desert and then in again to circle the city. Mizhael rose and stood shielding the dish with his body as they clattered along beside the ridge, well below the level where he and Nigel were standing. The horsemen on the plain below had stopped to watch.

"Probably just a show of strength," he muttered, hurriedly stuffing the leads and cables loose into the case. He fitted the dish into the bulge in the lid, crammed it shut and clipped the case onto the rack.

"Sort it out when we're home," he said, handing Nigel the collapsed tripod. "You're going to have to cope with this. Hop on."

By the time he started the engine the helicopters had completed their circuit of Sodalka and were beginning another. Two of them swung on along the same course as before, but the third peeled off and climbed directly towards the quad-bike as it jolted down the hill.

"Don't worry," Mizhael shouted over his shoulder. "They can't land on this slope."

The bike bucked and tilted. Nigel clung to Mizhael's waist with his right arm while his left cuddled the tripod uncomfortably into his stomach. His shoulder was starting to hurt again. The helicopter came directly at them, passing only a few feet above them, with the battering downdraught of its rotors sending the dust and grit of the hillside stingingly into their faces.

Then it was gone. A bit of grit had got under Nigel's left eyelid, blinding him with tears, but through the growl of the bike's engine he heard the helicopter clatter away, turn, turn twice more, and now it was on their tail, directly above them…And staying there. Deliberately keeping them in its hideous downdraught, as if it was trying to batter them into surrender.

"Hold tight! Lean left!" yelled Mizhael.

Nigel let go of him, grabbed the side of his saddle and moved with Mizhael as he swung his whole body-weight inwards and the bike lurched violently to the left.

He'd misjudged it! They were going over!

But then they were bumping along the slope, momentarily out of the awful storm, with the thunder of the rotors below them on their right. Somehow the grit had wept itself out from under Nigel's eyelid. He wiped the side of his face against Mizhael's shoulder and now through the blur of tears he could see the dark shape edging back towards them, tilted to an angle where it looked as if the pilot was trying to slice their heads off with the rotor tips as he passed over them.

"Right!" yelled Mizhael.

That meant letting go of both saddle and tripod and swapping hands, then grabbing the tripod as it slithered from his lap. They charged downhill through the edge of the storm. When Nigel opened his eyes the helicopter was behind them, but already turning to head them off again.

The manoeuvre repeated itself, once, twice, three times, with variations, the pilot getting better at the game each time. That was obviously how he thought of it. He was having fun, the cat tormenting the helpless wren. Once, when the helicopter passed close beside him, Nigel thought he could see jeering faces at the small windows. Louts in a street gang watching some of their mates beat up a passer-by.

Mizhael had headed directly down the hill, avoiding the road where the helicopter could land. Out on the slope they could dodge and weave as they bucketed slantwise down towards the gates of the city. They'd only a few hundred yards to go, with the helicopter on their tail again, when Mizhael steered them just below a larger than usual boulder, yelled "Left!", swung round it and roared up the slope.

Deafened by the combined clamour of their engine and the rotors, and wrestling to keep his seat and hang on to the tripod, Nigel didn't realise anything had happened until Mizhael slowed, turned and looked over his shoulder. Nigel did the same, and stared.

The wreckage of the helicopter lay beside the boulder with the dust of the crash still settling round it. There was no sign of any other movement. Mizhael cut the engine.

"Bloody idiots," he said. "Must have caught a rotor. We'd better get out of here. The other two will be back any minute. You OK?"

"Suppose so," Nigel muttered, still staring. Those jeering faces.

They'd belonged to real people, full of life.

The helicopter exploded. A glaring ball, blinding sight. A bellowing roar and a blast of searing air, riddled with grit, lashing into his face.

"Hold tight," said Mizhael and drove off, stopping again when they were well clear of the wreck. Nigel forced his eyes open. His face was stinging sore. Something trickled into the corner of his mouth. He licked, and found that it was blood.

He twisted round and looked back. The wreck was now a normal blaze, the flames bright orange despite the strong sunlight. Oily black smoke roiled up into the limpid air. And the men were all dead. Dead.

"You've got a cut," said Mizhael.

"Yes, I know. So've you. On your left cheek…Higher. It isn't bleeding much. My face is pretty sore."

"Mine too. Alinu will have something. Hey! They're coming back! We'd better get under cover."

Nigel twisted round to look. The other two helicopters had swung round and were heading straight for them. A moment later the clatter of their rotors was joined by another as a line of horsemen crossed the ridge and raced towards them, riding without reins on the treacherous terrain and loosing off with their AKs as they came. The Akhlavals liked to put on a show all right.

By the time they reached the shelter of the gateway the helicopters were hovering over the wreck and the citizens of Sodalka were massed along the walls, cheering like a football crowd as the quad bike drove through, with their cavalry escort behind them firing triumphant volleys into the air.

CHAPTER 19

Taeela, still in black, brought Janey to supper so that Nigel could tell her the bad news. She listened, stony-faced, and turned to Mizhael.

"Tomorrow I go to Dahn, talk to Nardu for lending you boat," she said. "You choose a good man for coming with me. Money too I will need. I may go, Khanazhana?"

The conversation switched to Dirzhani as she and Mizhael made arrangements. Spicy smells drifted from Lily-Jo's cooking.

"What do you think of the new me?" muttered Nigel. "I like it a lot."

Taeela had stared at him when she had first come in, and then laughed, but Janey had come first.

"I like both yous," she said. "Your face looks sore."

"The helicopter chucked up a lot of gravel and stuff at us, but it's not too bad now, since Alinu got at it."

"You spoke with your father? Lucy is well?"

"She was out, but he told me some other stuff. I'll tell you as soon as Mizhael's stopped talking to Janey. I wanted to tell her about Rick first."

"Yes. Poor Janey...You are sad, Nigel? It was scary what happened to you. So stupid, these men! This never could happen if my father is alive."

"I suppose it was scary, but there wasn't really time for that. I'd got stuff to do, just staying on. No, it was…I didn't see the actual crash, so that wasn't too bad. But when it went up. Those men… They'd been alive just a moment before, laughing at us. Alive. To see them die like that…"

"This is war, Nigel. One little bit of war. If the Varaki fight the Dirzh, many, many times it will happen. We must stop that."

"You think you can take the palace without killing anyone? Sesslizh? Madzhalid? Mr Dikhtar?"

(Take the palace? Crazy. Gameboy fantasy. But it was real for her. Mizhael too, seemingly. It couldn't work, even in Dirzhan. But he'd promised himself that he'd stick by her. And he'd promised his father he'd stay out of it. And nothing would bring the dead men back. He felt really depressed.)

Taeela was looking at him as if she was expecting an answer to something she'd said.

"Sorry," he muttered. "I was thinking about those stupid guys in the helicopter."

"Sesslizh, Madzhalid, and Avron Dikhtar—they are different. They killed my father. I have sworn my vengeance on them. It is the word of the Khan."

"You don't have to kill them. You can put them on trial or something. Anyway you need Mr Dikhtar. He'll tell you all sorts of stuff if he thinks it'll save his skin—who else was in it, who put the money up, that sort of thing. "

Her face hardened.

"It is the word of the Khan, Nigel," she said. "They killed my father."

He couldn't meet her look. There seemed to be a huge gulf between them.

"Your dad tell you anything else, Nick?" said Mizhael.

Nigel pulled himself together and turned.

"Um…they've lifted the curfew a bit—he didn't say how long. There's rumours about a mutiny at Dor-something. Dorvadu?

Dad and the other ambassadors and people are trying to get the Colonels to sign a provisional constitution…"

"That could be useful. Did he say when? See if you can find out next time you talk to him. Not sure how we're going to do that. Don't want the same thing happening tomorrow. After dark tonight, maybe…"

"That would be good."

Lily-Jo came in to tell them that supper was almost ready, and to take Doglu off for Darzha to bathe.

"We will help to bring supper in," said Taeela when she returned. Lily-Jo looked surprised and started to protest, but Taeela spoke to Janey, and Nigel and Mizhael were left alone in the living room. They moved over to the window and stood looking down on the central courtyard.

"Couldn't help hearing what you were talking about," said Mizhael. "I'm afraid she's right, Nick. These guys killed her father. Got to avenge that. Fat chance her brothers will do it, so it's down to her—with her own hands, if she can. No Dirzhak's going to think she's worth anything without that. Let alone have her for Khan. Tell you the truth, I feel that way myself. Not think, Nick. Feel. It's in our genes."

"The vengeance of the Khan."

Taeela's voice, a barely audible whisper, came from behind them.

She was standing by the table, staring at nothing, with a steaming bowl of noodles in her hands. Slowly she turned her head and looked at him. The gulf was still there, but the hardness was gone, and her eyes were sad.

"Do you stop helping me?" she said.

There wasn't a right answer.

"No. No I guess not," he said. "I can't come with you. I've promised Dad I won't get involved. But I'll try and sort that map out for you."

"Best thing you could do," said Mizhael.

They ate mainly in silence. When they sat down the minarets of the city were golden with sunset. When they finished the stars were out behind them.

"Better go and make your call," said Mizhael, pushing his chair back.

"Don't have any more adventures," said Lily-Jo.

The gate of the city was closed and barred, but an armed guard opened it and closed it behind them. They drove quietly up to the ridge, where Nigel held the torch for Mizhael while he set up his dish. The embassy line was engaged, so they sat in silence looking out over the moonlit distances. Invisible below them lay the wreck of the helicopter and the charred bodies of young men.

Second try, they got through, and his father answered.

"British Embassy in Dirzhan. Ambassador speaking."

He sounded tired.

"Hi, Dad. Sorry to call now. Thing is I can't tomorrow. Any chance of talking to Mum?"

"Later. You'll need to do it on the other line. I'll explain in a moment. First though, the interruption this afternoon—had that anything to do with a helicopter, or helicopters?"

"Uh…Uh…"

"I'm sorry, Niggles. I urgently need to know. Two hours ago I received a formal protest from the regime about one of their helicopters on a reconnaissance mission being brought down by insurgents using a ground-to-air missile supplied by the British."

"That's ridiculous!"

"Of course it is. It is clearly a first shot in a campaign to break off negotiations with us over the Vamar dam so that the contract can be taken over by some probably criminal organisation which will have been behind the assassination of the President in the first place."

"That's disgusting! Those men are dead, Dad, and all the bastards can think about…"

"I'm afraid the world's like that, Niggles. All we can do is try to see they don't get away with it. Anything you can tell me may be useful."

"Oh…Well, we'd gone up on the hillside so we could use a special bit of kit—don't tell anyone this part—so that we could get a secure line. Then these helicopters showed up…"

He found it difficult to explain coherently. He was actually shuddering with a of sick, helpless fury that men had died horribly, here on the naked hillside, and someone sitting at a desk in Dara Dahn (or Moscow, or Naples, or whatever) had simply jumped at the chance of using those deaths to help them in a multi-million dollar scam.

"Well, that's a start," said his father. "Any witnesses?"

"Oh, hundreds. They were watching from the walls…Hold it. I bet somebody videoed it. We could download that and e-mail it to you."

"Now, that would be really useful. I await results eagerly. Meanwhile I'd better put what you've told me through to London. I won't say anything about what you were doing on the hill. If you come up with a video of the accident it shouldn't be necessary.

"Now, your call to your mother. I want it on the open line in order to reinforce the idea that you are in Kyrgyzstan. You escaped with the Khanazhana and friends of hers arranged for you to be sent on to Kyrgyzstan for your own safety. You saw the President assassinated in front of your eyes and your escape and journey north were also harrowing experiences…"

"He wasn't the only one."

"Good god! You mean…? No, tell me later. The point is, Niggles, that you aren't in any state to talk to journalists or anyone else. Meanwhile wherever you are you're going to have to do your best not to be recognised…Niggles…?"

"Uh…"

There had been a moment, just that one instant when his father had seemed to understand...He pulled himself together.

"Sorry, Dad. It was something you said. It's all right. I've had my hair dyed, and I've got sunglasses and Dirzhani clothes to wear."

"Good for you. Right, so you give me five minutes to explain to your mother what's up, and then you call her on the open line and tell you're in safe hands and fundamentally OK, only a bit shaken by everything you've been through, and no wonder, from what you tell me. You can ham it up a bit if you like, and I'll tell her that you seem to be in much better nick than you're going to make out for the benefit of listening ears. Think you can manage that, Niggles?"

"I suppose so. When can I talk to her for real? It's not like I can just pick up the phone, Dad. We've got to get all the kit together and come up here and set it up."

"Not tonight, I'm afraid, Niggles. I need to keep this line open. Tomorrow, same time?"

"Thanks, Dad. See you."

"Good luck, Niggles. You're being remarkably useful. Doesn't sound as there's much point telling you to keep out of trouble."

"Doing my best, honestly. See you, Dad."

"Think I got most of that," said Mizhael as soon as he'd signed off. "Should be able to find a video of the crash—see about it soon as we're back. Gather you've got a call to make on an open line."

"Dad wants me to try and make it look as if I'm in Kyrgyzstan."

"Sound notion. See if you can hint so's the Khanazhana—just enough to keep 'em guessing. What was that your dad told you right at the start? Ridiculous, you called it. Then disgusting."

Nigel explained, and he laughed.

"Not much you can't do with a fancy mobile these days," he said. "But bringing down helicopters...Pentagon's probably working on it. Right. Make your call and we'll get out of here."

Nigel's mother answered at the first ring.

"Nigel?"

There was a faint echo on the sound of her voice.

"Hi, Mum."

"Oh, darling! You know you're all over the papers back home. They keep calling up asking me for photos. Helen says you're on TV too."

"That's crazy!"

"Of course it is, but you know what they're like. There's probably not much else happening this time of year. What I want to know is are you all right?"

"I'm OK…. I suppose. I mean people are looking after me, only they don't want me to say where I am. I'm not sick or anything, except I got a bash on my shoulder, but it's stopped hurting, almost. But I've had the hell of a time, Mum. I don't want to talk about it. I don't like being scared, running and hiding, seeing people getting beaten up, killed…"

There wasn't any need to fake it. His voice started to shake. It was difficult to stay in control, to remember the listening ears…

He shook himself and gathered his wits.

"I'm sorry, Mum. I didn't mean to…"

"No, darling. I'm glad you told me. It's important not to bottle that sort of thing up. You've had a hideous time. Let's hope it's over. You really think you're safe where you are now?"

"Safe as can be. They're good guys. One of them was at Balliol."

(Hell! He shouldn't have said that. Listening-ears might be able to work it out.)

"Good lord! Have you told your father?"

"Not yet. Have you been to Sodalka, Mum?"

"I was saving it up to go with you. I'd love to see it."

"I thought it was really cool. Like Dahn must've been when it was just the old city—like a dragon was going to show up any minute. You've got to get Dad to take you there."

Apart from that first outburst it all sounded fake to Nigel's ears, as if they were rehearsing for a play when they'd only just learnt their lines. They managed to chat for a bit about the birds at Forghal, but it was a relief to finish.

At breakfast Mizhael said, "Afraid I'll be tied up mostly today. People to talk to. In Dirzhani mostly. Khanazhana the same. No point your tagging along. Best thing you can do is get on with the map of the palace. Lily-Jo's made you some large-scale outlines of the palace to work on. She's raring to go. Anything you want from Dr. G.?"

"Could you ask him for a list of Old Script numbers?"

"There should be a book in library. I'll come and see what I can find."

Drearily he settled to work. His heart wasn't in it, but at least it was something to stop him thinking about the dead men on the hillside, and how many more dead people there were going to be before this stupid adventure was over, with men like Adzhar Taerzha and Colonel Sesslizh running Dirzhan, and the domes of Sodalka shattered and smoke drifting up from the ruins.

And Taeela made to marry some bastard who was calling himself Khan.

He transferred what he'd worked out yesterday onto one of Lily-Jo's enlarged outlines and pencilled in the stone-counts in Arabic numbers. It was slow work. That done, he guessed how many stones it would take to cross the Hare Room and the passage beyond, doubled it for the opposite wing and added that to the number of stones in the long passage. That gave him the full width of the palace, measured in stones. They were about fifty centimetres wide, but there was no point in converting them. Stones would be fine as a basic measure.

His imagination started to reconstruct the passages as he worked, breathing the chill, unused air with its faint odour of old stonework, seeing Taeela and Fohdrahko moving silently away through the darkness silhouetted against the glow of their torch, with the eerie shadows of long-dead eunuchs watching them pass.

Soon he was absorbed by the task for its own sake. The table was in shadow again when Mizhael came to collect him for lunch.

"Yes," said Lily-Jo. "It's got to be a lot simpler than it looked. Secret passages are like that. If they wandered all over the place the people using the rooms and corridors wouldn't be able to move about, because there'd always be a secret passage in the way. What is this?"

"That's one of the symbols I haven't worked out. I think those lines might be rungs."

"Yes, with a crawl-space between them, to get over a corridor or something. And look. This bit here."

She traced a line along with the tip of her knife.

"When we've straightened it out and opened it up it'll be just one long passage with a few short branches that don't go anywhere. And they're all on one side. These are spy-holes, you say? They're all on that side too. And here's a crawl-space, but no rungs. That will be to get under a window on the other side. You can do that because outside walls are thicker in a building like the palace. And another. And...Look. All the way along. And no corners. So what you've got here is a passage running all along one side of a building. Windows on your left and rooms on your right. A narrow building, or the side-branches would be longer... How many entrances? One, two, three, four, five. Three entrances close together this end, and one in the middle and one at the end. But—how many?—nine spy-holes. So three small rooms and two long ones. Where can we fit that in...?"

"Along the side of the courtyard?" said Nigel. "Look, here. It would have to be this side if that's an outside wall. There's a sort of balcony running the whole way round on the inside."

"You've seen it," said Lily-Jo. "Did you see any doors?"

"Yes, I think so. And windows. All the way along."

"Barracks?" said Mizhael. "Guards got to sleep somewhere. Two rooms for the men and three for the officers. That's the sort of thing we're looking for. Nigel's made a great start, but it's only a start. Not much use our attack party knowing their way round the passages if they're lost soon as they're out of them. So first you get them drawn in as a skeleton, and then you work out how the rooms fit in round them. Right up your street, darling."

"Rahdan'll know about the barracks and stuff," said Nigel. "And Taeela will know how a lot of the other rooms go."

"Right. I'll try and lay that on for tomorrow morning. Thing is, it's becoming a bit urgent. That mutiny at Dorvadu your dad told you about, that wasn't the only one. Some of the Varaki units are beginning to show up back home, fodder for the hot-heads. It'll only take a skirmish or two for the Colonels to send the bombers up. We can't afford to hang about, and none of the guys I want to recruit is going to commit himself without a working plan of the palace.

"Other thing is, we've got to have a target date, Nick. A day we know if the bastards are going to be there, in the palace. They've told us they're keeping Urvdahn Idzhak and the rest of our people in Dara Dahn to sign their draft constitution soon as it's ready. They'll want to make a big show of it, in the Great Hall, in front of the cameras, show the world what good boys they're being. That's our best chance. They'll ask your dad to come along?"

"I expect so."

"OK. I've got hold of two videos of the crash for him. We can e-mail the files off from the ridge tonight, and you can tell him they're on the way, and while you're at it you can see if he knows anything about the date."

"I suppose so."

"You don't like it?"

"If there's going to be fighting…Mum and Dad will be there…"

"Last-minute diplomatic illness, maybe?"

"It'll look as if he knew."

"See what you mean. Tricky. Have to think about it."

"I'd like to call them anyway."

"What would you like to do this afternoon?" said Lily-Jo.

"Go back to the library, I suppose."

"You can't do that all day. You'll go mad. I've got to look for a birthday present for Mike to give one of his sisters. Why don't you come with me? Doglu loves shopping. There might be something you'd like to buy. Ear-rings for your mother? There's several stalls with fun stuff."

"Oh, OK. You'll have to help me choose."

Nigel was reaching for a small amber brooch when someone standing beside him reached out towards the same tray, but instead of picking anything up touched him firmly on the wrist with three fingers and withdrew. He snatched his hand back, thinking he must have done something wrong, but the man had already turned away.

A few minutes later it happened again, this time a brief firm touch on the side of his neck, just behind the ear. He spun round. It was a woman, but again he wasn't quick enough to see her face. Three or four other people were standing there watching him. He smiled and held out his arm.

"Anyone else want a go?" he said.

They stared at him blankly and looked away.

"What on earth was that about?" he said.

"No idea," said Lily-Jo. "I'll ask Darzha."

She'd hardly got three words out when Darzha cut her short with a warning frown and a shake of the head.

"Some sort of superstition, I guess," said Lily-Jo. "Better pretend not to notice if it happens again."

It did, three times. Lily-Jo was on the look-out now.

"They don't mind me watching," she said. "It's you who mustn't see who they are. They pick their moment, and turn away as soon as they've touched you. It's always three fingers laid together like this. One girl had a couple of friends watching. It was like it was a bit of a joke, only it mattered."

In the end Nigel chose a matching brooch and ear-rings, dark brown stones with glints of red deep inside them, like embers. The stall-holder was all smiles, but refused to let him pay for them, and when Nigel tried to insist Darzha dragged him away.

Mizhael laughed when they asked him about it.

"Seems they've decided you're the Khanazhana's baizhan," he said.

"Uh?"

"It means Greek. Byzantine. All the great Khans had baizhani. Didn't have to be human. Morval had an eagle and Diraki had a white mule, but the first one was Agran Alk's favourite Greek slave-boy. Nothing special about him till the battle at Lake Ingru. Boy begged to be let fight. Alk laughed at him and put him under guard, but the boy slipped his guards. Slaves didn't get to use swords but he took one off a dead man and got to Alk's side somehow.

"Battle going badly till then—Chinese archers had 'em pinned against the lake and were picking 'em off one by one—but the moment the boy showed up the clouds broke and the sun shone dazzling off the water straight in the archers' eyes so Alk could storm their position and win the battle."

"You mean I'm a sort of mascot! Taeela's teddy bear?"

"'Fraid so, Nick. You shouldn't have brought that helicopter down. Just the sort of stupid bit of luck sets something like this off. And you'd breathed darm. That'd open you up to this sort of thing People can get a share of the luck if they touch you, but it's the Khan's luck they're stealing. When Alk caught them trying it he had their hand cut off. So they mustn't let you see who's taken it. And you can't just let them touch you because the luck isn't yours to give, it's the Khan's."

"That's really stupid. How do I resign…? What's the problem?"

"Sorry. Just thought. Better take this seriously, because people do here. You know how the Chinese try to get their babies born in the year of the ox? They know it's a superstition, but that doesn't stop them acting on it."

"Darzha wouldn't even let us ask her about it."

"That figures. Unlucky to talk about, specially to you. Even me—now I'm telling you, well, I'd sooner it was someone else. Anyway, no, you can't resign, Nick. Point is, if the Khanazhana's got her own baizhan, that shows she really is the Khan. That's how we think in Dirzhan. The guys I've been talking to about are keen to go, but they've all told me they're going to need something extra to bring enough of their mates in. This might be it. Or part of it"

"The crash was an accident, Mike! I didn't make it happen. If anyone did, it was you, dodging round that rock!"

"I don't suppose Alk's baizhan struck a single blow at Ingru. Luck's like that."

"Well, if you think I'm going to show up at the palace with somebody's sword in my hand, you're wrong."

That night they sent their e-mails from the ridge under a starry sky, and Nigel made his call. As it turned out his father wanted to know anything he could tell him about Varaki attitudes to the constitution and mentioned the date in passing. They had eight days.

CHAPTER 20

Back in the library next morning Nigel carried on where he'd left off, until Mizhael turned up with fresh outline plans of the different floors of the palace, including the stuff he and Lily-Jo had worked out yesterday. He drew in what he'd just done and carried on. Images of the passages, their darkness, their stillness, formed unwilled in his mind as he drew them in.

He was working on the area round the President's offices when Mizhael came back with Taeela, Rahdan, two men about his own age and one greybeard. Janey was on her way to Dara Dahn, so Taeela's companion was a veiled woman called Satila who waited in the background, not uttering a word.

Rahdan, it turned out, couldn't read or write, and the greybeard was there to do it for him. But he got what was wanted of him almost at once and took it seriously, sucking his pencil as he frowned at the plan, and then deliberately and neatly drawing in a line or two and sucking his pencil again. They had been right in their guess about the barracks, which was encouraging.

The two younger men were the Akhlaval brothers. Urvan asked most of the questions. He was taller and skinnier than Mizhael, quick-eyed, with a hard, intelligent face. Izhvan was the younger one, a couple of inches shorter, his face broader and flatter, with prominent cheek-bones. He greeted Nigel with a mutter and an unsettling stare.

Urvan spoke almost entirely to Mizhael, though it was usually Taeela who knew the answers. He would look at her without expression while she told him what he wanted to know and immediately turn back to Mizhael. Taeela gave no sign that she noticed this treatment, but Nigel minded for her, so as soon as he could he moved across to the other table.

He minded for himself too, feeling left out, on the fringe of things, though he'd have been useless in the palace, except for knowing his way around a few of the secret passages. And scared stiff. Still, it was hard to become absorbed in the task again. Taeela's presence and the voices at the other table disturbed his concentration. He glanced across and saw the Akhlaval brothers, their heads close together, frowning down at one of the outline plans. Izhvan looked up and caught his eye and didn't look away. When he returned to the passages Izhvan was there, leading his comrades through the maze in secrecy and darkness, peering about him with that unnerving gaze.

Mizhael's voice scattered the vision.

"They're going to need a base, Nick. A room where the advance party can hole up, find their way around, check if the opposition have got into the passages beyond the bit we know about, etcetera, etcetera. Khanazhana says there are rooms on this side like the one you call the Hare Room over that side, but she doesn't know which…"

"We've done that bit—I've got it here," said Nigel and waited for them to come over. "Look. Here it is on Fohdrahko's map—this one. The beetle means there's a room there. That's its entrance, and that's a spy-hole into it. You reach it by this shaft. So here it is on the plan we're doing. There's the corner of the palace. There's the shaft. There's that bit of passage. There's the entrance and the spy-hole. So the Beetle Room's got to be in here, but we haven't worked out how big it is yet. We're doing the passages first."

Muttering doubtfully to each other, the brothers stared to and fro between the two plans. Eventually Urvan's frown cleared. He looked directly at Nigel and nodded: If you say so.

"OK," said Mizhael. "You go and have lunch now, and we'll see what Lily-Jo can make of it. Tell her you've got three days. Think you can do it, Nick?"

Three days?

"Guess we'll have to," he said.

Lily-Jo seemed able to carry whole stretches of a plan in her head, as if she'd lifted the roof off a doll's-house. Nigel worked with her all afternoon, sorting out the rest of the level he'd started on. Taeela had already roughed in the Khan's private apartments and offices. On the top three floors a single basic passage ran along either side of the palace, hidden in the outer walls of the building, with occasional short side-branches. The only passage across the front of the building was the one on the hidden level which they had used in their escape.

The section between the great hall and the courtyard was much deeper and more complicated. The main passage twisted to and fro through it, with side branches right and left, several times converting into crawl-ways to get past some obstacle. Taeela had sketched in a few of the rooms, but the puzzle would have been insoluble without the Google Earth image, which showed three small courtyards acting as light-wells for internal rooms that otherwise would have been windowless. Fohdrahko's map gave no hint of their existence.

They had worked steadily for over three hours when Lily-Jo pushed her chair back, yawned and stretched.

"Time for a break," she said. "My brain's dead. Yours too, I guess."

"Yeah. Bad as chess, almost."

"OK, we'll take Doglu out shopping. If there's anything you

want, just tell me. If you try to buy it yourself, looks like they'll give it to you."

That didn't work. They wandered round Sodalka for almost an hour in the golden, dusty late afternoon. Not one of the stall-holders would accept any payment. Some of them even darted out as Nigel approached and thrust a gift into his hands. All he could do was thank them and smile and wish them luck. Five times he felt the light touch of fingers on the side of his neck, but after the first start of surprise he walked on as if he hadn't noticed. In a shady little square the owner of a stall with a few tables in front of it pulled out chairs as they approached, imploringly inviting them to sit.

"Better had," said Lily-Jo. "Treat for Doglu. I don't usually let him."

The stall-holder brought them tall, strange-shaped blue tumblers—made from melted-down medicine-bottles, Lily-Jo said—of an ice-cold bittersweet fruit drink, and a mound of sticky little cakes, which Doglu studied intently for at least a minute, as if the fate of the world depended on his choice, before delicately picking one out.

There had been only two other customers when they arrived, but by the time they rose to go every chair was full and a dozen people were standing around sipping their drinks and looking away the moment Nigel turned in their direction. He did his best to hide his discomfort and wished the stall-holder good luck, as usual.

"You've brought him that already," whispered Lily-Jo as they left. "That's got to be his best afternoon for months. Are you up for another stint on the maps?"

"I suppose so if you are. And if you've got the time."

"I'll send out for a take-away. I want to get this done. It's for Mike. So that he doesn't feel guilty about not going along with the others. That makes two of us, I guess."

"Sort of."

"Doglu's perfectly happy with Darzha. Besides it's good for me to practise. I'm hot stuff at this kind of thing, and I don't want to lose that."

They worked on until Mizhael brought Taeela and Satila, her silent companion, in for supper, but in fact nobody spoke much more than she did. There was only one subject on everyone's mind, but none of them seemed to want to talk about it.

"What did you two do this afternoon?" said Mizhael.

"We got on with the plans for a bit," said Lily-Jo. "Then we took Doglu out and did a bit of shopping; only people kept trying to give poor Nick stuff. Old Dahdbu in Olzha Square stood us primh and a mountain of seed-cakes. Doglu thought he'd hit heaven. Then we came back and got on some more. We'll show you after supper."

"People seem to have decided Nick is your baizhan, Khanazhana," said Mizhael.

Taeela turned slowly to Nigel and looked him in the eye.

"I knew this before we came to Sodalka," she said.

"No you didn't," said Nigel. "It's nonsense. It makes me feel a total phoney. Can't you tell them to stop, Mike?"

"Inside my father's house, maybe. In Sodalka, no."

"It is not good to talk about it," said Taeela, in an almost-whisper.

Nigel stared at her. She nodded seriously.

"OK, forget it," he said. "It's only a few more days, I guess."

They ate on in silence.

Next day Lily-Jo and Nigel worked steadily on the plans all morning, broke off to have lunch and play with Doglu for a while, and did another solid stint through the heat of the afternoon. Then Lily-Jo drove him, with Doglu and Darzha, several miles out across the plain to a solitary reed-fringed pool fed by some underground spring. Two boys were watering a flock of goats along its further edge. Birds came and went. The reeds were noisy with their strange calls. Meanwhile Doglu crouched at the water's edge with Darzha gripping his collar while he tickled the water with the tip of a reed Lily-Jo had cut for him and watched the ripples move.

Driving back to Sodalka it struck Nigel that it had been the first normal peaceful, stress-free time he'd known since those shots had cracked across the Great Hall of the palace and the President had crumpled onto the stairs.

After supper Mizhael drove Nigel up the hill to call the embassy. His father was out, so Roger and put the call through to his mother.

"Hi, Mum. How's things?"

"Oh, darling! Are you all right?"

"I'm fine. They're looking after me very well. It's just a bit boring being stuck here, not seeing you, and worrying about you worrying about me. Any news about the girls?"

For several minutes they managed to talk family stuff, but even that seemed forced and strained.

"I think that's enough, don't you, darling?" she said after a while. "Give my love to Taeela. I'll tell Nick you called and you're all right."

"What's he up to?"

"It's a sort of get-together with some of the other ambassadors to agree a common front about the famous constitution. They've twisted the brutes' arms to get them to sign one at all. It'll be a complete sham, of course, but…"

"I hope you're not going, Mum."

"No, of course not! Sit in the room where I saw him murdered and watch the men who did it preening and posturing! I'd sooner die!"

"Good for you. I suppose Dad's got to go."

"He thinks so. It's all about the stupid dam, of course. It's sickening!"

"Right."

They said goodbye and signed off. Nigel's sigh as he gave Mizhael back the handset was a mixture of worry and relief. How to get the Akhlavals and their wild followers to understand that they mustn't go loosing off their guns at random in the Great Hall?

"OK," said Lily-Jo next morning. "We're not going to get it all done. Let's see how long it takes us to finish the lower floor. I've had a couple of ideas about that. If there's any time left we'll have a go at the top storey, and then that's it. They shouldn't need anything else, and it'd take another day to finish the lot."

In fact it took them all morning and two hours into the afternoon to sort out the maze of outer rooms and windowless cells below the Great Hall, and the corridors and secret passages threading their way among them. By the time they broke off they had a complete floor-plan of the palace apart from the top floor, where the old khans' wives and children had lived, and the palace servants' quarters running along the western wing of the courtyard.

"I guess that'll have to do," said Lily-Jo. "I'll call Mike, and then I'll take Doglu out. Want to come?"

All those furtively watching eyes?

"No thanks. Tell him to bring Taeela up, if she's free. And Rahdan. They'd better check it over."

"That is wonderful," said Taeela. "Thank you, Nigel. You have worked so hard."

"Well, I wanted to do something."

He got it wrong. He could hear the undertone of ruefulness and resentment even as he spoke the words.

"Yes, it has been hard for you at Sodalka," she murmured, so quietly that she might have been speaking to herself.

"I guess so. Can't be helped."

"Hard for me too. I think of you every day. And Lucy."

"I talked to her last night. She sent you her love."

"When this is finished we will all go to the hunting lodge again and be happy together."

"If only."

"No, Nigel. Not if only. One day. Soon."

The moment Nigel turned out the light the great maze started swimming and shifting behind his eyelids. Deliberately he chose a passage and worked his way along it, spy-holes, entrances, shafts, booby-traps…they were all there, inside his head, many of the slab-counts, even, as if his brain had been some kind of memory stick slotted into Lily-Jo's PC for her to send the file to.

He wasn't aware of falling asleep, only now he was feeling his way through the almost-dark, followed by a line of armed men, all of them relying on him to find the way, each one as tense as a hunted animal. He had one hand on the masonry at his side, the other holding his torch pointed down at the slabs as he numbered them off. Ten, eleven, twelve, and there was the spy-hole into the Ibex Room, where they could relax and rest. The entrance would be three slabs beyond it. He rose on tip-toe to peer through…

And he was looking not into the Ibex Room but into a dungeon cell, with a known figure hunched on the bench—known by the ash-blond hair bowed despairing over the knees. He turned, but the men who had been following him were gone, lost somewhere else in the haunted maze. Where was the Ibex Room? Where was he? As he stood fumbling with the folds of the map three chill fingers were laid against the side of his neck. His torch went out.

Only a nightmare. He knew that before he woke. He wouldn't be there.

"Crunch moment," said Mizhael as he led Nigel across the courtyard next morning. "Everyone's coming."

"Who's everyone?"

"The Khanazhana, of course," said Mizhael. "The Akhlavals. Varat Vulnad and Benni Dorzh from the West Dirzh, Ammun Amla from the East Dirzh and old Uncle Doglu to help the hold everything together."

"I thought they all hated each other."

"Not as bad as that. Varat's my first cousin. Several Akhlavals have married Dirzhi over the years. A lot of people, not just us Varaki, aren't at all happy about the coup. President did pretty well by the country at large, provided you toed the line. More in people's pockets, crime way down, corruption a tenth what it used to be, good hospitals, schools for the kids, food in the markets, etcetera, etcetera. Everyone knows these bastards aren't interested in any of that. All they want is to do well by themselves. And the Khanazhana's got this bee in her bonnet about Dirzh being her people too—can't only be us getting rid of the bastards, got to bring them in somehow if the countercoup's going to stick. Uncle Doglu's backed her up on that."

"I thought he..."

"Yeah, I was surprised. Old boy's got bloody good intelligence. Says Adzhar Taerzha's dead set on having a go at Sodalka and he's talked the colonels into making an example of us, keep the rest in line. Doglu says we've got to get our blow in first, and this looks like our best chance."

"If it works. Everything's got to go dead right."

"Yeah. Better had. In here, Nick."

By now they had turned in through a door under main arch of the courtyard, climbed a stairway and reached an impressive pair of doors.

"Council chamber," muttered Mizhael. "Good big table. Doglu fixed it. Don't know what he told Dad. Doesn't matter. Dad doesn't want to know."

Inside the room the prickle of argument hung in the air. Several pairs of eyes swung to stare at Nigel. Only Izhvan Akhlaval didn't instantly look away.

Mizhael introduced the three strangers: Varat Vulnad was about Mizhael's age, serious looking; Ammun Amla was younger and smiled shyly when Nigel said hello; Benni Dorzh was small, wiry, bright-eyed, at least ten years older than any of the others. He answered Nigel's greeting English.

"Good morning, Mister Nick."

The accent was Dirzhani crossed with American.

"Right," said Mizhael. "Let's have a look at these plans."

Nigel opened Lily-Jo's portfolio and laid the sheets out on the table in the order the attackers would come to them.

"These are the dungeons," he said. "You come in from the river up beside the sewer. There's a gate here. You use it to climb across, and open it this side. Taee…The Khanazhana's got the key. Then you come along this side of the sewer to this door—the key's hidden in the wall, here…"

And so on, with long pauses while Mizhael translated, until they had climbed the first shaft. He laid the next three sheets out one above the other, with a small scale one beside them to show how they fitted together.

"That's the shaft you've been in," he explained. "Lily-Jo's marked all the shafts in green and the secret passages in red. You're in one now, on the level below the Great Hall…"

Mutters of doubt broke began as Mizhael translated.

"It's all right. The other levels are much simpler. Look. This is the courtyard back here. You can see there's just one passage running all along this side, with a few short ones branching off. Most of the palace is like that, round the Great Hall. And it's not that difficult to find your way about once…"

He dried up. No one was listening. The mutters were louder now, and not just doubt. Dismay. Somebody asked a question. Mizhael answered without translating, explaining something, trying to calm things down. All the men answered at once, except Uncle Doglu. Mizhael gestured desperately, his voice unheard. Izhvan Akhlaval snatched up two sheets of the plan, ripped them across and across and stared at Nigel with that half-mad gaze.

Taeela seized the moment of silence and started to speak, just as Nigel had heard her speak to her father in the hide at the owl sanctuary, pleading and passionate. They listened, shaking their heads. She turned to Uncle Doglu and asked a question. He replied calmly, sensibly, telling her she was wrong. She looked at Nigel.

"Trouble?" he said, ridiculously. Even if he hadn't heard the anger in the men's voices he would have seen the answer in her face.

"They say you must go with them, Nigel. If you don't, they will not do it. I told them I will go. I know the passages better than you. They say that is no good. It must be you."

"You've told them I can't. I promised Dad. Honestly, the plans aren't that difficult, nothing like as bad as they…"

"It is not about the plans, Nigel…"

"You remember what happened to you in the market?" said Mizhael.

"Oh, not that! It's rubbish!"

"They won't talk about it—that's bad luck in itself—but… Look, this is a risky business, going to need a lot of luck. They're staking their lives on it…"

Mizhael's voice trailed away. Nigel barely noticed. He was watching Taeela. She returned his look, deliberately blank-faced, not pitiful or pleading or trying to put any pressure on him. But behind the mask…

He had seen her weeping after her father's death, but even in the pit of misery she had been undefeated, defiant. Not now. Her one chance was gone, and she knew it.

A moment ago he had heard her arguing with all her soul-force that he must be allowed to keep his promise to his father. She'd stood by him, though she must have known what it might mean. He swallowed.

"All right," he croaked. "I'll come."

They understood without translation. The tension eased.

Murmurings began.

"Wait," he said. "Tell them I'm breaking my promise to my father…That's a big deal. I want something in exchange…"

The pauses for translation gave him time to think.

"I know why you really want me in on this. I don't believe in it myself, but that doesn't make any difference…It isn't going to work, is it, if you have to tie me up and drag me along with you? I have to come of my own free will…And there's got be a reason for me being there, like helping you find your way around the secret passages…

"Well, I'll do all that provided you promise me that there'll be as little fighting as possible, and you won't shoot anyone unless you absolutely have to…If they start shooting at you you'll have to shoot back I suppose, but like I say, as little as possible…Stuff like settling old feuds, that's out. Right…?"

He waited, letting them take it in. The Akhlavals didn't like it at all. Judging his moment he went on.

"You too, Khanazhana. You talked about taking vengeance on your father's murderers… With your own hands… That's out… You can arrest them and put them on trial—I hope you do—but that's it… I think they're total bastards and they deserve everything that's coming to them, but not like that… If you can't promise me that, then I'm out… Is it a deal, Khanazhana?"

They stared at each other. The men muttered among themselves and fell silent. Nigel was strongly conscious of them, full-grown adults, about to risk their lives on the outcome of what might have been a playground argument between two children.

Taeela nodded slowly, twice.

"It is a deal, Nigel," she whispered.

He walked round the table and offered her his hand, palm up.

"Word of the Khan, Taeela?" he said.

She took it between both of hers.

"Word of the Khan, Nigel," she said firmly, and repeated the oath in Dirzhani.

There was a thin moon setting in the western sky as the quad bike climbed the spur and halted at the platform.

"What are you going to tell them?" said Mizhael as he set up the dish.

This was the moment Nigel had felt sick in his stomach about from the moment Taeela had given him her word, worse even than the whole hideous business of going along on this crazy, impossible adventure. He couldn't tell his parents the truth. He loathed the idea of lying to them.

"We're going somewhere else and there isn't a secure line there, so whoever's listening will know where we are. Best I could do—sort of true—but I don't like it. They'll know."

"Tough," said Mizhael off-handedly.

Even he hadn't got it. He was too wrapped up in his own plans. Nigel felt utterly alone as he took the handset.

The usual clicks and whistles and silences.

"Ambass—"

Piano music.

He almost dropped the handset in his haste to ring off.

"What's up?" said Mizhael.

"Someone listening."

"Let me try."

He dialled, spoke briefly, listened and rang off.

"Hell, you're right," he said. "You can usually tell. Wonder how they did that. Bloody nuisance. Never mind, Nick. I'll get a message to your parents somehow. Anyway we won't be using this system for a while."

He wasn't a good liar. He had got it, after all. He must have fixed for this to happen so as to let Nigel off the hook. It was still a sort of lying, but at least he didn't have to tell the lie himself.

"Thanks anyway," he said.

He spent his last day in Sodalka bringing his blog up to date. He knew he was never going to be able to post it, whatever happened, but at least Mizhael would be able to send it on to his parents one day so that they'd know what had happened to him, and why he'd done what he'd done.

CHAPTER 21

Somebody shook Nigel out of his dream.

"Boat coming now, Nick." whispered a voice. Benni Dorzh.

Achingly he pushed himself into a sitting position, and found that he had been lying on somebody's coat with his head on his bag. His shoulder was acting up. The last he could remember was sitting by the tailgate in the back of the pick-up watching the dusty road reel away behind them in the almost-dusk, just as it had been doing all through the blazing day.

Now it was full night, a half moon rising in the east, the sky above dark velvet and full of stars. The rippled waters of the lake twinkled with their reflections, streaked here and there with the brighter gleam of a light-lure on one of the boats. Another darkness jutted out a little way over the water. The shapes of men moved to and fro on it.

Benni helped Nigel to his feet, picked up the coat and gave him his shoulder bag, and then helped him stumble down onto what turned out to be a rough old timber quay. Chugging softly, the approaching boat nosed in. The gunwale bumped against timber. Ropes were thrown and hauled tight. With a few low-voiced words the men loaded the guns and stores and climbed aboard, leaving only the driver to take the pick-up away.

There seemed to be eight of them now, the five who'd come

from Sodalka, two crewmen from the boat, and one who turned out to be Rick's friend Nardu, the boat-owner, who had been waiting for the Sodalka party at the quay. The boat was oddly broad in the beam with a foremast and a short deck fore and aft, but was otherwise open. A stubby pole, not a mast, rose from the centre of the well. A small pile of something gleamed around its foot. A tarpaulin covered the three boxes of guns close to the foredeck. An uninterpretable darkness filled the further end of the well

They chugged a little way clear of the shore and drifted to a standstill. Nardu said something. Benni tugged at Nigel's sleeve.

"Now he light his light," he said. "We gotta get down so guys in other boats not see us."

Nigel crouched alongside the others. With a fizz and a crackle a light blazed, blinding, at the top of the pole. It sparked and popped as insects flung themselves against it. The dark mass beyond turned out to be fair-sized inflatable.

Almost at once the reason for the boat's odd shape became apparent. There was a splash from nearby followed by a slap as a fish landed in the well of the boat. Before it had finished flopping about another one joined it.

Nardu laughed and spoke. Nigel, conscious of eyes switched towards him and instantly away, didn't need to wait for Benni's translation.

"He say someone bring him luck."

Mercifully it didn't go on like that. The fish leaped in erratically in a brief, gleaming arc, two or three almost together and then none for several minutes. They were about the size of small mackerel, with blunt heads and silvery-green bodies. The crewmen sorted them out as they flopped and gasped, throwing the larger ones onto the gleaming pile round the foot of the mast and the rest back into the water.

This lasted an hour or so, until one by one the engines of the other boats woke to life and they chugged away. Their engine-notes rose as they drove into the river current. Nardu waited a few minutes before he followed and the passengers could rise with sighs of relief and stretch their limbs.

All the way back to Dara Dahn Nigel yawned with weariness and tension. The crewmen got on with their normal night's work of sorting their catch into wicker baskets. The lake narrowed and became the river, and the passengers had to hide again, huddling together beneath the tiny foredeck as they passed under the bridges.

Nigel could hear the tension in the men's voices as they muttered in the darkness. Peering over the stack of baskets he counted the bridges. There were nine of them on the street map. The Iskan bridge must be about the fifth or sixth. The one below it had been modern, brutally plain. That one? Yes.

The crewmen heaved the inflatable to the side of the boat and slid it into the water. Now, with the sky overhead suffused with the glow of the palace floodlights, it was natural for Nardu to take advantage of the slack of the current by sailing upstream in the deep shadow cast by the tall embankment. Izhvan and Benni shoved the baskets away, crawled out from under the foredeck and dragged the tarpaulin off the boxes of guns and stores. Nigel waited for the others to follow and felt his way out as the boat passed into the darkness beneath the second arch of the bridge. By the time he reached the gunwale Izhvan and Benni were already in the inflatable and the crewmen were lowering the boxes to them.

Hands guided him down and settled him onto one of the boxes. The boat chugged softly towards the growing arch of sky, letting the inflatable drift backwards in the slight current until it lay astern and was being towed upstream. Out in the open Nigel saw that Izhvan was in the water beside them, with the faint light glistening off his naked shoulders. Even without his weight the inflatable seemed dangerously low in the water.

Once clear of the archway, Nardu steered close enough to the bank for the crewmen to cast the inflatable loose and let it drift back with the current while Izhvan shoved at its side until it fetched up in the corner where the tangle of driftwood that had lodged against the grating met the river wall, well in under the overhang of the arch.

Nigel reached for the lip of the ledge and tension slipped away at the touch of the stonework. He was no longer just a lucky mascot, a passenger tagging along with a lot of guys he couldn't even talk to. Now there was stuff for him to do. He scrambled onto one of the boxes, stood and shoved his bag onto the ledge, got his elbows onto the surface and swung his legs up.

"I'll tie up, Benni," he whispered and took the rope and made it fast to the grating.

A locksmith in Sodalka had made several copies of Taeela's key to the hidden entrances, and a leather-worker had made head-straps for the party's torches Nigel fished his out, adjusted it and used it to find the slot to on the section of grating, but like Taeela had trouble getting the key to engage. He felt it grate home, levered and tugged. The mechanism clicked, and the bar he was holding with his right hand shifted slightly in his grasp.

He rose, took a fresh grip and heaved. The bars refused to budge. When he threw his full weight on them they shifted a fraction, and the next jerk came with a rush that almost sent him backwards into the water. He rose panting, and stared at the opening.

It was too small for the boxes to go through. His own stupid fault. He was the only one who'd seen both the boxes and the opening.

Benni didn't seem at all put out.

"We see what is in there," he said, pointing at the tunnel.

They explored briefly and returned. Benni explained the problem to Izhvan as he rubbed himself down. He nodded, unperturbed, and started to dress. Benni opened the first box and passed the guns through to Nigel to stack against the wall, until Izhvan joined them, stared at Nigel and spoke.

"He is right," said Benni. "Now you sleep, Nick. Soon we are needing you."

"OK," he said and climbed down into the inflatable, made himself comfortable and slept without dreams till Benni woke him at one in the morning. He'd had had less than two hours, though it felt like ten and he could have done with a dozen more.

While he slept the other three had arrived from the fish quay, with Nardu's son to take the inflatable away, loaded with the empty boxes. They had ferried the guns and stores across the stream, and now needed him to open the inner gate for them.

He adjusted his torch in its head-strap while they fetched the guns and stores through, then closed and locked the gate and showed them the hiding place for the key. Benni drew a white cross on the brick with a piece of chalk so that any of them could find it. Then on beside the stinking stream, counting the forty-seven slabs to the entrance to the shaft.

He knelt to open it, and paused. He'd known all along that he was going to have to face this moment, but his mind had shied away from thinking about it. Another ghastly death. Fohdrahko lying in the pool of his own blood. The rats would have found his body by now. It would stink...

At least if he warned the men they wouldn't think it was a bad omen. Then they could face it with him. He rose and turned to Benni.

"There's a dead man in there," he whispered. "Fohdrahko. He looked after the Khanazhana. He helped us escape, then he came back here and cut his wrists. That's what the eunuchs did when they weren't going to be any use to their masters anymore."

"What is 'eunuchs'?"

"They looked after the Khans' women. They had been...you know..."

Nigel gestured towards his groin. Benni's eyebrows rose. He nodded dismissively and started to turn.

"Wait," said Nigel. "Tell them he was a hero. And the Khanazhana loved him."

Fohdrahko sat almost he had last seen him, propped between the ladder and the side wall of the shaft. His head had fallen forward and his hands were folded on his lap. His blood, black in the torchlight, had soaked his thighs and spread across the floor of the shaft. There was no sign of anyone having stepped in it, or of rats having come anywhere near him. The reek of the stream and the musky scent he wore disguised the stench of death. It looked as if he had simply fallen asleep and chosen not to wake up, ever. Not ghastly at all.

Nigel rose and stood aside, wiping his eyes while one by one the men came and peered through the opening. The slow tears wouldn't stop coming.

Benni turned to him.

"Now we go up, you, me, find the place we wait. You ready?"

Nigel wiped his eyes on his sleeve yet again,

"Sure," he said. "Sorry. I can't help this. He was my friend."

"It is good you cry for a friend. The others, they bring guns. Then they make your friend right for Khanazhana seeing him."

"Great. Thank you."

Again and again Nigel had mentally rehearsed the next stage. He counted fourteen rungs up, found the slot, slid the tool in and worked the lock. Its click seemed horribly audible. He listened. Nothing.

He eased the slab open an inch and listened again. Again nothing.

Cautiously he pushed the slab fully open and turned his head to shine the torch-beam along the floor of the passage, sighing with relief to see the dust undisturbed. Everything depended on how far the soldiers had managed to explore the maze. They must have tried, surely, even if they were short-handed. They knew about the Hare Room. If they hadn't found a way past the open drop-trap they could still have broken through from Taeela's living-room. How much further had they got? Not this far, at least.

Benni chalked crosses on the slab, inside and out, and Nigel led the way towards the back of the palace, holding his torch with just enough light showing between his fingers to let him count the slabs. Now he was in the palace of his dreams, the maze he had built up step by step in his mind as Lily-Jo drew it out on her computer. The tension was still there, twanging taut, but changed. In the boat it had been the approaching dangers, the thousand things waiting to go wrong, felt in the churn of his imaginings, in the chill hollow of his stomach. Now they were all around him, just the other side of the passage wall, where a sleeper might wake to the sound of a careless movement, or in the actual stonework, where some ancient booby-trap might have been left primed to do its deadly work. His skin crawled, as if it were trying to wake some extra sense that would reach out through the dark and warn him.

...Fifteen. Sixteen. Seventeen...

He switched off the torch, ran his hand over the right-hand wall, and found the spy-hole. The left pocket of his jacket was stuffed with little squares of cloth. He rolled one up, doubled it and crammed it into the hole. The entrance to that room was four slabs further on. Benni marked it with a circle, because it wasn't a room they expected to use, but might need to find.

Faint moonlight gleamed ahead. They crept forward and reached a T-junction, where the passage to the left ran off into the total darkness under the Great Hall but the one to the right ended a few paces further on in moonlit stone tracery. In the far left corner Nigel found and opened the entrance to a tunnel that ran beneath the windows of a room called the Fox room. They crawled through on hands and knees. Through a spy-hole Nigel saw by the moonlight that the room was full of filing cabinets, their drawers wide open and files and papers littered across the floor. At the further end of the tunnel another short side-arm led into the main passage that from here on snaked past the rooms all along the west side of the Palace.

Two more spy-holes to block, two more entrances to locate and mark, and then the Lizard Room. On tip-toe Nigel peered through the spy-hole. There was only a faint glow of moonlight, much less than in the ransacked office, but he made out what looked like a stool and the corner of a table.

"I think it's OK," he whispered, and counted the slabs to the door.

"Yes, for six men only, is good," said Benni, as Nigel swung his torch round the little room, revealing two stools, a small table, and a canvas cot, all covered with dust. A curtain in the corner hid the latrine. Beside it stood a water-barrel. There was one small barred window and a shackle in the wall above the cot. A prison cell.

Benni sniffed the water in the barrel and nodded.

"You are knowing this is here," he said. Not a question, a statement.

"It just looked like it. There'd got to be a room here, because they'd given it a name, but there was no way it could have a door leading anywhere except into these passages. The room where we hid after the President was killed was like that."

"OK," said Benni, unconvinced. It wasn't Nigel's job to be that sort of smart. He was there to bring them luck, luck like finding this room straight off, the luck of the ancient khans. They were going to need it.

"Now you sleep again, Nick," he added. "I go bring the others."

"I'm fine," said Nigel. "I could easily come."

"No, you must sleep. Is coming long day."

"You're sure you can find the way?"

"Sure," said Benni and crawled out.

Even the few movements they'd made had stirred up clouds of dust. Nigel ran water from the barrel into his cupped hand and slung it hither and thither across the room until the air cleared, then tilted the cot onto its side and used one of the cloths in his pocket to sweep as much of the damp dust as he could off onto the floor. Finally he spread his anorak out on the filthy canvas, curled up on it with his bag for a pillow, and was asleep before he had time to start thinking about tomorrow.

His shoulder woke him just after six, with daylight outside the window. Ammun Amla, a plump, earnest-looking young man, was sitting at the table, rolling dice, using a piece of cloth to muffle their rattle on the bare wood. The four others were sprawled on the floor, asleep. Boxes and bags were piled in a corner, with the guns leaning against the wall beside them. It didn't leave much room to move around.

Ammun looked up, raised a hand in greeting and returned to his dice. Nigel picked his way between the sleepers to use the latrine, then rinsed his face with water from the barrel and dried it on his sleeves. He was furiously hungry.

"Is there anything to eat?" he whispered, pointing at his mouth.

He breakfasted off greasy dark bread, salt fish, dried apricots and water. One by one the men woke and joined him. He answered their greetings with a grunt and a smile, and they stood round talking in low, serious voices while they ate. His apprehension grew and grew until he found it hard to swallow.

Benni turned to him at last.

"Good," he said. "Is much for doing this day. First we find room for when others come here. Then you show us all these hided ways..."

They'd gone through all this several times, before they'd left Sodalka, but Benni was like that. The business of looking for an extra room had unsettled him, and he wanted to make sure everything was still in place. Nigel forced his exasperation down.

"OK," he said, as soon as he got the chance. "We'll check out some of the rooms the other side of the passage in case that's the best we can do, but they're all inside rooms. No windows. No water-butt, probably. Our best bet is two floors up, in the hidden level. There's a couple of rooms there might do. We'll have a look at them, and the passage across the front of the Great Hall, and then we'll move up a level."

Benni translated. The men picked up their guns and waited for Nigel to lead the way out.

On Fohdrahko's map the rooms in the mysterious area beneath the Great Hall had letters and numbers, not names. The spy-holes revealed nothing but darkness, and when Nigel opened a slab and shone his torch into one he saw a dusty corridor with closed doors either side—store rooms, at a guess.

The next entrance opened into a large strange room, bare apart from about twenty raised slabs ranged opposite each other down its length. It looked like a hospital ward with no privacy and very uncomfortable beds. The slanting beam of Nigel's torch picked out scraps of writing scratched deep into the walls, and he realised what he was looking at was a different kind of store-room. This was where the khans had stored their slaves. There was a water barrel and a latrine hole in the corner but no curtain. The men gazed doubtfully round.

"Maybe, maybe no," said Benni. "We go up now, see there?"

"Fine," said Nigel, and headed for the shaft in the south west corner of the palace. They climbed to the hidden level and began to wind their way back towards the river, the men stooping beneath the low ceiling. Lily-Jo had been right. Fohdrahko's map of this level showed only two named rooms along all this side of the Great Hall, because they could only be fitted in where the room below was low enough to have a false ceiling. Elsewhere the spy-holes looked out into the Great Hall or down through the inward-curving ceilings of the rooms on the floor below, as the passage snaked between them. Nothing much was happening in any of them this early in the day.

The Scorpion Room turned out to be a bleak unfurnished space, barely larger than the cell where they had spent the night. Something had died beneath the floor and the air was rank with its reek. But the Beetle Room, further on, was a smaller version of the Hare Room, with water-butt, latrine, a few worm-eaten furnishings and a window in the side wall of the Palace. The dust lay thick and undisturbed. Urvan poked his head in, withdrew and nodded, Benni marked the entrance and Nigel led them on, pausing to show the men the shaft down which he and the others had escaped. To his relief the faint trail of the cloth-roll he had dragged this far was unmarked by any later footprint.

Two more turns, and the passage ended at a seemingly blank wall. He put his ear against it and listened. Nothing, and still nothing stirred at the click of his key in the entrance-catch. He switched off his torch, swung the slabs apart and peered out. To his right a few pale patches of daylight receded down the long passage across the façade of the palace. To his left, impenetrable dark. He switched the torch on. The dusty paving was scuffled with footprints.

His heart thumped and steadied. First contact. The searchers had come this far, not found this entrance and gone past. Even before he looked to his left he knew what he would see. A dozen paces further on a whole section of paving had risen to block the passage. This side lay the black mouth of a trap-shaft. More dead men. He withdrew and turned to Benni.

"You'd better all see this," he whispered. "We can't go any further for the mo. Just look. Don't go right out."

He waited while they peered out one by one, then closed the slabs. They gathered round him in the dark and he explained what they'd seen.

"That's the passage that runs across the front of the Great Hall. It's a nuisance they've found it, because it's the best way across to the other side of the palace. They must've got into the room we'd been hiding in, and then found their way out into that passage..."

A murmur of interruption. Benni translated.

"They had dog. Izhvan sees mark from dog-foot."

"That makes sense. It was following Fohdrahko. He wore

scent, and he'd gone on along the passage to set the drop-trap. I told you about drop-traps at Sodalka. That was one you saw out there. If the dog was following him it'd have fallen down the drop-trap, and some of the men too, probably. They couldn't get any further without it. They can't keep losing men. They must be pretty scared about using the passages at all."

He thought about the dog while they discussed it among themselves. Why should he mind almost as much as he did about the men? It was as if it had been a dog he'd known.

"OK," said Benni. "Now we go up, find attack room for us."

This was the main thing they were here to do. Back in Sodalka the first idea had been that the attackers would muster in the passage behind some chosen room on the main floor, and at the right moment rush in and burst out into the Great Hall. But from what Taeela had told them they'd realised that those rooms were too large and busy. Not everyone in the palace would be watching the ceremony. How could thirty men burst through a small opening on hands and knees and take over a room that size without someone giving the alarm? So they'd decided to attack down the stairs from one of the smaller rooms above, where their guns could command the whole hall once they were out onto the arcade.

They climbed two floors to rooms Nigel had already seen and started to work their way back round to the far wing of the palace as it began to wake to its daytime life. Two young army officers were lounging in the President's outer office. Their chat sounded more like gossip than work. A bored guard slouched in the lobby using his mobile, with his gun propped against the wall beside him. The spy-hole into the President's private office was sealed off. They crept on in silence through the casual noises of the day, the twitter of a call-tone hushed by an answering voice, a vacuum cleaner, a query and its bored reply, uninterpretable knocks and rustlings, all as ordinary as the daylight streaming through the windows of those rooms and glimmering through each spy-hole into the darkness of the haunted passages.

Though this was the world of Nigel's dreams, in one way it was very different. A rattle of gunfire startled the silence, but turned out to come from a shoot-'em-up someone was playing on his desk-top computer. An unwatched monitor was running a porn video in an empty room. A guard chatted up a cleaner while an officer strolled past uncaring. Another guard was smoking.

If the palace had come to life, it wasn't the life Nigel had sensed all around him when the President was still alive, humming with his energies, busy fulfilling his demands, tense with the dread of his displeasure. Now its life was the life of a zombie. Power had gone elsewhere.

But in the passages the tension was still unrelenting, as the intruders stole along, the men so silently that Nigel had to fight the urge to look back and check that they were still there. Those idlers had ears, ears that might startle to the knock of a gun-butt against the stone-work or the cough of a throat tickled by the dusty air, and wake the zombie into murderous life.

It was slow work. They all looked through every spy-hole, then Varat would block it and Benni would mark the entrance, while Ammun made notes about it before they moved on. It took most of the morning to work their way through the complex maze running across the back of the Great Hall to the passage along the further wing of the Palace. Weary through and through, Nigel knelt, worked the entrance-lock and eased the slabs apart. Several pairs of foot-prints were clear in the dust beyond.

He snapped the torch off and waited, straining for the whisper of any movement nearer than the casual noises from the unseen rooms on either side.

Nothing.

He peered out. The faint light seeping through spy-holes only emphasised the darkness. Yes, of course. Once they'd broken into the passage past Taeela's room there'd been nothing to stop the soldiers exploring back in this direction. It didn't mean they were still there. No telling.

He switched on his torch again and edged aside so that the men could see what he had seen, but sat slumped against the wall waited while they worked it out for themselves. He felt utterly done for. He'd had only scraps of sleep last night after an endless-seeming day, and had woken still bone-tired. All morning tension had kept him going. Every step forward had been into possible danger, forcing him alert for each next step, denying him any moment to notice what was happening inside himself. Finding the footprints—that sudden extra demand—had taken all he'd got. His mind filled with a picture of a sodden and exhausted dog paddling in a foul dark stream, searching for a place where it could climb to land. The picture became a dream.

"Nick?"

"Uh?"

"Nick. You hear me? You are ill?"

"Sorry. Fell asleep. I'm all right…uh…"

Benni put a hand under his arm and heaved to his feet, then helped him all the way back through the maze, their two shoulders scraping against the passage walls. He was yawning uncontrollably by the time Benni unfastened his torch-strap and helped him onto the bed in the Lizard Room. Someone took off his sneakers. His last thought was that Fohdrahko hadn't come out alive.

Benni woke him after a couple of hours and sat him down in front of some food. He'd thought he wasn't hungry, but after a couple of mouthfuls found he was wrong.

"Where are the others?" he said.

"They take guns up to other room," said Benni. "This room for Khanazhana. Then they look again where we are this morning."

"She's coming tonight?"

"I hope. When you finish eat, we go look down at below ways.

You are strong for that?"

"I'm fine."

"Nick, you been here in palace when President is live. These soldiers we see, no good."

"You can say that again. No, his guards were a crack lot, and dead loyal to him. The bastards would never have got away with it if they'd been here, but they tricked him into sending a lot them up to Lake Vamar so they could put their own men in. They haven't got a lot of guys they can trust, and they need them to do other stuff. There's nothing much to guard in the palace now, so I suppose they thought it doesn't matter who does it."

"Maybe they bring gooder men in tomorrow."

"They won't know their way around."

Benni nodded. It didn't seem to cross his mind to ask how Nigel knew the stuff he came up with. Maybe he didn't mind if he was just guessing, because his guesses would be right. He was the Khanazhana's baizhan.

He was still eating when the Akhlavals came back. They glanced at Nigel and Urvan asked a question which Benni answered briefly. The same thing happened when the other two showed up, and this time round Nigel recognised his own name. He could hear a strain in their voices that hadn't been there before, as if there'd been some kind of furious, whispered argument out in the passages. The atmosphere in the room had soured. Old animosities had come to the surface. Urvan Akhlaval and Varat Vulnad wouldn't look at each other.

Ever since they'd left Sodalka things had been going unbelievably well, but now, suddenly, they weren't. They couldn't find a room from which to launch their attack and they couldn't agree what to do about it. At the crucial moment their baizhan had failed them. The feeble little wimp had flaked out. So now they stood around and waited for him to finish his meal and pull himself together and summon up his non-existent powers and get them out of this.

If only, he thought, chewing sullenly on because he knew he

needed the food, though it no longer seemed to taste of anything. Why had he ever agreed to come on this horrible adventure? If he'd refused the others wouldn't have come without him and the whole mad plan would have been off.

Except that it wouldn't. Somehow or other Taeela would have scraped a gang of even crazier guys together and given it a go and they'd all be dead.

He shoved the remains of his food away and lurched to his feet.

"OK," he said. "Let's go and see what we can find downstairs."

The larger rooms at floor-level with the Great Hall made for a simpler lay-out than on those above and below, and Taeela and Rahdan between them had known what they were used for. The shaft emerged into the main passage between the guard room in the corner of the Great Hall and the rooms down that side, and ran along the outer wall of the palace, ducking below their high-silled windows. Fohdrahko's map showed a couple of spy-holes and a hidden entrance into each room, and three sets of rungs running up to crawl-ways that led to spy-holes looking out across the Great Hall. The central set came on a fold in the plan and the original markings were illegible, so Lily-Jo had marked it with a query, but she said that was the only thing that made sense.

The first room was used by the palace officials as a general purpose office, with people coming and going. Even during the signing ceremony it was likely to be occupied. Next came the first set of rungs. Ammun climbed to investigate, and found that the spy-hole was one of the ones that looked as if it was designed to let a gun to be fired through it. He sounded excited about it. The Akhlavals were scornful.

Listlessly Nigel led them on, automatically counting the slabs between each feature. He could hear the men following him, moving less carefully than they had before, as if it didn't matter. The whole idea was hopeless anyway.

The next room used to be the old khans' audience room. It was now used as a council room and looked more promising, with a big central table, chairs, shelves of books, computer consoles and so on. But the entrance was blocked by some large piece of furniture, invisible through the spy-holes.

Then a smaller room that used to be the antechamber to the audience room. There were people in it, setting up television equipment for the ceremony. No use. Still counting, Nigel crouched along beneath a window, beginning the count again when he reached the hidden entrance just beyond it. One, two, three, four, five...

He stopped dead and looked back. Three. The rungs Lily-Jo had marked with a query should have been above the third slab. He checked the map. Yes, three. He shone the torch ahead, along the passage. No sign of any rungs. But there must be something here, roughly opposite the wall of the antechamber, where he'd seen it through the last spy-hole.

A seemingly solid wall

"What happens?" whispered Benni.

"Wait. Keep your fingers crossed."

All the mortar around the third slab had the same rough texture, no sign of a slot in it. Lily-Jo had known there was a wall between the spy-holes either side of where he was standing because they had to look into two different rooms, but, misled by the different sizes of the rooms, probably, she'd printed it further to the left, in blue to show she couldn't be sure of its position.

But if it was exactly behind slab three there was something else that made sense. Course by course, Nigel ran his finger-tips over the mortar. Four courses up he found a few inches with a smoother texture.

He pressed his key against the left end and the strip grated round. It can't have been used for years, centuries even, but when he engaged the key and levered the catch clicked sweetly.

He pulled, using the key as a handle. Nothing happened, not even when he threw as much of his weight on it as his grip would stand. Still nothing. In desperation he shoved and felt the stone-work shift.

Benni joined him and they shifted it another half inch. A crack, not straight like the edge of a normal door but following the lines of mortar, had opened all the way up from the floor to a bit above Nigel's height. He stood clear to let two of the others join Benni. Under their full weight the door gave with a rush and they tumbled on top of each other through the gap.

Surely someone had heard the flurry of thumps. No alarm sounded. They rose and turned to see what they had found.

A single straight passage, without any visible opening on either side, ran towards a glimmer of light at the far end. The spy-hole was too high for Nigel. Close by, his fingers found a strip of smoother mortar. The key slid easily in.

"It's another door," he whispered. "The lock's here,"

Benni edged past and peered through the spy-hole.

"Is the big room," he said. "Too many people now. We come again tonight."

The men all took their turn at the spy-hole while Nigel waited further back, leaning against the wall. Why on earth? What was it for, this place? It was almost as if the men who had built the palace four centuries ago had put it here, ready for them to use. No. Tomorrow wouldn't be the first time, anything like. Many times before this the mosaics of the grand stairs must have been soaked in blood – a rebellious chieftain, trusting in his safe conduct, while armed eunuchs mustered in this passage, ready to rush out and slaughter him in the middle of his bodyguard. There'd been a lot of that sort of stuff in the history of Dirzhan, according to Google. The chill of the stones he was leaning against seemed to seep into his body. He shuddered.

The men returned towards him. He could hear in the tone of their whispers, in the lightness of their movements, how their mood had changed. Their confidence had returned. They were a team once more, agreeing with each other, working together. Yet again, against all the apparent odds, something had gone dead right. Their baizhan had come up with the goods and they would succeed. Benni even said as much, good as.

"This is very OK. This is what we look for. Thank you, Nick."

"No problem," he muttered balefully.

They explored the rest of that floor almost light-heartedly. A muffled murmur of angry voices greeted them as they stole back the way they had come. In the old antechamber two army officers and a tribesman wearing the black and orange of Adzhar Taerzha were having some kind of a conference with two of the television people. It wasn't going well. The men crowded round the spy-hole, listening intently. Nigel settled onto the floor and waited.

The voices stilled as a newcomer came into the room, then rose as all three tried to put their cases at the same time. The newcomer answered calmly, ignoring grumbles of interruption. The argument dwindled into discussion.

"Nick, who this man?" Benni whispered.

He didn't need to look. The voice was unmistakable.

"Avron Dikhtar. He was the President's secretary. What's their problem?"

"They fight for who come first down stair for to sign constitution—Adzhar Taerzha, Sesslizh, Madzhalid. This man fix it."

"They're doing it like the Tribute of the Chieftains? That's useful."

"Yes. Is good, Nick."

(Bastards. Deliberately going through their stupid ceremony on the very spot where the President's blood had stained the stairs.)

They waited for the discussion to end in case they learnt anything else useful, then made their way back to their new base in the Beetle Room.

For Nigel the evening became a time of waiting. They ate together in friendship, like a hunting party home from the field. They were all in this thing together, and on a roll, and they were going to pull it off. Even Nigel found himself infected with the same crazy optimism, at least to the extent that though he didn't think they were right he was no longer sure they were wrong.

The men finished their meal and left to prepare the slave room for overflow sleepers, but they wouldn't let Nigel come with them. He thought of sneaking off down to the dungeons to see if Rick was there, but it wasn't worth the risk. He was far more likely being held in a barracks somewhere. Besides, suppose the men came back and found him gone...On the way out, perhaps, when it was all over...If they came this way...If he was still alive...

His last thought as he drifted off to sleep was that by the time he woke Taeela would be here. He hadn't seen her for four days, and wouldn't much tomorrow, but at least they'd be under the same roof.

CHAPTER 22

He slept erratically. The room seemed to be filled with stirrings and whisperings. His worries faded into dreams which roused back into worries. He'd be planning an imaginary escape with Taeela…and he'd be scuttling through a series of crawl-ways and panting up shafts, looking for the room where two veiled women were holding her pinioned by the arms while a man he couldn't see through the spy-hole stalked towards her…and then awake and rehearsing a conversation with his father about why he'd broken his promise…The window was pallid with dawn when Benni woke him.

Achingly he rose, sorted himself out and made his way down to the Lizard Room. Rahdan was sleeping across the entrance, with the slabs slightly ajar and his gun on the floor beside him. He woke groaning and rolled onto his knees, swung a slab open and spoke to somebody inside the room. Still groaning under his breath, he stumbled off towards the slave room. Time passed, and Taeela crawled out of the entrance. Her mourning dress was all smeared with the dust of the passages. She rose and flung her arms round Nigel all in one smooth movement. Gratefully he hugged her back. This was the first time ever, a real hug of pure affection. And probably the last.

"Oh, Nigel!" she whispered. "I have been so worried for you!

You are all right?"

"Fine. A bit short on sleep. Otherwise it's gone pretty well."

"Last night the men tell…told me everything. You have been wonderful."

"Wasn't me. Everything's just gone dead right for us, that's all. What about you?"

She must have been up half the short night and it was now barely dawn. There were dark patches beneath her eyes, made darker yet by the shadow-casting torchlight, but the eyes themselves glittered with energy. Before she could answer she was interrupted by a soft cough from the passage behind him. He dropped his arms to let her stand clear but she didn't let go.

"You will be there with me, Nigel? We will watch together, two sisters. I have brought a dahl for you."

"When it happens…? Uh…I'd thought…"

He couldn't say it, not to her face. OK, he'd promised his father…but that was only an excuse. He'd already broken that promise. The truth was he couldn't bear to stay and watch the whole thing come unstuck, with Taeela struggling in the grip of her captors and an ash-blond patch among the blood-soaked bodies on the floor of the hall.

"Two good men will go straight to your father and keep him safe," she said. "It is arranged."

He stared at her, shaking his head.

"You will stay, Nigel? I will not make you."

She already had. Behind him Rahdan coughed again. Time was racing away.

"Uh…I guess I'll stay," he muttered. "I've got to go. See you later."

"Be careful, Nigel."

Through a gap between two jars on a set of open shelves Nigel watched Rahdan stroll towards the stove. A raucous sort of Dirzhani rockabilly on a tinny little radio drowned the sound of his footsteps. Despite what must have been a rough night he looked pretty good. The uniform the tailor in Sodalka had made for him fitted him as well as an officer's. The butt of his AK dangled comfortably beside his hip. The bald cook stirring a pot at the enormous stove never heard him coming and when Rahdan tapped him on the shoulder jumped like startled frog, almost dropping his spoon.

Rahdan laughed and spread his hands in apology. He spoke. The cook shook his head crossly and returned to stirring. Rahdan took a dirzh note out of his wallet and laid it on the stove. The cook looked at it and pointedly went on stirring. Rahdan added another note. The cook picked both notes up, handed him the spoon and strutted away.

Stirring with one hand Rahdan took a glass flask out of his jacket pocket, pulled the cork out with his teeth, tipped some of the contents into the pot, checked the level in the flask, re-corked it and slipped it back into his pocket. He continued stirring until the cook came back with a pewter tankard. Rahdan swapped spoon for drink, took a good long pull, swallowed and sighed with satisfaction, then drank slowly, chatting between mouthfuls.

Nigel should have been twanging with nerves. All this was unrehearsed. He hadn't had a chance to explore the passages along the east wing of the courtyard yesterday and they'd turned out trickier than they'd looked on the plan, mostly under ceilings so low that they were almost crawl-ways. The soldiers in the barrack-rooms were rousing as they'd passed. They'd cut it too fine, but now he waited for Rahdan in a dreamy daze. It was as if the last two days had numbed his capacity for tension.

He'd talked to Taeela, held her in his arms, she'd made him feel he mattered to her as much as everything else put together. That was enough.

Rahdan put the tankard down, wiped his mouth on the back of his hand and came strolling back. He opened the kitchen door, closed it with a bang and followed Nigel into the storeroom from which they'd emerged. The barrack-rooms upstairs were emptying as they crept past.

The next two hours sauntered by, untroubled. Nigel breakfasted slowly and repacked his bag ready for a quick getaway, got out his chess set and explored a variation on the Queen's Indian. Men crawled in, glanced at him, muttered to each other and left. After a bit of this he shifted his chair to face away from the entrance and wasn't surprised when the next visitor seemed to stay longer and before he left something brushed lightly against the nape of his neck.

This time he didn't mind. It seemed to be an expression of their togetherness, like the comradeship among their five leaders that had suddenly renewed itself when they had found their attack-point yesterday. Nigel had never been a natural joiner-in, a foreigner in Santiago and almost that back in England, with his stupid looks and hoity-toity accent. Even in the chess team, with the other players older than he was, he never felt he really belonged. He used to tell himself he was a loner, anyway. Not now.

Only when the men began to muster to their posts, departing a few at a time so as not to clog the shafts, did tension return. He followed the last of them along the passage to the foot of the shaft and waited there, yawning and sighing, until Taeela appeared from below, already in her dahl. She checked over her shoulder that he was there and climbed on, followed by Satila and then Rahdan. Nigel joined himself on at the tail.

When they emerged on the gallery level she took charge and led them to the left, then to Nigel's dismay knelt at an entrance he had tried yesterday and found blocked on the inside. By the time he had pushed past Rahdan and Satila to warn her she had swung the slabs apart and was crawling through. They emerged into what looked like a store-room for office stuff.

"What happened?" he whispered. "I tried this…"

"We came up in the night to see. Me, Satila and Rahdan. This is the best room for us. The women will watch from the gallery, and they will leave their cloaks in the room outside, so we came through Ditta's office to clear the way. Now you put on your woman's clothes and we go through."

There was a silk undershirt, dark green with lacy white cuffs. The dahl was a classy garment, rich brown, beautifully soft and supple, with a pattern of glittery bits on the shoulders and round the arm-slits, and a little handbag to match. There was even a pair of fancy shoes he could get into.

"You must practise to walk like a girl, Nigel" she said, giggling as he tittupped awkwardly across the room. She seemed to be in terrific spirits, as if she were getting ready for a fancy dress party, preening this way and that while Satila fussed round her brushing away the dust of the passages and picking off invisible scraps of fluff. Her outfit was the same as his with the colours reversed, showing they belonged to some clan or other.

"We're some rich guy's daughters, right?" he said.

"Tahrin Farzhna. West Dirzh. He works in Vladivostok. He has two daughters. They have never been to Dirzhan. No one will speak to you."

"Bet they haven't got blue eyes."

"In your bag, Nigel. I think of everything. No, don't put them on. Satila must do your face."

"There's only about six square centimetres anyone's going to see."

"They must see a girl."

"Someone in Sodalka made all this kit? The stupid shoes even?"

"Sure. Alinu had felt your feet. She knew the size for them."

"You couldn't know I'd be was coming up here with you."

"I knew."

Suddenly he wanted to yell at her. She didn't! She didn't! She didn't! Any more than she knew that in twenty minutes' time the whole enterprise wouldn't have ended in a bloody shambles!

She reached out and stroked the back of his hand.

"I knew you'd do what is right, Nigel," she said gently.

There wasn't an answer, not here, not now in this swirl of fear and excitement, this longing to be out of it all, anywhere else in the world, provided she was there too. He pulled back the hood of his dahl and let Satila start work.

She did his whole face, lip-stick and all, working steadily, absorbed in the task. People were moving about now in the room outside. He heard women's voices, a burst of laughter. Satila finished his face and picked up his hand, too pale for a Dirzhak's, too large for a girl's, with short unvarnished nails.

"There isn't time!" he whispered. "I'll keep them under my dahl."

"Yes, we must go soon," said Taeela, and explained to Satila.

She raised his hood and fastened the veil, careful not to smear her work. He picked up his hand-bag and strutted round the small space between the shelves, getting used to the shoes, while Taeela listened at the door.

"Now," she whispered. "We are two shy girls. Hold my hand, Nigel."

She turned the key, and they slipped out behind the cover of a conveniently placed coat-rack. No, she'd probably shifted it there on her reconnaissance visit that morning. She relocked the door and gave him the key.

Yes, of course. He'd be coming back this way most likely. She probably wouldn't. Whatever happened.

With their joined hands invisible in the folds of their dahli they edged out from behind the rack, followed by Satila. A couple of women were checking their make-up in wall mirrors. Several others were chatting in small groups. Only three were wearing dahli, the rest elegant head-scarves. Nobody did more than glance at the newcomers as they slipped out into the gallery.

The spaces along the balustrade were filling up, mainly towards the front of the Great Hall, where the spectators could look more directly towards the staircase. As if too shy to join them Taeela headed for the corner where the gallery turned along the back of the hall. Still hand in hand they leaned on the balustrade and studied the scene below, vivid under the television lights.

The lay-out was a copy of the Tribute ceremony, minus the fancy dress. There was a table on the dais with three microphones and chairs. The band with its weird instruments had been replaced by four buglers and a drummer. A dozen men in tribal dress, chieftains by the look of them, were lined up on one side of the table. The ambassadors and other bigwigs, along with half-a-dozen senior officers, were seated either side of the stage, with two ragged lines of palace guards behind the chairs. Nigel could see the back of an ash-blond head in the front row below him.

Now another gap appeared as a guard on the far side laid his gun on the floor and scuttled off towards the guard-room, his hands already feeling for his belt-buckle. A different soldier appeared, picked up his gun and filled one of the gaps, grey-faced and swaying. An officer strode up and snarled at the guard-sergeant. The poor guy was obviously suffering as badly as any of his men. The officer looked at his watch. Too late to do anything about it. He snarled again and stalked up onto the dais in front of buglers. Another thing going right. The timing had been tricky. Veela had had to show Rahdan several sizes of pot and how much of Alinu's mixture to put in each of them.

Nigel sneaked a glance at his watch. Three minutes to twelve. He tried to count seconds but the hammer of his heartbeat muddled his timing. Mr Dikhtar appeared at the top of the stairs with a shiny leather folder under his arm. He walked quietly down to the dais, took three documents out of the folder, laid them on the table ready for signing, and stood to one side.

The band readied their instruments. The huge room stilled. The officer raised a hand, one finger pointing at the dome, took a quick glance up the stairs and brought it smartly down. The drums rattled. The bugles squawked. Adzhar Taerzha, flanked by two of his personal guards, strode out from the shadows of the gallery into the lamp-glare and raised a hand in greeting. The two colonels appeared either side of him, halted and saluted. The stricken soldiers raised a feeble cheer and the audience clapped. Both sounds were immediately drowned by the roar of canned applause.

The colonels started down the stairs. Adzhar Taerzha followed a couple of steps behind them.

Now! thought Nigel.

Taeela's fingers squirmed in his tightening grip. Her nails dug into the back of his hand. A burst of gunfire broke through the canned clamour. Immediately below Nigel a stream of tribesmen wearing black and orange sashes poured out across the floor, whooping and waving their guns as they rushed towards the dais. The party on the stairs halted and stared. Mr Dikhtar went scuttling up past them. Colonel Sesslizh spun round, snatched his gun from its holster, aimed two-handed and shot Adzhar Taerzha in the face.

He fired again as the big man fell, and again as he hit the stairs, out of sight behind the balustrade from where Nigel was standing, and then both colonels were flung backwards by a burst of fire from the two bodyguards.

At that point someone in the control room switched off the applause. It had all taken less than thirty seconds.

Nigel turned to look at Taeela. She wasn't there. He hadn't even noticed her letting go of his hand. Satila had gone too.

There were screams to his left where most of the women had left the balustrade and were crowding towards the cloakroom, though a few were still where they'd been, staring down at the chaos below. Where was his father? There, crouched in his chair with his hands clasped behind his head in the emergency-landing posture. Most of the male audience were on their feet, heading for the main doors or simply staring around. Three of the attackers had their guns trained on the group of officers.

Over on the far side the soldiers seemed to have melted away. The officer was barking orders at the ones below Nigel. The men stared mutinously at him, broke apart and shambled off out of sight beneath the gallery.

Up on the dais the chieftains had split into two gesticulating groups. The attackers were in confusion. What had just happened wasn't in the script. That first warning burst of gunfire had been meant to be the only shots fired. They would storm the dais and arrest and Adzhar Taerzha and the two colonels, while others racing in along the gallery blocked their escape up the stairs. Taeela would then make her grand entrance from there. Dead bodies sprawled on the stairway were not part of the scenario.

More confusion now, a scuffle of some sort, at the top of the stairs. An elderly woman pushed her way out of it, staggered down and flung herself on her knees at the back of the dais, wailing and tearing her hair. Oh, no! But of course they would have been there to see their men in their moment of triumph—the mothers, the wives, the sons and daughters...

Unable to watch, Nigel turned away. Unthinkingly he headed for the cloakroom but the doorway was choked with women trying to get through. He heaved a slow sigh and came to his senses. Not time yet. He had to stay there, to see it through. He'd promised. He forced himself back to the balustrade.

From this new angle he could see Adzhar Taerzha lying face down, with a pool of blood beneath his head, glistening beneath the lights and dripping down in a thin stream from step to step. Further down Colonel Madzhalid was sprawled on his side like a sleeping man, his wounds invisible. Colonel Sesslizh had rolled down to the dais and lay there with the woman crouched over him, moaning and wailing, then throwing her head back and raising her fists and yelling her curses towards the dome. She could have been Lady Finching's sister. There is no bottom to the pool of grief. It can never be filled.

Around her the attackers were sorting themselves out. They'd stripped off their black and orange colours and were handing round the purple sashes of the khans. Two of last night's new arrivals seemed to be in charge and were lining the rest up on either side of the stairs, like a ceremonial guard at a wedding, with the dead bodies at their feet. The ones at the top faced outwards, watchful for any sign of a counter-attack.

One of the men in charge walked over to the grieving woman, took hold of her arm and started to heave her to her feet. She was trying to fight him off, still wailing, when Satila came hurrying down the stairs and spoke to him. He nodded, let go and stood back. Two palace servants arrived carrying a makeshift stretcher–it might have been a door ripped off a cupboard–rolled Colonel Sesslizh's body onto it and carried him up into the gallery and out of sight, with the woman stumbling beside him wrapped in her noisy desolation. A door closed and the wailing died away.

That changed things. There was no need of a signal. The whole huge room seemed to become aware that something new was about to happen. The gaps along the balustrade had almost filled and the bodies were gone from the stairs when Taeela walked quietly out of the shadows of the gallery into the television lights. She had been wearing full mourning under her dahl and stood there, jet black amid the glitter and glare, a figure of tragedy

There was a brief, astonished silence. Nigel hadn't expected any applause. Almost everybody in the Great Hall must either have supported the coup or else couldn't afford to take sides, one way or the other. But somebody clapped and several others joined in. The women around him were whispering excitedly. A few cheers had started when the canned applause took over.

With Satila and Rahdan a couple of steps behind, Taeela came slowly down the stairs, stopping on the final step above the dais so as to give herself the extra height. Two of the men picked up the table, carried it bodily towards her, adjusted one of the microphones for her and removed the other two. The canned applause stopped abruptly and the scattering of cheers died away. She fiddled with the microphone and was clearly about to speak when she was interrupted by a fresh disturbance at the top of the stairs.

With deliberate slowness she turned to see two of the men standing under the archway with Avron Dikhtar sagging in their grasp.

Idiots! At this moment of all moments!

No, it hadn't been like that. He must have been there all along. They'd've collared him almost at once. He'd raced up the stairs and run straight into their arms. Taeela had arrived in time to decide what to do about the captive before she made her entrance. This was the result. She'd been expecting the interruption, chosen the moment.

She beckoned. The men virtually carried Mr Dikhtar down towards her—he'd have fallen if they'd let go of his arms. She climbed to meet them, stopping several steps up and turning half-sideways so that audience and cameras could see the confrontation.

The men forced him to his knees on the step below her and stood back. He stared up at her, grey-faced, streaming with sweat. Still with deliberate slowness she drew her pistol out of her jacket and weighed it up and down, holding it two-handed so that everybody could see what it was.

Every Dirzhak in the room knew what to expect. Three of her father's murderers were already dead. The last one cowered at her feet.

Her thumb moved on the safety. She began to raise the gun, paused, lowered it again, closed the safety, put it away and turned to face the room. She took a deep breath and called out two short sentences in Dirzhani, waited, and repeated them in English.

"The vengeance of the Khan is the mercy of the Khan.

"There will be no more killing."

Nigel watched, strangely detached. The rest of the room may have been shuddering with the release of tension. Even the half-dozen men who'd heard her give him the Word of the Khan couldn't have been sure she'd keep it. Only he can have been certain, or known what it had cost her to forgo her vengeance. To stand there and act her agonising change of heart right to the hilt, laying it on for all she was worth.

And why not? She was fighting with everything she'd got—for herself, for her father, for Dirzhan—and she hadn't got much, forty-odd crazies from the wild clans in the north, and herself, the Khanazhana. And the people of Dara Dahn who'd poured rioting into the streets that night to protest against the coup, and had had to be driven back by tanks and gunfire. She was appealing directly to them. It would make great television. Mutineers from the Dorvadu barracks were supposed to be taking over the TV and radio station just about now, providing nothing had gone wrong…

Something had, though, here. For the first time Taeela seemed to be hesitating, unsure of herself. She was looking up at the gallery to his right…

Hell! He'd moved. She'd looked for him where he should have been as if to say "There! I kept my word, right?" and he wasn't there. Automatically he raised his arm and waved. She caught the signal, smiled and walked back down to the microphone.

And meanwhile everyone round him had seen the pale coarse hand and big macho wrist-watch protruding from the elegant sleeve. Quite a few of those below too had turned to see what she was looking for. Hurriedly he lowered his arm out of sight and turned away. There were mutters and whispers all around him but a pathway opened before him.

By the time he reached the cloakroom door Taeela was speaking into the microphone. Her voice filled the Great Hall.

CHAPTER 23

Fohdrahko's body lay against the wall with his eyes closed and his arms neatly folded across his chest. The entrance slabs were still open. From the direction of the dungeon came a curious muffled uproar. Nigel hesitated at the door, but the key-ring was still in its hiding-place, five keys, three plain and two with more elaborate business ends—skeleton keys for the cells presumably. One of the plain ones fitted the door.

The din burst through as he inched it open, men's hoarse voices yelling, mixed with metallic bangs and clanks. The bars the far end were silhouetted against the weak dungeon lighting. He unslung his dahl from his shoulder-bag and pulled it on over his ordinary clothes, fastened the veil and crept forward, almost invisible now in the darkness of the tunnel. A cell door came into view, with a man's face pressed close the bars, lined, haggard, mouth open in a scream, like a horrible old painting of a soul in hell.

He hesitated again. But if there was any chance Rick was there, screaming like that…

More doors came into view, more faces, snarling or yelling or grimly silent. The third one on the left was black.

No point in sneaking about. The other plain key fitted the lock on the grille. The yelling changed tone as he opened the gate and with quick, short girl-steps crossed to Rick's cell. Rick cut his yell short and stared at him. Nigel had to shout to be heard..

"It's OK, it's me, Nigel. Tell you later."

The second of the fancy keys fitted. Shouts rose to screams as the other prisoners saw Rick lurch out into the open. What had happened to the warders? They must have heard.

"We'd better get out of here," he shouted.

"Janey? The girls?"

"Up at Sodalka. They're fine. Tell you later. Know any of these guys?"

"Sure. Vandi. That one."

"OK. Those two are the skeleton keys Tell him to let the others out. We've got to go. That gate I came out of."

He headed for the tunnel and stripped off and refolded his dahl. The shouts from the dungeons were dying away as Rick came limping back. Nobody tried to follow him. The released prisoners were moving towards the far end of the dungeons. Nigel hurried on. He was almost at the end of the sewer-tunnel before he realised Rick was having trouble keeping up.

"Are you all right," he said.

"I'll do. It's my ankle, mainly. Bastards knocked me around a bit, trying to get it out of me where you'd got to. As if I knew. Diplomatic immunity, hell. I passed out 'fore they'd done."

"But they were all yelling just now, and…"

"That's the warders they were yelling at. Hadn't brought breakfast round. Gone off somewhere, 'parently."

"They were short of guards…Tell you later. Think you can make it across here? It's using your arms, mostly, but you've got to reach with your leg on the far side. Shall I go first, show you? I can give you a hand that last bit."

Rick eyed the sewer-crossing.

"Give it a go," he said.

He just made it, managing to reach the ledge with his left leg so that Nigel could heave him across, gasping for breath and in obvious pain.

"Bastards must've cracked a rib," he muttered. "Reckon I've bust it now. How far've we got to go?"

"Do you think you can get as far as the fish-quay? We're just coming out under the Iskan Bridge."

"Give it a go. Guys there know me. Pals of old Nardu."

He staggered on, groaning at every step and leaning more and more heavily on Nigel's shoulder, then passed out just as they reached the gate. Nigel eased him down and ran. In the office shed three men were watching the scene in the Great Hall on the TV, but Nigel didn't pause to look.

"Please...," he said urgently. The men glanced irritably round. Their faces changed as they stared at his western clothes and his painted face

"Rick's hurt himself," he said, pointing towards the gate. "Nardu's friend. Please help."

Perhaps the names meant something. One of them came to the door to look, said something and strode off. The others followed. Nigel snatched the portable telephone off the table and raced back to the gate, where the men were about to roll Rick over onto his back.

"Watch it!" he shouted. "He's bust a rib! Hurt!"

He mimed a hurt side and made gestures of carefulness. They copied the gestures to show they'd got it.

He stepped a few paces away, called the embassy and waited, tense for the piano music. Then Roger's voice.

"British embassy, Dara Dahn."

"It's me, Nigel."

"Nigel! Where are you?"

"At the fish quay—you know, near the Iskan Bridge. I've got Rick here. He's badly hurt. We think he's broken a rib. The guys here are helping, but I can't speak Dirzhani and Rick's passed out. Can you talk to them?"

"OK. You're aware of what's been happening at the palace,

I take it?"

"Some of it. Here you are."

He passed the telephone to one of the men, who spoke briefly, listened, answered for a bit longer and listened again. The other two went back to the shed. That's torn it, Nigel thought. Roger had got it at once that he'd been in the palace. He wouldn't have to lie to his father after all. In some ways it was a relief.

The man gave him back the telephone and hurried off.

"It's me again," he said.

"OK," said Roger. "I'll call the hospital and try and get an ambulance down there straight off. Got a number I can call you on?"

"45796," said Nigel, reading it off the handset.

"OK. Then I'll get straight back to you and tell you what I've managed and maybe talk to your friends. Got time to talk to your mother while I'm doing that?"

"If that's all right. You told me keep it as short as possible, in case..."

"Looks like the system's broken down in the confusion. Here's your mother."

"Nigel!"

"Hi, Mum."

"Oh, darling! Are you all right? Where are you?"

"I'm fine. Just a bit tired. I'm at the fish quay, near the palace. I've got Rick. I found him in the dungeons. He's badly hurt. They'd beaten him up. Roger's trying to get an ambulance down here."

"Dungeons! You were in the palace! You said..."

"Couldn't help it. I kept right in the background. Tell you later."

"We've all been watching it on the telly. It's amazing. And you're really all right still?"

"I was just up in the gallery, mostly, wearing a dahl. Have you still got the telly on? Can you see Dad? He was OK last I saw."

"He's still there. It was agony for a bit. Those horrible men were just coming down the stairs when these other men came charging in loosing off their guns and then the screen went blank. I was worried sick of course. Thank heavens I didn't know you were there too! And we waited and waited and all of a sudden the telly came on again and there was Taeela with…"

"Hang on. Looks like Rick's coming round. Bye, Mum. I should be home soon."

"Oh, please!"

Rick was lying on his back with a rolled-up coat under his head. He fidgeted about, trying to get more comfortable but wincing with almost every move. His face was the colour of dirty tarmac. He stared as Nigel knelt beside him. His lips moved.

"Who…? What…?"

Even that seemed to hurt.

"It's me, Nigel. We're at the fish quay. I've called Roger. He's trying to get an ambulance down here. I found you in the dungeons, told you Janey and the girls were OK, remember. They're up at Sodalka. Mizhael Baladzhin's looking after them. I'll tell you…"

The telephone rang. It was Roger.

"Right, Nigel, I think I've got that sorted. They took a bit of persuading—they're all glued to the telly. Should be there in about ten minutes. May get a bit held up. Everyone's out on the streets, judging by the racket. Got any money?"

"Lots. How much do you want me to give them?"

"I've told them fifty each. That's to take you and Rick to the hospital. I and your mother will pick you up there. We'll wait for you at the main entrance. OK?"

"Right. Thanks. See you."

He took the telephone back to the shed and tried to give the men twenty dirzh, but they turned away from the television just long enough to refuse it with smiles. By the time he returned to the gate Rick was asleep.

He settled down to wait with his back against the gatepost,

noticing for the first time the noises reaching him, mainly from across the river, though this time it wasn't the angry mutter of a protesting crowd, rumblings of tanks and the dull jar of cannon fire, but cries just as loud but lighter in tone, mingled with the incessant hooting of car-horns. Dara Dahn rejoicing.

The ambulance showed up in twenty minutes. Nigel gave the men their fifty dirzh and sat in front with the driver. As they drove out to the ring road they saw pedestrians and cars streaming in the other direction, mostly saving their vocal cords and batteries until they were nearer to the palace.

His mother was getting out of Roger's car as the ambulance drew up at the hospital. She glanced at him as he approached and looked away, then turned and stared.

"Hi, Mum."

"My darling! What have you done to yourself?"

"It's the new me, Mum. What do you think?"

"I didn't want another girl. I'd got two already."

"I haven't seen the face. It'll wash off, won't it? Can you take a photograph first? I like the hair, though."

"Well, if…Good Lord! Is that Rick? He looks awful!"

The ambulance men had lifted the stretcher onto a trolley and were getting ready to drive off while an orderly wheeled it away. Rick managed a kind of smile and a weak mutter as Nigel and his mother caught up, then Roger went in to see him through the system while they waited outside on a shady bench. People came past in clumps, four or five of them at a time trying to watch the screen of a single mobile.

"Don't tell me now," she said. "Wait till your father gets home. Just tell me what happened in the bit we missed after the screen went blank. Next thing we saw was a spokesman person explaining about some kind of agreement making the three head chieftains a—what's it called?—Council of Regency or something—until Taeela's old enough to be Khan. And then there she was with a lot of—chieftains, I suppose—doing oath-taking and stuff, though some of them didn't look all that happy about it. How on earth…? Where were the men we saw coming down the stairs?"

"Dead, I'm afraid. The one in the middle was a chieftain called Adzhar Taerzha, and the other two were…"

She listened, frowning, and shook her head in bewilderment when he finished.

"How too extraordinary!" she said. "It's almost as if Taeela had some kind of good fairy looking after her."

Nigel sighed.

"We've just been dead lucky," he said, and changed the subject.

He was telling her about the birds at the desert pool when Roger came back and said Rick had broken a rib and they were going to X-ray him and see if it had pierced his lung. If it had, it was going to be touch and go. They'd ring the embassy as soon as they knew.

Taeela had called to check that Nigel was OK. He called back, but couldn't get hold of her, had a long shower, tried again without luck and collapsed onto his bed, meaning just to lie there for a few minutes and have another go. It was almost dark when his mother woke him.

"I thought I'd better," she said, "or you won't get to sleep tonight. Taeela called and I told her you were all right, but she said not to wake you."

"Thanks, I suppose. What about Rick?"

"That's why I came now. They just called. It's serious but not ghastly. The rib's broken all right, but it's only sort of scratched his lung, not gone right in. Is there any way we can get hold of his wife?"

"Wait…Here you are. You'll need the code for Sodalka. Ask for Mizhael or Lily-Jo. They both speak English. When's supper?"

"We're having it cold in the living room so we can watch the TV."

"Give me two mins."

His mother was on the telephone, talking to Janey. His father eyed him up and down.

"I'm glad to see you in your own hair," he said. "Your mother showed me the photograph. I can't say I thought it an improvement."

"I gave it three goes in the shower," said Nigel. "Dad…er…I hope I haven't messed things up for you too much."

"So do I, but in any case I shan't hold it against you. The Khanazhana tells me they forced you to go with them because you were the only one who understood the map of some secret passages they needed to use."

"It wasn't like that. She took my side. She knew I'd promised you I wouldn't get involved. But I think they'd have tied me up and taken me anyway, so I did a deal with them. I wasn't going to be much use to them tied up, except as some kind of hostage maybe, but I said I'd help them find their way round the passages provide they swore they wouldn't kill anyone they didn't absolutely have to. That was a big deal for the Akhlavals. They've got a blood feud with Adzhar Taerzha's lot they were planning to settle."

"Not to mention that you yourself had a certain…ah… emotional involvement in the success of the enterprise?"

"No I didn't! I didn't want her to go! I thought it was absolutely crazy. They hadn't got a hope."

"I'll take your word for it. Ah, well. Let's regard it as water under the bridge. We'll just have to hope that no one makes the connection. If they do…I don't like to think.

"I take it that's why you dyed your hair. What chance is there that anyone recognised you, do you reckon?"

"I don't think anyone except Mizhael Baladzhin. Pretty well all the way up to Sodalka I was wearing a dahl, pretending to be a girl. I had to take it off to say hello to Chief Baladzhin, but I pulled my cap right down over my hair. Then Mizhael fixed me up with Dirzhani clothes and a turban until we could get it dyed. And I called myself Nick Riddle. Mizhael spotted who I was, but he doesn't want it coming out any more than you do. They've got to show they didn't get any help from us or anyone else."

Nigel's mother put the handset down and turned.

"She's going to try and come straight back," she said. "Anything new?"

The TV was showing what looked like some kind of enormous street party filling the Iskan Bridge, with stray fireworks, loosed off at random, soaring over the water.

"They showed us that bit they blacked out yesterday, darling," said his mother. "The part you told me about. I expect they'll show it again if you want to see it."

"Not much," said Nigel. "I don't like watching people getting killed."

"They're telling us rather more than I'd have expected," said his father. "I'm afraid the pledge you were given had its limits. There were several casualties on both sides in the attack on the television station."

"One poor woman got killed by a stray bullet," said his mother.

"That wasn't us," said Nigel. "That was a lot of deserters from one of the barracks Mizhael roped in."

"But on the whole they seem to have been remarkably efficient," said his father. "Of course all the colonels' most committed troops are away from Dara Dahn, dealing with various pockets of unrest. There's no news yet about how they're reacting."

"But it's nothing like all over, is it?" said Nigel. "Not the way that lot on the bridge seem to think it is."

"Popular support is all very well, as far as it goes," said his father. "But there's a lot of powerful people who won't be too happy about what your friends have done. As far as they're concerned it's nothing like over. It'll be a year or two before we can expect to see anything like a functioning parliamentary democracy."

"For God's sake, Dad, this is Dirzhan! They wouldn't know

what do with a functioning democracy. Let them do it their own way. They'll work something out."

"You may well be right, Niggles, but if they do they will be very much the exception. I will put your point of view to my superiors, though I'm afraid you mustn't expect them to listen."

"Do you want me to tell you about what happened to us after the President got shot?" said Nigel.

"Tell us while we're eating," said his mother. "It's cold, because I didn't know when you'd wake up."

"Do you mind if I record what you say?" said his father. "There'll be useful stuff in it and I don't want to keep stopping you while I take notes. And I'd like Roger and Tim to listen to it later."

It was midnight before Nigel got to bed. From his window he could see that the party on the Iskan Bridge was still in full swing, with people dancing round a huge bonfire in front of the palace. The great building glowed in its floodlighting, making it impossible to tell which windows were lit from behind. He wondered whether Taeela was asleep yet, and if so where. Her old bedroom had probably been ransacked. She mightn't want to use it anyway.

He was home, if anywhere was home for him since Santiago. But everything was strange.

CHAPTER 24

Hi! Here I am again. At last. How long has it been? 13 days I make it. Sorry about that, but stuff's been happening. I've seen the Brit papers, so it's probably been on TV. Just remember a lot of what they say about me is wrong…

Nigel slept late. His mother had finished her breakfast but was still in the dining room, reading. The TV was on with the sound turned down.

"Anything new?" said Nigel.

"I don't think so," she said. "We decided there wasn't any point in Ivahni hanging around to tell me what they were saying when they weren't really saying anything. Three planes came over about half an hour ago—I don't know if you heard them. They just screamed round a couple of times and whizzed off. To show they could, I suppose.

"Ivahni's called the hospital. They operated on Rick last night, and he's doing fine. We tried to call your friend Janey but she's already on her way back.

"How are you feeling, darling?"

The right answer would still have been "Strange," but he didn't feel like explaining. He couldn't have, anyway, even to himself.

"Hungry," he said, and helped himself to scrambled eggs.

He ate slowly, in silence, thinking about yesterday. It already seemed to be much longer ago than that, as if it was fading into the past, becoming just memory. Over. Like his old school in Santiago. When he looked up he saw that his mother had stopped reading and was just sitting there, watching him.

"You've grown up," she said. "It wasn't just the hair."

"Yes, I suppose so," he said. Perhaps that was what was strange. She sounded as if she thought so. Things were different between them now.

"No wonder," she said.

"Well, you might tell Dad. Then he might stop calling me by my baby name."

She laughed, but before she could answer the telephone rang beside him on the table.

"Nigel?"

His heart bounced at the sound of her voice.

"Hi. How are you? Did you sleep OK? When am I going to see you?"

"I sleep…slept little. How can I? But I am well… Nigel…"

"What's up? What's happened?"

"My regents…They are afraid of the Russians. My brother is in Moscow, my father's oldest son. Perhaps they will say he is the true Khan. Avron Dikhtar has said—you were right, Nigel, he tells us so much—he's said it is a very rich Russian building man who pays Sesslizh and Madzhalid for killing of my father so that he will build our dam. Already the television in Moscow has news about my vengeance. They say the British meddle too much in Dirzhan. They say the British ambassador visits with my father in his private hunting lodge…"

"Do they say anything about me being in the palace with you yesterday?"

"They don't know. They mustn't know. I did not tell my regents this, even. Now I must do what they want. So you were not in Dara Dahn, Nigel. You were all the time in Sodalka. You must go in secret back there for a few days. Then you come to Dara Dahn."

"I'm going back to England next week."

"I know. It is best. You spend few days in Sodalka and then... Oh, Nigel...!"

"And anyway, what about the guys who were with us in the palace?"

"They will not tell, Nigel. Think who you are. It will be terrible for them to tell your secrets."

"They can't all believe that."

"Of course they believe. They saw what happened yesterday. I believe also. We cannot chance to be so lucky. Don't you believe?"

Nigel laughed uncomfortably.

"Not really," he said, but he wasn't sure if it was true.

"Who else has seen you?" she said.

"Nardu and his sons. The people at the fish quay. No, it was just Rick and me there, so they wouldn't have made the connection...Hang on."

His father had come in and was hovering, clearly waiting for him to finish.

"It's Taeela," he said. "She wants me to sneak back to Sodalka and make like I've been there all along."

"Now that's not at all a bad idea...provided we can get away with it. It depends who else..."

"She says the guys who were with us in the passages won't talk. Tell you later. Hello, you still there? Dad's all in favour."

"You will need bodyguards still. Wait...Yes, I will call Chief Baladzhin so that he can send bodyguards to bring Lucy to Sodalka to fetch you and say thank-you to him for looking after you. You can go with her so nobody sees you. Can she do this, Nigel?"

"I'll ask her. I wanted to take her to Sodalka anyway. Hang on."

"No, I will talk to her."

He carried the hand-set over. His father beckoned him back.

"This would solve a lot of problems, Niggles," he muttered. "We'd need to fix how to smuggle you up there…"

"She's got that sorted, if Mum can do it," said Nigel, and explained.

"Amazing child," said her father. "But I hope she doesn't imagine she can run the country like that on her own."

"I think she's letting the regents take over. She said she's got to start doing what they want."

"Yes…Listen, Niggles. You're not going to like this, but I think you'd better stay up there almost till you're due to go home."

"But…"

"I'm anxious to quash the perception that there might be anything on between the two of you, which is of course what everybody wants to think. I imagine Taeela's regents feel even more strongly about this. We'll put it about that you found the whole experience pretty traumatic, and we need to give you peace and quiet to recover. OK?"

"No…. Oh, hell!…Let's see what Taeela says."

"Right…Tell me, how sure can we be that the men who were with you in the palace will keep their mouths shut?"

"Dead sure, almost. It's that baizhan thing I told you about. Especially after yesterday, when everything went pretty well impossibly right. You could almost feel the way they believed in it, like…I don't know what."

"I'll take your word for it."

Across the room Nigel's mother had been talking cheerfully to Taeela, just as if it had been an ordinary, everyday chat, the sort he wished he could have had. Now she said goodbye and held the handset out for him.

"Hi. I'm back."

"Oh, I am sorry…I wish, Nigel…"

"OK, you needn't go on. I get it. We're supposed to be like we aren't friends any more."

"We are friends, Nigel. It is for a few days only, and then…

Wait. Somebody comes. I'll call you when I am able."

"OK. See you."

He went and stared out of the window. Tiny figures were moving about in front of the palace, raking the litter into mounds, shovelling the ashes of the glorious bonfire into barrows and carting them away. Him too. He was a bit of litter being cleared away up to Sodalka after the party was over. He tried to tell himself that Taeela was as unhappy about it as he was. It didn't help much.

She didn't call back.

Dara Dahn was having one of its hotter-than-hell days, so there wasn't any excuse for not bringing his blog up to date. He yelped with astonishment when he saw how many hits he'd had in his absence. There'd never been more than maybe a word or two from Mr. Udall, and a snide remark from some kid in his class doing his own blog. Now there were 12,387, with the count going up even as he watched. And pages of comments about entries he'd posted before stuff had really started happening, mostly from kids wanting to be his friends, or to know more about Taeela, or to put him down one way or another.

He glanced at a few of them, but forgot about them as soon as he started to sort out the stuff on his memory stick, since that last morning when Rick had driven him down to the palace. He'd been at it for over an hour when Roger came in with the printouts from the London papers.

The main story in the serious ones was about some big bank going bust, but they'd all got the same grainy picture next to it, lifted from Dara Dahn TV, Taeela standing on the grand stairway, side on to the camera, with her pistol half raised and Mr Dikhtar cowering at her feet. The headlines ranged from TEENAGE PRINCESS STAGES SUCCESSFUL COUNTER-COUP IN DARA DAHN to TAEELA GET YOUR GUN. All the stories had at least one thing wrong. Several of them said things like "Nigel Ridgewell son of the British ambassador, who had been with the Khanazhana at the time of the coup and had participated in her escape, was previously reported as being safe in an undisclosed location, thought to be Kyrgyzstan. He will be returning to Dara Dahn as soon as it is safe to travel."

He carried on with the blog until he got to the peach orchard. He'd need to ask Taeela about that, and anyway he was pretty well brain dead, so he just wrote "More next time," and printed it out for his father to check over.

"Spot on," said his father. "Plenty for people to get their teeth into, and no toes trodden on, to mix a metaphor or two. Something I wanted to ask you, though. This baizhan thing..."

"I'm not going to say anything about it. The Dirzhaki would think I'm ruining Taeela's luck."

"Yes, of course. But have you thought about what's going to happen here when you have to go back to home, Nigg...Nigel?"

"Thanks,. Dad."

"High time, I suppose. Where were we? Oh, yes, we may think of it as irrational nonsense, but if it's part of the Khanazhana's mystique it has to be taken seriously. Can it be passed on? If so does your successor have to be another person? One of the old khans had a white mule, I think you said."

"Yeah, I know. It's been bothering me. She won't talk about it, and I guess nobody else will. Even Mizhael said he felt iffy telling me. Anyway, I'll ask him when we're in Sodalka. Doctor Ghulidzh might know, I suppose."

The afternoon shuffled dully away. Beneath their windows Dara Dahn slept in the blanketing heat. Only as the lights came on did life begin to stir. At last Taeela called.

"Great," he said. "Something I want to ask you. It's for my blog. There's thousands of people reading it now. Is that scary or is that scary?"

"I have thousands of people watching me Nigel. Tens of thousands. All of the time."

She sounded tired and low-spirited. She wasn't putting him down.

"Yeah," he said. "That must be really tough. This is the same sort of thing, I suppose. That stuff on the way to Sodalka, when you had to shoot…"

"Tell them what happened, Nigel. Everything."

"Are you sure?"

"I am sure. Let us…let's talk about something else."

It didn't work. He hadn't done anything worth talking about, and she'd endured a series of dispiriting hassles and frustrations which she didn't want to think about.

"I think we will stop," she said at last. "Oh, Nigel, it will never be the same! Perhaps it will be better when you are in Sodalka."

She rang off without giving him time to answer.

Next morning two SUVs carrying five armed guards drew up at the Embassy with the Baladzhin pennant fluttering from their aerials. Wearing his dahl, sunglasses and a pair of his mother's sandals Nigel tittupped down the steps and climbed shyly in beside her. Nobody seemed to be watching.

Twice they were stopped at dodgy-looking road-blocks on their way north, but their guards carried passes from Chief Baladzhin and made it clear that they were prepared to back them up with their own fire-power, so there was no serious trouble.

They were lunching beside a rocky stream half way up a pass when Nigel's mother said dreamily "I've had an idea about what you were talking to your Dad about yesterday. He would have to persuade Herr Fettler, of course."

"Herr Fett…? Mum, that's brilliant!"

"I thought so. You'd still have to find out how to do it."

A little way short of Sodalka they halted again for Nigel to change cars. The one he was in went on ahead, entered the town by a different gate and drove round to the back of Chief Baladzhin's house so that he could be out at the front gate with him to greet his mother. A television crew was waiting to film him running forward, regardless of protocol, even before her car had drawn to a halt, and then flinging his arms round her as she emerged.

She threw herself into the act, laughing and crying as he dragged her back up the steps to introduce her to a beaming Chief Baladzhin.

They spent six good days at Sodalka. In the mornings they poked around in market stalls with Lily-Jo and Doglu, or explored wonderful over-the-top buildings and streets where hardly a house looked less than hundreds of years old, or sat under awnings sipping ice-cold juices and nibbling Dirzhani snacks. Though nobody now sneaked up to try to touch him he was all the time conscious of the pressure of suppressed excitement at his presence. "It's creepy the way they won't quite look at you," said his mother.

On the second day the journalists started to show up, trying to interview Nigel, and when they didn't get anywhere with that just asking people about him. They didn't get anywhere with that either. One woman spotted him and his mother leaving the market and rushed up with a microphone, but an angry crowd gathered round her before she reached him and his mother had to wade in and rescue her. Next day the embassy announced he would be giving a press conference when he got back to Dara Dahn so they went away to wait for that.

They spent the heat of the day indoors and summoned the real world back for an hour or so by watching the Dara Dahn television news and phoning Nigel's father. Taeela phoned them too, when she could, and she and Nigel got better at keeping a conversation going. At one point he was telling her how he and his mother had used the cool of the previous evening to take the four girls up into the hills to look for birds. Lisa and Natalie were teaching the other two English, competitively and in a Leeds accent, with a lot of teasing and giggling, all four working together to bury, if only for the moment, the horrors they had been through.

"It isn't fair, Nigel!" she said. "You have fun. You do these things with Lucy and the girls, and I work, work, work. And it is not—what do you say?—proper work. Anyone who has a smiley face can do it. I will find a girl looking the same as me..."

"A double? That's a great idea! And then you can sneak up here and do fun stuff with us."

"When did I last ride my beautiful horses, Nigel? My poor horses! They will be so bored. They will forget me."

"You're right. Seriously, Taeela, it isn't good for you. You must tell your regents..."

"I do not tell them, Nigel. They tell me. They tell me I must show everybody my smiley face so they all say 'Yes, this is a good government.'"

"Come off it. You tell them, don't you?"

"A little bit. It is like a difficult horse. Three difficult horses..."

Her tone had changed. The flash of her old self was over.

She hadn't been exaggerating about her work-load. There were always at least a couple of items about her doings on any news bulletin, talking to patients in hospitals, visiting the makeshift camps of refugees from the three patches of fighting still going on, inspecting troops, welcoming a UN peace delegation and so on. She did a very genuine-seeming smiley face.

Doctor Ghulidzh couldn't find anything in any of his books about switching baizhani. Alinu just shook her head warningly.

"Guess you'll just have to make something up," said Mizhael.

"What would you do in one of your fantasy games?"

"Don't ask me. I just market them. Any ideas, love?"

"A magical apple, maybe," said Lily-Jo. "The tree guarded by a dragon. The old baizhan takes a bite and passes it to the new baizhan. Or…"

"If Zhanni's going to eat it it's got to be fish," said Nigel.

"A magical pool, then," said Lily-Jo. "A grim guardian in the depths."

"Cool," said Mizhael.

On the fourth morning Nigel and his mother went to the market alone and bought a sheaf of brilliant red-purple flowers like miniature gladioli. They left the town by the west gate with the sun already roasting on their backs and climbed the short distance to the place where the helicopter had come down. The wreckage had been cleared away but the circle of blackened hillside was there, spreading away from the fatal boulder, and the clean hill air still reeked faintly of burnt aviation fuel and—or was this only imagination?—charred meat.

Nigel scrambled onto the boulder from above and his mother passed him the flowers. He crossed to the other side, laid them carefully down near the edge, moved a pace back and stood with his head bowed. The black circle was the pool of grief, and the dead soldiers were there, and the parents of Halli and Sulva, and the brutes who had killed them, and Adzhar Taerzha and Sesslizh and Madzhalid and the soldiers who'd fallen down the drop-traps, and their dog, and the unknown others who'd died in the fighting at the TV station, and the woman who'd just been in the way of a bullet. His flowers would wither by sunset, the black circle would be green next year, but the boulder would remain.

They walked down the hill in silence. A line of people were watching from the walls as they came through the gate.

Taeela called that same evening. The first thing she said was "The flowers, Nigel. Where the helicopter was crashed. Why did you do this? It was on the television. What does this mean, Nigel?"

"It doesn't mean anything! It's private! Look, if I hadn't wanted to talk to Mum those guys would a still be alive! I don't feel guilty, only sad. It isn't anything to do with anyone else, just me!"

"Everything you do has meanings, Nigel. I think this has good meanings for my people. It is because of who you are…No, what you are."

"Well, as far as I'm concerned it's still private. Oh, I suppose I'm glad you think it might be some use, but, tell you truth, I'm sick of all that! I can't wait to get out of Dirzhan…Hell! Sorry, I don't mean it like that. I still think you're terrific—the best thing that ever happened to me…"

"You really think this, Nigel?"

"Oh, sorry. I didn't mean…well, yeah…yeah, now I've said it, I guess so. But it's no use, is it? Not if we can't be together a bit. And Mum and me'll be flying out Friday. Look, I've got to see you before I go. Alone. Well, I suppose you'd better have Satila there, but no one else. It isn't because of what I just said. I mean, I really want to see you of course, but I've got to, too. Whether your regents like it or not. It's important for both of us. Thursday, if poss. We'll be back in the embassy Tuesday evening. You can call me there to tell me when. OK?"

"Good. I will make it possible…Wait…"

There was a long uninterpretable pause, then she spoke in a rapid mutter, as if she'd had to force herself to say it.

"Nigel, you are the best thing that ever happened to me."

She rang off before he could think of an answer.

There were newspaper printouts waiting at the embassy, but fewer and shorter than last time, as some kind of banking crisis was sweeping round the world like a tsunami, washing yesterday's news away as it went. But there were stories about Nigel himself being in the palace with the Khanazhana when her father was murdered and escaping with her up to Sodalka. They'd only got his blog to go on, plus a lot of rumours. They made a big thing of

Taeela shooting the two thugs at the peach orchard, of course. He was still looking at the printouts when she called.

At first they were back to where they'd started, heaving the conversation along through a series of awkward pauses. Nigel had very little to tell her apart from Chief Baladzhin giving his mother a huge turban pin in his household colours, and telling her that if she'd been free he'd have made it a wedding ring.

The return to Dahn had been an eventless seven-hour drive. He'd thought of asking if they could go back over the pass where they'd buried Halli and Sulva's murdered parents so that he could put flowers on their grave, without any photographers lurking around. He didn't tell Taeela that bit. It was too close to the emotional bog they'd fallen in yesterday.

She at least had something to talk about. She'd spent part of her morning being smiley to a delegation of East Dirzh rebels who'd come to negotiate with the regents about a cease-fire.

"That sounds like good news," he said.

"Yes, I am very happy for it. Oh, Nigel…"

She pulled herself up, teetering for a moment on the edge of another section of the bog.

"OK," he said in desperation. "Let's talk about that sort of stuff tomorrow, only not on the telephone, right? When am I going to see you?"

"Half after three. We have one hour and twenty-five minutes. Then I take you to meet my regents."

"I've got to do a press conference in the morning."

"I want to ask you about this. Nigel, those men I had to shoot. There are people who say they put their guns down, and then I shot them. It was in Moscow papers like this. We tell everyone it isn't true, and Rahdan saw it, and Janey, but they are my servants, so these people say of course they lie for me. You must tell them at your press conference what you see…saw."

"Right. Dad says he knows a friendly journalist. We'll get him to ask. Anything else? What about my bet with Zhiordzhio

Baladzhin? Do you want them to know about your dad's promise, and yours, and all that?"

That kept them going until they could decently ring off, in Nigel's case with a curious mixture of relief and disappointment.

CHAPTER 25

Day whatever-it-is.

Hi, there. We're off to England tomorrow, so this is my last from Dirzhan…

They held the press conference in the entrance hall of the embassy, which was another miniaturised clone of the Great Hall in the palace, with a fine staircase at the back leading to a gallery above. There were about twenty reporters there with two TV crews, one at the back of the room and the other up in the gallery. His father started things off.

"Good morning, ladies and gentlemen. I've only two things to say. First, that this is not an official occasion, sponsored by the British government. It is entirely Nigel's affair, as all his actions have been since the death of the late President. He got into his adventure entirely by accident, when the President asked me if he could spend some time with his daughter while he was in Dara Dahn, to help improve her English accent, and it was because of that that he happened to be with her in the palace at the time of her father's assassination. Apart from a few brief telephone calls to assure us of his continuing safety we had no contact with him until after the Khanazhana's dramatic return. For fear of compromising my position he had not even told me that anything of the sort might be afoot.

"Secondly I must ask you to remember that Nigel has been through a series of experiences that even an adult would have found traumatic, and not to press him too hard about anything he may say.

"When he has finished I will take advantage of your presence to answer any questions you may want to ask about the likely effect of the current financial upheaval in the banking sector on the construction of the Vamar dam.

"Nigel."

He waited while the man adjusted the microphone, and began.

"OK. Well, like Dad says, I was with the Khanazhana when… Look, I'm going to call her Taeela because that's how I think of her. We were just friends, that's all. OK?"

The first part was mostly in his blog, but he went through it again, deliberately making it as dull as he could. The secret passages were simply there, with a few traps which Fohdrahko knew how to use, and a room to hide in, and a way down to the dungeons, and then out of the palace, but nothing about how creepy and scary it all was and how shattered Taeela had been by her father's death and how tough despite that. He said what an ace old man Fohdrahko had been, and how he'd died, because he wanted people to know, and it would give them something to write about that wouldn't cause any problems.

Escaping from Dara Dahn disguised as girls being people-trafficked should be good stuff too. Besides, it led on to what had happened at the peach orchard. Again he treated that as flatly as he could, just explaining that the President had given Taeela a gun and made sure she knew how to use it, and she'd got it out just in time to stop them killing Rahdan.

A hand went up in the middle of the room.

"Sorry," he said. "Did I say something wrong?"

A large bald man with a red beard stood up.

"Edwards, WPA," he said. "I'm sorry to interrupt, but I think this is an important point that needs to be clarified. There is a report in certain sections of the press that the Khanazhana shot these two men after they'd surrendered their weapons."

"That's crap! The guy had his gun up with the safety off and his finger on the trigger. She didn't even have time to think. And if she hadn't shot him in time Rahdan would be dead and Janey would be dead and the girls would be up in the hills somewhere being sold to guys who fancied having an extra wife to play with and the two thugs and their mates would be asking around to find who'd pay them the most for getting their hands on the Khanazhana and how much they could squeeze out of Dad for letting me come home.

"It was nothing like cold blood. She's not like her father that way. He'd've killed them straight off, no problem, but she was really upset after. Crying and shaking. OK?"

"How can you be sure that he would actually have pulled the trigger?" said a voice with some sort of an accent.

"I couldn't, not then. But I can now. Look, we found the guys' van the other side of the orchard. There were two girls tied up in the back. We found their parents' bodies in the orchard. They'd both been shot in the back of the head. That's what Dad means about traumatic experiences. Can we talk about something else, please?"

A chair scraped. A hand started to go up and came down. Nigel waited a little and went on. Sodalka. Taeela at the road-block. And at the Baladzhin palace. Laying it on what a star she was among the Varaki, so that they'd all get it what a big deal her marriage promise was. That stirred them up all right. Pencils raced over note-pads, fingers rattled away at lap-tops. He didn't bother with his chess match against Zhiordzhio Baladzhin. He hadn't done anything himself, just watched things happen.

He'd been worried about the next bit. How much had he known about the attack on the palace? Why hadn't he told his father? And so on. He'd got the answers ready but he didn't need them. He hadn't seen much of Taeela and they weren't interested in anything else. The conference fizzled out with a few stupid questions. Was he in love with the Khanazhana? Did she have a boy-friend? That sort of thing. It was a relief when it ended and he could go.

"What was that about the dam, Dad?" he said.

"It's a bit of a worry. A lot of the money behind the consortium comes from Brunfeld's, who seem to be pretty heavily involved in this property mess. We'll just have to see. If the worst comes to the worst I may be out of a job."

Outwardly Nigel's final visit to the palace began exactly like his first, with the Rover drawing up at the foot of the steps, his driver opening the door for him and saluting as he got out, and an official waiting for him beside the guards at the top. Inwardly it was totally different. This time he was in control.

The official introduced himself as the Khanazhana's private secretary, and the guard would have waved Nigel through if he hadn't opened his bag and shoved it under the man's nose, and then opened the box he was carrying and shown him its contents. The guard looked up, startled, as the contents cheeped pitifully in the sudden blaze of sunlight.

"It's for the Khanazhana," explained Nigel.

The guard caught the name, guessed the meaning, frowned briefly, then nodded and hurriedly closed the box.

How many people does it take to start a rumour without you actually talking about it, Nigel wondered as they crossed the great hall. One, if you're lucky, and the guard had obviously got it. The one outside the private apartments would make two, the secretary three, and Satila four, except that she might keep it to herself.

The mosaics of the stairs had been so fiercely scoured that they looked brand new. Otherwise little had changed. Only that background tension had gone out of the air. In the dimmer light of the gallery the contents of the box didn't protest at the inspection, but blinked in a bewildered way and then mewed when the lid was closed, as if it had been expecting something better.

The inner door, forced open by Colonel Sesslizh's soldiers, had been replaced and still smelt of fresh paint. The secretary was about to knock when Nigel stopped him.

"Wait a moment," he whispered, and laid the box gently down beside the door. "It's for later. Will you tell the guard it's meant to be there, and not to let anyone touch it? Thanks."

Satila must have been close inside the door, all set to swing it dramatically open the moment the secretary knocked and reveal Taeela standing in a fashion-plate pose a few paces into the room. She was wearing a pale green dress with a pattern of gold threads, long loose sleeves and high collar, wide gold belt with huge jewelled clasp – amethysts he guessed – with matching necklace and bracelet, and a purple headscarf. Also lipstick, eye-shadow, the lot. She looked terrific, and knew it. She also looked at least two years older than she was.

"Wow!" he said. "What's this in aid of?"

"Am I hot?"

"Wicked hot, and dead cool with it. That's some trick, Taeela. You've got the Dalai Lama coming to tea, then?"

"I have you coming to tea, Nigel. I want you to remember like I used to be, before all this. I told Satila Make me a little bit pretty, so my friend Nigel won't forget me. But she is an artist. She doesn't know 'a little.' We had good fun, Nigel."

"Fun for me too. Thanks. How've things been, then? Got to ride your horses yet."

"Next week I will ride. Come and sit, and we will have tea and talk, like we used to."

Deliberately, he thought, she curled herself into the corner of the sofa, as if she was trying to fit herself into the part of the child she'd been a couple of weeks ago and wasn't any longer. The classy get-up only added to the effect, and Satila made it odder still by pinning a starched linen napkin down her front like a child's bib.

She started to chat away, just as she used to do.

"Yes, next week I will ride my horses, and then it is my birthday when I must be smiley for everyone..."

"You don't have to be smiley for me, you know...I mean, if you want to talk about your dad..."

He'd got it wrong. She stared at him, open mouthed. The patches of rouge stood out suddenly as the blood left her cheeks. She seemed to shrink even further among the cushions and to lose the imaginary years.

"I cannot," she said. "I must not. I would do nothing, only weep. I must be strong. Strong for Dirzhan. On Sunday is his state funeral. Then I am allowed to weep. And at night, when I am alone...Not now, Nigel. Soon I must take you to meet my regents."

"OK, I get it. I'm sorry. But you can't keep bottling it up, you know. I'll...No, why don't you call Mum tonight? It doesn't matter how late—she sits up till all hours, reading. She'll be much more use than I would, anyway. And she's your friend, just as much as I am. OK? You'll do that? Promise?"

She nodded twice, her face blank, withdrawn.

He took things slowly, giving her time to recover. Gradually animation came back into her responses as he told her about the press conference. Satila wheeled the tea-trolley over, filled their cups and left them to help themselves to the same kind of little sweet cakes the cafes served in Sodalka.

"What is 'crap'?" she said.

"Rubbish. Nonsense. It really means, er, dung, I suppose."

She actually laughed.

"We say ardh," she said. "It is rude."

"Yeah, I guess so. Not F.O.-speak, anyway. Whole point was that this was me telling it my way, not what Dad had put me up to."

"But you did not...didn't tell them how you fought the man so he couldn't kill Rahdan?"

"Not you too! I wish people would stop yakking on about that. It wasn't like that, honestly. More like a horse bolting and barging into whatever's in its way. OK, I hammed it up a bit. Said I'd just panicked and started to run, only I'd tripped over the hem of my dahl and hung onto the guy to stop myself falling. I'd rather look like a total idiot than any kind of a hero. BRIT HERO NIGEL SAVES THE DAY! I've got to go back to school, for God's sake!"

She laughed again.

"Nigel, you are hopeless! You forget, girls like heroes. How will you get yourself a girl?"

"Trouble is, I like girls who don't give a toss for heroes."

"They do not exist."

"Bet you."

"Nigel! You cheat me! You know this girl! You have a photograph, but you don't show me!"

"Not to say know. Fact is, I've hardly spoken to her. She's same age as me but she's very bright, so they've bumped her up a year. Her name's Ronnie – short for Veronique – she's half French. Not ordinary pretty—bit of a monkey face, but interesting. She plays soccer, got a lovely run, same kind Mum has—that's why I noticed her. Anyway, I thought I'd try and get alongside her next term. I haven't had the nerve before, but…I suppose I owe you that. I'll send you a photograph if I get anywhere."

They chatted on easily enough, about nothing much, drank tea, nibbled a couple of cakes. He kept an eye on the time and when they'd got half an hour to go he stood up and brushed the crumbs off.

"OK," he said. "It's your birthday in a couple of weeks, right? I've got a present for you, only we'll need the curtains closed, if that's all right. Tell Satila I haven't gone crazy. No, it's a surprise. I'm not going to tell you."

He crossed to the window and worked the cords of the huge curtains until there was only a strip of daylight showing, leaving the room in twilight. Then he fetched the box from outside the door, dropped on one knee in front of the sofa like a courtier in El Cid and offered it to her to open. Cautiously, as if it might be a jack-in-the-box or something, she raised the lid and peered inside, frowned for a moment and then laughed.

"A baby bird!" she said. "Oh…! A fish-owl?"

"That's right. Herr Fettler was pretty keen after Dad had talked to him. We thought if you took the fish-owls as your special bird, like your dad did with his eagles, it'll show people you're dead serious about them. Not just in Dirzhan, either. It'll help make the Greens ease off a bit over the dam."

"They will say…"

"No they won't. It's got a damaged wing, so there's no chance of it learning to fish. It'll never survive in the wild."

"Yes, that is good. Is it a boy or a girl?"

"Too early to say, Herr Fettler says."

"It is a boy."

"If you say so. Now, first thing you've got to feed it…him, so he starts getting the idea it's you he belongs to. Herr Fettler says he's too small to wear a hood yet. That's why I left it as long as I could and got it pretty well dark so he thinks it's feeding time."

"Cake?"

"No, fish of course. I've got some with me. There's a bit more to it than just feeding him. We've got to do this right. Listen. I call him Zhanni, but his real name is Zhan, Taeela. That's a sort of secret name. It's short for something…The second half of something."

"The second…? Oh…!"

She laughed delightedly.

"Yes, this is really, really cool!" she said. "You give him to me—that is enough?"

"No. We've all three got to feed from the same dish in the right order. Trouble is, Zhanni doesn't do dishes. He'll have to take it out of your mouth, so…No, wait. You'd better ask Satila to come and have a look so she sees and tell her enough to let her guess what it's about, and then maybe she won't want to actually watch while it's happening, if you get me. Maybe if she tucked herself in behind the curtain…"

Taeela nodded and spoke. Nigel took the little jar of fish-scraps out of his bag, unscrewed the lid and put it on the chess table beside them. Satila came silently over and exclaimed in amused surprise when she saw Zhanni, who responded with a bubbling chirrup.

"That's his feed-me noise," said Nigel. "We've timed it bang on. He's going to have to sit on your shoulder, so maybe she could shift your bib round so he doesn't poop on your dress… That's fine. Ready?"

He eased Zhanni out of the box and settled him onto the bib. The light fluctuated briefly as Satila slid behind the curtain. Zhanni chirruped again and nibbled experimentally at the corner of Taeela's mouth.

"Right," he said. "The next bit's tricky."

He took a morsel of fish out of the jar and showed it to her.

"I'm going to hold it between my teeth and you're going to take it with yours and give it to Zhanni the same way. We've got to be careful we don't bang our teeth together and one of us swallows it by accident, so…"

He put his arm round her shoulders as if to steady them both.

"Ready?" he said and nipped the morsel between his front teeth.

Zhanni started to chirrup eagerly. Taeela plucked the fish neatly from between Nigel's teeth and twisted her head to feed it into the gaping beak, then turned back smiling to him. The tip of her tongue licked delicately across her red lips.

"OK?" he whispered.

Still smiling, she tilted her face to be kissed. He could feel her hands moving gently over his back.

Far too soon Zhanni started to chirrup again. They ignored

him until the chirrups became urgent, and then repeated the process; but before long he became impatient with this leisurely manner of feeding and started to chirrup furiously the moment he'd swallowed his bit; and finally, when they didn't immediately respond, burrowed urgently between their faces in search of his share of whatever was passing between them.

"Ouch!" mumbled Taeela and pulled her head away. Above the corner of her mouth a bead of blood had appeared on the smudged make-up. She put her fingers to the place and stared at them.

"He bit me!" she whispered. "He has tasted my blood! We are tied."

"A sort of owl version of the blood oath, you mean?"

"It is a sign, Nigel. I know what I want. Zhanni knows what I must."

She was dead serious about it, not just playing with the baizhan idea as he had been, working out his moves in advance to get what he wanted, as if it had been a game of chess.

"I guess that's about it, then," he said. "This one had better be goodbye."

He chose the largest morsel he could find and they kissed for the last time. Ever, probably.

"You have lipstick on your cheek," she said as they separated. "You must clean yourself before you see my regents."

"What will Satila say?"

"Already she knows, Nigel. Of course she knows. She is not a fool. But she is a good friend. Yes, she must go behind the curtain, but she remembers how it was when she was a girl. Go and clean yourself and I'll call to her. I'll tell her that the bird did it. She will pretend she believes me."

She picked up the jar and fed Zhanni another morsel of fish, turning her head to smear it across her face as he took it. She called to Satila as he left the room.

When he came back Taeela Zhanni was back in his box, and

Taeela and Satila had vanished. He was at the window watching the river traffic when they returned, Taeela now back in full mourning with a clean white napkin pinned to her shoulder and her face made up much more soberly for the regents. Nigel picked Zhanni out of his box and settled him onto the napkin. He burbled contentedly as Taeela teased gently at the soft down under his neck and didn't seem at all put out when Satila bandaged his eyes with a length of the purple ribbon that Nigel had used to decorate the box, and tied it in a neat bow under his chin.

"How did you know to do this?" said Taeela as they came side by side down the grand stairs.

"I didn't actually. Nobody I asked did either, so I made it up. It seemed to work. At least it did for me, and then some."

"Nigel, this is wicked!"

She managed to make the word carry both meanings. He grinned at her but she just nodded and turned away.

The lift slowed and came to a stop. Zhanni ruffled his feathers uneasily. When the doors slid open the Khanazhana walked out into the Great Hall without a glance, as far as Nigel could see, towards the stairway where twenty-one days ago her father had died in his own blood.

THE END

About Peter Dickinson

PETER DICKINSON was born in Africa, but raised and educated in England. From 1952 to 1969 he was on the editorial staff of Punch, and since then has earned his living writing fiction of various kinds for adults and children.

Amongst many other awards, Peter Dickinson has been nine times short-listed for the prestigious Carnegie medal for children's literature and was the first author to win it twice. His books for children have also been published in many languages throughout the world. His latest collection of short stories, *Earth and Air*, was published by Small Beer Press in October 2012.

Peter Dickinson was the first author to win the Crime-Writers Golden Dagger for two books running: *Skin Deep* (1968), and *A Pride of Heroes* (1969). He has written twenty-one crime and mystery novels, which have been published in several languages.

He has been chairman of the Society of Authors and is a Fellow of the Royal Society of Literature. He was awarded an OBE for services to literature in 2009.

Peter Dickinson lives in Hampshire, England.

Books by Peter Dickinson

Crime and Mystery

Skin Deep (US: The Glass-Sided Ants' Nest) (1968)
A Pride of Heroes (US: The Old English Peep-Show) (1969)
The Seals (US: The Sinful Stones) (1970)
Sleep and His Brother (1971)
The Lizard in the Cup (1972)
The Green Gene (1973)
The Poison Oracle (1974)
The Lively Dead (1975)
King and Joker (1976)
Walking Dead (1977)
One Foot in the Grave (1979)
A Summer in the Twenties (1981)
The Last Houseparty (1982)
Hindsight (1983)
Death of a Unicorn (1984)
Tefuga (1985)
Skeleton-in-Waiting (1987)
Perfect Gallows (1988)
Play Dead (1991)
The Yellow Room Conspiracy (1992)
Some Deaths Before Dying (1999)

Books for children and young adults

The Weathermonger (1968)
Heartsease (1969)
The Devil's Children (1970)
Emma Tupper's Diary (1970)
The Dancing Bear (1972)
The Gift (1973)
The Iron Lion (*illustrated by Marc Brown*) (1973)
The Blue Hawk (1975)

Chance, Luck and Destiny (1975)
Annerton Pit (1977)
Hepzibah (1978)
Tulku (1979)
City of Gold (*illustrated by Michael Foreman*) (1980)
The Seventh Raven (1981)
Healer (1983)
Giant Cold (1984)
A Box of Nothing (1985)
Mole Hole (*illustrated by Jean Claverie*) (1987)
Eva (1988)
Merlin Dreams (*illustrated by Alan Lee*) (1988)
AK (1990)
A Bone from a Dry Sea (1992)
Shadow of a Hero (1993)
Time and the Clock Mice, Etcetera (*illustrated by Emma Chichester Clark*) (1993)
Chuck and Danielle (1996)
The Kin (1998)
Touch and Go (1999)
The Lion Tamer's Daughter (1999)
The Ropemaker (2001)
The Tears of the Salamander (2003)
The Gift Boat (US: Inside Granddad) (2004);
Angel Isle (2006)
Earth and Air (2012)
In the Palace of the Khans (2012)

With Robin McKinley
Water: Tales of the Elemental Spirits (2002)
Fire (2009)

Other books
The Flight of Dragons (*illustrated by Wayne Anderson*) (1979)
The Weir: Poems by Peter Dickinson (2007

CPSIA information can be obtained at www.ICGtesting.com
Printed in the USA
LVOW121605050513

332357LV00029BA/934/P